Beyond
the
Clouds

Books by Elizabeth Camden

Praise for Elizabeth Camden

"A sweeping saga of a historical romance, enhanced by complex characters and riveting period detail. A fascinating read."

Mimi Matthews, *USA Today* bestselling author
on *Written on the Wind*

"This intriguing and unique story took so many twists and turns, I couldn't look away—a must read!"

Gabrielle Meyer, bestselling author on *While the City Sleeps*

"Elizabeth Camden brings the bustling metropolis to living color like no one else. . . . A novel that will keep readers up late into the night."

Jocelyn Green, Christy Award–winning author
on *While the City Sleeps*

"Christy Award winner Camden presents another fabulous love story wrapped around compelling historical events."

Booklist on *The Spice King*

"An adventuresome, entertaining romance that blends themes of betrayal and forgiveness."

Foreword Reviews on *The Spice King*

"Camden is the master of historical inspirational romance, and she has delivered another fascinating read with complex, memorable characters and an interesting subplot."

Booklist starred review of *To the Farthest Shores*

"With fluid writing . . . Camden's delicately written romance—spiced with murder, superstition, and ancient secrets—will inspire readers."

Publishers Weekly on *Until the Dawn*

WOMEN OF MIDTOWN

Beyond the Clouds

ELIZABETH CAMDEN

BETHANYHOUSE
a division of Baker Publishing Group
Minneapolis, Minnesota

© 2026 by Elizabeth Camden

Published by Bethany House Publishers
Minneapolis, Minnesota
BethanyHouse.com

Bethany House Publishers is a division of
Baker Publishing Group, Grand Rapids, Michigan

Printed in the United States of America

Library of Congress Cataloging-in-Publication Data
Names: Camden, Elizabeth, author.
Title: Beyond the clouds / Elizabeth Camden.
Description: Minneapolis, Minnesota : Bethany House, a division of Baker Publishing Group, 2026. | Series: Women of Midtown
Identifiers: LCCN 2025025330 | ISBN 9780764241734 (paperback) | ISBN 9780764246050 (casebound) | ISBN 9781493452439 (ebook)
Subjects: LCGFT: Fiction | Christian fiction | Romance fiction | Novels
Classification: LCC PS3553.A429 B496 2025 | DDC 813/.54—dc23/eng/20250626
LC record available at https://lccn.loc.gov/2025025330

Scripture quotations are from the Holy Bible, New International Version®, NIV®. Copyright © 1973, 1978, 1984, 2011 by Biblica, Inc.® Used by permission of Zondervan. All rights reserved worldwide. www.zondervan.com. The "NIV" and "New International Version" are trademarks registered in the United States Patent and Trademark Office by Biblica, Inc.®

This is a work of historical reconstruction; the appearances of certain historical figures are therefore inevitable. All other characters, however, are products of the author's imagination, and any resemblance to actual persons, living or dead, is coincidental.

Cover design by Design Source Creative Services, Dan Thornberg

Baker Publishing Group publications use paper produced from sustainable forestry practices and postconsumer waste whenever possible.

26 27 28 29 30 31 32   7 6 5 4 3 2 1

Prologue

Finn dragged himself another yard in the mud as agony shot through his mangled leg. He needed to hide. The pilot who shot him down had probably already landed at the German airfield two miles away, and it wouldn't be long before a search party was sent to capture him. Finn's airplane had burst into flames moments after he crashed, and now it billowed sooty clouds of smoke that acted as a signal to the Germans. And Germans sometimes shot downed pilots rather than take them prisoner.

A village was only a few acres away, but Finn's chances of getting there with a busted-up leg weren't good. He clenched his teeth and elbowed another few feet through the sludge, struggling to keep his head up so he wouldn't suffocate.

He couldn't die now. Delia hadn't forgiven him yet. She was the best, purest part of him, the shining inspiration that fueled his dreams ever since he was a kid. He *had* to survive, if only to get home and win her forgiveness. He crawled through the mud with renewed determination.

"*Monsieur, laissez-moi vous aider.*"

7

The urgent whisper startled him, and he lifted his eyes to see a woman hunkered beside him. Frizzy copper hair surrounded a face filled with fear, for the Germans would shoot her too if they caught her helping him.

She repeated herself, and his pain-addled brain struggled to make sense of the French words. She was offering to help him. A boy stood behind her, who looked barely old enough to shave.

"Run," he gasped. "They'll be here soon. *Run*."

The woman ignored him and crouched down, slipping an arm beneath his shoulder. "*Pieter, aidez-moi*."

Pieter rushed to his side, looping Finn's other arm over his own shoulders. Together they hauled him upright. Pain jolted through his body, and he nearly screamed. Instead, he gritted his teeth and forced his good leg to move while his right leg trailed uselessly behind.

The rumble of an automobile sounded in the distance. It was the Germans. Only Germans had gasoline rations, and they'd be here soon.

Waves of agony rolled through him as he focused on the timber-framed cottage straight ahead. A little girl held the front door open. The woman started issuing orders to other children inside.

"*Vite, remonte les planches*."

Quick, pull up the floorboards, she had ordered. Finn understood the words but couldn't make his brain work well enough to reply in French.

"Don't risk your life for me," he said. She had children. They'd be orphaned if the Germans found them.

The floorboards had been pulled up, revealing bundled newspapers and tins of beef hidden below. In short order the mother emptied it, and Finn rolled into the shallow hiding place. His spine slammed against the foundation stone, shooting another wave of pain down his leg.

He got a look at her panicked face as she prepared to cover him with the boards. "Madam, thank you. I owe you my life."

Darkness descended as she replaced the boards and dragged furniture over them. Lying there in total darkness, he started praying. The Germans were coming, and his odds of surviving the next few minutes weren't good. If by God's grace he managed to get home, he would find a way to thank this good woman, and then he would fight to win Delia's forgiveness.

New York City • September 1917

Today wasn't the first time Delia Byrne had to scrub congealed egg yolks from the front of the building, but it was the worst. In addition to the eggs spattered on the stately old law office, the vandals had scrawled slurs in red paint across the plate-glass window. *Kraut lover. Pacifist cowards. Traiter.*

"They misspelled *traitor*," Delia said with a nod to the word that obliterated the elegant gold stenciling of the Chandler Law office.

"I suppose we've been called worse," Reginald said as he surveyed the damage. As always, she and Reginald were the first to arrive at the office this morning. Wesley Chandler, the owner of the firm, usually arrived a few hours later. As a widowed father with a teenaged daughter who was running amok, Wesley made a point of having breakfast and dinner with his wayward daughter every day.

"Let's try to get this cleaned up before Wesley gets here," she said. They were due in court at eleven o'clock for the Baumeister case, and she didn't want Wesley distracted by this latest attack of vandalism. If they didn't get the egg off soon, the heat would bake it onto the bricks.

The law firm kept wire brushes, scrapers, soap, and buckets for precisely this sort of vandalism, which was becoming depressingly frequent ever since America entered the pointless European war. Defending the city's immigrants from anti-German hysteria carried a cost, and it was likely to get worse unless decent people stood up to the bullies.

Once armed with soapy water and a wire brush, Delia attacked the dried egg yolk with gusto. She hated this war. Actually, she hated *all* wars, but this one seemed especially tragic. It provoked knee-jerk hatred toward anything German, even though few people even understood why America had joined the war.

"And how much is the Baumeister case going to cost the firm?" Reginald asked as he watched her scrub. Reginald managed the finances for Chandler Law and cared too much for his manicure to help with the scrubbing. With his ruthlessly groomed Van Dyke beard and piercing black eyes, he reminded Delia of a hawk on the lookout for anything that could endanger the firm's bottom line.

"Wesley is donating his time, so it won't cost us anything."

"Wrong," Reginald said. "It's cost us the Darlington Hotel contract. Yesterday, Mr. Darlington notified us that he no longer wants Wesley to represent his hotel and has demanded a refund of his retainer fees."

Delia winced. The Darlington was a luxury hotel a few miles north of here. Wesley handled their legal issues, and it was a lucrative contract.

"How much are we going to lose?" she asked.

"Eight hundred dollars per month, plus two percent interest and a five percent sliding contingency rate." The answer was typical of Reginald's painstaking attention to detail when it came to money and financial security.

She and Reginald were kindred spirits in that area. After growing up in an orphanage, Delia paid scrupulous attention to her financial security, and losing the Darlington contract was going to hurt the firm. Wesley was a rich man, but he had been losing clients hand over fist ever since he publicly denounced the war.

"You probably put Wesley up to taking the Baumeister case," Reginald accused. "The two of you are always willing to put principles over profit."

Delia lifted her chin as she sloshed hot, soapy water on the congealed egg yolk. If anything, she was the one to rein Wesley in from pursuing his more chivalric impulses, but it wouldn't be wise to point that out to Reginald. There was already gossip in the office about the unusually close relationship she and Wesley shared.

"We'll simply need to find more business," she said primly.

"Or perhaps we ought to quit defending Germans."

That wasn't going to happen. Wesley was too high-minded to overlook blatant injustice, but they needed something to offset the witheringly bad publicity they'd been getting ever since they volunteered to defend German immigrants who'd been harassed after the war broke out in 1914. Everything got worse once President Wilson brought the United States into the war a mere five months ago.

"I'll bet you didn't account for cleaning up this mess in your awe-inspiring daily calendar," Reginald said.

She hid her smile at Reginald's backhanded compliment to her "awe-inspiring calendar." She kept columns for tasks, reminders, a correspondence log, color-coded priority tags, and a deadline tracker.

"I build in a fifteen-minute allowance for unexpected tasks every day," Delia said, but if she didn't get this mess cleaned up soon, she'd find herself behind schedule.

"I don't know why we should even bother scrubbing up," Reginald said. "We'll surely get hit again after today's court case."

Delia dropped the wire brush back into the bucket to let the blood flow back into her tired arms. A pair of businessmen sent disapproving looks at her as they walked past the law firm on their way to work. She smiled at them anyway. It was easier to let them believe this didn't hurt than to show the truth.

"We'll just have to endure the slings and arrows," she said with a teasing glance at Reginald. "We should be used to it by now."

"And yet it never gets easier," Reginal said before turning his back to retreat inside the office.

Delia's attempt to clean the building ahead of Wesley's arrival failed. Her employer showed up earlier than usual and stood before the spattered gunk and painted slurs with an inscrutable expression, yet she knew it had to hurt.

He was dressed for court in a formal charcoal suit, matching vest, and starched collar. His dark hair was immaculately groomed, with only a few strands of gray at his temples. The dismay in his dark eyes caused the faint lines surrounding them to appear a bit deeper.

"The price of business," he said in a matter-of-fact voice. "Are we prepared for the Baumeister case?"

She smiled. "We are," she said with confidence, although she'd need to tidy up first.

It was important to appear prim and businesslike when she sat beside Wesley in court. She always wore a crisp white blouse paired with a dark tie and slim skirt, the female version of a professional business suit. A smock had protected her clothes while she scrubbed the egg yolks, but tendrils of her ebony hair had escaped her chignon and would need to be restyled.

By eleven o'clock they were in court, Delia sitting at Wesley's right-hand side. As his legal assistant, she compiled case law, drafted preliminary legal documents, and assisted him in the courtroom during his arguments. Her biggest asset to Wesley was her unique memory, able to supply him with instant access to statistics, relevant case law, and catch opposing litigants in contradictions.

She fastened her eyes on Thaddeus Pettigrew, the city's attorney who was trying to shut down all German-language publications for the duration of the war. With his pale hair and a wispy mustache, Mr. Pettigrew looked like a callow youth. But his voice rang out like whip.

"Mr. Baumeister's newspaper is a clear and present danger to our republic," he said while pacing before the judge's bench in the walnut-paneled courtroom. "He could be sneaking articles into his paper to stoke anti-American sentiment. He must obey the city ordinance and start publishing his newspaper in English."

Delia kept her face expressionless as she listened to each word, but inside she cringed for Franz Baumeister who sat on Wesley's other side. Mr. Baumeister had lived in this country for thirty years. He worked hard, paid his taxes, and employed nine people at his newspaper that catered to the immigrant community. All of it could be lost because of an irrational fear that German language newspapers were disseminating enemy propaganda.

The only time Delia took her eyes off the city's attorney was to jot a case name on a slip of paper. Wesley was a brilliant attorney, but he didn't have a mind that could recall chapter and verse from two hundred years of legal tradition. Delia did.

When Mr. Pettigrew stated that the city was entitled to curtail civil liberties in time of war, she jotted down *Ex parte Milligan, Supreme Court, 1866*. It was a landmark case that ruled it was unconstitutional to suppress civil liberties during a time of war without specific evidence of danger.

Wesley glanced at the slip of paper she passed him. It caused a hint of a smile as he folded the note and slipped it inside his jacket, then cooly rose to his feet.

"Your Honor, I would call your attention to the Supreme Court's decision in the 1866 case of *Ex parte* Milligan. It firmly established that the government may not suspend the civil liberties of civilians while civil courts are still functioning."

He continued speaking while Delia settled back in her chair to watch Wesley in action as he eviscerated the competition. As always, they were a one-two punch. She supplied Wesley with ammunition, and he wielded it in battle. Over the years they had developed a well-oiled routine in which she did the initial research, and he deployed it in court. He was smart, principled, and the man she adored.

How much longer could she wait for him? On the rare times they had frank conversations about their relationship, he insisted that he was too old for her. Was nineteen years too big of an age gap? Delia was twenty-nine and always wanted to be married before she turned thirty, but Wesley remained resolute in claiming that a platonic working relationship was best.

It would be easy to turn her attention elsewhere if Wesley didn't care for her . . . *but he did*. He gave himself away in every stolen glance, every affectionate brush of his hand that lingered just a bit too long. He showed it to her one rainy afternoon when he drew the shade down over his office window and kissed her until she was breathless. They had been standing beside the floor globe when he closed in on her, cupped her face between his hands, and kissed her as if his life depended on it.

That had been more than a year ago. A year! And still she waited for Wesley to shed his inhibitions and begin a normal courtship without fear of their age difference or his spoiled daughter.

Delia shook off her annoyance and turned her attention back to the courtroom. She ought to be grateful to have become infatuated with such a thoroughly good man. After a disastrous teenaged love affair, Delia once feared she was incapable of falling in love again, but Wesley disproved that. Finn Delaney was a distant memory, and Wesley was her future.

By five o'clock it was all over. The judge issued a bench decision in Mr. Baumeister's favor; it was a complete and total victory.

Delia had no one to celebrate the victory with. Wesley went home to his daughter, Delia to the dining hall of her apartment building. In a restaurant crowded with hundreds of women, she ate alone.

The Martha Washington Apartments were designed for single women who might otherwise have difficulty finding a respectable place in which to live in Manhattan. When it opened in 1903, its twelve stories were immediately filled to capacity with five hundred female teachers, stenographers, nurses, and other professional women who could afford the rent. The first floor had an ice cream parlor, a library, and the dining hall where residents took their meals. Delia used to enjoy long, chatty dinners late into the evening, but that was all over. Now she ate as quickly as possible before heading up to her eighth-floor apartment to curl up with a good book.

She took another sip of tomato soup. Clattering utensils mingled with gossip and laughter from the women at nearby tables while Delia read the current issue of the *Saturday Evening Post* and pretended not to mind eating alone.

Hilde Wallace, with a clipboard propped in the crook of her arm, approached the neighboring table filled with schoolteachers.

Delia stiffened. With her cool, blond good looks and sharp features, Hilde was both pretty and mean. She was tall too. Was that why Hilde assumed leadership wherever she went? She certainly seemed to have a following at the Martha Washington. A gaggle of other women trailed after Hilde as she approached the teachers.

Delia returned to her magazine to study the advertisement for the newest Mary Pickford movie. Wesley once told Delia she resembled Mary Pickford, which was flattering given Pickford's heart-shaped face and sparkling eyes. She was still studying the magazine when Hilde and her entourage arrived at Delia's table. She set the spoon down and braced herself.

"Hello, Delia," Hilde said. "Care to donate to the war bond drive? Everyone else I've spoken to is chipping in."

War bonds were used to manufacture machine guns, battleships, and bombs. All across America, people like Hilde were shaking down civilians to collect funds. Contributing to the manufacture of weapons to murder people was abhorrent, but Delia kept her tone polite.

"No, thank you."

Hilde smirked. "Oh, yes, Delia the pacifist. You're obviously so much better than us. If you're too pure and holy to donate to the war, perhaps you can bring yourself to give something to the Red Cross. Blanche will be happy to take your donation."

Blanche Nesbit stood right behind Hilde. Blanche was the overnight desk clerk at the apartment building. Seeing her march in lockstep behind Hilde hurt because Blanche used to be Delia's friend. Now she was one of many who'd turned frosty over the political divide.

Delia met Blanche's eyes. "I'm sorry. I've been donating everything I can spare to the CRB since the first month of the war."

"What's the CRB?" Hilde asked in a challenging voice.

"The Commission for the Relief of Belgium," Delia answered. "When Germany attacked Belgium—"

"They didn't attack Belgium," Hilde interrupted. "If Belgium would have allowed German troops to cross through their land on the way to France, Germany wouldn't have had to attack them at all."

Delia tried not to roll her eyes at the contradictory statement. Belgium had the bad luck to be located between two warring nations. They tried to remain neutral, but two days after Germany declared war on France, the Germans started rolling through Belgium in a stampede of plunder and destruction. Belgium had been living under the boot of German occupation ever since.

"Belgium is starving," Delia added calmly. "Before the war they imported almost all of their food supply, but the German blockade put an end to that. They have no way of feeding themselves unless relief supplies are sent in from abroad."

Hilde's mouth thinned. "Why don't they just grow some crops like any hardworking American would do?"

Because Belgium was the most heavily industrialized nation in the world. Belgium had factories, shipyards, electrical plants, and steel mills, but those industries didn't produce food. As a densely populated nation with scant farmland, famine set in soon after Germany blockaded the nation. This wasn't the time or place to educate Hilde about the economic constraints of Belgium, so Delia moved straight to her point.

"The Commission for the Relief of Belgium is keeping nine million people from starvation. It costs a fortune to keep sending ships filled with relief supplies to them. Anything I can afford to donate goes to the CRB."

Hilde tossed her clipboard onto the table, sloshing tomato soup on the snowy-white linen. "So you're too holier-than-thou to spare a few pennies for the Red Cross?"

Others at neighboring tables had quieted to listen. They only heard Hilde's loud statement that Delia refused to support the universally admired Red Cross, nothing about the valiant cause of the struggling CRB.

"Hilde, if I live to be a hundred, I'll never learn to be as cleverly mean as you. Congratulations! You've won the day."

"Let's move on," Blanche said, for once standing up to Hilde.

"Yes, let's see if we can find someone who doesn't hate their country."

Tension unknotted from Delia's shoulders as they left, although women at the tables nearby cast sidelong glances her way as they whispered behind cupped hands.

Although Delia remained steadfast to her principles, it never got any easier to be a pariah.

2

Finn Delaney leaned heavily on the cane as he limped down the gangway in New York Harbor. He wanted to kiss the ground, but the splint encasing his leg made it impossible. The best he could do was stand at attention and salute the Statue of Liberty. Ever since he caught sight of Lady Liberty as the troopship neared the harbor, he'd been struggling with emotions that careened between joy and some other feeling he couldn't name. Guilt? Grief? Whatever it was, he needed to get back to his squadron in France as soon as he could convince the Army he was fit to fly once again.

But first he had been ordered to report to Camp Mills, the training and embarkation site for the American armed forces. A sergeant had been sent to drive him to the brand-new installation that had been hastily constructed on Long Island.

"I read about you," Sergeant Lewis said, admiration in his gaze. "It's an honor to drive you to the base, sir."

Finn suppressed a grin. "Thank you, Sergeant." He leaned heavily on his cane as he limped alongside the young soldier to an open-air Ford Model T painted army green.

Finn sat in the back seat as the automobile navigated around vendor stands, dockworkers, and lumbering carts. The harbor was a chaotic mess. Flatbed wagons rolled along embedded railway tracks to deliver cargo to ships. The smell of exhaust fumes mingled with those of salty air and warm tar.

A wiry man ran toward the automobile, waving a stack of pages and shouting, "No more war!" He panted as he tried to keep up with the car, shoving a flyer at Finn that he instinctively grabbed.

"Back off, yellowbelly filth," Sergeant Lewis growled, and then he increased the car's speed by means of the throttle lever, leaving the protester behind.

"Sorry about that, sir. You can throw that trash away. Or use it at the latrine."

It was an antiwar flyer filled with lies and claptrap about the war. Finn held the document aloft. "Is this common here?"

"Not at all, sir. Just a handful of cowards afraid to do their duty. Everybody hates those people."

Finn didn't hate the pacifists; they were just ignorant of what was going on over there. Nobody who'd seen the horrors Germany was inflicting upon Europe would spout such claptrap. He tossed the flyer over his shoulder, letting the wind carry it into the bay.

Soon they were out of the city and on their way to Long Island. Every bump and jolt over the uneven road shot pain up his leg. Medical facilities weren't all they could be in France, and the fracture in his leg wasn't healing properly. It ached all the time now, but he'd eat nails before complaining. The guys in the trenches had it worse than he did, although he thanked God when their automobile finally turned into Camp Mills an hour later.

The camp spread before him in an overwhelming panorama. Thousands of olive-green tents stretched as far as the eye could see. Though the hastily constructed camp was only three months old, the grass had already been worn away in the aisles cutting through the sea of tents.

They rattled along a dusty dirt path, kicking up clouds of grit that made his nose twitch. They veered around a supply truck laden with rolls of canvas for more tents and squadrons of men marching in formation. Other soldiers were laying down board-walks over the dirt paths, the noise of their clattering hammers filling the air.

"How many people are here?" he hollered to Sergeant Lewis.

"About ten thousand," he called back. "A ship with three thousand men from the Nebraska National Guard left for France yesterday, and we've got another five thousand arriving from Ohio and Indiana this weekend."

It was entirely different from what Finn had experienced in France. The old excitement he once felt took root. This was where he belonged, among men joined together in a common cause. After being trapped for six weeks in Belgium, followed by another week on a troopship, it was time to join the Army and fight for freedom.

Their automobile cleared the tent city, moving toward a row of wooden buildings housing the medical station, command head-quarters, and the supply depot.

"That's the administrative building," the driver said, pointing to a boxy structure with two wings stretching out from a central hub. "We'll have to go in through the back entrance since they're laying concrete for the front steps."

Everything about this place was new and smelled of fresh paint, sawdust, and wet concrete.

An orderly with a wheelchair awaited them at the back door, and Sergeant Lewis hopped out of the driver's seat to open Finn's door for him.

"I'll be okay," Finn said, grasping the handle of his cane and waving the wheelchair away. He wasn't about to meet his new commanding officer looking like a cripple.

For the last two years, Finn had been flying for France as part of the Lafayette Escadrille, a squadron of American volunteer pilots who had no patience for President Wilson's spineless stance on German aggression. Now that the United States had formally entered the war, the Lafayette Escadrille had been disbanded. He'd have to sign up with the aviation section in the U.S. Army before he could be sent back to France.

His commanding officer had a different idea. "Why aren't you in the wheelchair?" Captain Romano said the moment Finn limped into the office. Unpainted wood framed the tiny room, which hadn't been wired for electricity yet. The only light came from an open window, where the tent city could be seen in the distance. Captain Romano stood and pointed Finn to the chair opposite his desk.

"I'm not that bad," Finn said.

Captain Romano frowned. "I sent that wheelchair for a reason. From now on you will be expected to obey orders. The rules here are different from what you were used to in France, Lieutenant Delaney. The French were so grateful to have you volunteer pilots helping out that they overlooked the rowdy behavior of the Lafayette Escadrille. Now that we're finally in the war, the aviators from the Lafayette Escadrille will be folded into the 103rd Pursuit Squadron, answerable to the U.S. Army."

"Understood, sir," he replied. "I'm looking forward to returning to France and helping the 103rd get up to snuff." Finn and his fellow pilots from the Lafayette Escadrille were the only Americans with aerial combat experience. They were sure to be an essential asset to the new squadron.

Captain Romano shook his head. "We've got plans for you Stateside. News of your escape from occupied Belgium has been printed in newspapers from coast to coast. You're famous here."

People had been singing his praises ever since he staggered across the border between Belgium and France, but he never tired of hearing it. For an orphaned kid who had dropped out of school to work in a fish cannery, it was heady stuff.

"How famous?" Finn joked. "Don't be shy. I want to hear all about it."

The captain ignored Finn's grin and continued with his instructions. "The Army wants you to ride along tomorrow in a war bond parade. There will be floats and regiments and plenty of music. You'll be in the back of a truck, and all you have to do is smile and wave to the crowd. People love a war hero, especially one famous for evading the Krauts. Incidentally, how did you pull it off? The newspapers were vague on that point."

It was the question everyone asked, but Finn vowed never to answer it. He smiled and acted nonchalant. "Pull what off?"

"How did you escape from Belgium back to France? That border has the most barbed wire, watch towers, and machine gun nests anywhere on the Western Front. How in blazes did you get through?"

"I guess the luck of the Irish was with me," he said with a shrug.

Captain Romano folded his arms and waited. Finn didn't budge. The silence in the room stretched and became uncomfortable. The ticking of the clock emphasized the standoff, but Finn would swallow his own tongue before he revealed the truth.

"I could order you to talk," Captain Romano said.

"With respect, it wouldn't do any good." Maybe refusing orders wasn't the best way to make a positive first impression on his new commanding officer, yet the Army needed Finn more than he needed them. He hadn't formally enlisted as yet, but if push came to shove, he'd go back home rather than inform on the people who had helped him escape from Belgium.

Finally, Captain Romano banged the desk bell, and the clerk opened the door. "Lieutenant Delaney, you're dismissed. Go to the intake office and sign your enrollment papers. And use that wheelchair. Again, so long as you are under my command, you *will* obey orders."

Finn nodded. "Yes, sir." While he'd never been much for following rules, he'd have to choose his battles carefully if he was ever going to get back to France.

The enrollment office had dozens of desks pushed together like sardines in a tin. The rattle of typewriters and the hum of voices filled the cavernous space. Finn sat at one of the desks as a recruitment corporal fired off questions and typed Finn's responses onto the blank forms. Finn answered every question, agreed to all the rules, and signed away his freedom with ease. His commitment to the cause was unshakable.

It wasn't until the last form that he balked.

"Who shall we notify in the event of your death?" Corporal Nowak didn't even glance up from the typewriter as he awaited Finn's answer.

Heat gathered beneath Finn's collar, and his skin prickled. No one. There was nobody. All his life, Finn had been the most popular man wherever he lived, and yet he couldn't think of one person to put down on the form. He didn't have a single relative or truly close friend. He had precisely nobody.

But then why should he care? He'd be dead.

"Just skip that form," he said, glancing at the clock on the wall and wishing to get this over with.

"I can't skip it," Corporal Nowak rapped out. "The Army needs to know who to notify in the event of your death. I need a name and an address."

Did Nowak have to say it so loud? On either side of him, others were easily supplying names of family members and wives. Finn was tempted to reach across the desk and tear up the form. He scrambled for an excuse. "I'll fill it out later. I don't have the address."

"Then just give me a name," Corporal Nowak said in exasperation. "We can hunt them down and be sure they get the death benefit."

"How much is the death benefit?"

"Ten thousand dollars," the clerk replied. "Who do you want to get it?"

Delia. The only girl he'd ever loved. She was the first girl he'd kissed, and the only one he wanted to marry. He would go to his grave regretting the way things ended between them. He still owed her three hundred dollars. The last time they saw each other, he tried to repay her, but she hated him too much to take it. She'd probably refuse the death benefit too.

"The name is Delia Byrne," he answered. It had been ten years since he'd spoken her name out loud. It felt strange to say it, as though the name was forbidden for him to utter. They had once been everything to each other. Now he couldn't even speak her name without feeling a rush of pained nostalgia and old regrets.

He straightened his spine and spoke more clearly. "Her name is Delia Byrne, and if I die and you can find her, give her everything and tell her that I'm sorry."

3

Delia normally found the quarter-mile walk between the courthouse and the law office easy, but the massive parade down Broadway had brought the city to a standstill. Schools had been let out early, businesses were closed, and the judge had canceled all afternoon cases since the parade down Broadway blocked all through traffic.

This meant she and Wesley were free to return to their office, except the parade prevented them from doing so.

"Who thought a celebratory parade for a pointless war was a good idea?" she asked Wesley.

"It's to drum up publicity for war bonds," he replied. "Shall we stay and watch?"

They didn't have much choice. Getting across Broadway would be impossible until the parade was over. The bleachers lining both sides of Broadway were filled, but they found a spot near a lamppost that wasn't too crowded.

Next to her, an old man wore a faded Civil War uniform. He had a young boy around five or six balanced on his shoulders. "That's the Statue of Liberty," the man said to the boy, pointing to a float featuring a reproduction of the statue.

Women dressed as pilgrims tossed candy to the crowd while men dressed in Revolutionary War costumes walked alongside the float and handed out flyers for Liberty Bonds.

A line of snare drummers came next, thrumming out a steady cadence as they led a formation of soldiers at least a thousand men strong, all marching in grim precision. Now the crowd really cheered. The women dressed as pilgrims and men in tricorn hats were playacting. The soldiers, however, were quite real.

The troops, having just arrived from the hinterlands of America, marched in lockstep behind the drummers. They all had the same shorn haircut, same uniform, same proud expression gazing forward. Yet they *weren't* the same. They were farmers, teachers, accountants, fathers, and brothers. Soon they'd be cannon fodder.

"Is my daddy in there?" the boy next to them asked.

"He's right there," the vet said, pointing vaguely to the regiment of marching soldiers.

"Where? I can't see him." The boy started crying, bemoaning that he couldn't see his daddy to tell him goodbye.

"Don't cry," the old man said. "Your dad will be back before you know it. I promise!"

Delia shifted her attention back to the next group of soldiers marching past, her heart growing frosty.

Not all fathers returned home from war. Or if they did, sometimes they were only a pale shadow of the person they used to be. Sometimes a strong man, like a pipe fitter who could haul an eighty-pound hydraulic pump as though it were a loaf of bread, could become so weak that lifting a hand in greeting would sap his energy. And sometimes that same man could be in so much pain that even smiling at his daughter hurt. Sometimes that same, formerly strong man would try to comfort his frightened daughter on the morning that he died, only three months after coming home from Cuba, and never once in all that time was he able to get out of bed.

Not all fathers survived a war. Delia still put flowers on her father's grave every Fourth of July, along with a small American flag because he had carried a fierce love of his country until the end. Delia loved her country too. It was the stupidity of the Spanish-American War that had made her a pacifist.

She folded her arms and glared as the troops moved past. Those men couldn't help what was happening to them. Some of them had volunteered, but most had been drafted and had no choice as to their fate. That sweet young boy might be an orphan before the year was out.

Following the soldiers was a mixed group of men and women, each wearing a sash across their chest denoting their volunteer organizations. They were civilians working for the Red Cross, the YMCA, even librarians who were heading overseas to set up libraries for the troops.

Then came an open carriage with a lone man sitting on a raised platform as he waved to the crowd. Even from a hundred yards away, it was easy to see his appeal. He was blond and tanned, with a knee-weakening grin. He wasn't in uniform, but his battered leather jacket had a military rank embroidered on the arm. The white silk scarf casually looped around his neck made him look like a movie star.

"Who's that?" she asked Wesley.

"I've no idea, but the leather jacket comes from the Lafayette Escadrille," Wesley replied, and then he went on the explain how a few dozen American pilots, frustrated by their nation's refusal to join the war, had gone overseas to fly for the French Army.

"Then he's an idiot," she muttered under her breath. Anyone who signed up to fight before America had even entered the conflict was a mindless warmonger.

Young women ran after the carriage, flinging rose petals in its path, and the man seemed to relish every second of it. He waved at the crowd with a cocky air, seeming to soak up their adulation, his grin as bright as the midday sun.

He looked familiar. She stood on tiptoe to get a better view.

There was something familiar in the way he held himself, in the easy confidence of his wave. Her heart hammered against her ribs at the sight of him, stirring a whirlwind of old memories.

No, it couldn't be. It couldn't possibly be . . .

But it was, and her stomach gave a faint lurch. The friendly, wry grin that melted her teenaged heart was the same. The sandy-blond hair with the stubborn lock that fell over his forehead was the same. The cleft in his chin, the glint in his eyes . . .

It was Finn Delaney, the daredevil adventurer who had broken her heart and stolen her life savings!

4

Seeing Finn for the first time in ten years left Delia shaken and raw. As teenagers they fell in love over their mutual love of staring into the sky and dreaming of what it would be like to fly. Of all the fates she had imagined for Finn, learning that he had twisted his love of flight to become a war hawk was quite possibly the worst.

Instead of heading back to her desk at the law office, she trudged up six flights of stairs to the roof of the office building. The Chandler Law Firm occupied the first floor of the mid-rise building, and she often came up here for a clear view of the sky. The weather-beaten, tarred gravel was the only ugly part of the otherwise elegant building. She took a seat on the edge of a wooden cable spool and gazed at the sky, the breeze tugging at her hair.

Maybe seeing Finn again was a blessing in disguise. The only thing stopping her from falling headlong in love with Wesley was her lingering affection for Finn, a man who was Wesley's opposite in every way.

Delia was only thirteen when she landed at St. Michael's Home for Orphans, where she met Finn. He was two years older and popular, while she was new, shy, and *bald*. During her father's illness, she'd contracted a terrible case of head lice. Shaving off her long, silky black hair was the only solution. Her baldness made her a target for a pack of mean-spirited girls at the orphanage.

Avoiding these girls was all but impossible. There were only eight in her age group, so Delia was lumped in with them, both in the classroom and in the dormitory. They would snatch the scarf off her head, call her "Baldilocks," and giggle behind their hands.

It came to an end when Sister Bernadette witnessed the time Kristen Danvers threw Delia's headscarf into the latrine. Sister Bernadette almost never got mad, but that day she battled angry tears as she excoriated Kristen and the other girls. The girls immediately expressed shame and apologized to Delia. They even agreed to befriend her, and for a while it seemed to work. They let her join them at mealtimes and quit calling her names.

One day they lured her up to the roof of the orphanage. "Have you never been up there?" Kristen asked. "It's the best place in the whole building! You can see all the way to the East River. You can even see steamships coming into port."

Delia followed the three girls up the dim stairwell leading to the roof. Their footsteps clattered on the concrete steps, and Delia covered her nose against the dank smell in the echoey stairwell. Her sense of unease vanished the moment she stepped onto the wondrous rooftop.

It was filled with sunlight, and a refreshing breeze blew steadily. She took in the impressive view around her. "You really can see all the way to the river," she marveled. She could even smell the salt air drifting in from the bay. And the *sky*! Much of Manhattan was cast in perpetual shadow by the city's towering buildings, and from the alleyways it was impossible to see more than a sliver of sky. Up here, she had to crane her neck to take in the immensity of the blue expanse above. Wispy clouds stretched as though painted by an unseen artist onto a never-ending canvas. It was the most beautiful thing she'd ever seen. "I love this!" she whispered.

"Good," Kristen said. "You can stay here and enjoy it." The

girls giggled as they ran for the stairwell door. They raced through and slammed it behind them.

As much as Delia loved the rooftop, she didn't want to be left alone up here. She hurried to the door and twisted the knob. It was locked. She wiggled the knob again and was greeted by gales of laughter from the other side of the door.

"Open the door!" she yelled, pounding on the door. "Please!"

The girls' laughter grew distant as they descended the stairs. They had abandoned her on the rooftop with no way to get back inside the building.

How stupid she had been to trust them. She couldn't go to Sister Bernadette about this either, for she didn't want to be known as a tattletale. Now that she was alone, it suddenly felt scary being on the rooftop. It was almost lunchtime, and she had to go to the bathroom.

If she wet herself, there'd be no end to the teasing. Her hair was now two inches long, so people didn't tease her about being bald anymore. But if she wet herself, nobody would ever let her forget it. Her legs began trembling, making it difficult to stand.

Delia turned and slid down with her back against the door. She sat on the gravel and looked up at the sky. "Oh, Papa, why did you die and leave me in this awful place?"

Shame immediately flooded her. Papa had tried his hardest not to die. It wasn't his fault. It was the stupid war that killed him, and she should be ashamed for even thinking such things.

"I didn't mean it," she whispered into her clenched hands, even though she prayed he couldn't hear or see her. He would be so upset to see what had become of her.

It became hot as the sun rose higher. The smell of warm tar rose from the rooftop beneath her, but she was too afraid to stand. The low brick wall would probably stop her from falling off the building, but she was shaking so terribly that she didn't trust herself on her feet. How much more could she take?

A rhythmic clang sounded from the far side of the roof. One

clang after another, and then a head popped up on the other side of the roof. It was Finn Delaney. He hauled himself up and over the side of the roof. How stupid she had been not to realize there was a fire escape.

Finn was one of the older boys, good-looking and popular. They never spoke a single word to each other, but he looked at her strangely as he scrambled onto the roof, carrying a kite slung over his shoulder.

"Hey, Delia," he said in surprise. "What are you doing up here?"

It was surprising a boy as well-liked as Finn Delaney even knew her name. "I got locked out," she admitted as she pushed herself to her feet. "I came up here with Kristen Jones and some of the other girls, but I think they forgot me. I got locked out."

Finn didn't fall for her lie and seemed genuinely angry. "I thought Sister Bernadette put an end to all that."

"I thought so too." Her lower lip began to wobble. To start crying in front of the most popular boy at St. Michael's would be the ultimate mortification.

"You can get down on the fire escape," he said. "It opens up on the fourth floor. Or you can stay up here and watch me fly my kite." He held it out for her to see.

It was a basic kite of white fabric stretched over a diamond frame and tied to a string. She didn't have any interest in kites, but she didn't want to venture down the fire escape alone.

"Can I watch?" she said, and he grinned.

It took about five seconds for the kite to catch the wind, and they both stared in admiration as it lifted overhead. The kite seemed as though alive as it soared above the gritty Lower East Side neighborhood.

It was at that exact moment when Delia felt her life turn, opening a page to a new chapter. She wanted to laugh and cry at the same time, but mostly she was just happy. The kite was beautiful! The way Finn smiled as he watched it made her smile too.

"Sometimes I feel like the earth is holding me down," Finn said, his eyes fastened on the sky. "When I'm flying a kite, I imagine I'm up there with it among the clouds, soaring over buildings, rivers, and treetops. It's the best way in the world to escape."

Why would someone like Finn Delaney need to escape? He was popular and smart, although appearances could be deceiving. She'd heard that Finn's mother had been killed in a fire when he was only twelve. Now he was fifteen and had a part-time job at a fish cannery, which was on top of going to school. It was one of the reasons he always looked worn out. Yet everyone respected him because he was already starting to earn money and make his own way in the world.

Her friendship with Finn grew quickly as she routinely met him on the roof to watch him fly his kite. On her fourteenth birthday, Finn gave her a kite he had made with his own two hands. It was the best gift she'd ever been given, and now the two of them could fly together.

It was in her fourteenth year that Delia became a genuinely happy person. She still lived in the grim world of the orphanage, but everything got better. Schoolwork was more interesting because flying kites had sparked her curiosity. Science class became an opportunity to learn about wind and gravity and velocity. Sewing lessons gave her the chance to experiment with kite design. She and Finn went to the public library to look at books that had drawings of dragon kites, box kites, and delta kites.

And somewhere along the way, they fell in love. They shared their first kiss one summer evening on the top of the building as the setting sun lit the clouds in a fiery golden glow. At first it was hard to believe someone as outgoing as Finn would choose a loner like Delia, but as the months rolled by, there could be no doubt. They told each other *everything*. He confided his ongoing guilt over his mother's death and his dream of someday opening a kite shop.

"I don't want to work in a fish cannery all my life," he'd say as he lay on his back gazing at the clouds. "If I could do anything in the world, I'd build and sell my own kites."

"Why can't you?" Delia was good at planning and calculated what it would cost to build kites and rent shop space.

During long, sunbaked afternoons, they dreamed about what it would be like to own a kite shop. At night they charted the heavens using books checked out of the library. They snuck onto the rooftop to watch meteor showers and lunar eclipses. Finn used his money from the cannery to buy a wind gauge for measuring the velocity of the wind. Delia kept a notebook to record the data, while Finn talked about designing gigantic kites that could defy gravity.

More than anything, Finn wanted to make a box kite, which was the king of kites. Its long, rectangular frame provided more stability to lift it higher into the sky than any other kite.

Their first attempts at making their own box kite failed because it was too heavy. Finn saved enough money to buy silk fabric, although they still didn't know if their second attempt would be light enough to fly. It required two people to run at top speed to launch it, so Delia borrowed a pair of trousers from one of the younger boys at the orphanage. Now that their secret was out, a lot of the other kids tagged along to the park to watch. Even Sister Bernadette came to cheer them on.

They took the box kite to a field with a huge wide-open space for them to take a running start. They waited for a breeze, then jogged slowly in tandem, gradually working up to a run. Finn took the lead, holding the flying line, while Delia carried the box kite a few yards behind. The wind was strong in her face, and she angled the kite, running fast until the wind lifted it away.

"Run, Finn!" she yelled after him. He lengthened his stride, racing across the meadow as the cumbersome box kite struggled to gain altitude. It wobbled and hovered, and then it happened. Like magic! It was as if the hand of God lifted the kite to soar up into the air.

It was magnificent! Delia and Sister Bernadette held each other as Finn ran laps around the field. Others in the park stopped to watch and shout their praise. Finally, the kite stayed aloft on its own. Finn didn't need to run anymore. Instead, he just held the line, panting from the exertion, but she could see his smile from all the way across the park.

The day Finn launched the box kite gleamed like a diamond in Delia's memory. Even now, after all this time, it had been the happiest day of her life. She doubted another could ever touch the pure joy and innocence of that day.

Delia shook away the memories. She ought to be downstairs, helping Wesley prepare for next week's cases instead of wallowing in old dreams.

As much as she once loved Finn, she hated what he had become. To use his marvelous gift of flight as a weapon of destruction was an abomination. Even worse, she had spent the last ten years comparing other men to Finn and inevitably found them lacking. Even Wesley paled in comparison. Could a girl ever truly forget her first love? Finn rescued her during the worst part of her life. Even though he had let her down, a part of her would always love what they once had. Those early years were pristine, like the idyllic world inside a snow globe, untouched by the chaos outside.

Delia abruptly stood from the abandoned cable spool. She and Wesley were the perfect team, and it was time to make her move and convince him that their age difference didn't matter.

Finn was her past. Wesley was her future.

5

Finn braced himself for bad news after submitting to tests and X-rays of his damaged leg. Two different doctors and a surgeon had examined him, and afterward he was wheeled into the Army surgeon's office to get the results.

Dr. Sullivan sent him a tight smile as he took a seat behind his desk to face Finn. "I've got good news and bad news. Which do you want to hear first?"

"Am I going to lose my leg?"

"That depends on what we find when we operate," the doctor said. "The X-rays show that the fracture in your tibia isn't healing like it should. There's a gap between the fractured segments, and you're going to need surgery to correct it. I'll put you under a strong dose of anesthesia, then open up your leg. I will realign the tibia with screws and a metal plate. I'll stitch you back up and slap a cast on it. Then we wait to see if it heals properly."

The prospect of surgery terrified Finn. To be put under and let some sawbones slice him open and bust up whatever minor healing had already happened? It went against everything he knew.

"And if the screws don't work?"

"In that case, we may have to take the leg," Dr. Sullivan replied.

"What if I don't have the surgery?"

"At best you will live in pain for the rest of your life. At worst you'll get gangrene, lose the leg, and die from the infection."

Finn digested the information in silence. He had been lucky not to have died during the crash landing in Belgium. He'd been lucky Mathilde Verhaegen rescued him before the Germans got to him. He was lucky to have escaped the periodic search parties that had been sent out to find him during those pain-filled days hiding beneath Mathilde's floorboards. Following the crash, his leg was treated by the town's veterinarian, the only person with medical training Mathilde trusted with her dangerous secret.

"If the surgery works, how long before I can go back to France?"

"You're not going back to France," Dr. Sullivan said flatly. "Captain Romano told me you've been appointed to a Stateside assignment."

Finn rocked back in his seat, dumbfounded. "What's the assignment?"

"He wouldn't say, but he stressed that you're very important to the cause, and you're staying right here in New York."

He shouldn't have signed those papers to join the Army. Maybe it wasn't too late to get back to France and join up with the Frenchies again. Or he could sign up with the French Foreign Legion. He signed on to the war to fight the enemy, to do so while in the cockpit of an airplane, not stay home in New York while his brothers-in-arms did the heavy lifting. Though he was willing to lay his life on the line for a cause, he felt no obligation to Captain Romano and his Stateside assignment.

The problem was that he needed his leg fixed before he could do anything. Once it was fully healed, he'd figure out a way to shake off Captain Romano as well as his mysterious assignment.

Finn was risking a court martial by leaving Camp Mills without authorization, but he needed to check on Delia before his surgery tomorrow.

It had been ten years since he'd seen her, and he needed to be sure she was okay. Almost drowning in a muddy Belgian field brought old regrets roaring back to life with painful clarity. Before risking his life on an operating table, Finn needed to put things right.

Not that he hadn't already tried. The last time he saw Delia, she was so furious she wouldn't even take the money from his hand when he tried to repay her. Back then she'd been in secretarial school. Had she ever gotten her certificate? Or found a respectable job? Working as a fish gutter wasn't a fate he'd wish on anyone, but that was how he and Dee earned a living after they left the orphanage.

He was sweating when the streetcar stopped at the Lower East Side destination. It took forever to ease himself through the opening of the streetcar, but the driver was patient. Everyone treated wounded men in uniform as if they walked on air, and a nearby pretzel vendor rushed forward to lend a hand as Finn gingerly stepped down onto the pavement.

"Can I give you a lift somewhere, sir?" the vendor asked.

"Thanks, but no," Finn said. The Hester Street Secretarial School was straight ahead, and he could get there on his own steam. He grasped the head of his cane and limped forward, focusing on the school's front doors as he walked. It would be better if there hadn't been a short flight of stairs in front of the building, but he'd endured worse.

Five minutes later, he was seated on a hard bench in the administrative office, waiting for the secretary to flip through a box of index cards that tracked the school's graduates. The Hester Street Secretarial School boasted of their fine track record for placing their graduates in professional positions, and Finn prayed that had been the case for Delia.

"The Chandler Law Firm," the clerk said as she held a card aloft. "Miss Byrne has been working with them for six years."

A spurt of elation made him sit taller. "She is? What sort of job is it?"

"The card doesn't say, but I'm sure Miss Byrne is a credit to our school."

"Is she . . . does she still go by Miss Byrne?" He thought she would be married by now. Not that it was any of his business. Delia made it blindingly clear that she never wanted to see him again, and he intended to honor her request, but he still wanted to know.

"I'm sure I can't say," the clerk said as she wiggled Delia's card back into the file box.

It didn't matter whether she was married or not. Finn had lost his chance with her but still needed to assure himself she was doing well. Not all law firms were classy. New York was filled with shady lawyers who'd do anything to earn a fast buck. It was only three o'clock, and he could get a peek at the place where she worked and still make it back to Camp Mills before the evening roll call. Delia was worth the risk.

The Chandler Law Firm was located off Fifth Avenue in a ritzy part of Midtown. It took an hour for Finn to get there, and he parked himself at a café across the street to nurse a cup of coffee while scrutinizing the building. It had six stories, a big front window with gold stenciling, and all kinds of fancy molding on the stone facade. They probably had the money to pay their secretaries a decent wage.

At five o'clock the door opened, and a woman came out. Dark-haired, elegant, well-dressed. He snapped the newspaper open to hide behind and peeked around its edge.

There was no doubt. It was Delia.

He'd never seen her so finely dressed. When they were kids, they got handouts from the charity bin, but Delia's tailored dress was no handout. The blue gown with black piping looked custom-made for her. That pale shade of powder blue had always been Delia's favorite color. His too. It was the color of the sky. They used to lay on their backs on the orphanage rooftop, watching cloud formations drift and reshape against the cerulean sky.

Those afternoons on the rooftop felt like a million years ago.

It was a magnificent time. Wasn't that odd? Their years at the orphanage were hard, gritty, and tough, but they'd both been happy. He thought they were merely having a good time. He didn't know they were making memories that would become the foundation of his life.

He twisted in his chair, angling the paper so he could watch as Delia strode down the street, a spiffy leather case in her hand and a straw boater perched atop her head. She looked prosperous and successful, and he was so proud of her that he wanted to cheer.

They'd both come a long way after leaving the orphanage, back in the days when she looked at him as though he were a hero. He had confided all his flaws to Delia, and she still respected him. He could tell her *anything*. One cloudy summer day, he even told her how he got the burn marks on his right hand.

Instead of scowling, she cradled his hand and kissed the scars. "It's okay, Finn. I'm not perfect either." They held each other and wept. It was the most profound moment of his life. The communion of two souls—both needy, both wounded. It seemed as if the clouds that had hovered over him for years parted, and he was given a glimpse of a future with Delia at his side. He had found a soul mate whose wounds were as deep as his, and yet they still gazed beyond the clouds to build castles in the sky.

For a while they believed they could do anything, even though they were two orphans who possessed nothing but their dreams. If Delia hadn't been so timid, perhaps they could have made those dreams come true.

Was she still timid? She looked quite determined as she arrived at a streetcar stop a block away. It was tempting to grab his cane and hobble after her. Call out to her. Talk to her. He could reach her before the streetcar arrived, but he'd have to move quickly.

Except Delia had stated she never wanted to see him again, and so far he'd honored her request. He squeezed the handle of his cane, drinking in the sight of her. Was she still angry at him? Perhaps she'd forgiven him, and they could wish each other well.

Congratulate each other because, against all odds, they had both made something of themselves.

Then again, maybe she was still angry and his trying to speak with her would be ripping the bandage off a still-raw wound.

He settled back into his chair. It was easier to imagine Delia had made peace with what happened between them than to face the possibility that she still despised him.

It was time to go back to his world and let her go about her own. She looked healthy and prosperous. He couldn't ask for more.

A streetcar lumbered to a stop, and Delia joined the cluster of people waiting to board.

"Good luck, Delia," he whispered as the streetcar carried her away.

6

It was an ordinary Friday, and yet nothing felt normal as Delia went about her daily tasks at the office. Today was the day she intended to issue the long-overdue ultimatum to Wesley, and it loomed like the sword of Damocles over her head. Either Wesley would accept her into his heart, or she would leave him.

And leaving him meant leaving her job. With each passing hour, she wondered if this would be the last time she would fill in her calendar, tracking the firm's weekly progress. She commissioned the calendar using exact specifications to display color-coded columns, tabs, trial schedules, and outcomes. For six years she had taken pride in the tangible record of their accomplishments. This week she recorded their victory in a case defending conscientious objectors from being drafted into the war. Her satisfaction was marred when she noted a lapsed donation to the Commission for the Relief of Belgium. Their stance on the war had caused a downturn in business, and so Wesley had to curtail his donations to the struggling charity.

Delia had provided free secretarial services to the CRB whenever Bert Hoover, the charity's founder, came to New York on business. "Bertie," as he preferred to be known, was an extraordinary man.

He climbed out of an impoverished childhood to became one of the richest men in America through his work as a mining engineer and investor. Once he learned what was happening in Belgium, he walked away from his job mining gold to found the CRB. Delia and Wesley were enthusiastic supporters of the humanitarian mission, and Wesley gave Delia leave to work fifteen hours a week to handle CRB affairs.

A wistful smile curved her lips as she closed her calendar, running her hands along the soft leather cover. She loved this job but wouldn't remain if Wesley was determined to hold her at arm's length for the rest of her life.

Reginald had left early this evening, leaving her and Wesley the only people in the office. Their regular Friday meeting to discuss unfinished business loomed. At the top of the list was a meeting with the leaders of the CRB to discuss their worsening financial situation, and Wesley's legal advice was desperately needed. Delia gathered her paperwork for the meeting and headed to Wesley's office, her heart knocking like an out-of-control jackhammer.

This was it, the moment that was six years in the making, and there would be no turning back.

Wesley sat behind his desk, a lock of dark hair falling across his forehead. He was overdue for a haircut. Normally he visited the barber every third Tuesday of the month, but his work with the conscientious objectors had caused him to miss it.

She tapped on the open door. "Ready for me?"

He pushed the paperwork aside. "Of course. Have a seat."

She left the office door open because he always insisted on proper decorum, even though the rest of the office was empty. Delia set her clipboard on the edge of his desk, then wandered toward the standing globe beside the corner window because she was too nervous to sit. This was the exact spot of their first kiss.

She sent the globe spinning with a single nudge of her index finger. "The meeting with the board of directors for the CRB has been scheduled at the end of the month. Germany wants to cut off their access to the international shipping lanes, so I've pulled the global treaties you'll need to bolster their cause. We will be meeting at Bert Hoover's house with the rest of the board."

The silence lengthened, interrupted only by the squeak of the globe as she slowly twirled it. She rested her finger along the equator, watching the continents spin by.

"Delia, would you step away from the globe?"

His voice sounded tight. Uncomfortable. She could read his mind, and he remembered their kiss.

"Why?" she asked. "I like this globe. Immensely."

"I like the sight of you beside it. Too much."

It was a perfect opening. She left the globe to close the office door.

Wesley quirked a brow but didn't say anything, even when she pulled the roller blind down, then turned to confront him. She tilted her head and locked eyes with him.

He remained seated behind the desk, almost as if it were a shield. His knuckles were white as he held the arms of his chair, and he swallowed so hard his Adam's apple bobbed above his starched collar. "Delia, please—"

"Please what? Please stop admiring you? Stop wishing for more?"

He sighed and glanced away. "I'm nineteen years older than you. In two years I'm going to be *fifty*."

"Don't you think I can count? Yes, I'm twenty-nine and you are forty-eight. According to actuarial tables, a man in your situation can expect to live into his seventies. I like those odds. Twenty years to give into temptation and have a partner with whom to share a fulfilling life."

"Twenty years for you to regret shackling yourself to an old man."

"Oh, stop," she chided. "There will be no shackles in our relationship. We shall forever be side by side out of choice."

The side of his mouth quirked. "No shackles then. Perhaps there will be wheelchairs, arthritis creams, and hearing trumpets."

"Still not afraid, Wesley." She said it in jest, but he had sobered.

"Delia, by your own admission, you are prone to youthful infatuation."

She should never have told him about Finn. "Only once," she pointed out. And it wasn't an infatuation; it was real love. She'd loved Finn with the youthful fires of spring, but he had betrayed her. With the passing of years, she came to accept her own role in what had happened. If she hadn't been so timid, perhaps he wouldn't have betrayed her.

Wesley's steadfast dependability was a much better match for her cautious nature. She leaned against the door as his laughter faded. She didn't want to leave. Even if they never had anything more than a deep and abiding friendship, she didn't want to leave. But it was time to screw up her courage and ask for more.

"I won't go on like this any longer," she said, her voice gentle.

He appeared wounded but recovered quickly. "Where would you go?"

"There are other law firms where I could find work. The government is scrambling to hire clerks with legal experience."

Wesley adjusted the knot of his tie. "Well, if that's what you want . . ."

It's not what I want, she silently screamed inside. *I want to stay here with you. I want you to fight for me, to beg me to stay. To tell me you can't function without me and you look forward to seeing me first thing every morning.*

She bit her tongue and didn't say anything as she pushed away from the door, circled his desk, and approached him from behind. He still hadn't left his chair, but he watched her from the corner of his eye, a muscle in his jaw beginning to twitch.

She leaned over him to set her hands on the armrests. She was close enough to see the tiny bit of dark stubble forming along his jaw. "I want to stay right here," she whispered in his ear.

His breath left in a rush. Unbelievably, the hint of a smile tugged the corner of his mouth. "Do you?" His voice was rough with just a hint of flirtation. It sent her heart into triple time.

She straightened and rotated his chair until he faced her. "I do."

He stood, but she didn't step back. She tilted her head up to lock eyes with him again.

"Sometimes you can be shockingly forward, Delia."

"And you're maddeningly reticent," she said, her gaze traveling over his starched collar, buttoned-down vest, and his firm jawline.

His lips parted as he leaned toward her, his mouth only inches from her.

The door banged open, and she leapt back. Amy, Wesley's seventeen-year-old daughter, barged into the office, all brunette curls and lacy flounce. "Papa, everything is a disaster, and the whole world hates me."

Wesley jerked back, leaving a tingle along Delia's cheek where his nose had just been nuzzling her.

"Darling . . ." Wesley soothed, but the affectionate word was directed at Amy, not the woman who was ready to lay the world at his feet.

Wesley's only failing in the entire world was in spoiling his daughter rotten. After her mother's death ten years ago, Wesley lavished money, praise, and indulgence on Amy, who devoured it all with the ferocity of a hyena scavenging for new flesh.

"The Westchester ball is tomorrow night, and I don't have any opera gloves."

"But you do," Wesley assured her.

"No, I don't! I only have wrist-length gloves, and Gladys Conner says wrist gloves are for babies. Gimbels is sold out of opera gloves, and I won't go without them."

Delia glanced at the clock, wondering how she could fix this. The Gimbels flagship store was in Boston, and they could put a pair of opera gloves on the overnight steamship operated by the Fall River Line.

"I'll take care of it," Delia said, hating the capitulation in her voice. "If I leave now, I can get a telegram to the store in Boston and arrange to have them shipped overnight."

The gratitude shining in Wesley's eyes made her annoyance worthwhile. "Thank you," he said. "A million times, thank you, Delia. You're a miracle worker."

"Isn't that her job?" Amy pointed out, and at last Wesley showed a hint of backbone.

"Yes, it's her job, but Delia's quick thinking and efficiency is something you could learn from, Amy."

Amazingly, Amy looked properly cowed. Delia picked up her clipboard and eyed Wesley. "This isn't over," she said.

"I suspected as much," he said dryly, and she couldn't tell if he was pleased or worried.

Either way, the battle would begin again on Monday.

7

Finn couldn't understand why he was so terrified of surgery. He had never been afraid to hop in an airplane and risk his life in a dogfight with German pilots. When he was in the air, he had a fighting chance, and if he died in pursuit of a noble cause? Well, that was okay with him.

Surgery was different. Instead of relying on his own wits, he had to lie on a table and surrender his body into the care of strangers. People didn't always wake up from surgery. The drugs could stop his heart. The slip of a scalpel could sever a nerve or vein, leaving him to die on the table. Infection could get him.

In short, there were a lot of ways this surgery could kill him, and all of it was out of his control. It was why he called for a priest. If he died on the table, he wanted to be right with God before he went.

He lay on a gurney outside in the surgical waiting room, dressed in a thin cotton smock and shaking from the cold. Was he really trembling from the cold, or was it because he was scared out of his skull? The throb in his leg ached so badly he was certain the doctor would probably lop it off.

A nurse with one of those folded caps approached, smiling down at him. "Dr. Sullivan is ready. I'll just wheel you in, all right?"

He grasped her arm. "I asked for a priest. I want to make a confession before they put me under."

"Father Patrick hasn't been in to see you yet?" He shook his head, and the nurse frowned. "I'll see if I can find him."

Finn turned his face to the wall. This wasn't how he wanted to die. For the most part he'd lived a decent life, but he had regrets and it was time to quit running from them.

Father Patrick arrived a few minutes later. "You asked to see me?" The priest wore a clerical collar, round spectacles, and spoke with an Irish accent.

Finn nodded and got straight to the point. "Forgive me, Father, for I have sinned. It's been six months since my last confession. But the thing is . . . ."

His mouth went dry, and he clenched his fists. Confession was never much fun, but he had often gone since leaving the orphanage. He had confessed the sin of theft when he stole from Delia and for the sin of lust. Delia again. He had confessed to his bouts with envy. Heck, he had all the normal sins of any man, but there was one he'd never been able to confess.

"The thing is, Father, I've never been able to confess my biggest sin. I've always been too ashamed to admit it." And it had nagged him for twenty-one years. When he was eighteen, he told Delia about it. She'd said all the right things, but he still hadn't been able to forgive himself.

The scrape of metal sounded as Father Patrick drew a chair beside his bed and sat. "Let's hear it then."

Finn clenched his fists and averted his gaze. It was hard enough to resurrect shameful memories without looking a priest in the face. "When I was a kid, I wanted people to think I was a hero, and I ended up getting my mom killed because of it. I was twelve when a fire broke out in the tenement where we lived. It was a cooking fire that had started on the floor above us. The whole building was a firetrap, and it spread quickly. My mom and I got out okay, but I saw a little yellow cat yowling on the fifth floor."

The cat belonged to a girl Finn liked. The girl's name was Daisy, and she loved that cat. Daisy stood in the alley and cried as she looked up at her cat, trying to encourage it to jump.

"I wanted to be a hero," Finn said, gripping the cold metal of the gurney rail. "I raced inside to save the cat so that Daisy would like me."

His mother had tried to stop him. She raced inside the burning building after him, yelling at him to stop being a fool and get outside. He ignored her, running up the staircase. She followed him. The two of them were able to get to the cat and scoop her up. Clouds of smoke billowed up the stairwell, and the heat was scorching. They had almost made it to safety when his mother got clobbered by a falling timber. She was trapped, and Finn couldn't get the beam off her. He tried, but he wasn't strong enough, and the heat was getting to him. His right hand got burned, making it impossible to keep trying. He ran outside for help, but she died before they could get her out of the building.

He told it all to Father Patrick. "My mother was the best," he finally concluded. "She looked after everybody in the building. She was the only one everybody trusted because she was smart and funny and wise. And she died a horrible death because I wanted to impress a girl."

"You were only a child," Father Patrick said, but Finn cut him off.

"I was old enough to know better," he said, unable to block the bitterness in his tone. "I did it because I wanted to be a hero, and my mom paid the price for it. I'll never forgive myself for that. I keep thinking that I owe the world for killing my mom. I try to do good. I stand up to bullies. I went to France so I could shove the Jerries back where they came from."

"So you're still trying to be a hero?"

He folded his arms across his chest. "Maybe," he admitted. It wasn't so much for the glory. It was because a good woman had died, and it was his fault. He owed it to the world to keep proving himself.

Father Patrick's voice was understanding. "My son, if you are genuinely repentant and ask Christ Jesus for forgiveness, you are forgiven. You don't need to perform acts of heroism to earn that forgiveness. He gives it freely. Your pain and regret are valid, but remember that Jesus came to save us sinners, to save us from our pride, foolishness, and vanity."

Finn turned his face to the wall, wishing he could believe it. The priest said his final blessing and left. Guilt still ate at his soul as the nurse wheeled him into the operating room.

His leg hurt. A heavy, dark fog surrounded him, making him weightless except for the sharp ache in his leg. Did that mean he still *had* a leg? Or had they lopped it off?

Finn groaned, trying to shake the haze of drugs from his brain and open his eyes.

"Shh," a woman said. "Stay still. You don't want to injure your leg further."

"Do I still have it?" he croaked.

"Yes, of course," the woman said, and he sank back to the mattress. A tear leaked from his eye, and he didn't have the strength to brush it away. He didn't care. He still had his leg.

But he couldn't move it. Panic set in again, and this time he managed to open his eyes. "I can't move my leg."

"It's in a cast. Here, have some water." For an old lady, the nurse was surprisingly strong as she lifted his head. Cool water soothed his throat, a blessed trickle of relief, and he wanted more.

"That's enough for now," she said, lowering his head. He didn't have the strength to reach for the glass and soon slipped back into a doze.

It was dark when he awoke again, thirsty and hungry and craving a cigar. Someone must have smoked one nearby recently because the whole room smelled of cigar smoke. Finn hadn't had a cigar since the plane crash. He didn't even like them all that much, but the relaxing comfort of a smoke would be good right now.

He cracked his eyes open to look around. There was no sign of the old nurse, just a shadowy man in a fine suit, sitting in the corner with a magazine propped on his lap. He was smoking a fat, hand-rolled cigar.

"How are you feeling?" the man asked.

"Like I could use a cigar," Finn replied, his voice coming out like a croak.

The man reached into his breast pocket and produced one. His body had been neglected, broken, and abused, and Finn wanted the comfort of that cigar enough to prop up on an elbow for it. He clamped it between his teeth while the other man struck a match. It illuminated a surprisingly young man with a round, pleasant face. His hair was neatly groomed down the middle, and he had the wholesome look of an altar boy.

Finn took several quick draws to light the cigar, then sank back against the pillow, savoring the soothing hit of nicotine. "Thanks," he said.

"Say nothing of it," the man said.

"Are you a doctor?" Finn asked.

The man shook his head. "Just a concerned citizen who wants to see you healed. Dr. Sullivan reports that you are expected to make a complete recovery."

"You're not joshing me, are you?"

"I wouldn't joke about something like that. You're too important to my cause."

Finn drew another pull on the cigar. Maybe he was still muddleheaded because, aside from his ability to fly an airplane, he wasn't important to anyone. The sooner he could get back up in the air, he could regain the fraying threads of dignity and meaning in life.

"What's your cause?" he asked.

"I raise money for the Commission for the Relief of Belgium. I think you would make a convincing spokesman. You have an interesting story to tell."

"Sorry, friend. The only thing I want to do once I get out of this bed is get back to France and rejoin my squadron." The two dozen pilots he left behind there were his only family. He was letting them down by lying here abed in New York. Maybe he couldn't fly for a while, but he could help train new pilots.

"Your commanding officer has assigned you to me."

Finn coughed on a lungful of smoke. Captain Romano only became his commanding officer last week when he arrived in New York. "Who are you?" Finn asked.

"Bertie Hoover, chairman of the Commission for the Relief of Belgium."

Finn let out a low whistle and collapsed back onto the pillow. Bert Hoover was one of the richest men in America. Rumor had it that everything he touched turned to gold.

"You look a lot younger in person," Finn said. "Mr. Hoover, sir—"

"Please, call me Bertie. My wife says I have a baby face because it's round, but I'm forty-three and old enough to know who I want for an important assignment."

Now Finn felt guilty for accepting the fancy cigar since he was going to turn down the man's job offer. "Look, I don't know anything about public speaking. I dropped out of school in the ninth grade. You could do better with someone else."

"How did you escape from Belgium?"

The question took Finn by surprise. It was the one everyone had been asking, and so far Finn had rebuffed all their attempts to learn the truth. Bertie Hoover was the last man on the planet he'd confess it to. He gave a little shrug and said, "My memory on all that is a little blurry."

It was a lie. He remembered everything about the day he snuck into the hold of that river barge. Six hundred sacks of rolled oats had just been off-loaded, and grit still swirled in the air. Even now it seemed like he could smell the scent of dried oats.

Suddenly, Bertie Hoover wasn't so congenial anymore, and his voice grew accusatory. "You got to Rotterdam by illegally slipping aboard a barge that had just delivered relief supplies from the CRB."

"Maybe," he hedged.

Hoover leaned closer, with no sign of the baby face in his fierce expression. "You endangered the venture I've devoted my life and my fortune to. The *only* reason Germany permits my relief supplies into Belgium is because I swore on my honor I wouldn't allow my ships, trains, or barges to be used for anything other than humanitarian relief. Germany has been suspicious of the CRB since the beginning, and the instant they suspect I'm helping Allied pilots escape across the border, they'll slam the door on my operation and nine million people will be in danger of starvation. By using one of my barges to escape, you jeopardized an entire humanitarian relief mission."

Finn set the cigar on a plate and folded his arms, unable to look Bertie Hoover in the face because everything the man said was true. "I'm sorry," he said.

"Sorry isn't good enough."

Finn pushed himself into sitting position, wincing against the pain in his leg, but this conversation was too important to handle while lying down. He owed Bertie Hoover his life. The reason Mathilde had been able to feed and tend his injuries was all due to the supplies sent in by the CRB. Mathilde, her family, and millions of other decent people whose lives had been upended by the war had all been put at risk when Finn hitched a ride on the barge.

"I didn't understand the details of your operation or the risk

I was bringing to it. All I knew was that my presence endangered the woman who hid me in her house. The Germans execute people for such things. I needed to get back to France, but I wish now I'd found a different way of escape. I'm truly sorry."

"Prove it."

"How?"

"You're a celebrity. The first American hero of this war, and you were kept alive by the supplies sent in by the CRB. Ever since the U.S. entered the war, I've lost my government funding. My donors are being lured to other causes. The CRB is on the verge of collapse for want of funds. I need a charismatic face to get people to open their wallets to the tune of three million dollars a month."

Finn sagged against the pillow again. Three million dollars? He couldn't even get his mind around a number that big.

"You have to understand. I'm not good at that sort of thing. I can fly an airplane and face down the Germans in a dogfight, but don't ask me to speak in public."

Bertie used his cigar to point in Finn's face. "You *owe* me, and I'm not asking. I'm *telling* you that your new assignment is to raise funds for the CRB, and you begin immediately."

8

Delia's plans to press forward with Wesley were delayed first by his bout with a head cold, then by a trip with his daughter to visit colleges in Boston. Two weeks had passed, and he had barely been in the office at all. It was fortunate they had no court appearances until next month. The only truly pressing matter was their volunteer work regarding the Commission for the Relief of Belgium. The organization was hemorrhaging cash, and the charity's annual meeting loomed on Monday.

It was late Friday afternoon when the bombshell landed on Delia's desk. She and Reginald were the only people in the office, and the casual way Reginald set the CRB's budget on her desk gave no hint of the trouble it contained.

Delia gaped at the balance sheet. The humanitarian organization wasn't merely running a deficit; it was on the verge of bankruptcy. Reginald was an accountant and ought to have sounded the alarm immediately.

"Why didn't you show this to Wesley when he was here this morning?" she asked Reginald.

"Because Wesley was engaged in business that actually generates revenue for the firm. His charitable interest in the CRB ought to come after his obligations to paying clients."

Delia pursed her lips. She knew exactly how Wesley was going to react to this report: he would be incensed that it was allowed to gather dust while Reginald pinched pennies. She held the report aloft. "What caused the CRB's budget to plummet more than a million dollars in the space of a month?"

Reginald calmly took back the report. "Alfred Pollard informed us that he will be redirecting his donations to Liberty Bonds. As a patriotic American, he is more concerned with the health and safety of the troops marching into a war zone than freeloaders depending on the charity of others."

There was no point in her wasting time arguing with Reginald. Alfred Pollard was the largest donor to the CRB, and the organization might not survive without his generosity. She snatched the report back from Reginald and slipped it into her briefcase. "I want to get this to Wesley before he has dinner with his daughter."

Reginald smirked. "Still polishing the apple for Wesley?"

She ignored the taunt and hurried out the door. By the time she got to the subway and traveled across town, the sun was beginning to set. She still had three more blocks to go, hurrying along the treelined sidewalk, before reaching Wesley's town house.

Hints of prosperous domesticity were all around. Mothers pushing baby carriages, parents sitting on their front stoops to take in the sunset, lovers holding hands as they strolled down the walk. Would she someday live here? For a girl who had grown up in an orphanage, it seemed impossible. But with each passing week, she sensed Wesley's resistance to her continuing to slip. Hopefully, his obsession with the difference in their ages would fade soon because she was tired of waiting.

She quickened her pace, eager to get the budget report to him before he sat down to dinner with Amy. He might even ask her to join them. His town house was straight ahead. Window boxes filled with scarlet geraniums lent a cheery touch to the otherwise formal white limestone facade.

A carriage passed Delia and slowed near Wesley's house. It

was a nice carriage with brass fittings and glossy red spokes in the wheels. Before it rolled to a halt, Wesley appeared at the door and sprang down the short flight of steps. He arrived at the carriage just as its door swung open.

A woman alighted, laughing as she accepted Wesley's assistance to step down from the carriage. Delia caught her breath as she recognized Constance Beekman, a widow whom Wesley had helped settle a few thorny legal issues concerning her late husband's estate. She looked splendid in her lilac suit, its jacket and pleated skirt perfectly tailored. She even had on a matching silk beret pinned to her upswept chestnut hair.

A rock landed in Delia's stomach. Mrs. Beekman had already concluded her business with their firm, hadn't she? What other reason could she have for visiting Wesley?

Delia remained frozen on the sidewalk as Wesley clasped the other woman's hands and kissed her on both cheeks.

Both cheeks! This wasn't the way Wesley usually greeted women of his acquaintance. He was always gracious and polite, but never forward. Yet here he was, extending his arm to escort Mrs. Beekman into his home. As the door closed behind them, Delia still hadn't moved a muscle.

It would be wrong to assume something was going on between Wesley and the elegant widow just because he gave her a warm greeting. There could be an innocent explanation for this, but it still felt as though a thousand dreams were crumbling, the disenchantment making it hard for her to breathe.

She still needed to deliver the CRB's budget report to Wesley. She'd rather run away and conjure innocent explanations for what she'd just witnessed, but that wasn't an option. Her limbs were heavy with dread as she walked to the town house and climbed the front steps. The lacy curtains in Wesley's sitting room were open, allowing her to peer inside. Wesley and Mrs. Beekman were sitting together on the sofa in the parlor. Wesley's arm was around her shoulders, and she had a hand on his knee.

Delia jerked her gaze away as though she'd been burned. But she had to get this over with, so she banged the brass knocker on the door. As soon as she delivered the budget report, she could flee home and collapse, but not a moment before.

A maid answered the front door with a smile. "Miss Delia!" she greeted.

Over the maid's shoulder, Wesley shot to his feet, a guilt-ridden expression on his face. "Delia? Is something wrong?"

Only a broken heart, she thought as she straightened her shoulders and met his gaze. "Reginald has prepared the budget projections for the Commission for the Relief of Belgium. Alfred Pollard has withdrawn his support, and the situation is dire. I thought you should see it right away."

"Yes, of course," Wesley said, scrambling to assume a professional demeanor. He wasn't wearing a tie, and his shirtsleeves were rolled up. Usually he was painfully formal, and it hurt to see him so casually dressed. She said nothing as his gaze flicked over the CRB financial projections, but the corners of his mouth turned down.

"Where's Amy?" she asked. After all, Wesley's excuse for leaving the office early each afternoon was always so that he could share dinner with his daughter.

"She has been taking dinner at her boarding school of late," he said, an artificially congenial expression plastered on his face. It was Wesley's unmistakable habit when he felt uneasy.

Good. He ought to feel uneasy for allowing her to imagine that it was nothing but their age standing between them. How long had he been cavorting with Constance Beekman? Ever since last year when he handled her estate?

Mrs. Beekman wandered over, her gaze curious. "Delia, isn't it?"

"Yes," she replied stiffly.

"How lovely to see you again," the older woman said. "Would you like to join us for a drink? Wesley was just about to open a bottle of wine from when we visited my cousin's vineyard in the Hudson Valley last week."

Delia's mouth hardened. Wesley claimed to be taking Amy to visit colleges in Boston. Maybe he was, but he'd brought the lovely Mrs. Beekman along for the trip. Wesley had leaned on Delia for six years to manage his office, do his research, and even help raise his daughter. What had she gotten for it? Nothing but a secret thrill whenever he deigned to cast a heated glance her way, all while he was saving the best of himself for Constance Beekman or whoever else he'd been courting on the side.

"No, thank you," she said calmly, though she glared at Wesley. "I wouldn't want to intrude on your evening. After all, I've spent six years perfecting the art of staying out of the way."

Wesley blanched, and then she left the room and closed the front door with a gentle click.

9

Delia was still numb from Wesley's betrayal when she arrived back at the Martha Washington. The wound was too raw to touch or else she might start crying, and she never cried. Ever. Even after her father died. One of the last things he asked of her was to stay strong in the years ahead.

"*Promise me, Delia,*" he had whispered, his sunken chest barely able to draw a breath as he lay dying on that thin mattress, "*no matter how bad it gets, promise me you will stand firm. 'The one who stands firm to the end will be saved.'*"

She took him literally. She didn't cry when her father died; she stayed strong. She didn't cry when the mean girls at the orphanage tormented her. She didn't cry when she learned Finn stole the money she had earned from slaving in a fish cannery, and she wouldn't cry today. All she needed was to keep standing firm until someday the sun would rise again.

After getting off the subway in Midtown, Delia headed straight to the library of the Martha Washington to begin her job search. The library on the first floor was mostly used by residents for gossiping and playing card games. Still, the room had a few shelves of books and, more importantly, copies of the daily newspapers.

Remaining at Wesley's beck and call was no longer tolerable. She grabbed the *New York Times*, claimed a vacant table, and flipped to the classified ads in search of a new job.

Optimism bloomed at the sight of two whole pages of advertisements for office jobs. Wesley would have to survive without her. She wouldn't look back as she embarked upon a new and better adventure.

The first advertisement was at the Port of New York, coordinating the transfer of troops by ship from Camp Mills to various locations overseas. She would starve before helping send young men to their deaths.

Her optimism began to fade as she came to the end of the first column. Many of the openings were at the Army's and Navy's recruitment offices, so those were out. Ditto working for the war bonds office. A surprising number of the office jobs were in munitions factories and uniform supply companies, and so those were out too. Hope temporarily surged when she spotted an ad for a research assistant, but it was affiliated with the War Office. The few positions at law firms specified they were searching for male applicants only, so she didn't stand much chance there.

She might have to settle for retail work. It didn't pay as well as office work, and she cringed a little as she skimmed the openings. This was ironic because once, in another lifetime, her brightest dream had been to open a shop of her own. Memory of the day she approached Finn with her idea still glimmered with a bittersweet nostalgia.

It had been a warm Saturday afternoon as they relaxed in the shade of an old maple tree in the park. Finn had left the orphanage the previous year to work at the cannery, although they still met in the park each weekend to fly kites together.

She sat with her back to the tree trunk while Finn lay on the ground, his head resting in her lap as he gazed at the dappled sunlight above. She'd been screwing up the courage to share her idea with him, as normally she wasn't this bold. She was usually exquisitely careful, but she'd been researching her plan for weeks and was convinced they could make it work.

"You want us to *buy* a shop?" he asked. They'd always talked of renting a space in which to open a shop, but Delia thought that buying one outright was a real possibility.

"It will take two thousand dollars to qualify for a loan," she said. "We'll earn more money from owning instead of renting, and the shop will be *ours*."

Finn immediately latched on to the idea and rolled into sitting position. "I can take a second shift at the cannery. They're advertising for a night janitor."

"Do you think I can get a job there too? That way we can save even faster." She didn't plan on gutting fish for the rest of her life. No, it was merely a stepping-stone on the way to being a shop owner.

She already knew exactly what their shop would look like. It would have a plate-glass front window to display their best kites. They'd paint the inside of the shop a pale blue to match the color of the sky. The front of the store would have shelves filled with ready-made kites, but they would take orders for custom kites and make them right there in the shop.

Finn was even more ambitious. "We could host contests," he began. "We need more people to get interested in flying kites, so we could put a signboard out front announcing the start of a new club. We can meet in the park and host contests. We will offer a prize for the best kite."

Delia grinned. "And a prize for the most creative design."

"The highest-flying kite," Finn added.

Once they started dreaming, the goal of becoming a shop owner was within sight. With Finn at her side, the possibilities seemed endless.

Finn got a second job cleaning the cannery at night, and Delia started working ten hours a week while going to school during the days. The smell was atrocious, her hair and clothes stank like cod, but she earned thirty cents an hour. At the end of each week, she was able to add three more dollars into the Mason jar where they kept their money for the shop.

The only time she or Finn dipped into their savings was to buy supplies for making kites. Their store would require plenty of inventory, and on rainy days when they couldn't go to the park, she and Finn made kites. They cut, sawed, and sewed all manner of them, and Sister Bernadette let them use the attic at the orphanage to store their inventory.

Then in December of 1903, everything changed. The Wright Brothers completed their first flight in a faraway place called Kitty Hawk. Finn read every newspaper he could get his hands on. He still loved kites, but his passion for airplanes soon became an obsession.

And it was worrying for Delia. Finn reassured her that he still wanted to open the kite store, yet his enthusiasm waned. It seemed all he wanted to do was talk about airplanes. Every week she felt him slipping a little further away, like water dribbling through her cupped hands. His fading interest had awakened her deepest fear. She wasn't bold and confident like Finn. She could never keep up with him, for he had set his sights on airplanes and flying.

Most worrisome was a daring new aviation company located only a few hours north in Hammondsport, New York. Glenn Curtiss was the major rival of the Wright Brothers, and he was hiring. When Finn mentioned quitting at the fish cannery to move to Hammondsport, it was terrifying. What would happen to them if he moved so far away? There would be other girls there, prettier girls who didn't stink like fish or worry all the time. How could she hold on to their dreams if Finn abandoned her to chase after airplanes or any of the other temptations in Hammondsport?

Finn was determined to move there, which would be a disaster for them both. The skills necessary to fly or design an airplane had nothing to do with kites, and she didn't want Finn's heart to be crushed.

"People who work on airplanes have money and connections and degrees," she told him. "All we know how to do is gut fish. They won't be interested in you."

Finn hated it when she doubted him. "Quit trying to talk me out of it, Dee," he said. "What's the harm in trying? Why are you so afraid?"

She was afraid that if he moved away, he would never come back. She wanted to pursue the dream of their kite shop in their own neighborhood where it was familiar and safe. Why wasn't that enough for him?

Delia shook away the old memories. Finn certainly found a way to make his flying ambitions come true. It cost her three hundred dollars and her faith in him.

Owning a store had always been a whimsical dream; she just didn't realize it until Finn stole her money. Store ownership was risky and uncertain, and she was right to have found a safer means of supporting herself.

She folded the newspaper and returned it to the shelf. None of the employment openings was tempting, but she had a long weekend ahead of her during which to mull over her options before having to face Wesley on Monday.

10

Delia braced herself all weekend to confront Wesley on Monday morning. Fantasies about marching into his office to recklessly quit played over and over in her mind. *Perhaps you can hire Mrs. Beekman to be your assistant,* she dreamed of saying.

And yet she'd never do it. Instead, she would give the standard two weeks' notice because quitting abruptly would reveal the depth of her hurt. Delia's heart was in her throat as she entered the office, prepared to announce her intention to resign to Wesley's face.

Reginald let her know otherwise. "He telephoned this morning and said not to expect him today. He's spending the day with his daughter."

"That's convenient," she muttered, throwing her bag onto her desk and knocking over her pencil cup.

"Wesley asked me to remind you about the CRB board meeting this afternoon. You are to bring the file about international shipping lanes and meet him at Mr. Hoover's town house at four o'clock sharp."

She sighed while restoring order to her desk. Why couldn't Wesley come to the office to pick up the shipping lane documents?

Why did she have to continually jump and scurry and burn the midnight oil to keep him happy? There were important men on the CRB's board of directors, and Wesley would look flat-footed without the documents *she* prepared and for which he would surely take credit.

She left work well ahead of the appointed meeting, but the subway was running late, so she was ten minutes overdue as she hurried down the street toward Bertie's modest town house. It was a classic three-story design, with wrought-iron railings lining the steps before a discreet front door. Ever since the war began, Bertie had been sailing between New York, London, and Rotterdam to carry out CRB business. It meant he now lived in rented town houses rather than in his mansion in San Francisco.

She rapped the brass knocker and waited. To her surprise, Wesley himself answered the door.

"Where have you been?" he asked in a harsh whisper.

She handed him the briefcase and walked inside without a word. He ought to thank his lucky stars she came at all.

The main room was filled with wealthy men and reeked of cigar smoke. The men of the CRB's board of directors exuded money and power with their glinting watch chains, bespoke suits, and gold walking sticks. Among them were two bank presidents, the owner of the New York Yankees, and Congressman Donnelly, the representative for Manhattan who held the city in the palm of his hand.

Wesley grasped her arm and steered her farther into the room. "I'm sure you all remember my assistant, Miss Delia Byrne. She'll be taking notes of our meeting."

"Good to see you again, Delia," Bertie said warmly. "Can I get you something to drink?"

She demurred, and the meeting quickly got under way. There was only room for six people in the upholstered chairs circling the room. Delia automatically took the window seat that overlooked the lush greenery in the walled back garden.

She propped the clipboard in the crook of her elbow as the meeting began. She was primarily here to take notes and jog Wesley's memory of details regarding the international shipping lanes.

"What's this I hear about financial troubles?" Congressman Donnelly asked.

Bertie Hoover supplied the answer. "When the war began, I thought it would be over in a few months, and I planned on funding it from my own pocket. That was naive. Here we are three years later, and I rely on donations from wealthy men such as yourselves. We need three million dollars a month to keep sending steamships filled with food to Rotterdam, although our donations are drying up. Last year the U.S. government donated fifteen million dollars. With our entry into the war, those payments have ceased, and our largest personal donor, Alfred Pollard, will be ending his support as well."

News of the dire situation caused a ripple of murmured concern among those in the group. Bertie stood to pace before the fireplace as he continued. "The problem is that I am rich, and that is always the first thing people think when I ask for donations. Why should they open their wallets for a man they believe could buy Central Park on a whim? It's not true, of course, as I've already given most of my fortune away."

"What about fundraisers?" one of the men asked.

Bertie shook his head. "People would rather give their money to the Red Cross or buy war bonds. Nobody has ever heard of the CRB. They can't even find Belgium on a map. I need help drumming up new publicity to keep this drive going. I need a charismatic personality to encourage people to open their wallets."

"Don't look at me," Congressman Donnelly said. "I won reelection by only two hundred votes. *You* should do it, Bertie. Everyone likes you. You're the best natural leader I've ever met. The foreman of your mining crew in Australia said the men would follow you over a cliff if you asked it of them."

Bertie pointed to his face. "Look at me. I've got a baby face as interesting as a bowl of oatmeal. I'm not the right man for the job."

"What do you suggest?" Wesley asked.

Bertie held up a newspaper, folded into quarters to display a story. "This is the kind of man I need," he said. "He's an American pilot who was shot down and trapped in Belgium for six weeks. He's handsome and funny and courageous. Without the relief supplies shipped into Belgium, he would have died, and he knows it. He's got the potential to be the perfect spokesman for garnering public support."

Delia's heart began to thump. She couldn't see the newspaper, but it sounded like he was referring to Finn. Bertie passed the newspaper around the room and continued speaking. "I want to use this man to lure our former donors back, starting with Alfred Pollard. Finn Delaney's story is tailor-made to grab people's attention and highlight the importance of what our cause means to the innocent people of Belgium."

Delia's hands shook too badly to keep taking notes. She had consigned Finn to the deepest vault of her heart, a place she never intended to unlock. Now he was about to join the CRB? Bertie was chasing a pipe dream if he thought Finn could persuade hard-nosed millionaires to open their wallets.

"How can we help?" Wesley asked.

"I need help with legal documents to lock the donors in," Bertie said. "That was my problem before. I didn't foresee how the U.S. entering the war would cripple our donations, so in addition to finding new sources of revenue, I want contracts that will bind donors to their commitments for the duration of the war."

Delia cleared her throat, hoping to draw Wesley's attention. He mustn't commit them to working with Finn Delaney. The last time she'd trusted Finn, he cleaned out their bank account and stole her money.

"I'd be happy to help," Wesley said.

She cleared her throat, louder this time. Wesley shot her scolding glance, along with a tiny shake of his head before turning back to Bertie with a congenial nod of acceptance.

"We're happy to help however you need," he said.

Finn was *not* trustworthy and was completely ill-equipped for this task. She couldn't exactly blurt out how she knew that in front of all these people; she could only pray that Wesley would stop before he committed them any further.

"I also need help getting Lieutenant Delaney up to snuff," Bertie said. "He has tremendous charisma, but he is a stranger in the high-finance circles of New York. He's still using crutches, so he'll need help getting around the city. While he charms the donors, I need his partner to lock down the commitments by getting everything in writing to make it legal."

"Miss Byrne can begin working with Lieutenant Delaney immediately," Wesley offered. "She'll be an excellent choice to prepare a dossier of potential donors and help Lieutenant Delaney secure contributions."

Delia was so mad she could spit. Was Wesley so cowardly he was kicking her out of the office to escape her?

"It's settled then," Bertie Hoover said. "Now, let us proceed to the matter of international shipping lanes and enforcing our right to use them. Wesley, I gather you prepared a legal brief for persuading Germany to grant us safe passage across the Atlantic?"

She had prepared that brief. *She* was the one who had given up her weekend to summarize laws governing shipping lanes for humanitarian relief. Wesley gave a sage smile as he opened her brief and read word for word the opening argument she'd prepared.

The meeting concluded after an hour. Most of the men retreated to the far side of the room, where Bertie opened a humidor and produced cigars. Wesley did not smoke. He had the decency to look a little sheepish as he closed the folder, her brief inside.

"A carriage is waiting outside," he said. "Shall we?"

If they got into an enclosed carriage, she would strangle him. "Outside," she bit off. "In the garden."

"Oh, dear. I sense I am about to be read the riot act."

Delia held on to the edges of her fraying temper as she led the way to the garden behind Bertie's town house. An ivy-covered brick wall surrounded the dreadfully overgrown patch of land, with shrubs slumping over, hanging vines, and wild roses. A few stone benches were clustered near a leggy herb garden, but Delia was wound too tightly to sit. She set the case down and whirled to face him.

"Who gave you permission to volunteer me for an assignment I don't want?"

Wesley blanched. She never spoke to him so harshly, but then again, she never realized how Wesley had led her to believe her affection was returned, all while he escorted the lovely Widow Beekman around town.

"If you truly object, I suppose I can speak with Bertie . . ." The tone of his voice implied he'd rather have a tooth pulled than withdraw his commitment.

"Do it," she snapped. "I have a history with Finn Delaney, and I refuse to work with him."

Wesley frowned. "How do you know him?"

Heat prickled across her skin. How could she explain the countless adolescent dreams, or the soaring but irrational joy that was felt when two lonely people found each other? Wesley cocked his head, watching her closely, but her tongue froze. She couldn't bring herself to form the words.

"Was he the boy from the orphanage?"

She nodded, grateful that he remembered the time Delia confided in him about the boy who had broken her heart.

"I see," Wesley said quietly.

"He stole my life savings," she managed to add. "He isn't trustworthy."

"We don't need him to be trustworthy—we need his *story*. He can help us raise funds. And he won't have access to any monies raised."

Delia sighed in frustration. "He's a poor choice to be a spokesman for the CRB. You need to tell Bertie to keep away from him."

"Really? Why?"

"Let's start with the fact that he is a warmonger," she said. "The man couldn't even wait for the United States to enter the war before he volunteered to fly for France, all so he could drop bombs on people."

"Delia . . ." The condescension in the way he drawled her name was maddening.

"Don't 'Delia' me. You're sending me on this assignment because I found out about Constance Beekman. I care for you and gave everything to your firm. You took advantage of that, and now you're sending me away because you're too cowardly to face me. Admit it."

He turned away to pace in the garden, only it was crowded by towering rhododendrons overhanging into the space. "I think a little distance between us might be for the best."

"Why didn't you have the guts to tell me that earlier?" she demanded. "How long have you been toying with me while squiring Constance Beekman all over the city?"

"Delia, I was always honest with you. I am nineteen years older than you and—"

"That hardly mattered when you kissed me beside the globe. Or the thousand times we both stayed late to work on cases and shared meals in your office."

"You were paid for those hours."

"That's beside the point, Wesley."

Finn lay flat on the stone bench behind the wall of overgrown shrubbery, covering his eyes and listening to Delia pour her heart out to a man who didn't deserve her.

Had there ever been a worse form of torture than this? He'd been cooling his heels in the garden until Bertie finished with his business meeting. Then he was supposed to join the other men on the board of the CRB for dinner.

He'd been casually smoking a cigar while lounging on the bench when they entered the garden. At first he hadn't recognized Delia's voice. Now he did, and waves of grief descended each time she spoke. He didn't realize he'd been holding his breath until dark pinpricks floated in his vision. He forced himself to drag in a lungful of air and unclench his fists. And not break anything. As much as he wanted to tear his hair out and howl at the moon, he'd survive this.

He'd lost Delia long ago but had always harbored a sliver of hope that somewhere deep inside, she remembered their years together with fondness. That sliver of hope flickered out and died while listening to her enumerate his crimes as he lay trapped on this awful stone bench.

Delia must never learn he'd overheard her conversation. She was a proud woman and would hate it if she knew he'd heard everything. The cigar smoke could give him away. He was about to rub out the glowing tip on the damp brick, but the man's voice made him freeze because it sounded like he was getting closer.

"Delia, I had no idea this was even an issue," the man on the other side of the shrubbery said. "Bertie needs help getting his ace flyer spiffed up to face the crowds, and you will be perfect for it."

"Forget it. I told you that I know Finn Delaney, and I wouldn't trust him to make me a ham sandwich. He is reckless, impulsive, and a thief."

Every word was like a sledgehammer. Finn stared at the sky, unable to believe this was actually happening.

Then another voice joined the fray. "Wesley? Delia?"

It was Bertie. The fiery argument between Delia and her companion stopped abruptly, as if doused by a bucket of cold water.

"Have you seen our pilot?" Bertie continued. "I asked him to stay in the garden during the meeting."

This was about to get awkward. Finn remained motionless,

hoping they would head back inside to continue the conversation. Then he could figure out a way to escape the garden, and Delia would never be the wiser.

"There's nobody out here," Delia said.

"Are you sure?" Bertie asked. "He's still using crutches, so he can't have gone very far."

There was no avoiding it. Finn clamped the cigar between his teeth so he could use both hands to push himself into a sitting position. The healthy leg was easy to swing to the ground, but he needed both hands to position the other.

A rapid pattering of footsteps and an audible female gasp sounded as three people rounded the overgrown shrubbery to see him on the bench, caught in the act. It was going to hurt, but he hoisted himself into a standing position, all his weight on the good leg as he shouldered the pair of crutches.

"Hello, Delia," he said, smiling as best he could with a cigar clamped between his teeth.

He wished she didn't look so horrified to see him, but she had cause. The roundness of youth had faded from her face, giving her a more refined look. Her raven-black hair was swept atop her head, and her blue eyes held cold fury. Bertie seemed mildly amused while the other man looked outraged.

Yeah, the guy was too old for her. Wesley was right, Delia flat-out wrong. These two were a mismatch for sure.

Bertie tried to smooth things over. "Please, Finn, don't hurt yourself. I'd like to introduce you to Delia Byrne, the lady who will be assisting you in our fundraising campaign."

"We've already met, though it was a long time ago," he said, extending a hand. "Nice to see you again, Delia."

Delia refused his hand. "Can't you at least remove the cigar from your mouth before speaking?"

The old Delia looked at him with hero worship, while this one sounded like a sour-tempered schoolmarm. Nevertheless, she had good cause to resent him. He removed the cigar from his lips and said, "I apologize for hiding out back here. I wasn't sure what was the right thing to do."

"How about simply announcing your presence?" Wesley said. "Or does doing the right thing not come easily?"

Finn refused to look at the old guy who had captured Delia's heart. Instead, he gave a self-deprecating smile. "If there's one thing I've always been good at, it's making a spectacle of myself. Honestly, Dee, I'm sorry. I never intended to overhear, and you've got cause to be mad. You can add it to the tally I'm running up with you."

He winked at her. He shouldn't have, but the old habit just reappeared, reminding him of all the years he'd flashed a wink at her across the classroom, in the orphanage dining room, or anytime he wanted to comfort her when the nuns made privacy all but impossible.

Wesley caught the wink and stiffened. "I may have been too hasty," he said. "Delia, you don't have to do this. Reginald can handle the tasks Bertie just outlined, and you can take over the accounting duties at the office."

"So everything will go back to the status quo?" Delia asked, her chin jutted out in a challenging pose.

"Yes, we will continue exactly like before."

Her pretty blue eyes narrowed. "I wouldn't dream of it," she said, then swiveled her attention back to Bertie. "I will be honored to assist Lieutenant Delaney however he needs."

"Excellent!" Bertie said. "Why don't we return to the drawing room and toast our new venture."

It sounded good to Finn, but Delia had other ideas. "First, I'd like a moment alone with Lieutenant Delaney. We will join you inside shortly."

11

The old guy Delia fancied pierced Finn with an acidic look that could peel paint before he left to follow Bertie inside, and Finn instinctively bristled. It had been a long time since he'd been on the receiving end of that kind of contempt from a complete stranger, and it stung.

Once they were alone, he tried to calm down as he turned his attention back to Delia. "Dee, I'm sorry for not speaking up right away. I just didn't know what to do."

"How much of my personal conversation did you overhear?" Her voice was frosty, her expression just as cold.

"All of it," he said.

"Fine," she bit out. "We need never discuss it again. *Ever.*"

"Yes, ma'am," he said, a hint of amusement in his voice as he saluted her. His impetuous act ten years ago had cost him Delia's love, but he could still regain her respect. They'd both come a million miles from flying kites on the roof of the orphanage. They ought to be proud of how far they'd come, not sit here trading barbs with each other.

"You look great, by the way," he said with a nod to her nifty clothes and the sleek leather case. "I'll bet that working at a law firm pays a lot better than gutting fish, am I right?"

A stiff shrug was all the answer he got, and he scrambled for traction. "I finally became a pilot," he said, though the comment didn't impress her as much as he'd expected.

"Yes, I saw you at the Liberty Bond parade."

He tried not to smile too widely. "You did? I hadn't expected that sort of homecoming, but it was great."

If anything, her expression got colder. "Congratulations. You must be very proud."

What was wrong with her? He'd survived a plane crash and the crucible of hiding from the Germans for six weeks. Maybe she simply didn't understand.

"I thought I was a goner for a while there. Hiding out in Belgium was rough, but I knew I had to survive so I could rejoin my squadron and fight another day."

Delia's eyes narrowed. "Fight? Why don't you simply say 'drop bombs on innocent people'?"

He blanched. "That wasn't what I was doing. When I dropped bombs, it was on German soldiers who were occupying land they stole from the Belgians."

"It's war, Finn. It's a filthy, inhumane war, and you shouldn't have any part of it."

He clenched his fists and looked away. He wouldn't lash out. This wasn't the first time he'd heard pacifists mouth off about things they didn't understand, and Delia had good cause to hold such a view. Her father had died in a pointless war. Yet this war was different.

"Delia, do you know what's going on over there? It's in all the papers."

"About how the kaiser bayonets innocent women and children? It's just propaganda meant to stir up hatred and keep the war going."

"I'm trying to *end* the war, not keep it going."

For once, something he said seemed to get through to her. She sucked in a quick breath and leaned in toward him.

"Then use your voice to speak out against it. People will listen to you. You can make a difference."

"By getting America to call for a truce and let the Krauts get away with what they're doing?"

He hated the scorn he saw in her expression. Delia used to look at him with love and admiration. That innocent girl was gone, replaced by this hard, cold woman who looked at him with contempt.

It wasn't her fault she didn't understand about the war. He should thank God she didn't! He would carry the images from Belgium until his dying day and wouldn't wish it on anyone. She might not even believe it if he tried to tell her. She was certainly prepared to dismiss anything she saw reported in the newspapers.

But he could tell her about Mathilde, the woman who had rescued him. What happened to Mathilde and her family wasn't propaganda cooked up in a newspaper office to stoke sentiment. Mathilde's life was a fate shared by millions of innocent people in Belgium.

"After I got shot down, a woman named Mathilde let me hide in her house," he began. Delia said nothing, but at least she was listening, so he continued. "Mathilde and her husband have three kids, but after the Germans rolled through her town, they scooped up all the able-bodied men and carted them off for war work. They took her husband. To this day she doesn't know what happened to him. He was a pharmacist, so it's likely he's been working treating soldiers so they can be turned around and sent back to the front. Meanwhile, she's sitting at home with three kids and barely enough to eat."

Although Mathilde did a lot more than sit around at home. Mathilde was up to her neck in resistance work, and any day could be her last if the Germans got wind of what she was up to.

Delia wandered to the edge of the garden, her shoulders

slumped. "Dropping bombs won't help people like Mathilde. Only getting politicians to the negotiating table can do that. And, Finn, you can help. If you renounce the war, maybe others will follow."

She was so naive, although pointing that out would only get her madder. He summoned a smile. "Let's talk about something else. Do you still fly kites? I saw there's a new kite shop in the East Village."

It was the wrong thing to say. If he hadn't impulsively taken the money she had saved, he and Delia might be married and running their own kite shop now. Given the hint of sadness in her eyes, it was exactly what she was thinking too.

"No, I don't fly kites anymore," she said. "I used to love flying kites with you because I could daydream about what it would be like to soar above and beyond the clouds. Instead of flying for joy, you do it to kill people. You took the best of us and turned it into something hideous. To kill and maim."

"To defend and protect and save."

"You want glory and accolades for what you do. I saw you in that parade. You loved every moment of it."

"Dee, stop—"

"I will *never* stop. Not while this war continues."

He turned his face away, wanting to weep at the sight of what she had become. The youthful dreamer was gone, replaced by this bitter harpy who didn't know what she was ranting about. Still, three years of war had trained him to ignore his feelings. Lock it down, push it away, and stay calm. He focused his attention on a rose vine climbing a trellis as he spoke.

"Dee, I wish I could heal the war that's tearing the world apart. I don't know how. You don't either. Let's stop attacking each other and work out a plan, okay?"

"Does this plan involve you getting in a plane and dropping bombs on people?"

Anger surged anew, but he tamped it down and met her gaze. "I want peace. So do you. We're not going to get there by attacking each other. I promised Bertie six months to help raise funds for the CRB. I have no idea how to do that, and apparently people wiser than me think you can help with that, but it's not going to happen tonight."

Delia ran a hand through her hair and wiped the contempt from her expression. Her face was now as calm and emotionless as a cameo. "I apologize," she said without emotion. "I can continue."

"I can't," he said. He was due back at Camp Mills before taps, and he'd already stressed his leg enough for the day. He grabbed his crutches and faced the door. "Let's meet again tomorrow when we'll both have cooler heads. Can you come out to Camp Mills? There's a Red Cross Hostess House on the base. You can find me there tomorrow morning at nine o'clock."

He headed toward the garden gate. Disappointment and frustration simmered inside, and he could only pray that their meeting tomorrow morning would go better.

Delia returned to the town house and went to the kitchen to help Louisa, Bertie's wife, set out the buffet dinner. Louisa was a strong-jawed woman who had met Bertie while they were both in college earning degrees in geology. She later followed him around the world to various gold and silver mines. Tonight she supported him by hosting a casual dinner, arranging cheese and tomatoes on a tray while Delia rolled slices of turkey, chicken, and roast beef for the sandwich platter.

All the while Delia eavesdropped on the men in the other room, smoking cigars and gossiping about yacht racing, but mostly she was listening for Wesley's voice. He didn't even like sailing, and yet he joined in the discussion with gusto.

"Would you please fill bowls with mayonnaise and mustard sauce?" Louisa asked.

"Of course," Delia said. "Is there any horseradish?" The question was out of her mouth before Delia realized she needed to quit fussing over Wesley. He loved horseradish on roast beef, and she would always bring some when she fetched their meals from the delicatessen. But she could hardly change her mind once Louisa pulled a jar of horseradish from the icebox. Delia scooped some of it into a small dish and set it beside the meat platter.

Bertie arrived to help carry everything to the sideboard. "You've worked the details out with Lieutenant Delaney?"

"Of course," she replied calmly. "Our first meeting is scheduled for tomorrow morning at Camp Mills."

"Excellent," Bertie said before carrying the platter away.

She and Louisa waited while the men had served themselves from the buffet, and Wesley complimented Mrs. Hoover on the fine array of offerings.

"I love horseradish," he said with a smile at Mrs. Hoover as he helped himself at the sideboard.

Soon they were all settled around the dining table. Louisa gamely joined in the conversation about an upcoming yacht race scheduled over Thanksgiving weekend. Laughter mingled with good-natured rivalry as Bertie jested with Congressman Donnelly about whose yacht ruled the seas. Given his flushed face and overly loud voice, it appeared that Congressman Donnelly might have had one too many glasses of sherry.

"Wesley!" he called from the end of the dining table. "Tell us you'll join me on my crew for the Thanksgiving race. There's no other yacht as fine as my *Aurora*, but Bertie paid a fortune to refit his *Sequoia*, so the competition will be tough."

Welsey cleared his throat. "I won't be available this Thanksgiving."

Bertie sent Wesley an engaging smile. "I heard you and your daughter would be heading up to the Hudson Valley at Thanksgiving. Tell us, is the lovely Mrs. Beekman involved? I gather her estate is up near Tarrytown."

Delia scowled at the mention of Mrs. Beekman, and Wesley cast her a nervous glance. He seemed momentarily tongue-tied, and tiny beads of sweat formed on his brow as he cleared his throat.

"Yes, I expect I shall pay a visit to the Beekman estate," he said. "But your yacht race sounds exciting. Tell me more about improvements to the *Sequoia*."

Wesley's attempt to change the topic completely failed. Bertie continued his train of thought without pause. "I always thought Horace Beekman should have dredged a deeper pier at his estate. It would be the perfect place in which to launch a yacht."

"Try to convince Mrs. Beekman to deepen the pier," Congressman Donnelly said to Wesley. "I heard that wedding bells might be in the offing."

A wave of heat flooded Delia while Wesley let out a stiff laugh. "There is no such understanding," he said. "You'll have to appeal to the lady herself if you wish the pier to be improved."

Louisa joined in the conversation. "When I saw the two of you at the Henderson gala last month, the pair of you looked as happy as two lovebirds."

"Marry her," Congressman Donnelly said. "Anything to get that prime river frontage made suitable for an afternoon on the water."

"No," Louisa said in a teasing voice. "He should marry her because it would be lovely to see two widowed people find a second chance at happiness."

Congressman Donnelly shook his head. "No, marry her for the river frontage."

Everyone, even Wesley, laughed.

Delia silently fumed as the ribbing continued. It seemed the entire population of Manhattan knew about the relationship between Wesley and the lovely Constance Beekman. While Delia stayed late at the office to tend to business, Wesley was galivanting around town indulging in a high-society courtship.

Bertie brought the hilarity down to earth. "Wesley can't disappear at Thanksgiving," he pointed out. "Isn't November the month you handle all the insurance policy renewals?"

"Actually, we work on those throughout the last several months every year," Wesley said.

It was the work *Delia* did for the last several months every year. Insurance renewals were run-of-the-mill tasks she'd been staying late to complete all month, with Wesley cutting out early so he could enjoy dinner with Amy and Mrs. Beekman.

"Still, don't let Congressman Donnelly pressure you to be gone at Thanksgiving," Bertie said. "You may find yourself shorthanded in light of Delia's additional services to the CRB."

"Delia will find it no burden," Wesley said, raising his glass and sending her a complimentary smile. "She is the embodiment of competence. For the past six years, she has been my right hand for completing my annual contract renewals, and this year shall be no different."

"To Delia!" Congressman Donnelly said, raising his glass as well.

Everyone around the table joined in the toast. Delia managed a smile, although she clenched her teeth so hard it made her jaw ache. She never minded hard work. Hard work and making Wesley's law firm thrive gave purpose and meaning to her world. And if it meant that she worked late five nights a week or lost out on the chance to meet a suitable young man and form a romantic partnership, none of it mattered because she always believed her purpose in life was to keep Wesley Chandler and his law firm afloat.

Now she knew better, and her long hours merely bought Wesley the freedom to court Mrs. Beekman. What a mistake she had made.

"How long will you need Delia's services?" Wesley asked.

"I've asked for a six-month commitment from Lieutenant Delaney. I would like for Delia to be on hand for his initial meetings with potential donors and to draft the legal agreements."

"Done!" Wesley replied. "Think no more of it. Delia will conjure a solution to your problem before you even know it exists."

Delia felt like a potted plant the way Wesley discussed her. Bertie cast a worried glance her way. "Perhaps we should ask the lady if she would be amenable to the task. It seems we are asking a great deal of her in addition to her normal responsibilities."

How ironic that Mr. Hoover showed more compassion for her welfare than Wesley. It hardened her resolve. She stood to fetch the pitcher of iced tea to refill everyone's glasses.

"Please, you don't need to fear for me," she said to Bertie. "I've worked with Wesley for six years and managed to keep his office afloat because I have no social life and few needs."

She proceeded around the table, filling glasses, all the while watching Wesley from the corner of her eye. He had frozen, watching her through cautious eyes as if he feared she were a bomb about to explode.

"I gave everything I had to Wesley's law firm, but now I look forward to working for the CRB. You don't need to worry that I will be stretched too thin to accomplish the job. I will contact you by this time tomorrow with a preliminary plan for myself and Lieutenant Delaney to begin the fundraising."

Delia reached Wesley's side and leaned across him to refill his glass. The entire room turned silent as the slosh of ice cubes and tea poured into his crystal goblet.

"Wesley," she added, keeping her voice as pleasant as a springtime breeze, "please take this as my notice that I resign, effective immediately." With that, she thumped the pitcher of tea beside his plate and strode out of the town house without a backward glance.

12

Finn didn't want to admit it, but Delia's antiwar stance had gotten beneath his skin. She was acting like one of those rigid pacifists so committed to their position that they demonized the opposition rather than try to understand them. Did she believe he was ignorant of the horrors of war? He'd held the hands of men as they died. He'd seen women strapped to plows, tilling the fields because their horses had been requisitioned by the Army. Those women didn't complain or criticize the men in uniform. They were grateful to the soldiers for protecting their farms and way of life.

He was still mulling over Delia's hostility as he arrived back at Camp Mills. It was almost midnight, and flickering lanterns created pools of light among the tents. Hushed voices and the occasional clink of chains mingled with crickets as he propelled himself on crutches through the sprawling encampment.

The glow of a lantern illuminated Finn's tent. Daniel Richardson, his tentmate from Kansas, always read late into the night. Permission to keep a lantern burning after taps was one of the few privileges afforded to officers.

Finn opened the flap of the tent, and Daniel rolled off his cot to help with the crutches. "How did it go?"

The last thing Finn wanted to discuss was seeing the love of his life again and hearing her disdain for everything he fought for over the past three years.

"Fine," he said. The canvas of his cot let out a sharp squeak as he lowered himself onto it. The tent smelled of damp earth and wool uniforms. "It looks as if I'll be doing fundraising for the next several months. I still should have some time to help you train the student pilots a few days per week."

"Do you mind if I keep reading?" Daniel asked, and Finn shook his head. It was a warm night, and after shucking his uniform, he lay back on his cot in his skivvies, staring at the canvas tent sloping above him. The lantern cast flickering shadows, and the low murmur of voices drifted in from outside, punctuated by the occasional clatter of boots or the distant laugh of a soldier.

Meanwhile, Daniel read letter after letter. The guy was so homesick, he reread the letters from his wife almost every evening. Though Daniel was only twenty-five, he'd been married for eight years and had two kids.

"Do you ever regret getting married so young?"

"Nope," Daniel said. "I started being truly happy on the day Amy Wells agreed to marry me. I never looked back."

What would have happened if Finn hadn't messed up but instead had married Delia like they planned? If he hadn't taken her three hundred dollars, would it have been possible to escape the cannery and make a go of things? He took a big risk with her money, but it paid off. Within a year he had four thousand dollars to show for it, although Delia never forgave him for gambling with her money without permission.

His bitter reunion with Delia led to a restless night, and he was bleary-eyed upon awakening. While he didn't need Delia to agree about the money or his views on the war, they were going to be working together. They needed to respect each other, and that meant opening her eyes to what was going on overseas.

He rose early and headed to the camp library in search of a particular publication. Camp Mills carried a number of newspapers shipped in from all over Europe, but there was only one he was interested in, and he prayed they had a copy.

The screen door creaked as he entered the hastily constructed library that smelled of sawdust and printer's ink. The bare plank floors squeaked as he entered, and the young soldier manning the library desk snapped to attention, saluting Finn with brisk precision.

"At ease," Finn said, still uncomfortable with his new status as an Army officer. He moved to the rack of newspapers on the far wall. The American press was doing a decent job of publicizing German atrocities, even though Delia dismissed it as propaganda. She'd probably feel the same about what was written in the British and French newspapers. While the American newspapers were all current, the foreign papers shipped from France were at least two weeks old, and none of them were from Belgium.

Maybe the library hadn't gotten their hands on any issues of the specific newspaper he needed. He pulled up a chair, set his crutches aside, and began searching the stacks of newspapers.

"Can I help you, sir?" the desk clerk asked.

"Have you got any issues of *La Libre Belgique*?"

"La what?" the younger man asked.

"It's a clandestine newspaper circulated by the resistance fighters in Belgium. A few copies usually find their way to the French newsstands. Have you seen it?"

"No, but I've only been here three days, sir."

Finn *needed* that newspaper. It contained the best insight into occupied Belgium, and since Delia wouldn't believe him, perhaps she would believe the Belgians.

"I'll help you, sir." The clerk stepped forward to look through the various newspapers. Dust swirled into the air, and Finn watched with growing dismay as the piles of newspapers grew shorter.

"There!" the clerk said. Buried behind a stack of imported French newspapers was a single issue of *La Libre Belgique*. It was two months old. The flimsy issue, only eight pages long, had yellowed and was stiff. Cheap paper aged quickly, but this newspaper was rare and precious. People had risked their lives producing this newspaper.

His heart thudded as he stared at the newspaper. "Can I have it?"

"People are supposed to check them out," the soldier said, and Finn gladly complied.

He tucked the paper beneath his arm as he made his way across the camp to meet Delia. People from New York had no experience of what it was like to be a prisoner in their own homeland, gasping for breath while being crushed by an iron fist. *La Libre Belgique* reported everything ordinary Belgians experienced on a daily basis.

A little bell rang as he entered the Hostess House run by the Red Cross. It was a good place for a quick snack, a friendly card game, and a little relaxation. The scent of freshly baked bread and hot coffee got his blood going as he entered the large A-frame building. Men occupied wicker chairs arranged around card tables, where they read newspapers or played board games with each other. Finn ordered a cup of coffee and a doughnut, then headed to a seating area near the back to start reading. After three years of living in France, Finn could speak the language, but reading French was still a struggle.

Just as he'd hoped, General Ryckman featured prominently in many of the articles. There was only one person in the world Finn deeply and thoroughly loathed, and his name was General Hans Ryckman, the German officer currently serving as the commandant over occupied Belgium. War was never pretty, but General Ryckman used unnecessarily harsh methods to keep Belgium compliant beneath his steel-toed boot.

Finn concentrated on translating the article. The commandant's latest edict required all Belgians to obey a six o'clock curfew each evening. The next line said something about random inspections of people's homes in search of contraband. He didn't even look up when the waitress refilled his coffee because all of a sudden it felt as though he were back in Belgium, huddled in the front room of Mathilde's cottage.

A single candle flickered, and the curtains were drawn as he listened to men of the Belgian resistance strategize ways to avoid the general's henchmen. A fine sheen of clammy sweat broke out across his skin. Even now, the friends Finn had made in Belgium were suffering under Ryckman's oppressive rule. His stomach soured. Here he sat eating a doughnut while his friends in Belgium couldn't enjoy a single breath of freedom. He blotted the sweat from his face with a jittery hand.

The trembling was odd. Maybe his hands shook because of the coffee. Or maybe it was that Delia was on her way, and he needed this morning's meeting to go better than the one yesterday.

He closed his eyes. *Dear God, please give me the patience to keep my head when Delia gets here. I did her wrong, I know that. I've tried to make it up to her, but I don't know how best to do that. I wanted her forgiveness for selfish reasons, but now we've got to work together to save Mathilde and millions of other Belgians from starvation. And that's not going to happen if she can't look at me without wanting to sock me in the jaw. Please give me patience.*

He opened his eyes, relieved that his trembling had eased, and returned to reading the news from Belgium.

At dawn the next morning, Delia set off for Camp Mills with her best friend, Inga, recently back in New York after three years of working at the American Embassy in Berlin. Inga had married an American diplomat during her time abroad and now worked as a telegraph operator for the Red Cross. Temporarily assigned to the new station near Camp Mills, Inga accompanied Delia to the U.S. Army base on Long Island.

The first leg of the journey was a ferry ride to Long Island. The benches were all filled, leaving the two of them to grip the cold metal railing of the ferry as it crossed the East River. Chilly mist gathered on her cheeks, and the murky air carried the scent of salt and industry.

"How does Finn feel about working with you?" Inga asked.

Delia winced at the memory of how they had parted last night. No matter their history or her disapproval of the war, she shouldn't have insulted a man who had been wounded in combat.

"We argued," she confessed. "He's so convinced the war is right and refuses to see reason. We'll both do our jobs, but I'll be counting down the hours for it to end."

"And then you'll go back working for Wesley?"

Inga's question hung in the air. Delia still couldn't quite believe her audacity of the night before. Standing in front of Wesley and the entire board of the CRB while she cleanly severed her ties to Wesley still didn't feel real.

She drew a steadying breath and met Inga's gaze. "I've finished with Wesley. Last night I told him I quit."

Inga gasped. "*No!*"

"I thought you'd be pleased," Delia said. "You're the one who told me I was squandering my life waiting for Wesley."

"Yes, but I didn't think you'd ever summon the nerve to actually walk away." A smile broke across Inga's winsome face. "Congratulations! This is going to give you a clean break and the chance for a new future. It's so exciting!"

No, it was terrifying. Working for Wesley had been safe. She knew exactly what to expect, and she was thoroughly competent at her job. Now she was facing an uncertain future and a mission she wasn't confident she could accomplish.

"Bertie walked me to the subway stop last night after I quit," she said. Their awkward conversation was still fresh in her mind.

He'd offered to pay her a salary in light of resigning her position with Wesley, and Delia had gratefully accepted. It felt awful to be yet another burden on the CRB's struggling finances, but she couldn't afford to go months without any means of income. Taking payment from the CRB strengthened her determination to refill its coffers, even if it meant working alongside Finn.

To the bottom of her soul, she wished Finn hadn't overheard her argument with Wesley. The pity in his eyes had been unmistakable, and it was humiliating. For years she wondered what it would be like if she ever met Finn again. She imagined being a successful businesswoman or perhaps the wife of a congressman or an aristocrat. The best fantasy was being the sole owner of her very own kite store, proving to Finn she didn't need his help to make their dream come true. Having Finn witness her mortifying rejection by Wesley had never been on her list of fantasies.

Delia's first sight of Camp Mills showed a vast landscape filled with thousands of tents. This was another world, a masculine one of marching soldiers and snare drums and officers shouting orders. Somewhere behind the miles of fencing, Finn was waiting for her, and she was going to have to fake a calm, poised demeanor as she met him to begin their joint mission of aiding the CRB.

"This is where we part," Inga said. "The Red Cross station is down the street, but you'll need to go to the checkpoint at the west gate to get inside the camp."

After they exchanged a quick hug, Delia went to the booth, where an enlisted soldier manned the checkpoint. This wasn't her world; she didn't belong here. Rows of khaki-clad soldiers marched the parade grounds while a cavalry officer led a row of trotting horses in formation. Even from the other side of the gate, the sheer magnitude of the operation was intimidating.

She straightened her collar and cleared her throat before approaching. "I have an appointment with Lieutenant Delaney," she said, the sound of Finn's rank sounding awkward on her tongue. "I'm supposed to meet him at the Hostess House."

"Yes, ma'am," the soldier shot back with rigid precision. She wished he wouldn't call her *ma'am*. She didn't want any part of this military world, where men barked out orders instead of speaking normally.

A few moments later, an open-carriage automobile arrived to take her to the appointed meeting place. She was told to settle into the back seat while the driver started the engine and put the auto into gear. The noisy motor chugged as they passed acres of tents, then rounded a row of wooden buildings housing the medical station, command headquarters, and the supply depot. The auto then made a sharp curve toward a tall A-frame building.

"That's the Hostess House," the driver said as he pulled to a stop and killed the engine.

Dozens of men in uniform milled about outside, some lounging in rocking chairs on the wide front porch while others kicked a ball around in the dirt yard.

Delia followed her escort inside the building, jumping when the rickety screen door slapped shut behind them. Their footsteps thudded on the wooden floorboards as she arrived at a spacious living room, furnished with tables and chairs for card playing. The far end was set up with upholstered chairs for reading and tables for letter writing or study. Rattan chairs were grouped around a long coffee table strewn with newspapers.

She spotted Finn sitting in a rattan chair, his crutches propped beside him. Her heart gave an involuntary squeeze at the sight of him. A battered leather aviator's jacket was slung over the back of his chair. He wore an ordinary open-collared shirt, a white silk scarf draped around his neck.

He looked even more handsome today than he did last night. Unlike the other soldiers with their shorn heads and close shaves, Finn's hair was long enough to brush against his collar, and he needed a shave. His slouchy, relaxed aura reminded her of the carefree boy she once knew. She'd probably always have this instinctive attraction to him, but inconvenient feelings could be ignored.

They *must* be ignored. Finn probably had a wife or a sweetheart somewhere, and she had no business hankering after such a man.

She closed the distance between them and sent a pointed glance at his tatty scarf. "That scarf has seen better days," she said. It was an understatement. The white silk was dingy, speckled with burn marks and frayed at the ends.

Finn beamed as he touched it. "This scarf has flown sixty-three missions with me and was around my neck the day I got shot down. I'll never get rid of it." He braced his hands on the arms of his chair and prepared to stand.

"Don't get up," she rushed to say, but he ignored her. Soon he was standing before her, six feet tall and radiating raw, masculine energy.

"Dee, before you say anything, I want to apologize for last night."

She stiffened. The less she had to dwell on the horror of last night, the happier she'd be. "There's no need."

"Yes, there is. If I had the ability to magically disappear from that garden, you'd have seen nothing but a little puff of smoke as I vanished."

She smothered the temptation to laugh and glanced about, looking for something to change the topic, and landed on the newspaper Finn had been reading.

"Do you know French?" she asked in surprise. Foreign languages certainly weren't anything taught at the orphanage.

"I learned enough to get by when I was over there," he answered as he gingerly lowered himself back onto the chair. He gestured toward the newspaper. "*La Libre Belgique* is a clandestine paper put out by a handful of brave people in Belgium. I was lucky enough to find a copy in the camp library. Yesterday you were pretty adamant that all the stuff printed in the American papers about how bad the Krauts are is just propaganda."

"Please don't say 'Kraut.'"

"The *Germans*," he amended with great exaggeration. "Maybe

some of the stuff in the newspapers is overblown, but I saw with my own eyes what's going on in Belgium, and believe me, it's bad. After the Germans rolled over the country, they seized everybody's horses and automobiles. They don't let people leave their neighborhoods unless they have a military pass. The telephone wires were cut, so they can't talk to each other. They made it illegal to fly the Belgian flag or to sing their national anthem. The newspaper offices were closed and the presses seized. Even so, some brave journalists cobbled together enough printing equipment to start publishing this newspaper." He held up the issue of *La Libre Belgique*. "This reports on ways to resist the occupation. It pokes fun at the kaiser and mocks the stiff-necked Germans stationed all over Belgium. It gives updates on rationing and tips for holding on through dark times. Delia, it gives people *hope*."

She took the paper, her eyes drawn to a pen-and-ink drawing of a handsome, albeit terribly intimidating officer in a German uniform. "Who is that?" she asked.

"That's General Ryckman, the Krau . . . that is, the German officer who is the commandant in occupied Belgium. He's the one who ordered a bounty on my head."

She gasped. "Really?"

"Really," Finn replied. "Everyone knew a plane had crashed near the village, and they searched the area high and low. The fact that I escaped gave General Ryckman a black eye, and to this day that bounty on my head is still there. He promised a thousand pounds to anyone who turned me in. He even offered amnesty if whoever helped me came forward, but Mathilde never did." Finn fiddled with the edges of the newspaper. "This Belgian paper is at the top of the list of things Ryckman hates. Anyone caught helping publish or distribute *La Libre Belgique* will be arrested on the spot. One of the guys delivering a crate of them to Antwerp was caught red-handed and sentenced to eight years' hard labor. He was sent to Germany in handcuffs, and nobody's heard from him since."

Delia's heart thudded. Had she known that Finn was fighting

overseas, she'd have been terrified on his behalf. Doubly so after he was shot down. And to know some awful general had put a bounty on his head? It made the horrors of war focus into harsh clarity.

"Finn, I'm not arguing that this isn't a tragedy, but I think the diplomats should take over. If the first shot had never been fired, none of this would be necessary."

Finn looked like he wanted to say more, but he shrugged it off. "Yeah, fine," he said. "Let's not argue about the war. Tell me about this Pollard fellow and how we can raise money to help Belgium."

Delia smoothed her collar and decided to follow Finn's civilized lead. "Alfred Pollard is a self-made millionaire," she began. "What Rockefeller is to oil, Pollard is to steamships. He has a reputation for being rigid in his ways, so we'll have to be on our best behavior when we meet with him. He doesn't drink or smoke, and he insists that every man who works for him be clean-shaven and refrain from swearing. You'll need a haircut and a shave before we approach him."

Finn raked a hand through his wavy blond hair. "They've been cutting me slack about that since I'm on convalescent leave. That's why I'm not required to wear my service uniform right now."

"Well, you'll need to be in uniform when we see Pollard. He makes all his employees, even the men in the steelworks, remain clean-shaven and in uniform. So that ratty silk scarf of yours will have to go."

"I've got others that aren't so bad," Finn said. "All the aviators wear them."

"Why?"

Finn pulled the scarf from his neck, then dangled it across the back of her hand. "Feel how silky that is. The scarves aren't fashion statements. We wear them around our necks while flying because the whole time we're in the air, we're looking up, down, and side to side, scanning both sky and land for enemy fighters. Without a soft scarf like this one, my neck would get scraped raw by my leather coat."

She nodded. "Is it cold up there?"

"It's *freezing*. The wind whips against your face and turns your breath into frost. And when you fly through the clouds, your face gets soaked. It's kind of great, though."

She shouldn't be discussing flying with Finn. It would only lead to her wanting to know more, such as what it felt like to be lifted off the ground or to zoom through a cloud. Or better yet, to fly above the clouds and gaze straight up into heaven. They'd often wondered such things when they were young, and revisiting those memories felt dangerous.

"You wore a proper uniform last night," she said. It was an olive-drab wool but tailored with a standing collar and shoulder straps embroidered with his officer's rank. It looked respectable, if not quite as dashing as the aviator's getup he'd worn in the parade.

"My Army dress uniform," he said. "I'll wear it if you think it will help."

"It will. Get a haircut and a shave too."

A teasing glint lit his eyes. "Yes, ma'am," he said, his tone carrying a hint of affection.

She needed to leave. It was too tempting being with him, even though little had changed. She needed safety and security, not a whirlwind ride with the man who had broken her trust.

"Yes, wear your dress uniform for our meeting with Pollard," she instructed. "Be prepared to share your story of how the CRB's food and medical supplies saved your life in Belgium. I'll handle the finance piece. Our meeting is at eleven o'clock tomorrow morning."

Then she cut the meeting short and fled as if the ghost of an old love affair had been awakened and threatened to lure her back into wondrous but risky territory.

13

Pollard Shipping dominated a sprawling complex of warehouses, piers, and office buildings on the east side of the New York Harbor. Unlike typical dockworkers, the men working for Pollard Shipping wore collared shirts with ties, even though their sleeves were rolled up as they loaded cargo, operated cranes, and hoisted crates on and off wooden pallets.

Delia stole a secretive glance at Finn, sitting opposite her in the carriage. Just as she'd asked, he had submitted to a short haircut and a close shave. Shorn of the tawny blond hair, he looked serious and disturbingly more manly. His jaw was sculpted, the column of his neck strong. His formal uniform consisted of a slim-fitting dark tunic adorned with his lieutenant's rank, brass buttons, and the Sam Browne belt strapped diagonally across his chest. Despite his fine appearance, he seemed uncomfortable as he continuously rotated a cigarette against his pant leg.

"Don't even *think* of lighting that cigarette," she said.

"I've been thinking about it ever since I boarded the carriage," he grumbled.

"When did you start smoking? It seems so unlike you."

The corner of his mouth tilted. "I don't even like the taste of tobacco, but I got hooked when I was in France. It turns out that when you're either bored or scared witless, a cigarette suddenly tastes like fine wine." He flashed her a grin. "And the cigarette smoke makes you forget how bad everything else smells." He pulled a pocket lighter flint from his coat and raised the cigarette.

"Finn," she said, warning in her tone.

"Why can't I sneak a smoke before we go in?" he asked. "We're a half hour early."

This was because Mr. Pollard was so obsessed with punctuality that he refused to see anyone even a few minutes late for an appointment. Delia intended to arrive with plenty of time to spare.

"If you smoke, your clothes and your breath will carry the stink. It will make a bad impression we can't afford. Nine million Belgians, Finn."

"And ten million reasons you're annoying," he muttered under his breath, which he fully intended for her to hear. He put the cigarette back in his coat pocket.

The carriage rolled to a halt before an imposing office building of granite stone. The once gray building had been stained black from years of soot coming from the nearby smokestacks. Delia clenched her briefcase with the legal documents she hoped to persuade Pollard to sign. She had no idea what sort of commitment they might wrest from Alfred Pollard, so she left the donation line blank, to be filled in if they were successful in securing a donation.

For a man still wrestling with a splint on his leg, Finn was surprisingly graceful as he twisted his large body out of the carriage. Delia handed him his crutches, then walked alongside him as they headed toward the front door.

"Remember, no swearing," she instructed. Thankfully, there was an elevator to take them to the sixth floor. With it being a warm day, the elevator operator looked overheated in his stiff collar, coat, and white gloves as he cranked the gate closed and pulled the lever for the sixth floor.

"Have you a meeting with Mr. Pollard?" he asked.

"Yes," Delia replied. "We're collecting for war donations."

"Good luck with that," the operator muttered.

Was it going to be that awful? Delia was accustomed to dealing with strict judges and demanding attorneys, but a corporate tycoon like Alfred Pollard? This was uncharted territory for her, and she began to perspire as they arrived at the sixth floor.

Mr. Pollard's secretary was an ancient man with a face that looked carved by a hatchet. "You're early," the secretary said with a frown as they entered the waiting area. It was as spartan as a government waiting room. Slatted wood benches with no cushioning sat against unadorned walls.

"I know of Mr. Pollard's respect for punctuality and thought it best not to cut it too close," she explained.

"Punctuality means arriving *on time*. Now the three of us must share this space until your meeting."

"We'll try not to interfere with your day," Delia said, then took a seat on a bench beside Finn. Would it have killed Mr. Pollard to have paid for a bench with a back? Finn shifted on the bench, the squeak echoing in the barren room. The secretary shot him a pointed glare. Good heavens, this was going to be a long twenty minutes.

At precisely eleven o'clock, the secretary stood. "Mr. Pollard will see you now."

Mr. Pollard's personal office wasn't much better than his waiting area. The furniture was made of the same plain oak, and practical filing cabinets lined the walls. The only luxuries were a large braided rug and the forest-green draperies framing the windows. Mr. Pollard's appearance, however, was as grim as his secretary's. His balding head gleamed from the desk lamp as he peered at them over his spectacles.

"I'm afraid you have wasted your time in coming here," he began. "I told Bertie I have no money left to give, and yet he still sends people hounding me for donations. Most annoying."

"I know," she said in a sympathetic but cheerful voice. "Mr.

Hoover understands your decision to fund Liberty Bonds instead of Belgian relief, but he thought you would appreciate hearing how your previous donations have been used. Lieutenant Delaney personally benefited from the supplies your donation helped make possible."

A spark of interest lit the old man's face as he swiveled his attention to Finn. "Are you the pilot who was in the parade last month? The one from the Lafayette Escadrille?"

"Yes, sir," Finn said, his voice strong and respectful, without a trace of his typical irreverence.

A wistful smile brightened Mr. Pollard's face. "If I were fifty years younger, I would have been in France with you."

"Really?" Finn straightened, leaning forward in his chair.

"I admire what you young men have accomplished over there. Knights of the sky, taking to the air to defend the weak. You didn't wait while the American government twiddled its thumbs. No, you went to Europe to do your bit. Please, tell me what it was like, and don't leave anything out."

Delia stayed silent. She didn't care if Alfred Pollard and Finn wanted to indulge in a romanticized version of war. If it encouraged the man to crack open his wallet on behalf of the CRB, it would be well worth it.

"The American flyers were all volunteers," Finn said, "and the French Army treated us like royalty. At first there was talk of making us sign on with the French Army, but they knew we were good for morale. It gave their people hope to know that men had come all the way from America to fight on their behalf. So they gave us our own unit and put us up in a fancy château in the country. We trained for seven months, and afterward we took to the air. Sometimes I'd go on scouting missions, while other times I'd escort bomber planes. I've flown missions to protect advancing troops. Ever since I joined up, I've felt as if each day is a gift."

"Weren't you ever scared?" Mr. Pollard asked.

"Sometimes," Finn admitted. "The trick is to transform the fear into determination. Each time I flew, I had a purpose. I was saving lives. The war made me stronger somehow; all of us felt that way. It's why I want to get back there as soon as I can get rid of this splint on my leg."

Mr. Pollard braced his hands on his desk and pushed himself upright. The palsied hands shook, and his head bobbed a little, but his eyes were keen as he met Finn's gaze. "Sir, I salute you," the old man said, then offered his hand.

Finn had to stretch across the desk to shake it. It seemed the bond between the two men occurred almost instantly, and Delia couldn't deny it. Bertie was right. Finn embodied the gallant, dashing figure that other men admired and aspired to emulate.

Mr. Pollard peppered him with an endless stream of questions. He wanted to know about dogfight maneuvers, the durability of aircraft under fire, and advances in propeller technology. Finn answered them all. Most of his responses were too technical for Delia to follow, but Mr. Pollard seemed captivated by the conversation.

"You know a lot about airplanes," Finn said.

Mr. Pollard nodded. "I've been studying ever since the Wright Brothers got off the ground." With an effort, Mr. Pollard's palsied hands gestured to the window across the room. "You see those train tracks out there? That's how my business began, shipping cargo by train all across America. Then I moved to steamships. I still have my trains, even though shipping generates most of my revenue. I suspect that someday airplanes will be used to transport goods. I probably won't be alive to see it, but I can't help dreaming about it."

"Have you ever been up in the air?" Finn asked.

Mr. Pollard coughed and shook his head. "Heavens, no. My wife cringes even when I climb a staircase. I'm afraid those days are behind me forever."

"Nah," Finn said with a good-natured smile. "If you've got a good pilot and the right airplane, you don't have to do anything except enjoy the ride. I'll take you up sometime. We can make a lap around the Manhattan skyscrapers like you've never seen them before."

A spray of lines appeared on Mr. Pollard's papery-thin skin as a magnificent smile transformed his face. "I never even considered it, but do you think it's really possible for me?"

Finn nodded and continued jabbering about flying, and Delia could only watch in dazed admiration. This was *exactly* the effect Bertie had hoped Finn would have on important donors. Glamorizing the war seemed wrong, but if it resulted in a large donation to keep the CRB alive, she'd stay silent.

After twenty minutes of their allotted thirty minutes talking about airplanes, it was time to lock down the donation Bertie needed. Delia pasted a serene expression on her face and interrupted the two men.

"We are so lucky to have Lieutenant Delaney helping us raise funds for Belgium. If it weren't for your donations to the CRB, he might not be alive today."

Her observation brought the conversation skidding to a halt. She felt like a spoilsport for interrupting their fun, but she was sent here on a mission, and it was time to secure a hefty donation.

"Ma'am, I know why Bertie sent you." For the first time, a hint of kindness tinged the old man's eyes when he looked at her. "I have diverted the limits of my charitable contribution to Liberty Bonds. It is the best way to bring this war to a swift end and stop the suffering."

"If the relief ships stop sailing, millions of people in Belgium will suffer."

Mr. Pollard shrugged. "That's not my war."

"It's *my* war," Finn said. "A lady named Mathilde risked her life to hide me in her home. The Germans put a bounty on my head, and people were in and out of Mathilde's house all day long, so I stayed put beneath the floorboards. All day I could hear voices and people moving around. A couple of times, German soldiers came looking for me, opening cupboards and checking under beds. Their footsteps were inches away from my face."

A chill raced through Delia, yet Finn spoke in his typically nonchalant manner.

"At night Mathilde pulled up the boards so I could get out. Her kids were fascinated by me and gathered all around. They didn't know any English, and my French isn't great, so we couldn't talk much. But I loved those kids all the same—their eagerness, their curiosity. The little girl was about five or six, and she kept trying to give me her cookies. Imagine that. A kid who didn't have much to eat saved her cookies to give to me. Mr. Pollard, I'm not fighting for the sake of nine million Belgians. I'm fighting for Mathilde Verhaegen and her three kids."

Mr. Pollard winced and turned away. He seemed genuinely moved and was surely wise enough to see the point of Finn's story. That little girl and her family had supplies, including cookies, because of Bertie Hoover. And if Bertie didn't get a fresh infusion of cash, his humanitarian shipments would grind to a halt.

Mr. Pollard sighed and pushed himself to his feet. He walked to the window and stared out at the freight yard, where trains funneled tons of cargo into the nearby port.

"It may look as if I'm rolling in money," Mr. Pollard said, "but the truth is I'm not. Everything you see out that window—the train tracks, the boxcars, the steamships—they all have my name on them, yet most of it is owned by banks and investors. They get the first cut of everything I earn. I also have six thousand employees whose wages I must pay, and they're a tough lot. While it would be nice if I could just snap my fingers so that little girl could get plenty of cookies and bread and jam, I simply don't have any more funds to give."

Delia understood enough about corporate financing to believe Mr. Pollard. The man's spartan office was proof that he didn't lavish money on himself. The regret carved into his careworn face convinced her that his coffers could no longer support a monthly million-dollar donation.

"What if you gave us something besides money?" Finn suggested.

"Such as?"

Finn snatched up his crutches and propelled himself over to the window. "What kind of ship is that?" he asked, pointing to a steamer docked in the harbor across from the freight yard.

"The *Athena* is a forty-ton cargo steamship," Mr. Pollard answered. "It crosses the Atlantic twice a month."

Finn's eyes took on a gleam. "If you can't give Bertie cash, how about you let him use a portion of that cargo ship to send food overseas?"

Delia caught her breath. Partial use of a ship wasn't as good as a cash donation, but at least they wouldn't leave empty-handed.

Mr. Pollard frowned. After a moment, he went to a filing cabinet to paw through some paperwork, then barked at his secretary to bring him the file on the *Athena*. The ticking of the wall clock sounded unbearably loud as they waited for the secretary to return. They waited some more while Mr. Pollard flipped through pages in the file.

A scowl darkened his face as he banged the keys of an adding machine, making careful notations in the *Athena* paperwork. He fidgeted and brooded while studying the ledger. Finally, he threw down his pencil. "I can let Bertie use three of the *Athena's* storage compartments with each crossing," he announced.

Delia couldn't guess the monetary value of such a grant, but Mr. Pollard didn't seem happy about it. No matter how big or small, it was vital his offer of cargo space remain in force even after his uncharacteristic generosity stirred by Finn's visit faded.

"Would you be willing to put that in writing?" she asked.

"What?" Mr. Pollard looked offended. "My word isn't good enough for you?"

It wasn't. If Bertie was to depend on this bequest, it needed to be spelled out, signed, and filed with the harbor master. "Bertie will want proof in case he encounters difficulty in the months to come," she explained. "You may not always be here in New York to assure the port authority of your permission to use the *Athena*. I'd be happy to draft a simple agreement."

Mr. Pollard didn't agree, but he didn't disagree either. None of the documents she'd brought with her was suitable to secure donated cargo space. It didn't matter. Delia had enough experience to write something up on the spot. Without delay, she opened her briefcase and took out some blank paper and a pen and began writing, paying scant attention as Finn started chatting Mr. Pollard up about the trains funneling into the port.

It was hard to concentrate when Finn wouldn't shut up. Why did he need to know the origin of each boxcar? Gondola cars carrying timber from Wisconsin and open-top hopper cars with coal from Pennsylvania. Boxcars from Kansas carrying wheat and so on. Nevertheless, she focused on drafting each word of the legal agreement to secure three storage compartments per sailing of the *Athena*. The language wasn't complicated, but she couldn't afford to make a mistake because Finn wouldn't stop talking.

"How much does it cost to attach an extra boxcar from Kansas and haul it out here?" Finn asked.

"Not much," Mr. Pollard said. "I own the boxcars outright, so the only real expense is a little extra fuel."

"So if you allowed Bertie to use a bunch of your boxcars to ship wheat from Kansas, it wouldn't cost you that much?"

Delia held her breath, suddenly realizing where Finn was headed.

"It would cost a fortune," Mr. Pollard corrected. "Wheat is a valuable commodity. It would cost thousands of dollars to fill a boxcar with wheat."

"Don't worry about the wheat," Finn said. "We'll figure out a way to pay for that. All I want is your promise to let us use a couple of your boxcars on every train coming in from the Midwest."

Mr. Pollard thrummed his fingers on the desktop, annoyance stamped across his face. Still, a hint of respect shone in his flinty gaze.

"Four boxcars," he snapped. "Bertie is responsible for buying the wheat and getting it to the station. I want that written into the agreement."

Delia nodded, although where they'd find the money to buy wheat was a mystery. She wouldn't look a gift horse in the mouth, but this was a major disappointment. Millions of dollars from Mr. Pollard would be flowing into Liberty Bonds to buy bombs and ammunition. Meanwhile, they had to settle for donated cargo space and the use of a few boxcars.

She started a fresh page to draft the railway commitment. They hadn't discussed how long the contract would last, and it would be pushing her luck to ask. She scrambled for the sort of language Wesley would have used for an open-ended commitment and wrote the words *Agreement shall remain in force until an armistice between warring nations is signed or until both parties arrive at a mutually agreeable date for termination.*

She handed the page to Mr. Pollard, watching as he scanned the document. There was no change in his expression as he read the short agreement.

"This is suitable," he finally said. "I shall ask my secretary to type two copies, and you shall have my signature before leaving." He tossed the document onto his desk, then turned his attention to Finn. "Now, about that airplane ride you promised me . . ."

14

Delia frowned out the carriage window as Finn hauled himself aboard. The carriage rocked as he plopped onto the bench opposite her.

"It could have been worse," Finn said, tugging at his tie to loosen it. "But it wasn't a complete bust, was it?"

She sighed. "It was mostly a bust. We've been given some free shipping, yes, but what Bertie really needs is cash."

"Well, that's the nature of tackling a hard challenge," Finn said. "We're going to suffer five losses for every victory. Don't lose hope so quickly. We'll just have to get back up, dust ourselves off, and live to fight another day."

Against her will, a smile tugged. Finn's buoyant optimism could always inspire her. Alfred Pollard was only their first of many appointments, and perhaps they'd have better luck with the next donor.

And yet Bertie was waiting for them at his town house. Disappointing him was not going to be easy. It took an hour to get across town and arrive at his brownstone, where Delia held Finn's crutches while he grasped the railing, hopping up each step on his good leg.

Bertie soon answered their knock, and the hopeful expression on his face turned to surprise when he saw Finn's new haircut and formal uniform. A rustle of silk came from down the hall as Mrs. Hoover joined them.

"You look different," Bertie said to Finn.

"Better?" Delia asked, a note of pride in her voice.

A diplomatic pause lengthened as Bertie scanned Finn's appearance from head to toe. "It's just . . . well, different. But enough of that! Come in and tell us about your meeting with Pollard."

"I'm afraid our meeting was a disappointment," she confessed as they stepped into the foyer. "Mr. Pollard told us he's fresh out of cash. He promised us some help, but no actual money."

Bertie grimaced and turned away while his wife summoned a resigned smile. "Let me get you something to drink. I know how exhausting Alfred Pollard can be."

Mrs. Hoover guided them into the large family room. The last time Delia was in this room, she confronted Wesley and quit her job. It felt like ages ago, and yet it was only three days earlier.

Bertie looked pensive as his wife poured lemonade. Once she joined them, he turned his troubled gaze to Finn. "I'm surprised to see you in that uniform. And with a military haircut. I expected to see you in your leather aviator's jacket."

"It's pretty beaten up," Finn said. "I didn't think it was right to show up at a fancy business meeting looking like something the cat dragged in."

Bertie tipped his head in acknowledgment. "Normally you'd be right, but these aren't normal times. You're an American hero and need to look like one. That battered-up leather jacket has panache. I suggest you wear it whenever you go out to shake the trees for donations."

Delia sagged. It had been her advice to spiff up Finn, and her instincts had been wrong. Bertie must have noticed her dismay because he gave her knee a pat.

"Don't take it so hard," Bertie said. "Raising money is a difficult task no matter who you ask. Let's get the unpleasant business out of the way. You said Pollard's donation didn't amount to much. Let's hear it."

"The best he could do was spare us space on his steamships and his trains coming in from the Midwest."

Bertie leaned forward. "How much space?"

"It's spelled out in the contract," she replied, handing him the documents.

Bertie's brows lowered as he studied the papers, but after a moment, he looked up. "Fetch me some paper and a pencil, would you?" he asked his wife.

Mrs. Hoover disappeared into the office in search of the requested items. Bertie set aside the contract after his wife returned, and he started jotting down numbers and formulas, chewing his bottom lip as he worked.

"I hope I didn't mess up," Delia whispered to Finn.

"You didn't," Bertie assured without looking up. He continued scribbling, the scratching of his pencil the only sound in the otherwise silent room. At last, he threw down the pencil, crossed his arms, and looked straight at Delia. "Do you know what you have done?" It was impossible to tell if Bertie was furious or about to burst with glee.

"No," Delia said, feeling mildly terrified. Even Mrs. Hoover looked confused by Bertie's strange behavior.

"I spend a fortune leasing cargo ships to send food to Belgium. I pay for fuel, the crew's wages, and rental fees tied to the ships. I pay port charges and for maritime insurance. You just secured generous cargo space *for free*. And boxcar space *for free*. Do you know the value of that donation?"

"No," Delia admitted, but hope was beginning to bloom.

Bertie clapped his hands together. "I don't either because you worded the contract to last until the end of the war, and who knows how long that will be? Delia, this is a definite victory. If the war lasts even a year longer, the value of this contract is worth millions!"

"How on earth did you make it happen?" Mrs. Hoover asked.

Elation coursed through Delia. "It was Finn's doing," she replied, and both Hoovers turned to look at Finn.

"Mr. Pollard wanted to know what it was like to fly," Finn said. "And what it was like being trapped in Belgium while the Jerries were looking for me. He couldn't get enough of it, so I just kept talking."

"And I want you to *keep* talking," Bertie said. "People are hungry for stories like yours. Rich folks have been hoarding cash because of the war, so ask each donor to donate a slice of his business. Get the cattlemen to donate beef. Get the millers to donate flour. The newspapermen can give us free advertising and so on."

Delia rocked back in her chair as understanding sank in. Finn flashed her a wink and a grin, and she grinned back.

"This calls for a celebration," Bertie said. "All over the world, humanity is sinking into darkness and despair, so we must celebrate these rare glimpses of joy. The CRB is proof that compassion knows no borders, and it shall be a beacon of light, reminding the world that goodness and mercy shall not be snuffed out by the winds of war."

Despite their triumph with Alfred Pollard, the CRB was still millions of dollars short of their monthly goal, so Delia couldn't afford to rest on her laurels. Most people had never even heard of the CRB, which meant they needed to drum up publicity before approaching any potential new donors.

She set up a meeting with Finn at the ice cream parlor on the first floor of her apartment building, even though she risked encountering cold shoulders from others who lived in the building. Finn loved ice cream, and this was a convenient place for them to meet. She wouldn't let the bullies interfere with her work, including Hilde and her gang who occupied a table near the front.

Delia chose a table at the back of the shop. The air was filled with the aroma of fresh waffle cones, and she casually read a newspaper while awaiting Finn's arrival. She was so engrossed in the lurid story of a show girl suspected of murdering her lover that she didn't notice Finn standing over her until he spoke.

"You really like that schlock?"

She held up the folded issue of the *New York Journal*. "This is research," she said, not at all embarrassed to be caught reading the trashy newspaper because Finn already knew she had lowbrow tastes when it came to literature. "In fact, this newspaper is going to play an important role in our fundraising."

Finn propped his crutches against the wall beside the booth and joined her. Something about a man in uniform was universally appealing, even to a pacifist like Delia. His khaki cotton shirt fit his broad shoulders perfectly. The matching trousers were folded into the brown leather lace-up boots, and he looked frightfully attractive. Other women in the ice cream parlor noticed, sending surreptitious glances his way.

Delia waited until a waitress took their order, and then she slid the newspaper across the table to Finn. "The *New York Journal* is William Randolph Hearst's newspaper, who's famous for splashing patriotic stories all over the front page. He'll gladly feature a profile of you, and we can mention how relief supplies from the CRB helped save you in Belgium."

"How do we make that happen?"

"I've already called and made an appointment. Mr. Hearst will host you at a private dinner with several of his journalists. You'll have plenty of time to tell your story."

And charm them. Finn could charm the birds out of a tree, and if he could manage to get on Hearst's good side, it would pay dividends for the duration of the war. Not only was the *New York Journal* the most popular newspaper in the city, its articles were syndicated to newspapers all across America. After they exhausted the donor class in New York, she and Finn could start approaching other wealthy donors from coast to coast.

The waitress brought their orders. Delia had a single scoop of strawberry ice cream, while Finn indulged in a banana split piled high with strawberry, chocolate, and vanilla ice cream.

Finn looked enraptured as he eyed the bowl before him. "Dee, I've seen the Eiffel Tower, the *Mona Lisa*, and the spires of Notre Dame, but nothing looks quite as good as this banana split."

He picked up his spoon and took a huge bite of ice cream, closing his eyes in delight. She left her own dish untouched. Sometimes the greatest joys in life came from witnessing someone else's happiness.

At the front of the ice cream parlor, Hilde suddenly stood, looking as pretty, cool, and blond as ever. She had a notebook propped in the crook of her arm and wore a sly smile as she wended through the tables toward them.

"Brace yourself," Delia whispered to Finn. "A wolf in sheep's clothing is heading our way."

Hilde approached Delia and preened before their table. "Care to donate to Liberty Bonds?"

"Thank you, but no," Delia said in an equally poised voice.

"Oh, yes, our local pacifist." Hilde swiveled her attention to Finn, a man in uniform and certainly no pacifist. "Did you know Delia here is a German sympathizer? She claims to hate the war and bores us all with her pacifist sermons."

Finn managed a smile that didn't quite reach his eyes. "Yeah, Delia's always been upfront about that."

"So you knew?" Hilde said, her nose wrinkling.

"Yeah. Dee and I go way back."

Hilde tucked a strand of hair behind her ear, looking annoyingly attractive as she focused on Finn and trailed her finger along the edge of the table. "I can't imagine staying neutral in times like these. Almost everyone at the Martha Washington has pulled out all the stops to do their part for the war effort, but I guess some people aren't cut out for it. Anyway, I want to thank you for your service, sir."

Finn tossed her a quick smile. "Thanks," he said, twisting on the bench to face away from Hilde, who didn't get the message.

"Can I coax you to join our table at the front of the parlor? I promise, we're much better company than the kaiser's little pet here."

Delia wanted to snatch away that notebook of hers and smack her with it.

Finn, however, seemed unfazed. "Hilde, if you would put as much effort into supporting our boys as you do into taking little digs at Delia, we may have won the war by now."

Hilde's fighting spirit was pricked, and she lowered her chin. "I've raised more money for Liberty Bonds than anyone else in this district."

"And yet somehow you still seem bankrupt of compassion," Finn shot back. "Now, if you'll excuse me, I'm on a date, and our ice cream is melting."

Watching Hilde's face seize with mortification was a guilty pleasure. Better still, all the women at Hilde's table had witnessed it. Delia shouldn't gloat, but it hadn't been easy being Hilde's pincushion, and it was nice to have someone defending her.

"What's *her* problem?" Finn quietly asked after Hilde had retreated.

Delia tried to sound as if it didn't bother her. "I'm something of a pariah around here. Most of the women have brothers or boyfriends who are suiting up for the war, so my being a pacifist doesn't go over very well."

"Do they come at you like that a lot?"

She shrugged. "Sticks and stones."

"Why don't you move somewhere else? There are lots of places to live in New York."

Her gaze trailed beyond the front windows of the ice cream shop and into the walnut-paneled lobby beyond. She used to love it here, and trying to find a new place to live would upend her world all over again.

"I hate change. I'd rather put up with it than move. Why should I move when I can keep enjoying the cold shoulders from the people here?"

Finn lightly kicked her under the table. "Because once again you're clinging to stability instead of striking out for something better."

The arrow found its mark. He didn't intend to be hurtful, but the charge was true. She shifted her attention to the newspaper to avoid the subject, checking the weather forecast printed at the top. Then, noticing the date, her heart froze, and she glanced back up at Finn. How could she have forgotten what day it was?

"Happy birthday," she said softly, knowing this was always a difficult day for him.

For a split second, Finn grimaced, a ghost of anguish flashing across his features. Yet it vanished as quickly as it appeared. "Thanks," he said, then dug back into his banana split.

Finn never celebrated his birthday. It was on his twelfth birthday that he tried to impress a girl by running into a burning building to rescue a cat. For a long time after his mother died, Finn wept every night. One of the nuns overheard him and coaxed him to turn his energies to good works instead. Finn went after it with both hands, volunteering for chores at school and sticking up for kids who needed help, and yet his guilt never eased.

"Finn, please quit blaming yourself. Your mother wouldn't want that for you."

Finn's mouth twisted with a bitter hint of a smile. "I know you mean well, but her death will always be on my conscience. The only way I can live with myself is to make the world a better place. That's why I agreed to work with Bertie. Mathilde reminds me of my mother, and I need to be sure she has everything she needs to raise those kids."

He pushed the bowl of half-eaten ice cream away. "I know I should be over it by now. Right before my surgery, I confessed everything to a priest, and he said all the right things. I was forgiven, but . . ."

His voice trailed off and Delia completed his sentence. "But you still haven't forgiven yourself."

"Bingo." He stood and grabbed his crutches. "I've got to get back to Camp Mills. When do we meet with this Hearst fellow?"

Delia ached to embrace him and soothe the anguish from his expression, but she couldn't go down that path again. She stood and managed a smile. "We meet with him for dinner at seven o'clock tomorrow. Meet me at the intersection of Broadway and 64th, and we'll head straight to the restaurant. Wear your debonaire pilot's gear."

Finn shook off his strange gloom and sent her a grin. "You think I'm debonaire, do you?"

"I think the leather jacket is debonaire. You I merely tolerate."

Her joke banished the lingering grief from his face, and his marvelous laughter lasted all the way out the ice cream parlor. Just before leaving, he turned to give her a salute and a wink.

The women at Hilde's table watched as he hobbled out the door, looking back at Delia in confusion.

Delia sat back down to finish her ice cream and secretly enjoyed their confusion.

15

Would he ever tire of the adoration? Finn ought to be used to it by now, but as he arrived at the restaurant, a photographer wanted him to pose beside the front door, standing alongside William Randolph Hearst, whose newspaper would print Finn's profile and distribute the story from coast to coast. Mr. Hearst posed as if opening the door to welcome Finn into the famed restaurant. Finn battled the temptation to gape at all the pedestrians who'd gathered at the street corner to watch. The photographer, meanwhile, demanded that the two men stand perfectly still so as to capture the evening shot.

Finn steadied himself as the photographer adjusted the focus on the large format camera. With the squeeze of a mechanical striker, the powder on the flash pan sent a burst of blinding light as his image was captured. Finn relaxed as the smell of the sulfuric powder tinged the air. He sent a wink to Delia, who watched amid the semicircle of onlookers.

"Let's try one more," the photographer said, walking his camera and tripod a few feet to the side. "Put your cane in front of your leg so I can get it in this next shot."

Finn complied. He'd switched to a cane this evening out of vanity. His leg was healing so well that he might not need the cane after a few more weeks, yet it was a part of his wounded pilot persona. He'd taken Bertie's advice and had reverted to wearing his leather pilot's jacket, along with a white silk scarf. Mr. Hearst clapped an arm around Finn's shoulder as though they were old friends.

Do you see me now, Ma?

She would be proud of him. He'd made something of himself after all. Though his task was far from over, Finn was committed to doing all he could so that the kids in Belgium would continue having food sent their way.

Another flash of light, another acrid tinge of sulfur, and then Mr. Hearst gestured for the group to step inside the restaurant. Three reporters, the mayor of New York, and a couple of officers from Camp Mills would be joining them for dinner.

Delia also joined the group following Finn and Mr. Hearst into Murray's Roman Garden, the city's splashiest restaurant. Its design was in the opulent style of ancient Rome, featuring ivy-draped columns surrounding a grotto with jetted fountains, marble statues, and frescoed walls. Laughter and music echoed off a barrel-vaulted ceiling two stories high. Living trees strung with fairy lights filled the interior that glittered with crystal and mosaics.

Finn was the guest of honor tonight, and with Delia on one arm and the cane in his other hand, he felt like a million bucks. Band music in the main room made it too noisy for an interview, but Mr. Hearst had reserved a private dining room. Textured wallpaper in hues of burgundy and gold adorned the enclosed room. A round dining table dominated most of the space, and a mahogany sideboard held an array of crystal decanters, wine bottles, and assorted spirits. Most impressive was a tall sculpture with tiers of tropical fruits, pears, and clusters of grapes.

Of course, none of this came free. Finn was expected to tell the reporters details of his crash landing and hiding from the enemy while under the floorboards of Mathilde Verhaegen's home. He would give them what they wanted, although his main objective was to highlight the importance of the lifesaving food and supplies provided by the Commission for the Relief of Belgium.

The first dish of stuffed olives and brandy-soaked figs arrived, and Thomas Brodsky was ready with a question. Brodsky was a reporter for Hearst's flagship newspaper, the *New York American*. But Delia had already warned Finn that anything he said publicly tonight would be shared across the countless newspapers owned by Hearst.

"Tell us about the circumstances of your crash," Brodsky asked, a notepad propped in his hand.

Reliving the crash wasn't fun, but he could do it, plus there wasn't any information he'd share that could endanger Mathilde or the CRB.

"I was patrolling an area along the Somme, looking for new German encampments over the border in Belgium. All of a sudden I heard the rattle of a machine gun. A German fighter plane had flown up behind me, unleashing a barrage of bullets."

Beside him, Delia had become very alert. He'd never told her any of this bitter memory, but talking about the crash was the cost of getting publicity for the CRB.

He assumed a cocksure smile and continued. "My odds were good because I was flying a Nieuport 21, which is the most agile airplane in the world. I could hear the bullets whizzing past my cockpit, but I executed a few sharp dives and turns to shake the enemy, although in the process my engine stalled."

Everyone around the table looked spellbound.

Finn paused and pointed at a humidor on the sideboard. "Say, could I have one of those cigars?"

Delia would prefer he didn't smoke, but his right hand started to tremble, and he didn't want anyone to see it. Mr. Hearst himself picked up a cigar and held the lighter for Finn.

Finn took three quick puffs, pretending to enjoy it as he settled back into the chair to continue his story. After his plane had stalled, he lost altitude fast. A spray of bullets struck the engine, sending sparks in every direction. It was only a matter of time before the fabric covering the wings caught fire. The squadron was flying over a densely populated city with nowhere to land. Finn had been close enough to the ground to spot a bunch of schoolchildren standing in a yard, staring up at him in horror as the plane trailed inky black smoke.

He was losing altitude by the second and didn't have long to make a decision. He couldn't aim for the field with all those kids around, but there was a canal in the distance, so he crashed on its narrow embankment.

Finn told the reporters everything. What crashing felt like, how his leg got mangled, and the panic of getting himself out the airplane, then nearly drowning in the muddy bank of the canal.

"After I dragged myself out of the airplane, I had only a minute or two to find a place to hide. The German pilot who'd shot me down was circling overhead, watching me. But the nearest landing strip was a couple of miles away. He veered off for it, and I knew the second he landed, he'd send a search party out to capture me."

He was sure to omit Mathilde's name or how many children she had, but he spoke about hiding in a sympathizer's house and the comradery he formed with the family.

"That's the thing about war," he said. "I would have given my life for any one of them. We never would have met except that my plane went down near their house. Yet knowing them, and sacrificing alongside them, was one of the most profound experiences of my life. The only way I can thank them is by making sure the shipments from the CRB to Belgium continue. That's why I'm here today."

The table before him held a bounty of rich food, but Finn had lost his appetite. He fiddled with the cigar in one hand and clenched the arm of his chair with the other. Beneath the table, Delia rested a hand on his knee. He was grateful for the assurance from her; that she knew what all this cost him and that she cared.

Finn nodded to the reporters across the table. "Anyway, thanks for listening to my story. I hope it will help raise support for the CRB and all the good that it does."

Thomas Brodsky, the reporter with the bald head and round spectacles, flipped the page in his notepad. "How did you make it back to France?"

It was the question Finn dreaded the most. "I was only a couple of miles over the border. It wasn't hard," he lied.

"Yes, but *how*," the other reporter pressed. "Every inch of the Western Front is bristling with barbed wire and land mines. There are observation posts armed with machine guns and searchlights. How did you get through?"

Finn ground out his cigar in a crystal dish. He was ready to end this and leave the restaurant. "You know what? Now might be a good time for you to put away that notepad and start minding your own business."

Delia sucked in a quick breath and withdrew her hand.

But Brodsky doubled down. "This is the most interesting part of your story," he insisted. "Everyone will want to know."

Across the table, Mr. Hearst stood and faced the reporters. "Come," he coaxed. "The cheese course is coming soon. We've plenty of time to hear about the splendid escape. Please, help yourselves to the cigars and relax."

Brodsky walked over to get a cigar. There was no way Finn was going to talk. It wasn't a "splendid escape." On the contrary, it was both terrifying and shameful. He'd sworn to Bertie that he'd never reveal the fact of his hiding aboard a CRB barge, especially not to journalists.

Brodsky gave a sly smile as he sauntered over to Finn with the additional cigar. "Pipe down, fly-boy."

Finn shot to his feet and grabbed Brodsky by both lapels, shoving him backward into the sideboard. Crystal decanters smashed to the floor, and the platter of fruit toppled. He drew back a fist to punch the lights out of Brodsky, but the older man made no move to defend himself. Instead, he leaned back against the sideboard, a look of horror mingled with pity on his face as he stared at Finn. It cut through the haze of red.

Finn gave the reporter a final shake before releasing him.

Delia rushed over to him, broken crystal crunching beneath her boots. She pressed in close to his face and spoke in a furious whisper, "Finn! You need to apologize. *Now.*"

What had come over him? Everyone in the room was standing now, staring at him as though he were a bomb about to explode.

"I'm sorry," he muttered, but nobody moved a muscle. He forced himself to look directly at an annoyed Thomas Brodsky, who was straightening and brushing off his disheveled coat. "I'm sorry," he said again. "I don't know what came over me. All this . . ." He gestured to the platters of food filling up the table, the mounds of chocolate, and the bottles of champagne chilling on ice. "All this makes me sick. It's a disgrace to pile up fancy food like that when people are starving all over Europe."

Delia stepped between Finn and Brodsky. "You didn't hear that," she said to the reporter. "Lieutenant Delaney is grateful to be safely back home but feels guilty over the people he had to leave behind."

Brodsky was still busy examining his jacket. "This is my best coat, and it's got brandy all over it."

Rescue came from an unexpected source. "I'll buy you a new coat," Mr. Hearst offered. "But I want the stories that each of you submit to accurately report the heroism of Lieutenant Delaney and nothing else. Is that understood?"

Delia tried to smooth things over. "We are very thankful for your hospitality, everyone, but I should get Finn back to the camp now. He isn't feeling well."

It was an understatement. He felt nauseous and was twitchy, hot and cold at the same time. Reaching for his cane, Finn walked with Delia out of the restaurant.

Finn still couldn't understand what had caused him to physically attack an innocent man. Delia sat opposite him in the carriage on the ride home, looking at him in confusion. The theaters had just let out, and the horse-drawn vehicle crawled slowly toward Broad Street. It was a damp November evening and chilly inside the enclosed carriage. It was so cramped, his knees bumped against Delia's.

"Well?" Delia asked pointedly.

"I promised Bertie I would never talk about how I got out of Belgium. Especially not to the press."

Bertie wouldn't mind sharing the story with Delia. Actually, he would probably urge Finn to inform her of the situation so that she could help prevent the truth from ever getting out. Anxiety made the damp chill feel even colder. He shifted on the bench to release some of the tension coiling in his muscles.

"I broke a lot of rules when I escaped from Belgium," he said, clenching his fist at the memory of those desperate two days of fleeing. "You've got to swear not to tell this to anyone, as it could ruin everything for the CRB."

"I promise," she said.

It would be a relief to tell her. Even Bertie didn't know exactly what had happened, and it was important for someone to know. Finn would rejoin the war soon, and if he died, nobody would ever know how a terrified fourteen-year-old kid worked up the courage to save Finn's life.

"Belgium has canals that run everywhere," he began. "They built those canals all the way back in medieval times, and they're still used today. The canals turned out to be a blessing."

Finn relayed how, after Germany had conquered Belgium, they seized control of the railroads, trains, horses, and automobiles. The canals were the only means by which the CRB could transport relief supplies to the interior of the country. They used barges to send sacks of wheat and oats from the Port of Rotterdam to distribution points throughout Belgium. When the local volunteers arrived to pick it up, they would always return the empty sacks from the previous week to be reused. The sacks were called "empties."

Finn got to a distribution point with the help of Mathilde's oldest son, Pieter, who was only fourteen, but war turned boys into men very quickly. He and Pieter hitched a ride on a wagon, which was heading to the distribution point loaded with hundreds of empties—canvas sacks to be returned to the barge.

It was a miserably cold, windy, and rainy night. They chose the night carefully, knowing the German guards were more likely to huddle inside the checkpoint shack rather than venture out for a close inspection of the barge.

Pain shot up Finn's leg as he hobbled toward the barge tied up to the landing. A flickering light from a single oil lamp cast dim illumination over the checkpoint. Water sloshed against the wooden sides of the barge, and chains emitted a rhythmic clank as it rocked in the choppy water. Rain spattered the riverbanks and sent up the loamy smell of mud and wet canvas.

Two guards sat inside the checkpoint shack, sipping from steaming mugs. The Germans were rigorous when inspecting goods as they were being off-loaded from the barge, though they paid little attention to the locals who returned the empties.

Finn had to hobble on his own two feet as he carried armfuls of canvas sacks aboard. He clenched his teeth against the pain as he twisted his body to climb down the short ladder onto the barge's deck that rose and fell with the waves. Pieter was right behind, carrying his own load of empties. The Dutch crew looked the other way as Finn went to the covered hold and eased himself down on the thick pile of sacks. The prickly canvas itched, and wheat dust swirled in the air.

"*Bonne chance*," Pieter said quietly as he mounded sacks atop Finn's.

Finn reached out to shake Pieter's hand. "You're a good kid," he whispered in French. "I've flown with a lot of daring pilots, and you're as brave as any of them."

Pieter's grin gleamed in the dim light. Their shared journey through darkness and danger would bind them together forever.

It took the better part of a day as donkeys pulled the barge slowly along the canal through a string of Belgian villages. Finn had no interaction with the Dutch crew. The helmsman and the line handler knew he was there, yet they never talked to him and instead kept their distance.

"Delia, those men risked their lives to get me out of Belgium. So did Pieter."

Delia had the strangest expression as she gazed at him. "I'm envious. I think I would be scared to pieces if I had to do what Pieter did. I wish I could be brave like that."

He laughed and swallowed back the lump in his throat. "Dee, we were *all* scared to pieces. Sometimes you have to saddle up anyway and get the job done."

"Why are you so worried about this story getting out? Nobody can identify those men on the barge, and there's no need to bring Pieter's name into it."

He shook his head. "The Germans have been suspicious of the CRB since the beginning, but they were getting such bad press about denying free food to the Belgians that they finally caved due to the pressure—provided nobody working for the CRB cooperated with the Allies. By hiding me on that barge, that was exactly what they were doing. The Germans have no proof I leaned on the CRB to escape, and I need to keep it that way."

At first Finn hadn't understood how he could have endangered the CRB's reputation for neutrality when he hitched that ride on the barge. Now he did, and he would do whatever was necessary to ensure Mathilde, Pieter, and all the other Belgians would continue to benefit from the humanitarian mission.

16

Fundraising over the next two weeks was more successful than Delia could have imagined. Despite Finn's flash of temper displayed at the restaurant, Mr. Hearst's newspapers came through for them in spectacular fashion. From coast to coast, Finn's dashing photograph graced the newspapers, and his exploits inspired a nation. Mr. Hearst loved the story of the little girl who had offered Finn her cookies, and he hired an artist to create a drawing of a barefoot girl with a forlorn face, offering a cookie to a wounded soldier.

New donations flooded in from across the country. Churches held fundraisers, corporations wrote hefty checks, and even the Red Cross kicked in a few dollars. Most of these were one-time donations, and yet Delia gladly marked them down in the ledger to help rebuild the CRB's bank account.

She and Finn made the rounds throughout New York City, locking down ongoing commitments. Mingling with rich people to ask for money wasn't exactly enjoyable, but they were good at it. Finn borrowed a Curtiss biplane to deliver on his promise of taking Alfred Pollard on a flight over Manhattan. It gave Delia the idea to hold a charity raffle, the prize being an airplane ride with America's hero. The raffle raised eight thousand dollars, and the winner was Mrs. Edna Orenburg, a middle-aged matron who arrived at the airfield with her four adult children and sixteen grandchildren to watch the spectacle.

Mrs. Orenburg looked frightened but excited as Delia helped the lady pull on a man's leather jacket over her plain brown frock. Once she had a scarf around her neck and a pair of goggles to protect her eyes, Finn placed a wooden crate outside the rear seat of the airplane for her to board.

It took both the lady's sons to steady their mother as she clambered first onto the lower wing, then into the back seat of the biplane. Painted a cheerful yellow with navy trim, the airplane still looked big and scary to Delia. Finn stood on the lower wing to holler last-minute instructions to the matron, and then he hopped into the cockpit and signaled to a man with the ground crew to crank the propeller.

The engine roared to life with a deafening rumble. The crew backed away, nodding and waving at Finn. Wind from the propeller whipped at Delia's hair, and thick exhaust fumes made her nose twitch. Then Finn increased power using a lever, causing the biplane to start rolling forward.

"Bon voyage!" Mrs. Orenburg called to her family, waving both hands wildly.

Delia's heart swelled with pride as the plane, with Finn at the controls, raced down the runway and took off into the air. The Orenburg family cheered and hooted, and Mrs. Orenburg's shriek of joy carried on the wind.

Delia shaded her eyes, watching the cheerful yellow biplane grow smaller as it veered to fly over the tallest buildings in Manhattan. *Oh, Finn.* Happiness mingled with shame as she watched him climb higher into the sky. Back when she lived at the orphanage, she'd tried everything to dissuade him from moving to Hammondsport to learn how to fly. She'd been so afraid of losing him that she stood in the way of his dreams, but thank heavens, he got there in the end. Finn was born to fly.

The flight lasted less than ten minutes, and Mrs. Orenburg's graying hair was a frazzled mess as she was helped out of the airplane and onto the ground. She beamed as her family swarmed around her.

"Want to go up for a ride?" Finn asked Delia. His face was wind-chapped, and his eyes sparkled.

"Heavens, no!" she said.

"You'll never forget it," Mrs. Orenburg said. She wobbled and leaned on one of her sons as he guided her away from the plane.

Finn nudged her arm, grinning with that devil-may-care charm of his. "Come on, Dee. Don't be such a scaredy-cat."

The word stung. He didn't mean to be cruel, but she *was* a scaredy-cat. It was one thing to imagine what it would be like to fly through the air, but when it came to actually doing it? The prospect made her want to run all the way back to the safety of her apartment. "I really don't want to, Finn."

The teasing glint faded from Finn's expression, and he tried to mask his disappointment, but she knew him too well. "Another time, then," he said, and she nodded in relief.

"Yes, another time," she said, knowing it would never happen. Yet they'd earned eight thousand dollars from the raffle. It was enough for her to be proud, even though she still felt like a bit of a coward.

Each week she and Finn visited Bertie's town house to present him with a list of new donations. By the end of November, she was happy to report that they'd raised two million dollars. It was still short of their goal, but Bertie had arranged for short-term loans to keep the ships supplied.

One evening in the first week of December, Bertie invited them inside for hot cider and conversation. The parlor was decorated with Christmas greenery and cinnamon-scented red candles, yet despite the cheery atmosphere, Bertie was clearly upset.

"I have a new request," he began, then strode to a standing globe in the corner of the room. He gestured them over and spun the globe to land a finger on a small country in northern Europe. "That's the Netherlands. It's a neutral country, which is why I've been using their port at Rotterdam to deliver supplies. Now that the United States has joined the war, the prime minister of the Netherlands wants to close the port to our ships."

"Why?" Delia asked.

Bertie's answer was diplomatic. "The Dutch know that if they show favor toward the Allies, the Germans are likely to invade, and in doing so, turn them into another Belgium. They are therefore adamant about maintaining their neutrality. The publicity about Finn's escape is beginning to backfire, and General Ryckman is rattling his saber."

Delia met Finn's worried gaze, remembering what he'd said about the despised German general who ruled over occupied Belgium. Bertie went on to report that General Ryckman was bitter about not succeeding with capturing Finn, as well as not apprehending the people who had helped him escape. All of this was made worse by the flurry of boastful newspaper articles coming out of America.

"General Ryckman has issued a bounty on the head of anyone who helped Finn escape. Although he has no proof, he is accusing the CRB with being complicit in Finn's escape."

Anxiety squeezed Delia's gut. Finn *did* use the CRB to escape.

"How can we help?" Finn asked.

"I want to lean on the prime minister of the Netherlands," Bertie said. "He might be persuaded to keep the Port of Rotterdam open to us. I've never met Prime Minister Jansen, but he was college roommates with William Howard Taft."

"The former president?" Finn asked.

Bertie nodded. "President Taft was stunned when he lost the last election, but he still has plenty of political capital. I don't know the man, but *you*," he said, clapping Finn on the shoulder, "well, you're a war hero, and Taft has great respect for men like you. I want you to make a personal appeal to President Taft. Get him to lean on Jansen and his other connections in the Netherlands to keep the Port of Rotterdam open to us."

"Are you able to arrange a meeting?" Finn asked.

"Already done!" Bertie replied, and Delia's heart started to beat faster. She'd met a lot of important people in the city, but no one close to the stature of an American president.

Bertie turned to Delia. "Ever since leaving the presidency, Taft has been at Yale, teaching classes on constitutional law. Head on up there, share Finn's story, and both of you convince Taft to put pressure on the prime minister to keep Rotterdam open to the CRB. Spare no effort. I *need* that port in the Netherlands."

17

Finn didn't know the first thing about President Taft, other than he lost a bitter three-way race against Teddy Roosevelt and Woodrow Wilson in the last election.

"Why isn't he relaxing on a yacht somewhere?" Finn asked as they stepped out into the bustle of Fifth Avenue. "Isn't that what rich people do after they retire?"

"I don't think he's that rich," Delia said. "Maybe he just likes working."

Either way, Finn didn't want to walk into a meeting with a former president, looking like someone who'd dropped out of school to work in a fish cannery. "Let's go get a cup of coffee, and you can tell me about him."

He bought a copy of the *New York Journal* from a newsboy, folded it under one arm, and offered Delia the other. Just because he didn't have much schooling was no excuse for not knowing anything about the world. He needed to do a better job keeping up with events.

His good intentions faded once they took their seats at a table in a café, where he opened the newspaper. "Hey, I know her," he said, gesturing to a photo of Blanche Scott, who looked dazzling and daring as she posed alongside an open-frame biplane. "We trained together in Hammondsport."

It was where Finn had learned to fly and where he'd gotten a job with the Curtiss Aeroplane Company, first as a janitor, then as a technician. As part of his salary, Finn got paid in flying lessons by Glenn Curtiss himself.

Curtiss was a pilot and engineer on his way to designing the world's best airplanes. In 1907, *Scientific American* announced a huge prize for the first person whose airplane could fly a kilometer. Curtiss needed money to design the innovative airplane, and when Finn asked Delia to use their kite-shop money to help fund the plane, she had refused. She wouldn't even hear him out. While he tried to explain how his cut of the prize money would be enough to pay her back tenfold, she still wouldn't budge.

Delia's opinion of his life in Hammondsport had always been a sticking point between them, and even now she frowned as she leaned closer to examine Blanche's photograph in the newspaper.

"Does she usually wear that much makeup?"

He shrugged. "Blanche was always a looker. You should have seen her when she wore her skintight flight pants and crawled into the cockpit. The sight was awe-inspiring."

Delia settled back in her chair. "While I was slaving away in the cannery, you were ogling female pilots?"

He shouldn't have said anything. Delia was always afraid he'd meet someone else when he moved to live in Hammondsport. Trying to reassure her was exhausting and fruitless. It was why he never mentioned Blanche before today.

"Dee, I was so busy working two jobs and dreaming of our kite shop that I was too dog-tired to go chasing after other women."

"And yet you found enough energy to sneak down to New York in the middle of the night to steal three hundred dollars." Her voice was sharp enough to cause other people in the café to glance at them.

He lowered his voice to a fierce whisper. "How often have I

tried to repay you, Delia? We could have opened our kite shop if you had only trusted me."

"You stole my money to gamble," she accused.

"I didn't steal your money—I *borrowed* it," he said tightly.

"Borrowed?" she scoffed. "Is that what you call gambling with my life savings?"

"*Our* life savings," he corrected. "There was twelve hundred dollars in that Mason jar, and I earned most of that."

"But three hundred of it came from me, and it was for the kite shop and the dream of getting us out of the Lower East Side. It wasn't for you to gamble on an unproven airplane."

Finn folded the newspaper closed and tried to speak calmly, to lower the temperature. "Delia, we would never have gotten out of the Lower East Side on fish-cannery wages. Do you know how much it costs to buy the kind of place we dreamed about?"

"So you stole from me."

He opened his mouth to again deny the accusation, then closed it as the details of that night flooded his mind. They'd kept their savings in a Mason jar that was locked up in Sister Bernadette's office. After Finn moved to Hammondsport, he still came back to the city every weekend to see Delia.

Except for the weekend he came for the money. Delia was too scared to ever take a risk, and he'd come to his wits' end. The only way to break their stalemate was to proceed without her. He waited until after midnight to head to the orphanage and climbed the trellis outside Sister Bernadette's office window on the second floor of the building. Night-blooming jasmine coiled around the trellis, and gummy petals stuck to his skin. Their cloying fragrance was nauseating as he climbed the trellis.

Sister Bernadette was too trusting. She kept her window cracked an inch, so that the scent of jasmine would drift into her office. Finn wiggled his hands into the opening and lifted the sash. He crawled inside, racked with guilt and hoping his mother wasn't watching from heaven.

The Mason jar was in the nun's bottom desk drawer. Finn's hands shook a little as he unscrewed the jar's lid; the metallic scraping sounded loud in the silence. He took every bill in the jar, leaving Delia a note saying that their money would be invested in the airplane contest, and he promised to pay her back soon.

The reek of jasmine clung to his clothes the entire way home. To this day, Finn hated the smell of jasmine. Even now, whenever he felt guilty about something, that haunting scent seemed to materialize out of thin air.

He could smell it right now, and it angered him. He stood from the café table and faced Delia. "Forget about lunch. Let's go to the bank, and I'll pay you back right now."

He strode out of the café, Delia following close behind. "You can't ever repay what you stole from me. You can't give me back the starry-eyed innocence you killed when you stole that money."

"You're looking for reasons to keep your anger stoked," he accused. "The gamble worked, and I got our investment back ten times over."

"It was luck," she retaliated. "Over a dozen teams were competing for that prize, and you could have lost everything."

"But I *didn't*," he pointed out. On a cloudless July morning in 1908, Glenn Curtiss piloted the *June Bug* twice the necessary distance to win the *Scientific American* prize. It was a glorious triumph, and Finn's cut of the prize money was enough to open their kite shop, if Delia hadn't been so incensed about the money.

He had apologized for taking it. He'd apologized until he was blue in the face, but nothing worked. He was done chasing after her, begging for a crumb of forgiveness. Winning that flying contest was the proudest accomplishment of Finn's life. He got to be part of a team of dreamers who put that plane together and took a huge leap forward in the world of aviation. Delia never even congratulated him.

Even today, the mere mention of Hammondsport was enough

to awaken all her old jealousies. She didn't even look at him as she walked away from him.

"I'll meet you at the train station tomorrow morning to go see Taft," he shouted at her retreating back. "I'll have three hundred dollars with me, and if you don't take it, it's proof that you're small, bitter, and petty."

Finn's shout echoed in Delia's ears as she marched away from him. His accusations stung because they were true. Instead of letting him pay her back ten years ago, she took out a loan to attend secretarial school. Each time he contacted her to pay her back, she had refused. Some of it was pride, but mostly it was self-protection.

She *had* wanted to keep her anger stoked. Keeping the debt between them was daily proof of Finn's reckless nature. No woman who valued stability should hitch her wagon to a man willing to gamble everything on a long shot. Finn's daredevil nature was partly why she found Wesley so appealing in comparison.

Delia was still wallowing in resentment when she arrived at the train station the following morning.

Finn was waiting on the platform, ready for their trip to Yale University. A gaggle of young ladies, probably on their way to work at the nearby woolen mills, clustered around him. He lapped up their attention and regaled them with tales of his exploits in France.

Delia sent him a dignified nod, which he returned. But she wasn't about to join his admirers and so took a seat on a wood bench, setting her leather case beside her. It was going to be a long day. It would take almost three hours to get to Yale by train, attend the meeting with President Taft, followed by another three hours for the journey home.

Ten minutes later, a train whistle sounded in the distance, and Delia stood for boarding. They would meet with President Taft, hopefully secure his agreement to intervene regarding shipping to the Port of Rotterdam, then return home and never again subject herself to the spectacle of Finn Delaney parading himself before the female population of Manhattan.

Finn strolled across the railway station platform like a peacock, deliberately soaking in the female attention coming from the other travelers, smiling and nodding at them.

"What a shame you must tear yourself away from your adoring entourage," she said.

"Not at all," he said. "Who wouldn't rather share a compartment with sour lemons instead of pretty smiles? Oh, wait. I've got three hundred dollars burning a hole in my pocket. Care to take it from me?"

The clanging bells and steam whistles as the train pulled into the station made it too loud for her to respond. Irritation still crackled as she boarded the train and settled onto the bench that had been allotted to them. The passenger carriage was full this morning, so they were stuck together.

"Well?" Finn asked as soon as the attendant slid the door to their compartment closed. They were alone now, and she needed to give him an answer about the money.

He was right. Her refusal to take it made her small and petty, and it was time to stop letting him have the high ground in this matter.

She put her hand out, palm up.

A fleeting look of surprise lit his face, but it vanished when her expression didn't soften. He rooted around in his pocket and came up with a fat wad of bills that he smacked into her palm.

"Thank you," she said coldly, tucking the roll into her purse and turning to gaze out the window. The money would go straight to the CRB. If she deposited it into her account, it would feel like a capitulation.

The train jerked as it pulled out of the station, and Finn brushed up against her.

"Could you please move over onto your side of the bench?" she asked.

"With pleasure," he muttered and scooted over.

It was going to be a long, difficult ride to New Haven.

18

Finn wasn't going to let Delia's snit get to him. She was still in a prissy mood when they arrived at the Yale campus, but he didn't let it throw him off course. If he could maintain his focus while German pilots fired machine guns at him, he could keep his head screwed on with Delia.

Even though it smarted. They'd been working so well together that he'd begun nurturing the stupid hope of her forgiving him.

She had finally accepted the three hundred dollars, and yet there was no thaw in her arctic blast as they walked along old brick paths on the campus, still slick after a cold morning rain. Leafless trees lined the walkways, their skeletal branches releasing occasional droplets. Still, nothing could mar the splendor of the Gothic architecture throughout the sprawling campus.

The law school was located in Hendrie Hall. It was large and elegant, though nothing like the White House. President Taft's office was on the second floor of the building.

Finn had been so busy silently enumerating Delia's flaws during the ride here that he forgot to be nervous about meeting the former president. He blotted his damp hair with his scarf, straightened his collar, and mentally kicked himself for arguing with Delia when access to the Port of Rotterdam was on the line. Mathilde and her family were dependent upon his success today.

President Taft opened the door, a cigar smoldering between his fingers. He was an enormous man: portly, broad, and even taller than Finn. The president stepped back to usher them into his surprisingly cluttered office with a genial wave. Stacks of papers and piles of books filled the large mahogany desktop. Leather-bound law texts lined the bookshelves, with slatted-wood blinds filtering the weak light coming into the jumbled space.

"So you're the pilot everyone is talking about," President Taft said as he shook Finn's hand firmly.

"Yes, sir. Lieutenant Finn Delaney, sir. And this is Miss Byrne, the woman who keeps me in line."

"Can I offer you a cigar?"

Who could have imagined a kid who grew up canning fish was about to smoke a cigar with a president of the United States! It would annoy Delia, but he wasn't going to pass this up.

"Thank you, sir."

President Taft retrieved a cigar from a humidor and clipped the end with a silver cutter. Finn clamped the cigar in his teeth, gently puffing as President Taft held a lit match to it.

"Now," President Taft said as he shook the match out, "tell me how I can help with CRB business."

Finn drew on his carefully prepared speech. "As a man who subsisted on CRB rations while trapped in Belgium, I have a personal interest in making sure the Port of Rotterdam remains open to the CRB." He proceeded to outline the reasons for their concern, as well as their hope that the president would agree to lean on Diederik Jensen, Taft's friend from college who was the prime minister of the Netherlands.

"I haven't spoken with Diederik Jensen in decades," President Taft said. "Frankly, I'm not sure I wish to spend my dwindling political capital to support Belgium. It's a shame the country has found itself so reliant on foreign aid."

Delia spoke up. "They don't have adequate farmland, as they're the most industrialized country in Europe. How could they have foreseen becoming a captive nation by Germany?"

President Taft remained unconvinced. "In light of that, they ought to have established better reserves to withstand such possibilities rather than have their hand permanently extended for aid from others."

Finn set his cigar down in defense of the people who had saved him. "Don't think of the Belgians as poor, downtrodden people. They're fighters, sir, and while I was trapped there, I saw the best of them. The Belgians are not looking for a handout. They're bankers and weavers and chocolate makers. In fact, it was Belgian engineers who designed and built the railways that crisscross Europe. They also designed the hydraulic systems used to manage canals for trade and industry."

Taft nodded. "I seem to have pricked a sensitive spot, and I'm sorry for that."

Finn looked away. He wasn't going to rescue Belgium by insulting President Taft, but he had to find some way to change the president's opinion.

"The Belgians are fighters," he repeated. "The lady who gave me shelter risks her life every week to distribute a newspaper called *La Libre Belgique* that reports on ways to resist the occupation. The newspaper gave people *hope*. Late at night, when all was silent, neighbors came to her house to talk about what they'd read in the forbidden paper. My French could barely keep up with what they said, but I could read their expressions. They were eager to fight and to resist the enemy. They leaned on each other and laughed together. The comradery in that room could power the sun, and it was a privilege to be among them."

A wave of painful nostalgia rose in his chest. They offered Finn shelter for six weeks, and he saw the best of humanity in them—in their generosity, in their sacrifice for each other and for their nation, and in their shared commitment. His lower lip started to wobble, but he fought it back so he could keep talking.

"One night a handful of resistance fighters gathered at the house, and they sang the Belgian national anthem. They sang softly because singing their anthem is illegal. They practically whispered the tune, but it hit me like a blast of trumpets. I don't think I've ever heard a more heartfelt song than that whispered anthem behind closed doors." Finn would remember the sacredness of that night until his dying day . . .

His heart started to race, his palms to sweat. A strange, unwieldy ache bloomed in his chest, and he drew a ragged breath, hoping it would ease. Without warning, his breath choked off and a sob escaped. Then another.

What was happening? He turned his face to the corner of the room, so that President Taft and Delia wouldn't see the tears welling in his eyes. He couldn't control his breathing. Tears spilled over, and he quickly swiped them away, but then a flood of blubbering sobs broke free, surging from deep inside him.

"Finn?" Delia's voice sounded as if it came from far away. "Finn, what's wrong?"

He couldn't answer her because he didn't know what was wrong. He was both hot and cold. He was twitching. He wanted to run from the room, but he couldn't leave without convincing Taft to contact his old friend, the prime minister, regarding the port in the Netherlands. Finn clutched a handkerchief over his face, holding it there so they couldn't see him weeping like an idiot.

Why was he crying? He knew plenty of men who'd been killed in the war, and he hadn't broken down like this. Mathilde and her family were fine. *He* was fine. He was one of the lucky ones, wounded but still alive to fight another day, and yet these blubbering sobs wouldn't stop. Delia hovered nearby, no doubt horrified by what was happening.

He had to stop sniveling and convince President Taft to use his influence on behalf of Belgium and the CRB. He needed to forget about the past and focus on the present. He had a mission to accomplish, and that meant getting ahold of himself.

Finn pressed the handkerchief hard against his face, willing himself to control the ragged gasps. Finally, his breathing calmed into a few broken, uneven breaths. Trembling and feeling embarrassed, he stuffed the damp cloth into his pocket, squared his shoulders, and turned to face the president.

"I apologize," he said, his voice a little watery. "If things had gone differently, you would still be sitting in the White House and helping direct the course of this war. But you still have influence. You can help keep the Port of Rotterdam open. Doing so will allow a couple million people to stay alive until this lousy war is over."

President Taft looked distinctly uneasy after witnessing Finn's breakdown, and he struggled to provide a semi-jovial reply. "I never said I wouldn't contact the prime minister. I will send a note to Jensen and let him know that America expects him and the Netherlands to do the right thing regarding their neighbor to the south. Consider it done."

Finn was exhausted as he walked beside Delia on the way back to the carriage. Hoisting himself onto the single step and collapsing on the bench drained the last of his energy. Delia clambered in next, and he briefly thought of offering her a hand, but the bone-deep exhaustion made him too lethargic to move a muscle.

"What happened in there?" she asked once settled on the bench opposite him.

He turned to gaze out the window. It would be easier to tell Delia that his outburst had been manufactured to win Taft's sympathy, but he couldn't lie to her. "I don't know," he answered honestly. "One moment I was fine, and the next an avalanche of memories rose up and I was drowning in them. Just about everything in Belgium was bad, and yet in a way things were good too. Does that make sense? Everyone was miserable, but they were united, bound together around a cause. I miss that. I got to see the very best in people. Mathilde and Pieter and so many others risked their lives to help a complete stranger. Thinking of their sacrifice got to me, and I fell apart. Right there in front of President Taft!"

Delia looked at him now in the same soft, admiring way she used to look at him when they were kids. Which was ironic since he wasn't behaving very heroic today.

He cleared his throat and patted her knee. "Thanks for not poking fun about . . . you know, my bawling like a baby."

Her palm was warm as she covered his hand with it. "Never," she said with a gentle smile.

He turned his hand to clasp hers, and they clung to each other during the entire carriage ride to the train station.

Delia had never seen Finn break down like he'd done in President Taft's office, and it was beyond upsetting. It was frightening. For it seemed as though he had no control over it, which wasn't like Finn.

It was late afternoon when the train pulled into Grand Central in Manhattan, where they would part ways. While the subway could get her home in ten minutes, Finn needed to take the ferry across the East River and then board another train to Camp Mills, and she was worried about him.

She walked with him to the Astoria Ferry ticket window. "I can go with you on the ferry," she offered, triggering a slight scowl from Finn.

"You don't need to," he said. "My crying jag is over for the day. Promise."

"It's not just that," she said, stepping with him in the line for the ferry. "I'm simply in the mood for a boat ride."

"You're a bad liar, Dee. Really, I'll be okay."

She wasn't so sure of that, yet the next ferry wouldn't be leaving for another thirty minutes, and she was starving. Enticing aromas coming from nearby vendor stalls selling roasted chestnuts, pretzels, and frankfurters made her mouth water.

"How about we each get a frankfurter?" she asked.

"They're called *hot dogs* these days," Finn said.

"*Some* people are calling them hot dogs," she teased. "I want a good, meaty frankfurter."

Five minutes later, they found a bench overlooking the harbor, where they ate the grilled frankfurters slathered with mustard and sauerkraut. The satisfying saltiness with just a hint of smoke made Delia's entire body happy.

So did the fact that Finn seemed to have shed his strange mood. He tossed a few bits of bread to the sea gulls and teased her for having said the word *sauerkraut*. "It sounds like a slur against the Jerries," he joked.

She laughed before she could stop herself. It felt as though the years and distance between them was dissolving, and she loved wallowing in his affectionate gaze. It sent a quiet flutter through her.

Finn had always been handsome, with a chiseled jaw and impossibly blue eyes. When he teased her, it pulled them back into their old rhythm as though no time had passed, and the tug she felt in her heart was hard to ignore. She longed to move closer to him, lean against his shoulder, and turn back the clock.

She should be careful, even though right now, sitting beside him in the fading light, she didn't want to be. What an idiot she'd been to nurture a grudge over money and for so long. All across the world, people struggled to survive, and she'd clung to a mistake made by a young man only a year out of the orphanage.

"What did you do before the war?" she asked him.

"Don't you know?" He had the strangest expression on his face. It was part amusement, part curiosity. A wheeling sea gull descended to snatch the last piece of her bread, but she couldn't tear her eyes from Finn.

"No. I never let myself think of it."

His smile was tender but sad when he said, "I own a kite shop on Long Island."

She gaped at him, surprised and amazed. She never should have doubted him. Finn could do *anything*. She listened with open-mouthed admiration as he continued.

"I opened the shop seven years ago. It's in a little town on the tip of Long Island called Windover. The town is pricey, but I bought the building and live above the store, so it works out okay."

Cascading emotions made it difficult for Delia to think straight: pride and joy that he'd made their dream come true, but sorrow as well because she hadn't been a part of it. "Is it like we always imagined it would be?"

The corners of his eyes crinkled, and just for a moment it looked like he might start crying again. But it vanished quickly, and he smiled and nudged her arm. "Nah," he said. "Nothing could ever be as good as what you and I dreamed up. But I'm doing all right. I have contests every summer when the tourists are in town, and they're all rich—they buy lots of kites. And the locals have been helping out by starting kite-flying clubs. I've got a club for kids, and another for those who like to get together to fly their kites. The wind in that area is out of this world. The beach is a great place for kite flying."

Regret mingled with wonder as she took it all in. Finn *was* the same boy she'd fallen in love with. He was open and friendly and still dreaming big, and suddenly it felt as though their teenaged love affair was so close she could touch it.

Together they stared out at the water, listening to the rhythmic lap of waves against the waterfront pilings and the cry of gulls.

Suddenly, Finn turned to her, a pensive look in his eyes. "Delia, are you still hung up on the old guy?"

She glanced away. Two months ago, the mere thought of Wesley awakened hurt and anger over Mrs. Beekman, but at present she felt nothing. Every scrap of her heart was full to overflowing with Finn.

"No," she replied, a smile beginning to tug at her lips because it was true. She'd been freed of her captivity to Wesley. "No, I'm not still hung up on the old guy."

"Good," he said, smiling tenderly at her. "Do you think you could ever forgive me for taking the kite money?"

They were less than a foot apart on the bench, and yet the wad of money in her purse was an old wound that had never healed. But it was *her* old wound. All these years it had been easier to cling to her resentment rather than forgive Finn and let herself be caught up in his risky, idealistic dreams.

Finn wasn't perfect. The dashing boy who had befriended her at the orphanage could charm the birds out of a tree and do just about anything he set his mind to, but it wasn't fair to assume he was perfect.

"I was wrong to nurse that grudge the way I did," she said. "Finn, I loved you then, and I love you now."

His eyes widened, and he swallowed hard. "Do you really mean that?"

Loving Finn was terrifying. His heart and soul contained a daring, impulsive streak woven into his very being, and he'd probably never change. Trying to mold him into someone careful and cautious would be like asking the wind to stop blowing. It simply wasn't in his nature. Expecting him to become anyone other than who God designed him to be wasn't fair. Perhaps their differences were a gift. She was a better, braver person when she was with Finn.

"Yes, I mean it," she said, starting to shiver. Her fingers were freezing, and her nose was so cold it felt as if it were about to fall off. Despite it all, letting Finn back into her life would be the biggest risk she'd ever taken.

He wrapped his warm hands around her icy fingers. "Dee, I've loved you since I was sixteen."

She tilted her face to meet his kiss. Once again the years fell away, and she was back in his arms, kissing the love of her life.

Gambling her heart on Finn was scary, but then she wasn't a

meek, frightened orphan anymore. Both she and Finn had matured a lot since those early days. If she was to fully participate in the wondrous world God had created, she needed to risk getting hurt. She was strong enough to survive whatever lay ahead. With Finn beside her, that world was about to bloom into a wonderful and terrifying adventure.

19

Finn began the following morning on his knees in the Camp Mills chapel, giving thanks for the miracles that had been happening in his life.

Dear God, thank you for bringing Delia back to me and for helping soften her heart. I don't deserve her forgiveness, or yours, but I thank you for it.

The gift of forgiveness had transformed his world, had washed his slate clean. He was the same man, with the same gimpy leg, but everything was different after last night. *Delia had forgiven him!* She was the Delia of old who looked at him with warmth and admiration, who believed in him, and they shared a heartfelt mission to save the CRB.

As for this morning, he had a few spare hours to continue working with the new pilots to get a little green off them. Memories of combat felt like another lifetime, and hopefully revisiting the past wouldn't trigger another bout of the strange weepiness that clobbered him yesterday in front of President Taft.

He bowed his head again. *Lord, I need your help as I work to prepare these pilots for what they will experience once they're in France. They're getting good training on how to fly, but I need to*

*teach them how to keep their heads when in combat, when the
Krauts . . . pardon me, when the Germans come after them and
attack them. And whatever happened to me yesterday, please don't
let it happen again in front of the new guys.*

Their instructor bawling like a baby wasn't what pilots-in-training needed to see. He still didn't understand why he'd melted
down like that, but he couldn't afford for such a thing to happen
again.

He got off his knees, grasped his cane, and stepped out into the
morning sunlight. His shin was finally mending, and the fact that
he could get on and off his knees was a big improvement. He nodded and traded salutes as he headed toward the classroom building. Confidence and a sense of purpose filled him. Delia believed
in him, and his leg was healing. God was good. This morning he
would share some insights with the new pilots, which might just
save their lives someday, and then this afternoon he and Delia
would set off to seek out more donations for the CRB.

He strolled past a number of hastily constructed wooden buildings toward the spartan shack that served as a classroom for pilot
training. His boots thudded on the wood floors as he entered to
face two dozen young men, chatting among the rows of plain
tables. Their uniforms consisted of olive-drab shirts and trousers,
and each man's hair was closely cropped.

They snapped to attention the moment Finn entered the classroom. This was partly due to his rank, but mostly because he
walked with a limp and had seen active duty. The deep respect
they showed him was still new to Finn, and he hid a smile as he
moved to the front of the room.

"At ease," he said, and the airmen shuffled to their seats behind
the tables that doubled as desks. Though there was no electricity in
the shack, the sunlight streaming in from the plate-glass windows
was enough to illuminate the space, including the blackboard at
the front.

Instead of technical drawings or rate-of-climb calculations, the blackboard displayed a series of cartoons. One showed the kaiser wearing a diaper and sucking his thumb. Another showed a German zeppelin with the caption *Retreat Airship* below it.

"Who's the artist?" Finn asked.

Silence hung over the classroom. They probably thought a reprimand was coming, yet Finn knew the importance of humor for letting airmen blow off steam by cutting the enemy down to size.

Finn waited, and still no answer came. That was good. The men before him were forming bonds of loyalty between them, and they didn't care to snitch on each other.

He wrapped a knuckle against the drawing of the kaiser. "This is wrong. When I saw the kaiser, he wasn't sucking his thumb. He had a pacifier in his mouth and was hiding behind his wife's skirts."

Laughter rippled among the men, unwinding the tension, so Finn asked his question again. "Who drew the kaiser?"

A freckle-faced man stood, who looked like he'd come straight from America's Heartland. "I did, sir."

"Nicely done. Did you draw the zeppelin too?"

"No, sir. That was the Third . . . I mean, Cadet Grayson, sir."

"Grayson, stand up." A square-jawed young man with round spectacles stood. "Why do they call you the Third?"

"Because I filled out my enrollment card as Charles Grayson the Third." Suppressed laughter rolled through the men. "It was a mistake," Grayson added in exasperation.

"Yes, it was," Finn agreed. Trying to cling to any sort of honorific status would be ripe for teasing among men who were in the midst of forming lifelong bonds. Cadet Grayson was going to have "the Third" slung around his neck for the duration of the war. "Now take your seat so we can get down to business. I'm not here to teach you to fly airplanes. I'm sure you're getting a first-class education over at the airfield. I'm here to teach you to keep your heads screwed on straight once the bullets start flying and you're ten thousand feet in the air."

Just speaking about it summoned the dull roar of his Nieuport biplane engine, the *rat-a-tat-tat* of machine-gun fire, the burst of bombs below. Finn clenched his fists, quickly checking himself for the telltale sign of the nerves that cropped up yesterday, but there was nothing. He was as calm as a summer's day.

Finn turned to the blackboard and tapped on a crude drawing of a Fokker Eindecker plane. The single-seat monoplanes manufactured by Germamy did not look impressive. They were boxy, blunt, and lacked panache and flair, but they were the most lethal planes in the sky.

"What makes this plane so different?" he asked, and all humor in the room fled. The men clearly knew the danger of this latest airplane developed by German engineers. Unlike American planes, the Fokker Eindecker had a synchronized firing mechanism so that their guns could shoot directly through the rotation of the propeller. It was the deadliest predator in the sky and had changed the course of aerial combat.

"Until one of our designers can develop a similar mechanism, the odds are against us," Finn said. "The only thing that will save you is to outsmart the Kraut."

Sorry, Delia, he silently thought for uttering the slur, but then continued.

"If you see one of these planes coming at you, it's important to keep your head. Use whatever advantages you have. Fly into the clouds so they can't see you. If there are no clouds, fly directly toward the sun. You can glance to the side, but he'll need to focus on you and stare into the sun, so try to blind him. But remember to keep your head. Stay calm."

Finn was perched on the edge of the teacher's desk at the front, facing the men. All watched him with the utmost seriousness. He spent the next hour fielding questions about what it was like to confront the enemy in the air. If the men were afraid, they gave no hint of it.

As he spoke to the men, Finn kept a close eye on the clock. He was to meet Delia for lunch, and then they were off on another fundraising mission. It was embarrassing how badly he wanted to see her again, especially when he owed these men every scrap of insight he could share.

Nevertheless, when he left the classroom an hour later, he had a smile on his face and new energy in his step. He was off to see the love of his life.

Not only that but he'd just relived some of the most harrowing memories of the war and hadn't suffered even a flicker of anxiety. Whatever strange mental lapse had stricken him yesterday was surely nothing more than a fluke, and he need not fear it happening again.

20

The next two months were the happiest of Delia's life. She had a *purpose*, and with Finn at her side, they pounded the pavement for donations and steadily refilled the coffers for the CRB. Bertie said they were surpassing his expectations, and thanks to President Taft's intervention, the Port of Rotterdam had remained open to them, accepting regular shipments from the CRB.

She and Finn visited at least three different venues each day to raise money. They attended charity galas arranged on behalf of the CRB, they sought out wealthy donors at their homes, and occasionally she was able to convince theater managers to allow Finn to give a speech before the shows began. He always showed up wearing his flight jacket and silk scarf. From grand opera houses to crowded vaudeville theaters, Finn took to the stage in his pilot's uniform to discuss how the good people of Belgium had sheltered him and had shared their food and other supplies—supplies that were sent to them from America.

Even with all the fundraising work, she and Finn were able to carve out time for themselves. On Christmas Eve they went to Central Park to admire the Christmas decorations and lights and listen to a brass band play carols. Fat snowflakes floated down as they walked arm in arm through the holiday market, sampling mulled cider and roasted chestnuts. Finn insisted on buying her a red knitted cap and arranged it on her head three different times until he had it to his liking. Each time he swiped it off, he pressed a trail of kisses along her neck.

"Let's try again, shall we?" She'd stand patiently as he angled the cap this way and that.

The only real bickering came when they approached the skating rink. Finn wanted to take a spin around the rink, but Delia didn't know how to skate.

"You go, and I'll watch," she said.

Finn ignored her objections and rented two pairs of skates. She sat on the bench beside him as he laced up his skates.

"C'mon, Dee," he cajoled. "I'll hold you with both hands and pull you around the rink. It'll be fun."

"I've always been a tremendous coward, you know that. I'm afraid I'll fall and break my neck."

"It's much safer than downhill skiing, and I've done a lot of that."

"Finn, you didn't!" she gasped.

He grinned. "I skied every winter in the French Alps near Chamonix. It was fantastic. Come on now. Put on your skates, and I'll lead you around the rink."

At times like these Delia realized how worldly Finn had become, but instead of being threatened by it like when he moved to Hammondsport, she admired him. What would it be like to be as daring as Finn, who never encountered a sport he wouldn't try or an adventure he wouldn't undertake?

She, on the other hand, was a cheerful coward and always would be. When she refused to put on the skates, Finn flagged down a passing boy and offered the skates to him. She stood watching as Finn guided the boy around the ice. The boy wobbled and teetered, but he seemed thrilled too, having fun while learning to skate. He looked at Finn with hero worship when they had come to the end of their skate, and who could blame him?

As December turned into a frigid January, Delia noticed the first hints that the daily rounds of public speaking were beginning to take a toll on Finn. It wasn't revisiting dark memories that got to him; it was fear for Mathilde and the Verhaegen children that haunted him. He confided in her one night as they sat in a Broadway delicatessen between shows.

"I'm worried they don't have enough fuel to keep the house warm," he said, staring at the radiator at the end of the front counter. Steam heat kept even modest places like this kosher deli toasty warm on chilly nights like tonight. "Winter can be brutally cold over there, making coal for heating about as prized as gold. And here I sit with a plate of hot pastrami and potato salad. They'll be lucky to get a bowl of oats."

He pushed the plate with his half-eaten sandwich away, as if he felt too guilty to eat another bite. "The little girl's name is Jeannette," he continued. "She's puny. I don't know if she's naturally little or if it's from malnutrition. If I ever have a daughter, I'm going to name her Jeannette and spoil her with candy and cake and toys. She'll never know a day of hunger or a night of cold."

His hands balled into fists. It wasn't like Finn to be so dark. She covered one of his clenched hands, stroking it gently. "Are you okay?"

He nodded. "Don't worry about me. I'm just mad the war is dragging on."

The Western Front was now an entrenched stalemate. Rumors of a major spring offensive by Germany had the Allied forces on edge, Finn included. He was tormented by guilt for remaining in New York while his fellow pilots fought on without him.

Ever since the day Finn was overtaken by waves of despair in President Taft's office, she'd kept a watchful eye on him. There had been no more uncontrollable fits of crying, and yet she remained worried. For all his cocksure charm as he retold his story over and over again, it all came at a cost, and she couldn't carry the load for him.

On the first of February, Delia set off with Finn to a remote town on the eastern tip of Long Island to secure a donation from a reclusive millionaire. Martin Galloway had made a fortune off his patent for a pencil eraser. After pulling up stakes in Cleveland, he bought a lonely house overlooking the cape, continuing to collect royalties on his invention while living in the middle of nowhere.

Delia hoped to persuade Mr. Galloway to part with a portion of his monthly eraser royalties. She had already prepared a legal form to shift the payments directly into the CRB bank account.

It hadn't been easy to get to Mr. Galloway. The journey began with a ferry ride across the choppy waters of the East River as the sleet fell sideways. Her hair and clothes were damp by the time she met Finn at Camp Mills, but at least the train was warm as they chugged farther east through barren fields and leafless forests. They rode the train as far east as they could go, at last arriving at a tiny town where they rented a horse and buggy to take them the final eight miles to the Galloway home.

The street outside the stables looked completely vacant. It was a touristy town, with white clapboard storefronts and a few restaurants. But tourist season was long over, and most of the shops were now closed. Aside from a few people leaving the post office, it appeared as though the livery yard was the only place doing any business.

Delia blew into her hands to warm them as she huddled on the seat of the buggy. The elderly man who owned the stables tossed a horse blanket over the back of the mare, and she hoped the poor horse wasn't as cold as she was. It seemed to take forever as the old man attached the leather straps and harnesses to prepare the buggy. Once done, Finn pressed a few dollars into the man's hands, then joined her on the bench and grabbed the reins.

"Do you know how to drive this thing?" he asked, and she turned to look at him in horror.

"I don't know anything about horses. I thought you did!"

Finn pulled back to gape at her. "Why would I know anything about horses?"

"Because you said we could rent a horse and buggy here," she said.

Mr. Galloway lived eight miles away, a difficult walk under any circumstances, but especially in this wind and sleet. Why did Finn rent a horse when he didn't have the foggiest idea of how to handle it? She wanted to shake him, but he looked so dejected. With the reins held awkwardly before him, and his face so pale she feared he was ill, she scrambled for a solution.

"Maybe we could hire a driver," she suggested.

"I already asked," Finn said, looking even more despondent. "The man working the stables said he doesn't have any help today, and he can't leave the stables untended . . ." The tail end of Finn's sentence was choked off, as if Finn was smothering a laugh.

"Why are you laughing?" she demanded.

"Because one of my jobs at the fish cannery was driving the wagon to deliver supplies. Don't you remember?" He practically howled with laughter as he deftly grasped the reins, gave a click of his tongue and a snap of the reins to start the horse trotting forward.

Now she really *did* want to strangle Finn but was too busy laughing.

As they rolled along, they reminisced about their wonderfully awful years at the cannery the entire ride to the Galloway home. Her nose was probably as bright red as Finn's, they both were wild-haired from the buffeting wind, and she could barely feel her feet, but who cared? They were having a grand time. With the narrowing stretch of land between Long Island Sound and the Atlantic Ocean, it felt as if they were heading toward the edge of the world.

When they finally reached the Galloway home, Delia clambered down from the buggy the moment it stopped moving. She stamped her boots, welcoming the tingle in her feet as she stared at the cottage.

It wasn't the sort of house she'd expected of a millionaire. The shingles covering the cottage sides and roof had weathered to a silvery gray. Dormer windows, a gabled roof, and large windows overlooking the sea made it look cozy, not imposing. She found it rather charming. Finn, however, wasn't looking at the house. He shaded his eyes with one hand as he stared out across the ocean. He was motionless and expressionless.

"Finn?"

He still didn't move. "Over there, beyond the horizon . . . the next piece of land is France."

She moved to stand beside him. The sea was a pale bluish-gray, blurring the line between water and sky. While France was thousands of miles away, it was calling to Finn.

The creak of a door swinging open caused her to turn. A slender man with a shaggy beard, unkempt hair, and round spectacles peered at them. The slow blink of his owlish eyes made her wonder if he ever left his house.

"Are you the fundraisers from New York?"

"We are," Finn said, turning toward the man.

Mr. Galloway nodded and beckoned them inside.

As charming as the cottage appeared on the outside, the interior was dark and claustrophobic. Overflowing bookshelves covered the walls and blocked the windows. Stacks of books took up much of the floor space as well, along with open crates brimming over with newspapers and magazines. The parlor had a sofa and two chairs, but they too were mounded with books. Only a single wooden chair with an old cushion on it was available.

The mustiness inside the cottage's main room made Delia sneeze.

"There's not much room here for us to sit," Mr. Galloway pointed out. "Come into the kitchen. We can talk there."

Delia held her skirts while navigating through an alley of books. She hoped Mr. Galloway wouldn't offer them anything to eat or drink. The coating of dust everywhere was triggering another sneeze, and consuming anything in this house could be a health hazard.

The kitchen wasn't much better. Clutter covered the counters and dining table, but at least the chairs were empty. The stove was cold, and when Mr. Galloway offered to light it to offer them tea, Finn came to her rescue.

"We wouldn't want to put you out," he said. "We're simply grateful for your time."

Delia took an offered chair and held her briefcase on her lap like a shield. Eccentric men could be generous too, and she had all the paperwork necessary to secure a sizable donation from Mr. Galloway should he agree to it.

The man seemed pleasant enough, listening to Finn's story with sympathy. When he got to the part about how Bertie needed three million dollars to keep the CRB in operation, Delia stepped in to describe how most donors structured their contributions.

"Some provide a large lump sum, while others prefer to contribute monthly. Both are appreciated."

"Of course I would like to help," Mr. Galloway said, a smile softening his face for the first time. "How does fifty dollars sound?"

She blinked. "A month?"

"Heavens, no. I couldn't afford that. But I can't bear the thought of those children going hungry during the cold winter months, and I'm more than happy to help as best I can."

They left ten minutes later with fifty dollars in her pocket, the total of Mr. Galloway's donation.

If possible, the weather had grown even worse during the ride back to town. "It wouldn't be so bad if it hadn't taken all day to get there," she said, turning to Finn.

He seemed remarkably placid. "We win some, and we lose some. At least the fifty dollars will cover the cost of our transportation today."

She burrowed deeper into her cloak as another gust of wind buffeted them. It snaked its way around her neck and triggered a round of shivers.

Finn drew the horse to a halt before the livery and climbed down from the buggy. He then moved to help her down.

"How come you don't look cold?" she asked. She could barely stand on her numb feet.

"I'm used to it," he replied, unwinding the scarf from his neck to drape it around hers. It was still warm from his body, and she enjoyed the way he fussed with the ends, tucking them snuggly beneath the folds of her cloak. "Now let's go get a cup of something hot before we catch the train."

Delia glanced up and down the quaint street. It lay deserted, its shuttered shops and empty boardwalks wrapped in the stillness of February, as if the town itself had fallen into hibernation after the tourists had left. "Is anything open?" she asked.

"I saw a place a couple of blocks down, and we've got plenty of time before the train. Let's go."

She tucked her hand inside his pocket as they hurried down the street in the sleet, which was now turning to rain. Now that she was moving, she didn't feel quite so cold, but she still kept a hand cupped around her eyes to keep out the rain.

She was breathless by the time they arrived at the end of the street. Finn held the door of a shop, and she slipped inside, grateful for the warmth. The scent of coffee was a balm to her soul. She used a handkerchief to wipe the rainwater from her face and hair, then swiped at the shoulders of her cloak. Then she looked up and saw a world of color.

Kites!

Her briefcase landed on the floor with a thud as she stared in wonder. Kites were everywhere, displayed on the walls, dangling overhead from the rafters. The walls and ceiling were painted sky-blue, just like they always imagined. A kaleidoscope of colors filled the shop, ranging from simple diamond kites to vibrantly painted Chinese dragons, the tails curled around to drape over the display aisles. Other kites resembled parrots with their wings stretched in flight or swans with long necks and arching wings supported by wires.

Finn watched her take in the shop, expectation in his eyes.

She broke into a huge smile. "Oh, Finn, you did it!" She cupped his face in her hands and kissed him, her heart expanding with so much pride she feared it might burst.

His eyes sparkled. "Well? Do you like it?"

"I *love* it. It's like stepping into a dream."

She slipped her hand in his as he began the tour. One wall had bins overflowing with skeins of string and scraps of fabric to make tail streamers. Inexpensive kites made of cotton fabric were stacked in the corner, yet the silk kites had the most artistry. While the shop wasn't large, it contained everything they had once talked about including in a kite shop.

She touched the delicate silk of an orange and scarlet kite, shot through with threads of golden yellow. It was made in the shape of a maple leaf.

"Those are one of my bestselling designs," Finn said. "Sometimes a bunch of people will fly them together, and it looks like a cascade of giant autumn leaves floating through the sky."

She moved deeper into the shop and spotted another important part of the dream: a worktable where she and Finn could make kites and chat with customers. Except now the worktable was staffed by a skinny young man, who was busy stitching diagonal silk panels to the end of a kite.

"Delia, this is Clyde Sommers. He's been running the shop since the day I went away to France."

"And making kites too," Delia said, glancing at a stack of kite

162

patterns. Clyde was making more maple-leaf kites, and she took up a nearby stool to watch him work.

Regret mingled with nostalgia and welled up inside her. If she had been a braver, more forgiving person, she could have been a part of this. Instead, she walked away from Finn and took a safe job in an office. It was a good life but a predictable one . . . and not the life she'd always dreamed of. And this beautiful shop had awakened a bittersweet ache.

Finn watched Delia as she experienced his kite shop for the first time, trying to judge her reaction. Did a part of her still dream about owning a kite shop or had that all been smothered out with her infatuation with the old guy? Her eagerness to listen to Clyde's explanation of how he joined the maple leaves into a kite train was a positive sign.

Yet Finn wanted more than a positive sign. He wanted Delia to say she loved the store and wanted to be a part of it. He wanted to show her his home above the store. It was a nice apartment even though it had only a large front room and two tiny bedrooms. The living area overlooked the main street, and the kitchen was nothing more than a sink, an icebox, and a stove pressed up against the parlor wall. It was an ordinary place, except for the spectacular view of the ocean from the back windows.

Clyde had made a pot of coffee earlier, so the whole shop smelled good. Delia had already finished her first cup, and he brought the carafe over for a refill.

Delia flashed him a smile as he filled her mug. "Do you keep the shop open all year?" she asked as she cupped the mug, sighing as the heat warmed her icy hands.

"I keep it open for the locals during the winter while also working to build up the kite supply. When the tourists arrive, it's hard to keep up with the demand."

Delia reached up to touch a scarlet panel on the tail of a Chinese dragon. "I would give my eyeteeth to fly this dragon kite."

Finn flashed her a smile. "Keep your teeth. I'll let you fly it for free."

"Right now?"

"Right now." The sleet had stopped, but it was still breezy. It had been more than ten years since they'd flown a kite together. Would it be possible to recapture the magic? He reached up to detach the dragon kite from the hook in the ceiling.

Delia shrugged back into her coat and, to his delight, wrapped his white silk scarf back around her neck. He liked the look of it on her. Anyone who knew what that scarf meant to him would see it as a sign that he wanted her for keeps.

The beach behind the shop was perfect for flying kites. Everywhere on the cape had good wind, but Finn and some of the locals had cleared the rocks from this stretch of beach so that kite flyers could run with abandon.

The sand churned beneath his feet as they trudged closer to the water. Gray clouds hung low in the sky, and the distant call of a lone sea gull sounded morose.

"I know it doesn't look like much now, but in the summer this place is wonderful," he said. "That's the thing about life. There are bleak, barren seasons, but then the sun comes out and the world shifts. The days lengthen, and the sunsets are amazing. I wish I could show you this place in June."

"Stop," Delia said. "I already love it."

"Do you? Because you're the person I always wished was with me on those long summer nights. I never stopped hoping that someday you and I could live here together. Raise kids here." He turned to point to the back of his shop. "You see those windows on the second floor? That's where I live. It's big enough for the two of us. I don't know if it's too late for us."

The wind tousled her hair as she hugged herself. Delia always struggled with change, and moving out here would be unlike her

164

normal, dependable life in New York City. The roar of the ocean and hiss of waves rushing ashore made it hard to hear, but finally she spoke.

"It's a big step," she said. "I need a little more time to be sure."

"I can give you time," he said. Her answer wasn't exactly what he wanted to hear, but it was good enough for now.

He handed her the kite, and the wind practically tugged it from her hands, sending it toward the sky. The multicolored dragon twisted and curled above them, its tail thrashing in the stiff breeze. He'd forgotten the beauty of Delia's laughter as it carried on the wind.

He held her the entire train ride back to Camp Mills. It had been a perfect day. They'd endured miserable weather, bad food, frozen feet and noses, and had gained only a piddly donation, but it didn't matter. It was the gift of being with Delia that had made it perfect.

Steam hissed and gears squealed as the train slowed outside the Camp Mills stop. He would disembark here while she rode the train the rest of the way to the Astoria Ferry, which would carry her back to Manhattan. He didn't want to let go of her.

"What time are we meeting tomorrow?" he asked. Delia always knew their schedule without having to consult her notes.

"No fundraisers tomorrow except for a meeting with the board of the CRB. We'll meet at Bertie's house at six o'clock."

"Sounds good," he said, but inside he braced himself. The board of the CRB included Wesley Chandler, and Finn suspected that Delia still harbored a lingering affection for Wesley, a man who was Finn's complete opposite.

She unwound his scarf from around her neck and moved to give it back to him. "Keep it," he said. "It looks better on you than on me."

He intended to start staking his claim for Delia's heart, and wanting her to wear his cherished scarf was a visible sign of his intentions.

21

Delia arrived with Finn at Bertie's town house a few minutes before the CRB meeting. She couldn't wait to present Bertie and the board of directors with the healthy balance sheet. Over the past two months, she and Finn had raised millions of dollars while also securing valuable donations of cargo space and fuel. Nothing in Delia's life made her prouder than the freshly inked balance sheet she would present tonight.

"Wesley is going to be here tonight," she quietly warned Finn.

Without a word, Finn extended his elbow and she gladly took it. This wasn't to make Wesley jealous; it was because she and Finn were a team now, and she wanted the world to see it. Together they mounted the front steps of the town house.

Inside, all nine members of the board were crowded into the formal living room. The scent of pine from the crackling fireplace mingled with the pungent smell of cigar smoke. The sofa and upholstered chairs were already occupied, and dining room chairs had been squeezed into the room, forming a circle. They were rapidly filling too.

"Let's take the window seat," Finn whispered in her ear, and she nodded. The window seat had only enough space for them to sit pressed close together. Holding her briefcase on her lap, she looked forward to presenting the all-important financial report to Bertie.

Wesley chatted with Congressman Donnelly near the fireplace. This was the first time she'd seen him since the night she quit in this very room. As ever, he looked the epitome of refinement in a perfectly tailored suit, but there were more strands of gray threaded through his dark hair. Had it changed that much in two months? Or maybe it had always been there, and she simply hadn't wanted to see it.

Bertie called the meeting to order, and conversations trickled to an end as the men settled back in their seats. Wesley chose a seat opposite her, and his eyes widened when he spotted her.

She gave a polite nod, and to her surprise he rose and closed the distance between them. "Delia . . ." he stammered, "it's nice to see you. Are you doing well?"

This was hardly the time to mend fences, but she couldn't resist a tiny dig. "I'm fine, thank you. How is Mrs. Beekman?"

Congressman Donelly chortled and turned. "You haven't heard?"

Delia wasn't privy to the rarefied gossip in this social circle, but Wesley looked distinctly uncomfortable. "Heard what?" she asked the congressman.

"Mrs. Beeckman got herself engaged to a physician from Up-state New York. She surprised everyone," Congressman Donelly said.

If Delia hadn't been sitting down, she would have fallen over in shock. Mrs. Beekman cast Wesley aside? It was difficult to believe, and yet the austere expression on Wesley's face said it was probably true.

Wesley hadn't taken his gaze off her face. "Delia, I just want to be sure you've landed on your feet. Are you sure you're okay?"

Bertie had been paying Delia a modest salary for her work on behalf of the CRB, but she sensed that wasn't what Wesley was getting at. She slipped her hand inside Finn's. "We're fine."

Wesley glanced down at their clasped hands. His face paled, and for once in his life he was at a loss for words. He opened his mouth to speak but nothing came out. Though this should have felt good, it didn't. She squeezed Finn's hand tighter so she wouldn't do something stupid like try to comfort Wesley.

Bertie tapped a glass with a spoon to again call the meeting to order, and Wesley retreated to a chair in the front of the room. Bertie remained standing near the entrance of the parlor, his expression grave. "I'm afraid we need to cancel our normal business meeting, as things have taken a turn for the worse overseas. Germany has announced they will no longer permit our ships to use the Port of Rotterdam."

Delia felt as if she'd been kicked in the stomach. Bertie sent her and Finn a sympathetic glance. "Although President Taft used his connections to keep the port open to us for several additional weeks, the Germans have since become suspicious of anything coming from the United States. Our ships are now prohibited from docking at Rotterdam. And we all know the Germans' reputation for employing their U-boats to stop a ship from entering a port."

It was a significant blow. The energy drained from her body as she set her briefcase on the floor with a thud. The financial report she was so proud of no longer mattered.

"What are we going to do?" Wesley asked.

"We'll have to start shipping the food to a neutral nation like Spain. The cargo will be off-loaded, inspected for contraband, and then loaded onto a Spanish ship to take it the rest of the way to Rotterdam. In addition to the extra time and manpower, we are going to lose the concessions we have won from men like Alfred Pollard. We don't have any arrangements with Spanish shipping, so it's going to cost a fortune."

While Bertie's tone was grim, Wesley sounded even more despondent. "We barely have enough fuel to keep the ships afloat, and each month we scramble for the last few dimes to stock the cargo space. How can we possibly find more money?"

Silence reigned in the room, until Finn suddenly chimed in. "I've found there are two types of people in the world. Those who say they can't succeed, and those who say they can. Both are usually right, so which one do we want to be?"

"We can do it," Bertie asserted. "It's not going to be easy, but this work is too important not to at least try. I intend to sail for Europe to find new partners to carry our food the final leg of the journey to Belgium."

"But will they allow you into Rotterdam?" Congressman Donnelly asked, and Bertie nodded.

"I'll sail on a Spanish ship, which shall have no problem landing in Rotterdam."

"What do you need from us?" Finn asked.

"Money," Bertie said bluntly. "We've already hit up the big donors in New York, so now I need you to travel to Chicago and St. Louis, perhaps even farther afield to California. Thanks to the Hearst newspapers, your story has been spread across the country. Still, nothing beats showing up in person to petition potential donors."

"I'll set off as soon as possible," Finn said.

Delia watched him, awestruck by the ease with which he'd volunteered. No hesitation, no second-guessing, but just a quiet, unshakable resolve to step forward and shoulder the burden. Men like Finn were the ones who kept the world spinning, and in that moment she vowed to do whatever it took to stand beside him, no matter the cost.

Specks of snow floated in the night air as they left Bertie's house. Finn held Delia's hand on their walk to the subway station, fearing this might be their last night together for a long time. Taking his fundraising appeals on the road was fine with him, but only if Delia came too. Wesley Chandler was now a free man, and the older man had been staring at Delia like a cat watching a goldfish.

He wanted her back, and Finn had no intention of being on the other side of the country when Wesley made his move.

"I want you to come with me to Chicago," he said.

"Just the two of us?" Her voice was heavy with skepticism. They'd both grown up on a diet of Sister Bernadette's cautionary tales, and it was obvious what Delia was getting at. Heck, he'd ask her to marry him and solve their problem that way if he thought she'd have him. Failing that, taking her with him to Chicago was the safest route for them.

"I need you, Dee. Who else will keep me in line and make sure I get to my appointments on time?"

"You don't need me anymore. Your stump speech is perfect."

"I'm not leaving you here while the old guy is roaming free and missing the world's best assistant."

"Don't you trust me?" Her voice sounded wounded in the cold night air.

They took several paces while he pondered the question. Delia was honest down to her bones. He was the reckless one who gambled on shortcuts and took risks. It wasn't that he didn't trust her, but a vague feeling of uneasiness plagued him nonetheless. He couldn't put a name to it, but he'd survived three years of the war by trusting his gut.

"It seems as though we're at a turning point," he began. "We've handled everything Bertie has thrown at us, and working with you has been great, but things are changing. Wesley is free again. I'm supposed to be heading off on my own, while you're back here and doing what? Going with Bertie to Rotterdam?" He paused and shook his head. "I want you to come with me to Chicago."

They were nearing her subway stop, and he wanted a commitment from her before boarding the ferry back to Long Island. "Dee, I want to plan a future with you. If you don't want me to be a pilot anymore, I'll try to get out of it. Bertie can probably help with that."

"You'd give up serving in the Army for me?"

"If it means staying here to rescue you from the clutches of the old guy, then yes, I would. Of course."

Her smile was like sunshine. "I don't need you to ride to my rescue, but I love that you'd be willing to do it."

"Are you sure? I can requisition an airplane and fly protective patrol around you to make sure he doesn't try anything."

She laughed. "You needn't worry about Wesley. The only person you need to fear is Thomas Babcock, chairman of the New York Stock Exchange. You have a meeting with him tomorrow morning, and he has a fearsome reputation."

"Oh? And why am I meeting with Mr. Babcock?"

"You're ringing the opening bell, and you have an interview with him beforehand in the hope of bringing in more donations. After that, if you still want to fly patrol above me, I think it would be flattering."

He turned to soak up the beauty of her face in the moonlight. Snowflakes dotted the air, mingling with the white puffs of their breath in the night. No matter what she said, leaving her alone in the city with Wesley Chandler on the prowl wasn't a good idea.

"Will you come to Chicago with me?"

She hugged her coat tighter around herself. "Did you know that until that day in December when we traveled to Yale, I had never set foot out of New York City?"

He tried to block the surprise from showing, but given the look of embarrassment on her face, he clearly failed.

"I've always been too cowardly to leave," she explained. "I never had money to waste when I was younger, and then after I started earning a good salary, I didn't want to let Wesley down by taking time off work. It seemed pointless to waste money on a vacation when my rainy-day fund could always use more."

"Do you still have a rainy-day fund?"

Her eyes twinkled. "It's more like a 'biblical flood fund.' I still save every spare dime, I suppose because it makes me feel safe."

For someone with as many dreams as Delia once had, to have

remained stuck in an office all these years because she feared risk seemed rather sad.

"Will you go with me to Chicago?" he asked for the third time. "I'll be there to protect you from gangsters and runaway streetcars, perhaps oversized rats and any other terrors Chicago might throw our way. And if a cow tries to start another great fire, I'll handle that too. I'm very strong and brave."

"And modest."

He nodded. "All those good things. Yes."

She huddled deeper into her coat as indecision rippled across her face. "Let me think about it," she said. "It's a big step."

He pressed a kiss to her temple. "I'll meet you tomorrow morning at the New York Stock Exchange," he murmured into her hair, and she nodded.

She pulled back to meet his eyes. "Nine-thirty sharp. The stock exchange opens at ten, and you'll be meeting with Mr. Babcock ahead of the bell."

He gave her a salute and a wink before heading off to catch the ferry.

It was after midnight when Finn got back to Camp Mills. A sleepy guard checked him in at the gatehouse, and then he walked past the endless rows of olive-green tents. Living in a tent hadn't been too miserable, but the dusting of snow on the tents guaranteed it was going to be a chilly night.

He lifted the flap of his tent, trying to move soundlessly, but crackling of the straw on the ground gave him away.

"I'm awake," his tentmate said in a groggy voice.

"Sorry," Finn whispered anyway. As he went to remove his boots, he bumped into the trunk in the center of the tent and bit back a curse.

"You can dial up the lamp," Daniel said. "By the way, you got a letter there on your cot."

That was a surprise. He received a handful of letters from the guys in France after he first arrived, but nothing lately. He struck the flint to light the wick in the lantern and dialed it to the lowest setting. The amber flame cast a dim circle of illumination, but it was enough to see the large manilla envelope lying on his cot.

The return address included the name Theo Montgomery, the opera-singing pilot Finn had served with in the Lafayette Escadrille.

Finn lowered himself onto the cot, his legs suddenly weak. What if one of his friends had been killed? His fingers trembled as he ripped open the envelope. It contained a copy of *La Libre Belgique*, along with a short note. His heart pounded as he scanned Theo's familiar handwriting.

Theo wrote that they'd all been folded into the U.S. Army and transferred to the Saint-Mihiel Training Center. They were learning new equipment, and he had nothing good to say about the food. The knot in Finn's shoulders began to ease as he neared the end of the letter. All seemed to be going well in France.

He turned the page over and read the final line of the letter: *I thought you would be interested in this issue of La Libre Belgique. I'm sorry, my friend.*

Finn's heart thudded as he dropped the letter and skimmed the newspaper. An article in the top left had been circled: *Une Femme Courageuse Arrêtée pour avoir Distribué un Journal.*

His mouth went dry. His French wasn't strong, but he knew the word *arrêtée* meant arrested, and Mathilde Verhaegen's name jumped off the page.

Then it got worse. His name was printed in the article as well. *Dans leur recherche du pilote américain abattu Finn Delaney, les Allemands ont fouillé le domicile de Mme Verhaegen et ont trouvé le journal.*

Panic-stricken, he struggled to translate the French. His heart thudded, and despite the chill, his entire body began sweating.

Keep your head, a voice silently warned. It was the first thing pilots were trained to do when danger threatened.

"Daniel, do you read French?"

"Nope."

The date printed at the top of the newspaper said it was three weeks old. Mathilde had been arrested three weeks ago! While he'd been dining in fancy restaurants and going to the theater, Mathilde was locked up in a German prison cell. Who was looking after her kids? Had they arrested Pieter too?

Finn needed to know exactly what had happened. He pulled on his boots, folded the newspaper under his arm, and bolted from the tent. The camp had in residence a French instructor, Lewis Hendra. Finn had visited the man during Hendra's first week in the camp but wasn't sure he could find his tent.

He raced to the east section of tents, his ragged breathing turning into white wisps in the cold air. The tents all looked alike, so he stopped at one and jerked a flap open. Two men lay asleep on their cots.

"Do either of you know Lewis Hendra?"

"Who?" one of the men said groggily from the shadowy interior of the tent.

"Lieutenant Hendra. He teaches French."

"Yeah, he lives a couple rows over. He's got a French flag pinned to the flap."

"Thanks!" Finn said and tore off in search of that flag. It didn't take him long to find it.

"Wake up, Hendra," Finn said as he entered the tent. "I need a newspaper article translated."

A muffled groan rose from a lump on the cot, buried beneath a mound of blankets. "What, now?"

"Please," Finn said. "It's urgent." He couldn't wait until daylight.

"Hang on," the man said, rolling upright in his cot. Finn lit a lantern while Lieutenant Hendra wiped the sleep from his eyes and put on his glasses.

"This is the article," Finn said, pointing to the circled headline. Hendra hunkered over the newspaper, turning it toward the glow of the lantern as he read.

Please, he silently prayed as Hendra scanned the article. *Please, God, let Mathilde be okay and her family safe. I'll do anything, pay any price, but please . . .*

"It says that a lady named Mathilde Verhaegen was arrested in connection with the escape of an American pilot, Finn Delaney. Hey, that's you, isn't it?"

Finn's breath froze in his throat, and he could only nod.

"It gets worse," Hendra said. "When they came to arrest her, they searched her house looking for where she hid you. They found a secret cache beneath the floorboards, and it was stuffed with issues of *La Libre Belgique*. The newspaper is forbidden, and anyone caught distributing it gets charged with sedition. She was caught red-handed, so her guilt is a foregone conclusion. The crime of sedition carries with it the death penalty."

An eerie calmness settled over Finn. This wasn't a hard decision. He knew exactly what he needed to do.

Mathilde Verhaegen had risked her life to save him. Now he would return the favor and no matter the cost.

He was going to Belgium.

22

Delia stood on the granite staircase leading up to the New York Stock Exchange Building, scanning the crowds of businessmen hustling down the sidewalks of Wall Street. It ought to be easy to pick out Finn's battered leather jacket amid the crush of black suits, but she'd been waiting for almost half an hour and there had been no sign of him.

They had less than fifteen minutes to meet with Mr. Babcock, and then Finn was expected to ring the opening bell. Photographers for the Hearst newspapers were already gathered on the trading floor, waiting to capture the moment on film. Mr. Babcock wasn't the friendliest of men, and Bertie had gone to great lengths to secure the honor for Finn. Striking the large brass bell with a mallet didn't exactly need a lot of instruction, but it wasn't polite of him to disregard the meeting with Mr. Babcock.

The opening of the stock exchange waited for no one, and so five minutes before ten o'clock, Delia raced inside to apologize to Mr. Babcock. After the glare of the morning sun on the white granite steps, it was hopelessly dim inside the building. She hurried down the crowded corridor, angling around clerks and traders to get to Mr. Babcock's office.

The secretary looked up from her desk as Delia barged in. "Have you seen Finn?" she asked, breathless.

The secretary shook her head. "Still no sign of him. Mr. Babcock has gone to ring the bell himself. Oh, and he's angry."

The man had a right to be angry. Such a ceremonial honor was rare and hard to come by, and failing to show up was unspeakably rude. Delia would have to figure out a way to smooth things over with Mr. Babcock. With luck, she might be able to move Finn's appointment to another day.

She arrived at the trading floor mere seconds before the ringing of the opening bell. A scowling man, presumably Mr. Babcock himself, stood on the podium, mallet poised beside the bell as he stared at an immense clock mounted on the wall across the room. Three photographers stood at the base of the podium, looking up at Mr. Babcock in confusion. They were here to photograph America's first war hero ringing the bell, not an ordinary businessman who looked as if he were sucking on a lemon.

The instant the clock's minute hand reached 10:00 a.m., Mr. Babcock banged the mallet against the brass bell. "Trading is open!" he announced, and the sea of stockbrokers flew into action, calling out orders and hurrying to their trading posts. Delia intercepted Mr. Babcock on his way to the administrative wing of the building.

"Mr. Babcock," she called as she hurried to reach him. He paused at the door of his office and spun around, peering down at her from his lofty height.

"My apologies for Lieutenant Delaney," she said, still struggling to catch her breath. "He comes all the way from Camp Mills, and there may have been a slowdown on the subway—"

"Every person in New York City knows there can be slowdowns on the subway. They make allowances for it and get to their appointments on time."

"Yes, but please keep in mind he's been wounded. He walks with a cane." In truth, Finn had been getting around quite well, but she wasn't beneath resorting to the wounded-hero angle if it could win Finn a second shot at this opportunity. "Could we reschedule his day to ring the opening bell? I will ensure he doesn't miss the appointment again."

Mr. Babcock frowned but agreed. "Contact my secretary," he grumbled. "And tell Bert Hoover he owes me a free round of golf for this one."

Delia nodded and thanked the man, wondering if it would be possible to reschedule Finn's appointment with Mr. Babcock before he had to leave for Chicago.

With nothing else to do, Delia returned to the Martha Washington and headed straight to the front counter. "Are there any messages for me?"

There was. A telephone message had been left for her earlier this morning but after Delia had already left for the stock exchange. She tore open the flap and read the clerk's message:

Finn Delaney called to say he had an unexpected meeting come up with an Army lawyer and is unable to keep his appointment this morning at the stock exchange building. He sends his apologies.

That was all.

Why on earth did Finn need to meet with a lawyer? Whatever the reason, it had to be serious for him to have skipped this morning's appointment.

She wouldn't waste time waiting for him to contact her. She was heading straight to Camp Mills to find out what was going on.

Finn's suitcase lay open on his cot as he tossed another plain white shirt inside it. He'd be traveling light and didn't have room in the single suitcase for his formal Army uniform. Besides, where he was going, being seen in an American uniform was likely to get him killed.

Sounds of a normal day filtered through the tent. The rumble of delivery trucks and of a sergeant leading the morning drill drifted in through the tent's flaps. Yet nothing could drown out the horrifying thoughts cycling through his mind.

Mathilde had been arrested and even now could be enduring torture in a German dungeon somewhere. No doubt the Germans were trying to pry from her the names of her fellow members of the resistance who had helped distribute *La Libre Belgique*. And being a woman wouldn't save her from their cruelty.

His hands shook as he balled up a pair of woolen socks. It was going to be cold over there, and he'd need to be ready for all kinds of weather. His silk scarves would come with him because he might need to pilot a plane. He didn't know how he was going to rescue Mathilde, only that he was going to do it.

"Finn? Finn, are you in there?"

Delia's voice sounded directly outside his tent. Facing her was the last thing he wanted this morning, but it had to be done. He untied the flap and pulled it back. Delia stood in her spiffy maroon business suit, a clipboard in the crook of her arm.

"Did you get my message in time?" he asked.

"No, I didn't. And I want to know why a meeting with an attorney took precedence over your appointment with the chairman of the New York Stock Exchange."

He turned away, a rush of acid filling his gut at the memory of his meeting with the Army lawyer. Captain Jacobs had confirmed his fears about Mathilde's dire situation. She'd been caught redhanded with a few hundred copies of the forbidden newspaper and charged with sedition, a death-penalty offense. The only good piece of news Captain Jacobs had been able to offer was that Mathilde was still alive. A flurry of telegrams had been sent between France and New York, confirming that Mathilde was being held at the Saint-Gilles Prison in Brussels, Belgium.

Finn motioned for Delia to step inside the tent. After lowering the flap, he said, "The woman who saved me has been arrested." He handed her the issue of *La Libre Belgique*, pointing to the news article. "Word of Mathilde's arrest is all over Belgium. I hadn't heard of it until I was shown that article—she was arrested *three weeks* ago."

The ire immediately drained from Delia's face. "Finn, I'm so sorry. Perhaps Bertie can do something to help."

"Ha!" he scoffed. "Bertie plays by the rules. He won't do anything to rock the boat with the Germans."

Delia's expression suddenly turned cautious. "What are you planning on doing?"

"I'm going over there. I can't just sit here in America while the person who saved my life ends up in front of a firing squad, all because of me."

"I don't understand," Delia said. "She's being held on the charge of distributing a forbidden newspaper, not for helping you, right?"

Finn shook his head. "Don't you see, Dee? All the fame I got over here, getting written up in newspapers and such, it got back to General Ryckman. My escape humiliated him, and he put a bounty on the heads of whoever helped me escape. They suspected Mathilde because her house was so close to where I crashed. They searched her place a dozen times but never found where she hid me. Somone must have taken the reward and turned her in. The Germans found the cache beneath the floorboards, which included a large stack of newspapers. This stupid, vain idea of making me a hero is probably going to cost Mathilde her life."

"Surely not," Delia said, coming to rest a hand on his shoulder. "She's a woman. They won't execute a woman."

His mouth twisted in bitterness. "Tell that to Edith Cavell's family." The brave English nurse had volunteered her services in Belgum and was caught helping Allied soldiers escape. They executed her two months after her arrest. "The Germans blindfolded her, stood her up against a wall, and shot her to death. They'll do the same to Mathilde."

Finn fumbled for a cigarette, his fingers shaking so badly it took a minute to get it lit. His heart and brain were racing. He took a long pull from the cigarette. "When I was twelve, I couldn't save my mom from the fire. I'm not going to have another good woman's death on my conscience. I'm going over there, and I'll save Mathilde Verhaegen if it's the last thing I do on this earth."

"That won't be possible, Finn. You've been ordered to take up a Stateside assignment."

"I'm quitting."

"You *can't* quit. You're in the Army!"

He never should have signed those papers. At the time, joining the U.S. Army was the only way to get to France and back into action. Now those papers had him trapped.

"Let them arrest me," he shot back. "They'll have to find me first, and that won't be easy to do once I get to France. Besides, they've got better things to do than hunt down a renegade pilot." He drew deeply on the cigarette, trying to calm his racing thoughts. It wasn't working.

Delia grabbed one of his silk scarves from the open suitcase. "Why do you need *this*?" Her meaning was clear. Thin silk scarves weren't for warmth; they were for pilots flying on a mission.

"I might need to fly an airplane." He wouldn't lie to Delia and kept his eyes locked on hers as his intent became clear.

She dropped the scarf back in the suitcase and grasped him by both elbows. "Sit down," she said, steering him to the cot.

He took another draw on the cigarette, then blew out the smoke on a shaky breath.

"Your hands are trembling," she pointed out, her face filled with concern.

"It's been a bad day."

"Maybe you should see a doctor."

He'd already seen one weeks ago. The doctor called his condition "war neurosis" and said there was no cure. Finn called these episodes "the tremblies." Regardless of the name, he wouldn't let a little trembling interfere when Mathilde was locked up in a prison.

"I don't need a doctor. The tremblies only happen when I'm thinking about Belgium, so it isn't a big deal."

But it was a big deal. His hands shook so hard, the tip of ash at the end of his cigarette broke off and landed on Delia's skirt. She brushed the ash away, took the cigarette from his hand, and snuffed it out in a dish already overflowing with butts.

"Finn, there are better ways of handling this than your boarding a ship back to Europe. We have connections in New York who can help. Slow down. Make a plan. Anything is better than going absent without leave and getting convicted of desertion."

He scoffed. "If I could turn the clock back and save my mother from that fire, do you think I would care about being absent without leave? I'm going to save Mathilde. I won't let her kids grow up as orphans."

The image of little Jeannette offering him a cookie rose in his mind. And Pieter smuggling him aboard the barge, already a man at fourteen. Finn clamped a hand over his knee to stop it from shaking.

Delia grabbed his hand. "Finn, there are nine million people in Belgium. They're depending on you."

He gave a heavy sigh. The image of Jeannette's sweet face preoccupied his mind. No kid should be as scrawny as her, and yet she still wanted to give him her cookie. "I know you're right, but I'm not going to sit on the sidelines. I can't." He closed the suitcase, buckled it, and hoisted it off the cot.

"What are you going to do once there?"

"Right now I'm going to book passage on a ship to France. I'll figure out the rest later." Finn couldn't bear to look her in the eye. Instead, he turned abruptly and left the tent.

Delia sensed her whole world crumbling beneath her feet as she watched Finn leave, his suitcase clutched in his hand. How could she just stand there while he went about destroying himself? If he didn't get killed trying to rescue Mathilde, he'd be court-martialed and would likely spend years in prison.

She stood in the aisle between the tents, watching him grow smaller as he walked away. To her left was the parade ground where new recruits marched in formation, and to her right was the administration building where she could report what Finn was doing. They would arrest him and send him to a military prison. It would ruin his career and his reputation, but it would save his life.

She mustn't do anything rash. Now more than ever, she needed to set emotion aside and approach this problem with analytical precision. There might be a legal way to free Mathilde and stop Finn from ruining his life.

And the best person to consult for help was Wesley Chandler.

23

The long trip back from Camp Mills meant it was late afternoon before Delia arrived at the office building where she'd spent six years working for Wesley. She hiked up her skirts and scurried up the front steps, desperate to catch Wesley before he left to have dinner with his daughter.

Had it been just last night that she'd seen him? The crowded meeting at Bertie's town house seemed another lifetime ago, before she knew of Finn's intention to destroy his future over an ill-conceived plan to rescue Mathilde. Wesley's disappointment at learning of her romance with Finn had been evident, but he was an honorable man and would still help to the best of his ability.

That didn't assuage the quivery feeling in her gut as she entered the building. She used to love working here. The scent of lemon polish on the mahogany wainscoting was the same. The hardwood floor creaked under her shoes at exactly the same spots. The cold brass doorknob was wonderfully familiar as she twisted it and walked into the spacious front room.

The sight of Amy Chandler sitting at Delia's old desk brought her up short. Wesley's daughter filed her nails as she casually twirled in the office chair.

It was a bit of an insult. Wesley had replaced Delia with the world's most pampered seventeen-year-old. "Hello, Amy," she said, a hint of a chill in her tone. "Why aren't you in school?"

Amy continued examining her fingernails. "Because school is pointless, and Papa pays me to do office work."

Hopefully, it wasn't the same wage Delia had received from Wesley. Amy's presence meant that he hadn't yet left for their father-daughter dinner, which was good.

At the far side of the office, Reginald Hawthorne stood. "Are you coming back to work for Wesley?" The note of hope in his voice was unmistakable.

"Sorry, no. Is he here? I need to speak with him."

Reginald took his seat. "You know where to find him."

Never had the sight of the closed door to Wesley's office looked quite so daunting. Coming to him for help was intensely awkward after last night. Nevertheless, there were few people in the city so well versed in humanitarian law. She squared her shoulders and knocked.

"Come in," he responded, his rich tenor painfully familiar. She opened the door, and surprise widened his eyes as he shot to his feet. "Delia, hello. Come in." He gestured toward a chair. "Please, have a seat."

"I have a legal problem. I wondered if you could help."

He smiled. "Of course."

She was too nervous to sit and instead paced the route circling his desk, the floor globe, and the chair near the window. It didn't take long to summarize Mathilde Verhaegen's arrest for her part in saving Finn. She explained the outlawed newspaper of the resistance and how Mathilde had been caught with hundreds of copies in her home, clearly intending to distribute the papers.

"Is her situation as bad as Finn believes it to be?" she asked.

Wesley remained seated at his desk, watching her through somber eyes. "It's bad, yes," he said. "Either one of those charges could potentially result in the death penalty. Both charges together is almost a certainty." He stood to retrieve a fat volume from a bookshelf. "This book contains the Hague Convention Treaties of 1899 and 1907—international agreements that govern the conduct of war and the rules for protecting civilians. Both Germany and the United States are signatories to them. This is Mathilde's best hope, albeit it's a slim one."

Delia took the heavy volume from him. "Any other ideas?"

Wesley returned to the desk and sat, thrumming his fingers while mulling the situation over for a moment, a gesture she'd watched hundreds of times over the years. She waited several minutes while he pondered. Finally, his head shot up. "Is there a photograph of Mathilde?" he asked.

"I don't know. Why?"

"It would be easier to rally public support if people can see her face. Edith Cavell's story caught fire because of her photograph—a lovely woman with classically beautiful features. It made her the ultimate heroine. Is there a photo available?"

But should support for a woman depend on her being "classically beautiful"? Finn never mentioned Mathilde's appearance, only that she was brave and that she loved her country. And yet if hunting down a photograph would help her cause, Delia would look for one.

"Finn once told me that she met her husband at the university in Ghent. Perhaps the university has a photo we can use."

"Find out," Wesley said.

Within moments they had reverted to their old rhythm, batting ideas around and generating angles for a legal defense. It was like slipping into a comfortable old glove. Wesley wanted to make Mathilde another cause célèbre, stoking public outrage much like had been done with Edith Cavell, but hopefully with a different outcome. Mathilde Verhaegen would be portrayed as a valiant mother, struggling to keep her children alive after her husband had been seized by the Germans and sent to an unknown fate.

"I'll get Amy to contact the local newspapers and start the process," Wesley added.

Delia frowned. "This is too important to entrust to Amy. Why did you hire her anyway?"

"I found myself short of staff when a reliable foot soldier disappeared without warning."

She quirked a brow. "Maybe you shouldn't have been running around behind said foot soldier's back if you wanted such unstinting support and loyalty. Why did you lie to me about Constance Beekman?"

"It wasn't a lie. It was an act of omission."

She waved her hand in the air, as if clearing the room of a bad smell. "Don't hide behind legal technicalities. You knew exactly what I wanted, and all the while you were escorting Mrs. Beekman to country vineyards in the Hudson Valley."

"It would have been improper for a lady of her status to gallivant around the state without an escort."

"How kind of you to sacrifice yourself on the altar of chivalry. Honestly, the halo above your head is practically glowing. Tell me this: if I offered to return to work here, would you hire me?"

"In an instant."

"And now that Mrs. Beekman is engaged to another man, would the age difference between us continue to be a problem for you?" She flicked the globe into motion with a single push of her finger.

Wesley stared at the rotating globe, his eyes both hopeful and calculating. The globe was the site of their first kiss. Several moments passed with only the squeak of the rotating globe to mark the passage of the seconds.

"No," he finally said. "I don't believe age should be an issue anymore. I'm sure we could reach an understanding, both in the office and outside of it."

Once upon a time, that statement was her deepest hope. Not anymore. She approached him slowly, her limbs feeling as heavy as stone. "And if Mrs. Beekman's engagement was to fall through, how fast would you toss me aside were she to reappear in your life?"

He glanced away, but only for a moment. "She is no longer in my life. You and I have always worked well together. I find you attractive. You have indicated similar feelings for me."

He opened the top drawer of his desk and removed a small ring box covered in royal blue velvet. He slid it across the desk toward her.

Her heart thumped. How many times had she dreamed about this? Her mouth went dry, and she could barely breathe.

"Open it," Wesley prompted.

She did. Inside lay an emerald-cut diamond ring. She set it back down on the desktop.

"Did you buy that for Mrs. Beekman?"

"I bought it for you."

It was impossible to know if that was true, but Wesley was an admirable man, intelligent and attractive and financially secure. She would be safe with him.

A knock at the door interrupted her thoughts. "Papa, it's late and I'm about to die from hunger," Amy said from the other side.

"Another few minutes, sugarplum," Wesley called out, though his eyes remained locked on Delia's. He lowered his voice to a whisper. "Amy has often mentioned how she enjoyed shopping with you."

"If you think that's sweetening the deal for me, you're sadly mistaken."

Wesley said nothing as a tangle of emotions warred inside her chest. Marriage to Wesley would be solid, secure. He would never dart off to France on dangerous rescue missions or gamble with their life savings. Yet she wanted to be valued for something other than being an excellent office manager or perhaps substitute mother for a spoiled young lady.

Delia stood, cradling the book of international treaties in her arms. She wouldn't be pressured into making a decision now, and moved to the door to open it. "Come in, Amy. Your father is look-ing forward to dinner."

Annoyance flashed across Wesley's features as Amy darted into the office and helped her father shrug into his coat.

"We shall continue this conversation at another time," Wesley said quietly in her ear as he left the room, Amy at his side.

Reginald was the only person left in the office. It felt like old times again when she and her nemesis shared this space, always the last ones to leave the office each day.

"Did you know about Mrs. Beekman?" she asked.

Reginald winced, then gave her a look of sympathy. "I knew," he admitted. "It was why I warned you away from Wesley. I often wondered if I ought to have told you but felt it wasn't my place. In any event, your departure was a great blow to the firm."

"He won his last two cases," she said. "I saw it reported in the newspaper."

"Those cases benefited from your assistance. Ever since then, we have begun to flounder. Amy is not all that one would hope for in an assistant, but Wesley doesn't like leaving her alone, and he has resisted hiring another qualified assistant. He hasn't even placed an advertisement for one."

Probably because he was expecting Delia to return.

Should she? Nostalgia rose inside her as she gazed at the shelves of lawbooks, the late afternoon sun casting an amber haze across the room. This place had once been her second home, a place where she'd been happy and felt safe.

Wesley had been safe. Maybe his romantic feelings for her would never call the moon down from the sky, but there was value in predictable safety. And falling in love with Finn Delaney had never been a safe bet.

Even so, she mustn't do anything hasty. Everything was hap-pening so fast, and she needed time to sort her feelings. She took a long, fond look around the office before she left, wondering if this would be the last time she'd see it or if she should accept Wesley's proposal after all.

When Delia got back to the Martha Washington, a telegram was waiting for her:

> *Sailing on the SS* Arabella *for France tomorrow morning. I love you, and I am sorry.*
>
> *Finn*

24

Delia arrived at the Chelsea Pier to say goodbye to Finn. The sun had just peeked above the horizon, and the *Arabella* loomed tall and imposing, her sleek hull rising above the boardwalk as the ship's crew prepared to set sail. Stevedores wheeled pallets of food and other supplies aboard. Fat rubber hoses watered and fueled the vessel as sea gulls circled overhead, their plaintive cries sounding as desperate and melancholy as Delia's spirit.

She huddled on a bench behind a rope barricade to watch people as they boarded. The *Arabella* was primarily a cargo ship, with room for only a few dozen passengers. Most would be men sailing to Europe on business. Nobody else would be foolish enough to risk the dangerous Atlantic crossing in time of war.

The moment she spotted Finn, she planned on springing into action to intercept him. She had to convince him to stay. They could sound the alarm about Mathilde's plight from right here in New York. He didn't have to risk his future. She silently rehearsed her arguments to persuade him not to go. He might do time in prison for desertion. He'd lose his kite shop and everything he'd ever achieved in his life.

The problem was that all her arguments were based on logic, while Finn was being led by his heart. His big, generous, good heart was about to be his downfall.

A few more businessmen arrived to board the ship, and she almost didn't recognize Finn. Dressed in an ill-fitting tweed suit with a bowler hat, he walked slowly down the boardwalk. No cane. No dashing pilot's uniform or jaunty silk scarf because he was smart enough to know he could be recognized if he wore his uniform.

She hiked up her skirts to run across the boardwalk, intercepting him before he reached the gangway. "Finn!" she cried as she rushed up behind him. "Were you really going to leave without saying goodbye?"

A fleeting look of happiness lit his face, but it was soon replaced by painful regret. He reached inside his coat pocket and pulled out an envelope. "I wrote you a letter. I was going to post it once I got on board."

She batted it away. "I don't want a letter. I want you to look me in the eyes and tell me you're prepared to betray everything we have together to go off on a quest you know is bound to fail."

"I have to try."

She wanted to shake him for his brave and terribly shortsighted gallantry. Her carefully prepared arguments had vanished from her mind. All she could do now was to dig deep and speak straight from her soul.

"Don't go, Finn," she said. "Please don't go. I'm begging you . . ."

He flinched with every word she spoke, and finally he interrupted her. "Delia, you've always been a rule follower. I'm not, and like I said, I can't stay here in New York when I know Mathilde is suffering in prison and could lose her life."

She wanted to shake him until his teeth rattled. "How can you possibly save her? I've seen photographs of that prison. It's a dungeon!"

"All the more reason to get her out of there."

"But how?" she demanded.

He shifted uneasily and looked toward the misty horizon. "I don't know, but I'll have six days during the crossing to think up something. I've got friends over there. Fellow pilots. Maybe even some people in Belgium."

An unsettling feeling took root in her gut. Aside from Mathilde and a few other resistance workers, the only people Finn knew in Belgium were affiliated with the CRB. If Finn used those connections to help Mathilde escape prison, he would be putting the entire operation in jeopardy.

"Please tell me you're not going to put the CRB at risk again."

"I won't," he assured her. "I learned enough about how the resistance in Belgium is organized to know how to get through to them without alerting the Germans."

The more Finn talked, the more hopeless his plans sounded. She had to suggest a better alternative. Wesley had already given her a few ideas.

"Do you have a photograph of Mathilde?"

"No. Why?"

She told him about her visit to Wesley's office to ask for his help, as well as his wanting to portray Mathilde as a heroic wife and mother, whose execution would no doubt inflame public opinion.

"You've seen Wesley again?" A trace of jealousy gave an edge to Finn's tone.

"I went to him to ask for legal advice," she rushed to explain. "He's one of the best attorneys in the country for taking on unpopular clients and figuring out a way to win on their behalf. We can't afford to turn his help down."

Finn's eyes crinkled in concern. "He's too old for you."

"At least he isn't abandoning me to sail across the ocean on a mission that will probably get himself killed or imprisoned."

He shrugged. "If you were in trouble, I'd do the same for you."

"Sister Bernadette would say you're letting your heart overrule your head."

"And I would remind Sister Bernadette that I'm a Samson, not a Solomon."

A reluctant chuckle lightened the mood, yet it vanished quickly. She put a hand on his forearm and said gently, "Finn, I had hoped we could have a future together, but if you board that ship, if you betray the Army and Bertie and me . . . well, I don't know if I'll ever be able to forgive you."

He sagged and turned away. "Delia, please . . ." His voice ached with longing, and it was terrible to hear, but she would remain firm. She wouldn't go through the rest of her life yoked to a man who couldn't control the wild, surging moods that drove him to near-suicidal risks.

"You don't need to go," she reminded him.

He cupped the side of her face with a warm palm, his expression a mask of regret. "I don't want to lose you, Dee, but I have to go."

He pulled her into an embrace. His entire body trembled. How could she let him go when he was a quivering mass of nerves? She scrambled for every possible reason to keep him home and safe.

"The Atlantic is swarming with U-boats," she choked out.

He squeezed her tighter. "I know."

"Tuberculosis is running rampant in France. There's no cure for it."

"I know that too."

This was probably the last time they would ever hold each other. His odds of coming back home were slim, and even if he did, she wouldn't be waiting for him. Despair filled her chest and squeezed her heart. There were a million things she wanted to say. To thank him for standing up to the bullies at the orphanage. Thank him for teaching her to fly kites and how to dream. Even though he'd let her down, Finn was a good man, and a part of her would always love him.

"Good luck," she whispered in his ear.

He clasped her face between his hands and kissed her with heartfelt desperation. This was their last kiss, and they both knew it.

"Thanks, Dee," he said into her hair. "Thanks for being the best friend I ever had."

She wasn't able to speak anymore. All she could do was embrace him one final time, heart to heart, friend to friend.

She disentangled herself and turned away so that Finn's last sight of her on this earth wouldn't show her face twisted with anguish.

Then she walked away without looking back.

elia's heart ached as she strode away from the port. It would be easier to bear if she didn't still love Finn, but his instinctive urge to rush to Mathilde's rescue was so characteristically him. The man believed he could do just about anything, often disregarding the consequences and his own safety. Loving Finn and knowing he was heading straight into the jaws of danger made it hard for her to put one foot in front of the other.

But her disillusionment didn't matter. She needed to tell Bertie what Finn intended, even though it felt like she was betraying him. *Finn* was the person who had betrayed them by walking away from his responsibilities to the Army and the CRB. And yet here she was, awash with guilt as she approached Bertie's town house. The railing was cold as she grasped it, barely finding the strength to trudge up the short flight of steps.

Mrs. Hoover opened the door. "Delia. Come in out of the wind, dear. Is Finn with you?"

"No," she replied, stepping inside and clutching her arms across her chest, her stomach churning with anxiety.

"I imagine he's busy preparing for his trip to Chicago," Mrs.

Hoover said. "Let me have your coat, and then you can tell us what brought you out on such a dreadful morning."

She held her arms tighter. "I'll keep my coat on, thank you. I feel so cold."

Mrs. Hoover closed the door. "Come inside. Let me get you something hot to drink. Bertie? Delia is here to see you," she called out, then lowered her voice to speak quietly to Delia. "He's getting ready to head back to Europe, and I'm worried sick about it. Those awful U-boats are everywhere. Did you hear that another of our ships got hit last week? Everyone was rescued, but nine hundred tons of grain is now at the bottom of the Atlantic. Such a terrible waste."

Delia stood in the kitchen as Mrs. Hoover set a kettle on the cast-iron stove. A hot drink might help to stop her shivering and the chattering of her teeth, for thinking of what Finn would be facing when he arrived in Europe had made her blood run cold.

Mrs. Hoover handed her a porcelain teacup lavishly embellished with blue-and-white Chinese figures. "A memento of our years in China, back when Bertie worked as a mining engineer," she said. "It seems so long ago now. The work was difficult, but nothing like what we deal with today."

Heavy footsteps thudded in the hallway. "What's got you looking so tragic?" Bertie asked, accepting a cup of tea from his wife.

"I saw Finn off at the port this morning. He's sailing to France."

Bertie stilled, the teacup halfway to his mouth. His face grew serious as he set it down with a gentle click. "Why isn't he on his way to Chicago?"

This was it. It was hard to keep her head up as she delivered the news. "Finn learned that the woman who rescued him in Belgium has been arrested, and he is determined to save her. He left for France an hour ago."

Delia watched as Bertie absorbed the news. Though his expression remained composed, the brief flicker of sadness in his eyes betrayed his disappointment.

"It appears we must continue operating on a reduced budget," he said. "That is a battle for another day. Far more urgent is getting the Port of Rotterdam reopened to our ships. You know Benedict Kincaid, don't you?"

She nodded. "He's the scary diplomat who married my best friend." Delia still couldn't believe sunny and cheerful Inga had married such a daunting person.

"A fair description," Bertie acknowledged. "He may be a cold fish, but there is no denying Benedict's uncanny ability to broker alliances. He was stationed in Berlin for eight years before the war and knows all the major players, both in Germany and on the Allied side. He's coming with me to Rotterdam to help with negotiations. I'll stay in Rotterdam while Benedict will travel on to Brussels to negotiate with the occupying German forces there. His wife will be accompanying him. I gather Inga is a skilled telegrapher and has agreed to facilitate communications between Rotterdam and Brussels."

Delia caught her breath. "I didn't realize women were allowed to go to the front lines like that."

"Not many have gone over, but there's a need for skilled clerks and secretaries," Bertie said. "I've always been short-staffed whenever I'm in Europe, so Inga will be worth her weight in solid gold."

"What about the U-boats?"

His smile was sad. "For every ship the Germans sink, around thirty make it through. In times like these, we must confront the danger, or inaction will harm our cause more than the enemy ever could."

He was right, of course. Whenever Delia was threatened with danger, she instinctively recoiled and told herself it wasn't fear but prudence that held her back. Yet it *was* fear, and the courage of those around her was humbling.

Inga and Benedict had sailed to Europe several times in the past few years on important diplomatic missions. Bertie was continually sailing to Europe ever since the war began. Although she vehemently disagreed with Finn's mission, he was the personification of courage in the face of danger. So far, Delia's efforts for peace had amounted to little other than shouting into the whirlwind. The cold shell of fear had blocked her from doing anything more meaningful.

"Can Benedict negotiate for Mathilde Verhaegen?" The question popped out before she had fully formulated a plan, but suddenly it made sense. "You said he was going to Brussels to negotiate with the Germans. That's where Mathilde is being held. Could he help get her released?"

Bertie looked mildly appalled. "Benedict and I will be wholly absorbed with talks to reopen the Port of Rotterdam. We cannot dilute our mission on behalf of an individual woman."

Delia didn't know much about international law, but it took six days to cross the Atlantic Ocean. She would not allow inaction to define her any longer. Women like Mathilde were risking everything for a cause while Delia never ventured outside the safety of a courtroom.

She wanted to be a better, braver person. She wanted to have at least a fraction of the courage that had guided Mathilde's life since the day Germany took control of Belgium. The time for action had come.

"If you need a secretary, I would be honored to accompany you to Rotterdam," she said.

And during the voyage, she would figure out a way to free Mathilde Verhaegen.

26

Delia stood beside Inga on the main deck of the SS *Infanta Isabella* as the ship left New York Harbor behind. She'd lived in New York her entire life but had never seen the skyline so clearly before. Every skyscraper, bridge, and church building was a landmark of her beloved city. Was it too early to feel homesick? Everything felt strange as the ship gently lifted and fell with the waves, and she prayed she wouldn't succumb to seasickness once they reached open water.

They were accompanied by Bertie and Benedict Kincaid, the diplomat Inga had married. The *Infanta Isabella* was a Spanish ship, so they would be permitted to dock at Rotterdam without incident since Spain was considered a neutral nation.

Wind buffeted Delia's face, and she had to shout to be heard. "Do you know how to swim?" she asked Inga.

"Nope," she replied with a cheerful smile. "Do you?"

"No." It was yet another reason to worry. U-boats had torpedoed plenty of neutral ships. A shiver raced through her, and she tugged the lapels of her coat tighter. Every major decision she'd made in her life had been influenced by fear. If she'd been more courageous, she would have gone to law school. She would have walked away from Wesley years ago. She would have given the three hundred dollars to Finn, and they would have opened the kite store together, as partners.

Courage wasn't the absence of fear; it was moving forward despite the fear.

Inga gave her a friendly nudge. "The crossing will be fun! We'll have six days until we reach Rotterdam, and we can relax the whole way there. Tonight we'll have dinner at the captain's table, and in three days there will be a party to celebrate Halfway Night. It's always such a fabulous party."

The crossing wouldn't be a party for Delia. She had six days to study and master the Hague Conventions of 1899 and 1907, which Wesley believed contained the best legal strategies for freeing Mathilde. The book contained four hundred pages of legal analysis, commentaries, and appendices. It would be dry reading, but the real challenge would be convincing Inga's husband to use his influence to help Mathilde.

"I still can't believe you're married," Delia said.

Inga wiggled her left hand, showing off her wedding band. "Six months next week!"

How a woman as cheerful as Inga could be happy with a wet blanket like Benedict Kincaid was baffling. Delia had never seen Benedict crack a smile, and yet he was the man she needed to help save Mathilde.

"Are there any special tricks to getting on Benedict's good side?"

Inga gave her a curious look. "Why do you need to get on his good side?"

"Because Bertie won't lend his influence to help Mathilde. I thought Benedict might be more open to it."

"Did Finn put you up to this?"

Delia shook her head. "I want to help Mathilde because I admire her. I'm not brave enough to have done the sort of things she accomplished, but I want to help nonetheless."

It seemed God made some people to be warriors, while others

were destined to work quietly behind the front lines. Both roles had their purpose, she supposed, and there was honor in each one.

"What are you hoping Benedict can do?" Inga asked, looking confused.

"He knows all sorts of government ministers and military people. He knows the right things to say and how to cut through red tape. I can do research and planning, but the Germans would never negotiate with a woman. I need a man like Benedict to carry the torch."

Inga's face softened as she delivered the bad news. "He won't do it. Benedict becomes very focused while on a mission, and he agrees with Bertie about this. Trying to save one person will muddy the waters when the primary goal is to persuade the Germans to reopen the port to the CRB—something that will help millions of people."

Delia nodded, shifting her attention to the skyline of New York as the ship carried them farther away. Before they reached Europe, she needed to succeed in winning over Benedict, convincing him to negotiate Mathilde's release from prison. How odd that Finn's quest had now become hers as well. She shivered as another gust of wind snaked beneath her coat and sent a chill straight through her. Had Finn made it safely to France? If all went well, he should be there by now. She prayed he hadn't done something quixotic like stealing an airplane to launch an improbable rescue mission.

If nothing else, she needed to persuade Benedict to lend his help in stopping Finn from getting himself killed.

Delia spent the first three days of the voyage locked inside her cabin, studying the Hague Conventions. The windowless cabin was sparsely furnished with a bunk bed, a washbasin, and no room for anything else aside from her luggage. A small electric bulb, its fixture bolted to the wall, was the only source of light, and a blinding headache set in each day after a few hours of squinting at the endless columns of small text while the ship gently swayed.

Every time she was tempted to join the others for afternoon tea or games in the cardroom, she thought of Mathilde suffering far worse in a prison cell. Delia would rise to her feet, say a prayer for Mathilde, stretch her shoulders, then settle back on her bunk to keep reading. The only time she left her cabin was for meals or to pester Benedict.

She had appealed to him twice about lending his assistance with Mathilde, and both times he'd firmly rejected her. Just as Inga predicted, he refused to entertain anything that deviated from securing port access for the CRB.

A banging on her cabin door startled her. She went and opened it to see Inga's shining face.

"You're coming with me to celebrate Halfway Night in the smoking lounge," she announced.

The Halfway Night party seemed a pointless waste of time when there was work to be done. The fact that it was taking place in the smoking lounge made it even less tempting. Why did men need to torture people with those awful cigars?

"I already told you. That sort of party isn't—"

"No excuses!" Inga said. "What's so bad about spending a few hours of companionship with fellow members of the human race? Honestly, you sound as dreary as Benedict. I had to twist his arm to get him to come as well."

If Benedict was going to attend the party, Delia suddenly had a good reason for being there. Perhaps a third try would be the charm. Ten minutes later, she had changed into a pretty mauve dress and accompanied Inga to the smoking lounge. It was a spacious wood-paneled room belowdecks, lit with brass lanterns that sent a warm amber glow over the space.

An oversized chart of the Atlantic Ocean hung on the far wall. The position of their ship was marked with a glittery ribbon. Benedict sat at a table with Bertie and a few of the ship's officers, where

Benedict nursed a glass of water while the others all smoked. Tall, lanky, and darkly handsome, Benedict had perfected the imposing look of a starchy diplomat.

"Throwing a party for being halfway through a voyage is like celebrating the midpoint of a tooth extraction," Benedict said. "Everything is still painful, and the worst may be yet to come."

Inga laughed as she approached the men's table. "Hello, dear. Cheerful as ever, I see."

A glint of humor flashed but quickly disappeared from Benedict's stern face. "Technically, we're not halfway into the voyage. That won't happen until six o-clock tomorrow morning. Celebrating at this point is mere wishful thinking."

Bertie stood and gestured for her and Inga to join them at the table. Delia slipped in front of Inga to snatch the empty chair beside Benedict. It wouldn't do to start nagging him about helping Mathilde right away, but she could at least start looking for his elusive good side.

"I imagine you must have made this crossing dozens of times," she began.

"You imagine correctly." Benedict rotated his glass of water, and Delia waited for him to add something more, but he wasn't the talkative type.

"That's very impressive," she added. "You worked in the American Embassy in Berlin, correct?"

"Yes."

Once again, a perfect opening for him to engage in conversation like a normal human being but getting this man to loosen up was like trying to squeeze water from a stone.

The awkward discussion was interrupted when the ship's captain arrived. Captain Alverez was surprisingly young, although his face was already showing the deeply weathered look of a man who lived at sea. He carried a card in his hand.

"We have just received a message wired to the ship for Mr. Hoover," the captain said.

Personal messages delivered at sea were rare, and Bertie rose in concern.

"Relax," the captain hurried to say. "This message is cause for celebration. It is from the king of England himself, and it reads: 'Congratulations on three years of heroic work for the people of Belgium, and good luck in Rotterdam. Sir, the civilized world stands behind you.'"

Absolute silence lasted for about two seconds before people began clapping and cheering. Bertie looked dumbfounded as the captain handed the telegram to him and shook his hand.

"You should ask for a knighthood," Inga enthused, and Bertie grinned.

"I'm an American, so I can't be a knight."

"Then become a congressman," Benedict said, "maybe a senator. Washington could use a truly great man like yourself."

Bertie flushed a little. "Perhaps someday," he said modestly.

Inga moved to the sideboard. "This calls for a toast," she announced.

It appeared that, in addition to celebrating the midpoint of their journey, they were also celebrating the king's message. More corks were popped, and more cigars emerged.

Delia fought to keep the pleasant expression on her face, but she hated the stench of cigar smoke. Benedict looked equally annoyed. Perhaps this was her chance. She strolled to his side and asked, "Can I have a few moments of your time? The air is easier to breathe up on the main deck."

If Benedict was surprised, it didn't show on his aloof face. He merely gestured toward the door, and she led the way.

The air was indeed fresher up on deck, but it was also cold and windy. She should have brought a coat but wouldn't risk leaving Benedict alone to dart off to her cabin. She hugged herself against the chill and faced him.

"Well?" Benedict said, lifting a quizzical eyebrow.

"If we can secure access to the Port of Rotterdam, would you be willing to intercede on behalf of Mathilde Verhaegen?"

"Once again, Miss Byrne, my answer is no. It's a hopeless case."

"I've been studying treaties, and I believe there is hope. Article forty-six of the Hague Convention of 1907 emphasizes the protection of civilian rights."

Benedict remained unmoved. "The Germans will say her work distributing enemy propaganda made her a combatant."

"No, the Hague Convention outlines the criteria for enemy combatants, and Mathilde doesn't qualify. I found it very persuasive. Of course, it would sound better coming from you."

"No doubt. However, *Acta est fabula, plaudit.*"

Delia narrowed her eyes. She'd heard Wesley quote the classic Latin phrase enough to know it meant that the show was over, applaud and be done with it.

"The show is *not* over, and I won't applaud," Delia said. "I'll do all the research. You just have to show up and present it to the German authorities in Brussels. You will be a hero. Think of it."

"*Tua causa est desperato.*"

Delia rattled through her memory bank of Latin legal terms but came up empty. "What does that mean?"

"It means your cause is hopeless. Give up."

She wanted to shake him. Benedict hadn't been any warmer on her earlier attempts, and it was hard to keep flattering him. "I shall never forgive you for marrying Inga."

He shrugged. "Half the male population of New York hasn't forgiven me for marrying Inga, so I shall not wither beneath your disapproval."

"You are completely unworthy of her."

His firm mouth quirked a bit. "At last, Miss Byrne, we are in complete agreement." He turned and departed, leaving Delia alone in the moonlight with a handful of long-shot legal arguments that might work but with nobody to champion them.

27

I can't believe you want me to eat boiled snails," Finn said. He sat across from Theo Montgomery in a French café, where they lounged in wicker chairs on a patio overlooking the Moselle River. They were in Toul, home of the American 1st Pursuit Group. This was where a number of Finn's former comrades from the Lafayette Escadrille had been assigned.

Finn and Theo had always been like-minded when it came to appreciating a view and so had chosen a table on the patio despite the chilly April evening. The clinking of silverware from inside the restaurant, as well as the Frenchwoman bringing in her laundry off the lines across the street, were touchstones of blessed normality.

"Escargot isn't boiled; it's simmered," Theo said, piercing a glossy black snail with a tiny fork and gesturing with it. "They're steeped in a broth of wine and herbs, then finished with a dash of garlic butter and parsley. They're delicious. You should try it."

Even in uniform, Theo had the look of an aristocrat: immaculately shaved and groomed, with Macassar oil making his dark hair gleam. As for Finn, he no longer looked like the dashing pilot whose photograph had appeared in newspapers across the United

States. He was now dressed like an ordinary civilian, wearing a secondhand winter coat and sporting a short beard for warmth.

"I'll eat escargot for a solid week if you would leverage your family's reputation to help me spring Mathilde Verhaegen from prison," Finn replied.

With delicate precision, Theo pried another snail from its shell and popped it into his mouth. "I won't do anything unless you promise not to waste your life in a foolhardy quest to rescue her. Besides, offering to exchange your freedom for Mathilde's release will not work."

It felt as if the weight of an elephant had landed on Finn's chest, making it hard to suck in a fortifying breath of air. "Nevertheless, I'm determined to do it."

Finn's initial impulse had been to commandeer an airplane and bomb the area surrounding the prison to create a distraction. Then he would find a way into the prison and free Mathilde. But during the long hours crossing the stormy Atlantic Ocean, he'd had the good sense to reconsider this plan. It wouldn't work. If the prison came under attack, the Germans' first response would be to increase security of the place even more, which meant additional guards and weapons. Finn needed to come up with another way to free Mathilde, and offering to take her place in the prison was the most likely to succeed.

Theo tossed the snail fork down with a clatter. "Look, you and I have walked through fire together, but I can't let you do this. General Ryckman is as bad as they come. Last month he executed ten innocent Belgians in retaliation for a single German officer who'd been assassinated. He won't be interested in a swap for Mathilde's release."

Finn's gut twisted with anxiety at the prospect of what he was about to do. Voluntarily walking into a prison cell and letting the door slam shut behind him went against every instinct, but if it meant that Mathilde could go home to her children, he would do it. While the Germans sometimes killed downed pilots in the process of escaping, they had never executed one they'd taken into custody.

"It's me they want, not Mathilde. Ryckman offered clemency to anyone who helped me escape, provided I was turned over. They will make the trade."

Theo shook his head. "That was before they found out she was distributing copies of *La Libre Belgique*. Her trial date has been set for June, and there will be no mercy for her. She'll be executed, Finn, and your sacrifice will come to nothing. They'll keep you locked up in that cell until the end of the war." Theo's expression darkened. "If you survive that long."

Finn crossed his arms, pondering Theo's point. The Germans suffered a firestorm of bad publicity when they executed Edith Cavell. Photographs of the martyred English nurse provoked fury among the people of England and America.

"I'll be offering General Ryckman a deal. Executing Mathilde would only stoke international outrage, just like it did with Edith Cavell. But if I surrender myself to the Germans and offer to take Mathilde's place in prison, Ryckman can then defuse the situation while still coming out on top. He will claim the moral high ground by releasing her. And he'll get to clap me in chains, which is what he wants more than anything."

"And if you die in prison?"

Finn's mouth went dry. He didn't want to die, but how could he keep hiding when the woman who had saved his life was suffering in prison? If he could win Mathilde's release, she could go home to her children.

"If I die in exchange for letting Mathilde live to be a wise old lady, it will be a fair trade."

"And you want me to use my family's influence to help you with this insane plan?"

Theo's family fortune had been built on tobacco. They owned cigar factories in Cuba and tobacco plantations in North Carolina for cigarettes. Trade in cigars and cigarettes were among the most prized luxury goods in the wartime black market, and Theo's uncle did brisk trade in Belgium. His traders used forged Spanish passports to move freely within Belgium. If Finn could get his hands on one of those passports, he'd be able to pass through the checkpoints with a wink and a nod. The Germans looked the other way when black-market merchants came through because their officers were the biggest beneficiaries of the goods. Posing as a black-market trader would give Finn the chance to get to Brussels, where he could strike a deal with General Ryckman.

Finn locked eyes with Theo. "Get me one of those forged passports," he said, "and a supply of the best cigars you can find, and we'll both be heroes."

Finn got into Belgium the same way other members of the black market did: with a forged passport, a greased palm, and a wink. The Germans loved Cuban cigars, and those tempting rolled tobacco leaves proved the key to slipping inside Belgium.

It took ten days of travel by barge and on foot to reach Brussels. Everything in his life had been leading up to this point. This was his chance for redemption, the chance for his life to mean something more than flying kites or dropping bombs. He couldn't save his mother, but he could save Mathilde. This would be both the hardest and the best thing he'd ever done.

He was tired, grubby, and his feet ached from hiking the dusty footpaths along the Belgian canals. Once in Brussels, the cobbled streets rang with the clatter of hooves and the occasional sputter of motorcars weaving through knots of pedestrians. But as Finn turned the final corner and stepped into the Grand-Place, it seemed a hush had fallen over the city. The grand square, once a jewel of civic pride, lay in eerie stillness, its elegance dimmed by the pall of German occupation.

The ornate guildhalls with their colorful facades, steep gables, and baroque flourishes framed the square. This had once been the city's bustling marketplace, alive with flower stalls and the cheerful din of merchants and townsfolk. Now it bristled with Germans in uniform. Soldiers with rifles slung over their backs loitered at the bases of statues and smoked beneath gilded balconies, going about their day as if they belonged there.

Theo had told him the Grand-Place was one of the most beautiful squares in Europe, and despite everything, Finn could see it was true. The town hall stood at one end like a Gothic cathedral, its soaring spire laced with stone filigrees, its facade filled with weathered statues of saints and statesmen. It had once welcomed King Albert and echoed with the voices of elected officials. Now it housed the German High Command. And Finn was here to walk straight into the lion's den.

Golden light from the setting sun played tricks on the elaborate facade, making the stone figures appear almost alive, as if they were silently watching Finn approach. The flag of Imperial Germany hung above the front entrance, waving limply in the breeze. The red, black, and white flag with its imposing iron cross ratcheted Finn's nerves tighter. Two guards flanked the entrance, rifles at the ready.

He hardened his resolve, the steady drumbeat of his heart ticking off his last moments of freedom. Could he actually see this through? Trade his life for Mathilde's? A gust of wind sent a shiver down his spine. It would be cold in prison, but summer would come soon. He mustn't let piddly fears of hunger or cold discourage him. Mathilde had been enduring hunger and cold ever since she was arrested in January.

Oh, Delia, please forgive me for this . . .

Both German soldiers had spotted him, and Finn raised the palms of his hands as he approached them. An older guard with a wiry frame eyed him with cool suspicion, while the other shouldered his rifle and aimed it directly at Finn's chest.

"*Was ist dein name und was machst du hier,*" the older guard demanded.

Finn halted. "I don't speak German," he said in English, then repeated the phrase in French.

The wiry guard shouted something over his shoulder, and more guards rushed toward the front entrance, all of them bearing rifles aimed at Finn.

Finn kept his hands high in the air. "I need to speak with General Ryckman," he said as calmly as possible. "My name is Lieutenant Finn Delaney. The general has been searching for me."

"*Was hat er gesagt?*" the wiry guard barked at a young soldier with hair the color of corn silk and whose wide-eyed look reminded Finn of Clyde, the assistant working at his kite shop back home. The German soldier carried on a short conversation with the older guard before turning his attention back to Finn.

"Sergeant Amsler says you are the American pilot who escaped from Belgium last year," the young man said in lightly accented English. "He demands to know why you are here."

"I've come to offer General Ryckman a deal. I will only discuss it with the general himself."

Finn's hands, still held uncomfortably over his head, began to tremble. The visible sign of his fear was embarrassing, but with four rifles trained on him, he dared not lower them. The young translator engaged in another flurry of harsh-sounding dialogue with the lead guard before turning his attention back to Finn.

"We must take you into custody before any further discussion," the translator said.

This was to be expected, but Finn held his ground. "You need to know that many high-ranking people have been informed of my plan to come here," he said. "I've come to offer General Ryckman a trade. High-ranking prisoners have been traded before. If I'm killed, there will be consequences."

The translator nodded but still gave the go-ahead to the guards. One of them grabbed Finn by the shoulders, spun him around, and jerked his hands behind his back to clap manacles on his wrists.

Welcome to German territory, Finn thought grimly as he was frog-marched through the imposing front doors. Perspiration prickled his skin despite the clammy air inside the ancient stone building. Instead of throwing him behind bars, Finn was taken to a room that looked like an ordinary office with desks and metal filing cabinets. The four German soldiers plus the translator made the room feel cramped and claustrophobic.

The young soldier spoke first, his voice unexpectedly kind. "I am Corporal Conrad Ekhart. I will be translating for you. The sergeant insists you must be searched. He will remove your handcuffs, and then you must take off all of your clothing so it can be inspected."

Finn hadn't expected this, but he should have. He wasn't a shy man, but stripping down buck naked in front of five armed guards was disconcerting. His skin was still damp with sweat, and he shivered once all his clothes had been shed. He stared at the clock on the wall as every item of his clothing was turned inside out and passed around among the soldiers for examination.

After a few moments, he was allowed to dress again, then was ordered into a chair where he had one wrist shackled to the handle of a desk drawer.

"I'm sorry for the precautions," the translator said. Aside from the accent, the kid even sounded like Clyde from back home. He was also surprisingly curious. "Did you fly a Nieuport 17?"

"Nieuport 21," Finn replied. Both were French airplanes and among the finest in the world.

The young man sat casually, his hands braced on his knees as he leaned forward. "Was it scary?"

Not as scary as this moment, but there are worse things than being afraid.

"It wasn't so bad," Finn said but refused to say anything else. He couldn't afford to trust anyone, and this fresh-faced kid could be gathering information.

It was pitch-dark before the guards finally came for him. He was allowed to flex his wrists once they unlocked him from the desk drawer, and this time he was handcuffed with his hands in front of him rather than behind. The chain rattled as he was escorted down a dim corridor, footsteps echoing against the stone walls. An eerie calmness came over him. *"Do not be afraid; do not be discouraged, for the LORD your God will be with you wherever you go."*

A guard banged an iron knocker against a wooden door, then opened it to reveal a lavishly decorated room lined with dark wood paneling. Opulent rugs warmed the floor, but Finn's blood ran cold at the sight of General Ryckman, sitting behind a massive desk.

The general wore a dark dress uniform, adorned with silver epaulettes, gold braid, and a high-stand collar. His angular face was framed by perfectly groomed steel-gray hair, which made his piercing blue eyes seem even brighter. Ryckman would be considered a fine-looking man if one did not know about the corrosion in his soul.

"Welcome to Brussels, Lieutenant Delaney," General Ryckman said in perfect English. For a man who went to Oxford, the general could ape British manners but still had three years of barbaric occupation over the people of Belgium to answer for.

Finn raised his manacled hands. "Your hospitality is legendary."

"We intended no disrespect," General Ryckman replied. "Your sudden appearance naturally aroused alarm about potential security risks. Now that the surrounding area has been searched and our concerns put at ease, I confess I am curious as to why you are here."

"Mathilde Verhaegen," he said simply. "I am here to offer myself in her place."

A single quirk of his brow was the general's only hint of surprise. "You don't really expect us to allow her to walk out of prison as a free woman, do you?"

"I expect you to do whatever is in Germany's best interests. You are turning Mathilde Verhaegen into another Edith Cavell. If harm comes to her, every Belgian resistance group will double their efforts and rally more support to fight for their freedom. The fact

I have come here on this mission is no secret. If neither Mathilde nor I return home within the week, my friends will assume the worst. And I have friends in very high places. If you choose not to trade Mathilde for me, Berlin will hear of it, and they won't be pleased that you threw away a clean, quiet resolution."

"The woman in question will be going to trial soon. It would be a corruption of our legal system for me to interfere."

"But you have that ability, General," Finn said. "As the military governor of Belgium, you are able to grant clemency."

General Ryckman nodded. "I do indeed. I can also order you to be imprisoned." He snapped his fingers, and the two guards near the door came to attention. "Escort Lieutenant Delaney to Saint-Gilles Prison and lock him up."

The abrupt command drove the breath from Finn's lungs. But there was nothing he could do as the guards seized him and forced him out the door.

28

Delia found Rotterdam to be a charming surprise. Warehouses along the waterfront were interspersed with stately homes and the spires of cathedrals. Although the war held most of Europe in its grasp, the neutral port of Rotterdam was a little haven of peace, albeit an uneasy peace.

Bertie reserved the top floor of a rooming house for the CRB delegation. The stairs creaked as Delia and Inga headed up a twisting staircase to the third floor, where four bedrooms led off a square landing. With narrow hallways, low ceilings, and wavering glass windows, the house was surely hundreds of years old. Her bedroom was charming, with a slanted roof and a window overlooking a walled garden behind the house. Ivy climbed on the old red bricks, a linden tree shaded the patio, and the first tulips of the season already provided splashes of red and yellow in the garden. Normally she would have loved the chance to savor the oasis of greenery, but the landlady had declared her garden strictly off-limits to guests.

It didn't matter. They were here on a mission that did not include springtime evenings in an enchanted garden.

Inga helped Delia unpack and was in a typically sunny mood. "My husband learned that Baron Werner von Eschenbach is on his way to Rotterdam to help with negotiations," Inga said as she lifted Delia's maroon walking suit from the trunk. "He's German and is willing to lean on General Ryckman to reopen the port to American shipments."

Inga went on to explain how Benedict had a long-standing friendship with the baron, who had been an Anglophile since birth. When war looked inevitable, Baron von Eschenbach traveled to London to negotiate for a delay before the formal declaration of war. He failed and ended up imprisoned for more than a year by the British. It took a good deal of diplomacy on Benedict's part to win the baron's release through a prisoner exchange.

Delia secretly hoped she might eventually persuade him to help with Mathilde, but CRB business came first.

The rooming house had only a cramped dining room with no windows, prompting Bertie to reserve an outdoor table at a bistro a few streets away. It was a warm spring evening, and their table overlooked a canal.

Evidence of Rotterdam's cosmopolitan atmosphere was everywhere. German voices mingled with Dutch, French, and English. The table beside them was filled with exiled Russian aristocrats, smoking cigarillos and engaged in zealous conversation. Benedict, who spoke a little Russian, said they were speculating on whether the dowager empress would attempt to flee Russia.

"Why hasn't she left already?" Inga asked.

"She refuses to believe her son is dead," Benedict replied. "Time is growing short, for the Bolsheviks will eventually conquer Crimea too. Then the dowager will end up dead like her son."

"Why must you always be so grim?" Inga said in exasperation.

Benedict slanted his wife a sardonic expression. "It is a thankless job, but someone must be the bearer of bad news."

The typically dour comment prompted Inga to lunge across the table and plant a series of quick kisses on Benedict's stern mouth. Delia had to move her teacup lest it fall victim to Inga's impulsive show of affection.

It was sweet actually. Even the usually sour Benedict was trying not to laugh as Inga planted a final peck on the top of his head before returning to her chair. It gave Delia an unobstructed view of the joy on Benedict's face as he gazed at his wife. It triggered an ache deep inside her.

Where are you, Finn? Why did you have to leave me?

Maybe it was simply the beauty of the evening that made her longing for Finn become a physical ache. She had been lonely most of her adult life, yet it was different now. To have known the warmth of his love, only to revert abruptly to her former solitude had left her feeling adrift in a colder, emptier world.

Bertie brought the meeting to order. "Let's get down to brass tacks," he said. "I propose we offer to hire Dutch citizens from Rotterdam to check the shipments coming in from America. It ought to reassure General Ryckman that we aren't smuggling armaments to the Belgians."

"Germans don't believe in simply *checking*," Benedict said curtly. "Either a thorough inspection is carried out or they consider it worthless."

"We can hardly demand thousands of crates be opened and searched on each incoming ship," Bertie said. "Random checks performed by neutral parties ought to prove our integrity."

"It won't," Benedict said. "Germany will be taking a risk by opening the port to us and will want something in exchange for letting CRB ships dock here. Baron von Eschenbach will join us soon, and he'll have an insider's view of what Germany wants."

"He'd better get here quickly," Bertie said. "We have tons of wheat waiting to be delivered, and with a damp spring, it is in danger of sprouting mold unless we can get it off-loaded quickly."

According to Inga, Baron von Eschenbach was well connected with everyone at the German court and had powerful sway in the military. Delia prayed he would arrive soon, so that she might formulate a plan for Mathilde before Finn got himself into trouble.

Finn jerked awake at the metallic sound of a lock being opened. He bolted upright on the cot, bracing himself for whoever was about to enter his cell. Even after the door creaked open, all he could see was the silhouette of a man standing in the opening. After endless days of imprisonment, his eyes were so accustomed to the dark that the sliver of light nearly blinded him.

"It's just me," the man said in lightly accented English. "Conrad Ekhart, the translator. Do you remember me?"

How could he forget? Finn had been in solitary confinement ever since that first day when he'd stupidly thought it might be possible to reason with General Ryckman. The days had melded together with nothing to do except count his regrets and dwell on how cold he was in this dank, underground cell. The only furnishings were a cot with canvas stretched between two iron supports, but with no mattress and no blanket. He wore the same grubby clothes he arrived in, and his toilet was a metal bowl in the corner.

Conrad seemed like a decent man, but a prickly sensation of fear zinged along Finn's nerve endings, making him clench his fists. They wouldn't have sent a translator unless something was about to happen.

"I remember you," Finn acknowledged, grateful to have someone to talk with. None of the guards who brought him food spoke English. They usually rattled off a few German words as they set a plate of boiled turnips on the floor, their staccato voices echoing off the stone walls of his cell. Finn tried to communicate using pantomime, along with basic French and English words. He was desperate to know what was going on in the world and if Mathilde's trial had happened. It had been scheduled for June, but Finn no longer knew what day it was.

"We are here to get you cleaned up," Conrad said, and for the first time Finn noticed two soldiers standing behind Conrad. They had their hands on their holstered pistols. "I gather it's been awhile since you had a shower."

Finn estimated that it had been more than a month. After infiltrating Belgium, he'd been too busy hiding in hedgerows and avoiding crowds to risk approaching a hotel for a bath and a bed. Once imprisoned, he was given only a few tin cups of water a day, and they were too precious to waste on bathing.

"I won't resist a shower," he said, still cautious. Something was about to take place, and they were cleaning him up for it.

After he'd been handcuffed, Finn trailed Conrad down a narrow corridor. Both guards were grim-faced and heavily armed. Finn concentrated on placing his footsteps carefully lest a stumble alarm the guards.

The lavatory was brightly lit and lined entirely with white tiles. A row of sinks lined one wall, with high spigots along the opposite wall for showers. Electric bulbs glowed overhead, and the only window was covered with iron bars, a stark reminder that he was still trapped in Saint-Gilles Prison.

"Once you have showered, you will be provided with clean clothes," Conrad said.

"Why?" He didn't want to look a gift horse in the mouth, but something was going on.

"General Ryckman wants a photograph of you so that he can prove to the world you are alive and not being mistreated."

That was a debatable point. Though Finn hadn't been beaten or starved, isolation in a dark, dank cell had tested his limits. As for food, he'd been given nothing but turnips. He'd lost so much weight that his trousers were in danger of slipping off his hips.

"Fine," he said agreeably. He wanted the shower but had no intention of sitting for a photograph. General Ryckman wanted a photograph for propaganda purposes only.

"Once you undress, we will take your clothing and give you privacy to bathe," Conrad said. "We will be right outside and will return with clean clothes."

Finn nodded his agreement, and one of the guards removed his handcuffs. Getting out of the filthy clothes was a relief. He no longer cared about modesty as he tugged off his remaining clothes and nudged them toward the guard, whose face twisted in disgust as he picked them up.

The tile was hard and cold beneath his feet as he padded to the shower area and twisted the knob. Water gurgled and knocked in the pipes, then hissed as spurts of water emerged high above Finn's head. After a moment, the noise stopped, and the warm water came through strong and steady.

Finn let out a breath he didn't realize he'd been holding as he let the water cascade over his head and down his body; rivulets of grime swirling down the drain.

Had anything ever felt so good? He soaped up quickly, scrubbing and rinsing his hair three times, praying the water would stay warm. It was harsh lye soap but still felt heavenly as he lathered every inch of his body. Warmth seeped into his aching muscles, which had grown stiff from disuse. The shower was a luxury beyond all words. If he was lucky enough to survive the war, he'd never take the gift of a hot shower for granted again.

He was turning his face back toward the spigot, savoring the fall of the water, when a knock on the door interrupted his enjoyment.

"Hurry up in there," Conrad said. "The photographer is here."

With reluctance, Finn twisted the knob for the shower. He remained beneath the spigot, letting the last trickle of water slide down his face and then his chest. He reached for a towel as Conrad returned.

"Here is a fresh set of clothes," Conrad said, dropping a bundle of clothing on the wood bench beneath the window.

Finn froze. Beneath the trousers, shirt, and undergarments was a leather jacket. A pilot's jacket. It was a clear indication that General Ryckman intended to make the most of capturing the pilot whose escape had proven such an embarrassment.

"You can bring my old clothes back," Finn said as he dried himself with the towel. "I don't mind wearing them."

Conrad gave little laugh. "But we mind smelling them. I think they've already been burned."

Finn, who wasn't about to walk out of the lavatory naked, tugged on the plain cotton drawers, then the trousers. The clothes were in good condition, although clearly not new. Finn tried not to think about the previous owner, probably a fellow prisoner who was now lying in a grave somewhere.

"Tell me about Mathilde Verhaegen." Finn had been kept ignorant of any developments, but her trial was probably drawing near.

Conrad gave a nervous laugh. "I'm afraid I don't keep well informed. I waste too much time reading novels instead of newspapers. At least that's what my mother always said."

"So the trial hasn't happened yet?"

"I don't know anything," Conrad said again with a shrug. "Come, you need to put that jacket on, and then we will visit the photographer."

Prickles of sweat broke out across Finn's body. Conrad seemed too emphatic. He had glanced away rather than meet Finn's eyes.

"Please," Finn implored, "could you find a newspaper or ask around about the case? I need to know." He'd sacrificed everything for Mathilde. He'd lost his freedom and a future in the Army. He'd lost *Delia*. He had to know if his sacrifice had meant anything at all.

Conrad sighed and met Finn's gaze. "Lieutenant Delaney, I truly don't know what has happened to the lady. Everything is censored here, so it should not be surprising that we are kept in the dark."

Finn's limbs felt unbearably heavy, and he dropped onto the wooden bench, unable to stand. He came to Belgium to rescue Mathilde and had lost everything. The Germans would keep him locked up until Mathilde's fate was decided. It would have been better to use his influence from his home in New York rather than be in prison, helpless under General Ryckman's control. Now his photograph was going to be circulated around the world, proof of his humiliation. He'd been reckless, arrogant, and stupid—a dangerous combination.

He raised his head and looked at Conrad. "Do you think I'm an idiot for trying to take her place?"

"I think you're the bravest man I know."

Finn grimaced. Yes, he had been brave, but it would have been better if he'd used a fraction of Delia's common sense before plowing ahead with his risky scheme. He scrubbed a hand over his jaw and stared at the pilot's jacket and white silk scarf. The silk lining of the jacket had a German label stitched to it, although the collar had been altered to look like an American-made jacket. The Germans were doing their best to stage this photo with utmost care.

"Please," Conrad said, "let them take the photo. It is going to go badly for you if you don't cooperate, and they will eventually get their photo anyway."

Finn stood, his spirit heavy as he scooped up the scarf and jacket. "Let's go."

The photographer was a woman. Wearing slim-fitting trousers, a man's shirt, and with her dark hair styled in a short bob, Fräulein Kolbe was surprisingly pretty. She spoke English as well. With one hand propped on her hip and holding a small box camera in the other, she flashed him a saucy smile.

"This won't take long," she said. "Just stand in front of that wall and look miserable. Then we can get out of here. Oh, and put the jacket on."

"No," he said. He still carried the jacket and scarf slung over his shoulder as he entered the private office. It was easy to see why they had brought him here. The room was an ordinary office with a wooden desk and a few chairs, but sunlight flooded through the large window, and the plain white wall opposite the desk worked as a suitable backdrop. The lighting and backdrop were perfect.

Now all they needed was a humiliated American pilot, but Finn wouldn't play along. He folded his arms across his chest, and Fräulein Kolbe sensed his unwillingness.

She spoke in a cajoling tone. "Come on, fly-boy. Don't make this difficult." She strolled to a tripod and screwed her camera into place. "The general is going to get his photograph whether you cooperate or not. Just put on the jacket and scarf and look dashing for the camera, or I can get those two thugs over there to help me out."

There wasn't much point in refusing to put on the jacket. There were other ways Finn could deprive General Ryckman of his propaganda photograph.

"All right," he said agreeably and shrugged into the jacket. It looked like an American pilot's jacket but felt all wrong. The leather was too stiff, too heavy. It smelled strange too. He ignored the smell and draped the white scarf around his neck.

"Where do you want me?" he asked, and Fräulein Kolbe flashed a lascivious smile his way.

"I'd take you anywhere I could get you, but for now, let's stand in front of the wall. Then give me your most mournful look. Think of a girl back home. Or maybe your mother. They're both probably missing you about now. Yes?"

Memories of Delia roared to life. So did guilt about his mother. Regret warred with yearning, but he didn't let it show as he took his place in front of the blank wall.

He met Fräulein Kolbe's frank gaze and flashed her a wink and a grin.

She captured the shot. "Very nice," she said. "I'll keep that one for myself. Now let's have a properly miserable one for General Ryckman, yes?"

Finn turned his shoulders a bit and slanted her a taunting smile.

"That's not doing it," Fräulein Kolbe said. "Come now. Surely it hasn't been fun being locked up in a dungeon for twelve days. Let's see some gloom."

It had been only twelve days? It felt much longer than that.

Fräulein Kolbe sighed and said something in German to one of the guards, who hopped off the edge of the desk and drove his fist deep into Finn's gut.

Stars flashed before his eyes, and he folded inward. Then came another fist, hard as iron, slamming into his side just above a kidney.

The air from his lungs violently expelled, and he went down on his knees. Everything blurred as a sharp pain rolled through his middle, making it impossible to draw another breath. Dimly, through a haze of agony, Conrad rambled out a string of angry orders to the guard. Was he egging the guard on or was it a reprimand?

The reality of the situation sank in. He was completely helpless, and they would probably get their miserable photo of him sooner or later.

But he wouldn't make it easy for them. He'd lose a piece of his soul if he cooperated. They could beat him to a pulp, but he wouldn't willingly give the Krauts the picture they wanted.

He flinched when another man knelt beside him, but it was Conrad, offering his shoulder to help him up. Finn got his right foot flat on the wooden floor and pushed himself upright. The soldier who had punched him watched with a smirk, while Fräulein Kolbe stood to the side, her face inscrutable as she watched events unfold.

"Want to try again?" he asked the woman. "I'll keep smiling through whatever you can dish out. If you want a photo of me looking small and humble, you'll have to beat me bloody, and that kind of thing shows up in photographs."

"You don't have to make it this hard," Conrad said. "All we want is a photo of you the general can use to help boost the morale of our people. It won't be circulated outside of Germany."

That was a lie. The general would send the photo to the four corners of the globe to show that they had triumphed over the American pilot, who briefly got the better of them.

"Forget it," Finn said. "Ryckman won't pass up the chance to humiliate me or Mathilde however he can."

A shadow crossed over Conrad's face. "Don't torture yourself over that woman, my friend. She is beyond your help." The breath froze in Finn's throat, and he stared at Conrad, who averted his eyes and said, "I lied when I told you I knew nothing of her fate. Mathilde Verhaegen was found guilty of sedition and aiding in the escape of an Allied pilot. She was executed three days ago. I'm sorry."

The strength left Finn's knees, and he slid down the wall to slump onto the floor. Mathilde, that brave woman . . . dead because she had rescued him. Her children would grow up without her. Little Jeannette was now an orphan.

The camera clicked, and Fräulein Kolbe smiled as she set her camera aside.

They had their photo.

29

After waiting three interminable days, Baron Werner von Eschenbach blew into Rotterdam with the force of a cheerful spring storm. The middle-aged man retained a trim physique, apparently from a life of sailing and playing polo. A few strands of silver in his chestnut hair were the only sign of his age. According to Inga, the baron's charm had been honed to perfection from flirting with ladies all across Europe, a skill he was determined to practice with their surly landlady in the hope of cajoling her into opening her garden to them.

"Come, Mrs. Holzhauer," the baron said to the thick-necked landlady, "your garden is a treasure that should be shared, especially in times like these. And look! You have five seats at your garden table, and there are five of us. Coincidence, yes?"

The landlady's eyes hardened. "No, sir. I once opened the garden to a visiting group of Italian diplomats, and by the end of the day, they'd trampled my daffodils."

Delia shifted impatiently. They needed to start their long-delayed discussions and could simply go across the street to a café rather than waste time haggling with Mrs. Holzhauer. Their entire group was crowded into the downstairs hallway, eager to get started. Who cared that the garden was so beautiful it could compete with Eden? Even the eternally good-natured Bertie Hoover was growing impatient with Baron von Eschenbach's determination to gather together in the walled garden instead of at a café.

"You need not fear the health of your daffodils," the baron told the landlady. "The daffodil is nature's way of smiling, and we all appreciate its delicate beauty. Mrs. Holzhauer, you are to be commended for the glory of this garden, and I, along with my fellow boarders, would like to use this blessed oasis to work toward bringing peace to the world."

The baron's lavish praise finally worked, but Mrs. Holzhauer still looked stern as she unlocked the door to her backyard garden and permitted them inside.

"Not one bloom is to be plucked," she warned, and Baron von Eschenbach bowed to kiss the back of the landlady's hand.

"Didn't I tell you he was good at negotiating?" Inga whispered to Delia, and a surge of optimism bloomed inside Delia's chest. She hurried forward to swipe a few cherry blossom petals from the seats, their faint, powdery scent lingering in the air.

The barrage of charm from Baron von Eschenbach continued when he brought out a bottle of champagne, a wedge of Gouda cheese, and a box of Swiss chocolates. "Compliments of the black market," he teased as he removed the wire cage from the top of the champagne bottle. Inga sliced the cheese while Bertie popped a square of dark chocolate into his mouth.

The baron's clipped British accent made it hard to believe he was German as he gestured for them to sit. "My friends, we have a challenging task ahead of us," he said while pouring champagne into the tumblers provided by the landlady. "But first, a toast. The friendship between us is genuine despite the differences between our nations. I pray to Almighty God that once peace has been found, we can reach across man-made borders and keep our friendships alive."

"Hear, hear," Bertie said, and all stood to clink their glasses.

Delia's nose wrinkled at the bite of tart champagne, yet everything else about their garden sanctuary was lovely. Bees droned as they whizzed among the blooms, and the sun was warm on her shoulders. A light breeze blew through the garden, causing more cherry petals to float to the ground. The beauty that surrounded them was a reminder of God's bounty, and yet, only a few miles outside of the neutral nation, the war cast a shadow of hunger, fear, and death.

"Don't expect your flattery to work so easily on General Ryckman," Benedict said. "Negotiating with Ryckman is a zero-sum game, and he views any concession as a sign of weakness. He will want something in return for allowing CRB shipments into Rotterdam, and we don't have the authority to give him anything."

"We can give him credit as a humanitarian," Bertie said. "Condemnation against Germany is gathering near universal momentum, and that will be exacerbated if he insists on blocking much-needed food and supplies from getting into Belgium."

"The problem is that Ryckman doesn't care," Benedict stressed. "Now that the revolution has knocked Russia out of the war, he has renewed hope that Germany can win."

"But Kaiser Wilhelm cares," Bertie said. "His concern is his reputation after the war is over—*that* is what he cares about. His cousin is the king of England. He doesn't want to be known as a leader who took bread out of the mouths of children."

"Then why can't we appeal directly to the kaiser?" Delia asked.

An abrupt silence descended among those gathered around the table. Given the amused expression on the men's faces, apparently she had said something stupid or naive, but perhaps her ignorance of diplomatic matters could be an advantage. Nine million starving people was worth their charting new territory to find solutions.

"Kaiser Wilhelm would consider such things beneath him," Benedict finally answered. "General Ryckman is the man overseeing occupied Belgium, and our request must begin and end with the general."

Baron von Eschenbach helped himself to another slice of cheese. "And the general ought to be in a good mood now that he has finally captured that American pilot."

The bottom dropped out of Delia's stomach, and she stared at the baron. "W-what American pilot?"

"That fellow who has been making a name for himself all over the United States," the baron said. "There are leaflets with the poor chap's photo all over Germany. He looks awful." He paused, a sudden note of concern on his face. "I'm sorry . . . have I said something amiss?"

"We are well acquainted with the American pilot of whom you speak," Bertie said.

Delia clenched the arms of her chair, but she must not panic. "What do you mean by 'he looks awful'?"

The churning in her stomach grew worse as the baron described the propaganda pamphlet that was circulating throughout Germany. It boasted how General Ryckman had captured and imprisoned the pilot who escaped last year, then recklessly entered Belgium to sabotage German lines of supplies. The supposedly heroic American had collapsed quickly once he'd been captured.

Delia turned her face away as the baron spoke but forced herself to keep listening to the excruciating details published in the pamphlet. The part about sabotage was clearly a lie to disguise Finn's true objective in trying to win Mathilde's freedom.

She wanted to smash something, flip the table over, yell at the sky. Instead, she ignored her anger and frustration and turned her gaze to Bertie. "We *have* to do something to save Finn," she insisted on a shaky breath.

"I'm sorry, Delia, but he's beyond our help," Bertie replied, not unkindly but the words still scorched. "Our mission in coming to Europe is to secure relief supplies for Belgium by seeing that the port is reopened. We can do nothing that will endanger or delay that objective."

Bertie was right, of course. Her mind told her that their mission was to keep relief supplies flowing into Belgium, but inside, her heart was breaking.

As soon as the shock of Finn's imprisonment faded, Delia and Inga headed into town in search of the German pamphlet boasting of Finn's capture. As a neutral country, the Netherlands allowed publications of propaganda from both sides of the war. Soon she had the terrible photograph in her hands. The dashing young man she had fallen in love with now looked defeated and destroyed as he slumped against a wall. She wanted to embrace him and soothe his fears, and at the same time she wanted to shake him until his teeth rattled.

They sat in the rooming house's garden, where Inga translated the article for her, which of course was written in German. It claimed Finn had been caught sabotaging German supply lines. It wasn't until after he'd been captured and brought to headquarters that the villain was recognized as Finn Delaney, the American pilot who had escaped from Belgium the previous year.

It was physically impossible for her to remain in cozy Rotterdam while Finn was being held in prison. It might not have been so bad if she hadn't seen the photograph, but nobody with a beating heart could see the desolation in Finn's eyes and remain unmoved.

"I'm going to Brussels," she announced to Inga. She set the pamphlet on the garden table, where only a few hours earlier she'd been sharing a festive meal with the others. Enjoying the beauty of this peaceful garden felt like a betrayal of Finn.

"Won't Bertie need you here in Rotterdam?"

Delia bit her lip. The entire reason she'd been brought to the Netherlands was because she was a skilled secretary knowledgeable about the CRB. But Inga was also a skilled secretary. She could step into Delia's shoes and even provide translation services for Bertie if necessary.

"Could we swap places?" she asked Inga. "You'll work for Bertie

231

in Rotterdam while I accompany Benedict and Baron von Eschenbach to Brussels?"

A guarded look came over Inga's face. "To what end?"

How could Delia explain? She shouldn't abandon her post to go on a personal mission, but she had a better understanding of what had compelled Finn's desire to rescue Mathilde. "I want to see Finn and let him know he hasn't been abandoned or forgotten." The last time she saw Finn was at the Port of New York, where she vowed never to forgive him if he left. That mustn't be the last time he saw her on this earth. "Will they let me visit him in the prison?"

Inga looked skeptical. "Benedict was able to visit Allied prisoners in Germany, but that was because the United States was still neutral and he had a diplomatic pass."

"He *still* has a diplomatic pass," Delia pointed out. "Perhaps I could accompany him as his secretary."

"They may not let him through now that we're at war," Inga cautioned. "Do you want to go all the way to Brussels and take the risk of being turned away?"

Delia would risk anything to see Finn again. "Absolutely. If I have to walk through fire or crawl over broken glass, I'm going to find a way to get through to Finn."

30

F inn braced his hands on the cold granite wall of his cell, standing on tiptoes to quietly speak through a rusty ventilation pipe near the ceiling. The pipe's opening was about the size of a baseball, and it had become his lifeline, a conduit connecting him to Father Gerhardt in the neighboring cell.

"Are you still praying for our enemies?" Finn whispered in a sardonic tone.

"Of course," the priest replied, his voice drifting softly through the pipe. If they spoke too loudly, it might alert the guards, and then Finn's only source of joy in this dank, dark world would be snatched away.

"Doesn't the Bible say that if your enemy is hungry, give him food to eat, and if he's thirsty, give him water to drink?" Finn asked. "I'm still waiting for the Krauts to give us more food and water."

"Perhaps they will if you stop referring to them as *Krauts*," the priest gently reprimanded from the other side of the ventilation pipe.

These rambling conversations had been going on since the morning after Finn arrived, when he was awakened by a harsh whisper in the night. *Is anybody there?* the voice asked repeatedly in French, and it was tinged with hope.

That was the beginning of a friendship built on hushed exchanges through the pipe at the top of his cell wall. The camaraderie Finn shared with his fellow prisoner was a gift from God, a reminder that even the darkest of nights held a glimmer of good in them.

Father Gerhardt had been here ever since being arrested six months ago. He was born and raised in Germany but slipped across the border into Belgium to carry messages of reconciliation to the Belgians. "The German Army called it treason, but Jesus said, 'Blessed are the peacemakers, for they will be called children of God.' I came to Belgium so that I might be a warrior for peace."

Finn gave a cynical laugh. "I'm the other kind of warrior. The kind called to take up arms and drive the invaders back to where they belong. I couldn't look the other way while the innocent suffered. It would be a betrayal of our duty to love our neighbor."

They could debate such philosophical questions for hours. When he and Delia discussed the war, all they did was argue. Father Gerhardt was different. He tried to convince Finn through using kind, gentle words of wisdom. "Violence begets violence, Finn. Turning the other cheek is not weakness, but the greatest act of courage. Words can build bridges where bombs can only destroy."

Finn pondered the priest's words during his endless hours of captivity. Never had he needed Father Gerhardt's companionship more than after learning of Mathilde's execution. The bravest woman in all of Belgium had been shot to death by a firing squad, and it was entirely Finn's fault.

As usual, Father Gerhardt had a unique angle for understanding what happened. "Finn, we cannot know the depths of God's plan or why you and Mathilde were set on a path that collided in that muddy field. Mathilde's sacrifice and your role in her life are threads woven into the tapestry of God's greater design.

The world is unfolding as it should. Mathilde fought the good fight, she has finished her race, and now she is with God as her reward."

Though the priest's wise counsel helped some, Finn still wanted revenge. He itched to escape his cell, hop back into an airplane, and bomb every German encampment in Belgium to smithereens.

Still, Father Gerhardt did help him with seeing the other side of the story. He was the only German friend Finn ever had, and listening to the old man talk about his life growing up in a small village was fascinating. Gerhardt came of age hiking in the Black Forest, fishing in its streams, and learning woodworking skills in the village's cuckoo-clock workshops.

"My job was to carve wooden leaves and acorns to decorate the clocks," Father Gerhardt reminisced. "I loved celebrating nature in the carvings because there is nowhere more beautiful than the forests of Germany."

"Are they different from other forests?"

He chuckled. "Maybe not," he conceded. "But when I imagine heaven, I believe it will look much like the Black Forest with its great canopy of leaves and sunlit glades. I dream of those wonderful forests at night and long to return to them."

The patter of footsteps sounded outside his cell. Finn dropped onto the mattress, praying that whoever was coming hadn't heard the whispered conversation. He held his breath as the clank of a key turned in his cell-door lock.

"*Hoch!*" the guard ordered.

It probably meant *up*. Finn didn't know German, but whenever a guard opened his door, they always shouted *hoch*, and Finn always rose, which seemed the proper response.

It wasn't time for the daily delivery of turnips, so he stood there motionless, straining to see if a translator was with the guard. But the thin sliver of light shining behind the guard almost completely blinded him.

"*Kommen*," the guard said. When Finn didn't respond, the

guard repeated the word and gestured for him to come out of the cell. There were in fact other men behind the guard. He could make out their silhouettes, and it looked as though they had weapons trained on him.

Finn cautiously stepped from the cell, squinting against the glare. After clamping handcuffs on him, they nudged him forward.

Father Gerhardt, please pray for me, he thought.

Aside from the delivery of turnips and water each morning, Finn had been ignored since the day they'd told him of Mathilde's execution. That had been, what, ten days ago? Fifteen maybe? It was impossible to guess in his cell where he never saw the sun as the days blended into nights.

Something was about to happen. He feared it as much as he was desperate for change. All his senses went on alert as they neared the end of the dim hallway. Keys jangled as the guard unlocked another door, and then he was led up a stairway.

He quickly grew winded from the climb. Once at the top of the stairs, guards on either side of him seized his arms and steered him toward a door at the end of a corridor. They opened the door and led him into a room flooded with sunlight glaring off white walls. Lots of people were inside. He squinted, trying to determine if they were soldiers or civilians, but still couldn't see much aside from their silhouettes.

One of them had the frame of a woman, and she approached him.

"Finn?" she asked.

He jerked to attention. That was definitely a female voice. His eyes slowly adjusted, and he blinked rapidly against the sun streaming through the windows. She was slim, had dark hair and a heart-shaped face. She reminded him of Delia, and a sad, wistful feeling arose within him.

"You look like my girl from back home," he said.

"Oh, Finn . . . I *am* your girl from back home."

He would have fallen over if the guards didn't have him by both his arms. A million thoughts cascaded through his brain. How did she get here? Was the war over? The chain on his handcuffs rattled as he reached out for her.

Instantly, guards jerked him backward, and Delia winced. A flurry of German commands was pretty good indication that he'd done something wrong.

"We're not allowed to touch each other," Delia hurried to say. "It was part of the conditions we agreed to for the visit to occur."

"We?" He glanced at the other men in the room, all of them wearing the ordinary attire of civilians. Not one of the men was familiar.

"This is Benedict Kincaid and Baron von Eschenbach," she said, gesturing to two of the men. "The others are here from the German Consulate. Benedict was able to get authorization for a visit based on the Hague Convention of 1907."

Finn had no idea what the Hague Convention was, but if it allowed him to see Delia, he'd say it was the greatest document in the history of mankind.

"It's good to see you," he finally stammered in what was surely the understatement of the century.

Finn was directed to sit in a hard-backed chair at a plain wooden table. Delia took a seat opposite him, sitting between her two companions.

The man named Benedict spoke first. "Are you being treated well?"

Finn glanced at the Germans standing at the far side of the room, watching. Did they speak English? It was impossible to know, so he took care with his response.

"I'm being fed," he said. "I doubt I'll have much of an appetite for turnips after this is all over, but I haven't been beaten or deprived of sleep."

"I saw a photograph of you taken in the prison," Delia said. "You didn't look good."

He should have expected it but knowing she'd seen the pathetic photograph was humiliating. No man wanted to be seen at the worst moment of his life.

"That was right after they told me about Mathilde's execution," he said, the words sour in his mouth.

Benedict leaned closer, and his eyes flashed. "Did you say 'Mathilde's execution'?"

"Yes. They told me about the guilty verdict in her case, and how they executed her right after, just like they did with Edith Cavell."

Delia's jaw dropped. "They didn't execute Mathilde, Finn. She's alive and well in this very prison. We met with her just this morning."

For a moment, the words didn't register. It was too strange, too impossible. He stared at Delia, the only person in the room he trusted.

"What? Repeat that please?"

"Mathilde is alive. Her trial isn't until next week."

"You're sure? It wasn't some woman they had dressed up like her to fool you?"

Delia gave a little laugh. "We're sure. We brought her attorney to the meeting to discuss the charges against her. Yes, we're quite sure it was Mathilde."

A shuddering breath escaped Finn, relief warring with anger. He should never have trusted anything the Germans told him. They had manipulated him just to get that lousy photo. They'd lied to him, and he fell for it. He'd been mourning Mathilde when all along she had been right here under the same roof as him.

"What are her odds of beating the charges?" he asked, knowing she was still in a dire situation.

"Not good," Benedict said. "She was caught red-handed with the illicit newspapers hidden in her house. She has not denied knowledge of them or of aiding in your escape."

Finn glanced at Delia. "Is there anything you can do for her? Get Bertie to appeal for clemency? Or maybe the Red Cross?"

Delia was about to say something, but Benedict raised a hand, cutting her off. "We've come to Brussels to appeal to General

Ryckman to reopen the Port of Rotterdam. We can't muddy the waters with personal appeals."

A tightening in Finn's chest became painful. He should have realized that Delia was here on CRB business, but he couldn't stop fighting for Mathilde. "Dee? Is there nothing you can do?"

"We're meeting with General Ryckman tomorrow," she said. "I'll try to—"

Again, Benedict raised a hand and shot her a glare. "Our mission with Ryckman has a single objective," he reiterated. "We *must* get the port made accessible again to the CRB, and that's all that can be said on the matter. You only have ten minutes to speak with Delia, so don't squander your time. I'm sorry we aren't able to grant you privacy, but please don't waste these few minutes worrying about Mathilde."

Delia managed a brave smile for him, and all of a sudden each second felt precious. After weeks of agony, languishing in his cell, God had smiled on him and let him gaze at the most precious sight in the entire world.

"You look good, Dee."

"Thank you." Humor and sympathy glowed in her impossibly blue eyes. "I wish I could say the same about you."

He rubbed the stubble on his jaw. "You're not a fan of the beard? I've been aiming for the rugged hero look. How am I doing?"

Her face softened, and she smiled. "You're pulling it off, Finn. Even in here, you look like a hero to me."

There were a million things he wanted to ask her. But their time was short, so he got straight to the point of what he wanted to say. "I'm sorry about how things worked out. If I could go back in time, I wouldn't be so stupidly reckless."

Her eyes took on a sheen of tears, which made them even more blue. "Expecting you to quit being reckless would be like asking the sun not to shine. It's simply who you are, Finn." She didn't sound bitter or resigned, just loving, and it split his heart wide open. He wished he could give her the world.

"Dee, I want you to have my kite shop."

She blanched. "What?"

"If I don't live to see the end of the war, there's no one on earth I'd rather—"

"Finn, stop," she interrupted. "You're going to be fine. Someday the war will end, and then you'll sail back home and everything will go on like before."

She was so naive. Anything could happen to a man in prison. Contagious diseases. Violent guards. A quirk of fate in which he could be hauled out of his cell and executed for political purposes. But he didn't want her to worry about him. He smiled and met her eyes, which reminded him of a cloudless summer sky.

"I hope you're right," he said and exhaled sharply. "But if for some reason I don't make it out of here, I need you to know that I never stopped loving you. I hope you don't hate me for leaving New York the way I did."

Delia's voice was quiet but steady. "Oh, Finn, do you think I crossed the ocean to tell you that I'm mad at you?" She shook her head. There was something fragile yet fierce in her eyes. "I forgave you long before I arrived here. And I've never stopped loving you either—not for a single second."

Their time together was over all too soon. Had it really been ten minutes? It was humiliating for him to have to obey the guard's order like a dog on a leash, but it would be worse if he didn't.

He flashed Delia a cheerful wink before being led away back to his dark cell.

31

It turned out that Benedict Kincaid wasn't a completely heartless block of ice after all. During the train ride from Rotterdam to Brussels, Delia finally came up with an argument that persuaded him to make an effort on behalf of Finn and Mathilde.

"I've spent the last three years battling anti-German bigotry in New York," she told him as the train headed south toward Brussels. "You've been back in America long enough to see it. If we can make progress on Finn or Mathilde's behalf, it will help lower the temperature of anti-German hysteria in New York."

Baron von Eschenbach backed her up. "Being the personification of evil is getting tiresome for ordinary Germans," he said, only half in jest. "Give the Germans a chance to show some benevolence. We can publicize our humanity by showing mercy to the Verhaegen woman."

It took a lot of nagging before Benedict finally budged. "If we succeed in reopening the port, I'll do my best for Mathilde . . . but *only* if we first succeed with the port."

Delia wanted to cheer but held her composure. "And Finn?"

"I can probably finagle a visit," he said, and indeed he won her that brief ten-minute visit.

Seeing Finn had been bittersweet. She wanted to weep after seeing his thin frame and the beaten expression on his face as he was led into the room. Finn used to face storms with a grin and relish any challenge. Yesterday he looked like a shadow of himself.

And today was the meeting she both anticipated and dreaded. The looming encounter with General Ryckman intimidated her like no other legal challenge of her life. The stakes for winning access to Rotterdam for CRB ships were already high, made more so because if they succeeded, Benedict promised to open negotiations on behalf of Mathilde and Finn.

The town hall of Brussels had been commandeered by General Ryckman to serve as his headquarters, where he ruled over occupied Belgium. German guards led the CRB delegation through the ornately decorated corridors toward the appointed meeting room.

Delia walked a few paces behind Benedict and Baron von Eschenbach, the sound of their footsteps absorbed by the royal-blue silk carpet. Gilded cherubs anchored near the top of the walls held lamps dripping with crystal. Rococo murals covered the arched ceilings and giant tapestries depicting scenes of classical mythology spoke of bygone eras. All of this was stolen from the Belgians for the occupying forces to enjoy.

The meeting room itself consisted of a long, dark mahogany table surrounded by cumbersome antique chairs. Scarlet wallpaper covered all four walls, darkening the room even more.

General Ryckman stood as they approached the table. With cheekbones as sharp as blades and his gray hair swept back from his forehead, he reminded Delia of an eagle looking down his beak at them.

He greeted them in English but directed his attention solely to Baron von Eschenbach. "Welcome to Brussels," he said cordially. "I trust your journey from Berlin was uneventful?"

"Indeed," the baron replied. "It looks as though you've recently earned another promotion," he said with a nod to the general's uniform.

General Ryckman's eyes gleamed, and he touched the silver stars on his shoulder board. "Yes, the third star was awarded last week at a ceremony in Munich. The promotion of the kaiser's senior officers was magnificent. Fireworks and music and dancing, although I could have done without the accordion playing. Next week there will be another celebration for promotion of the mid-level officers."

"All well-deserved, I'm sure," Baron von Eschenbach said politely.

"I expect they will enjoy the accordion music more than I," the general said, then gestured for them to sit.

Delia tugged at a chair, but it was so heavy it barely budged. Benedict wordlessly drew the chair back, and she sent him a brief nod of thanks as she sat.

As Americans, she and Benedict were probably not worthy of the general's regard. Even so, she knew the Hague Convention inside and out, and it would be their best weapon today. She opened her leather satchel and withdrew two files, one for each of the Hague treaties that Germany had agreed to. She handed a page that outlined Section II, Article 23 of the 1907 treaty and slid it in front of Benedict.

His voice was calm as he opened negotiations. "As we begin this discussion, I would be remiss not to acknowledge Germany's admirable humanitarian sentiments when they signed the Hague Treaty in 1899, and again in 1907."

General Ryckman gave a single nod of his head but said nothing. He surely knew what was coming, and Benedict cut straight to the point.

"Article 23 of the treaty states an occupying force may not block or seize the property of civilians, and this includes relief supplies. It is our position that the food sent by the Commission for the Relief of Belgium is the property of Belgian citizens, and by blocking our access to the Port of Rotterdam, you are in violation of Article 23."

The general stated that military necessity was a suitably legal reason for Germany denying shipments from America, and this trounced anything written in the Hague Conventions. He hadn't finished speaking when Delia flipped to the relevant passage to counter the general's argument and passed it to Benedict. He took it without missing a beat and immediately responded to the general, referring to the passage shown him by Delia.

The hour-long negotiation was filled with sparring back and forth. The days she'd spent studying the Hague Conventions during the Atlantic crossing paid off as she was quickly able to land on key clauses to bolster their case.

The general swiveled his attention to Baron von Eschenbach, speaking in German with a scolding tone. The baron replied in the same language, but his voice was more congenial.

Benedict leaned toward Delia and translated. "He's demanding to know why a civilized German aristocrat would consort with American peasants."

The general sent a surprised glance at Benedict. "I was not aware you spoke German."

"I lived in Berlin for ten years," he replied. "I was stationed only a stone's throw away from Charité Hospital, a hospital that speaks well of Germany's long commitment to the betterment of humanity. It is one of the reasons I remain hopeful for a positive outcome today."

"*Ja,*" the general said tersely. "Charité Hospital is the finest in all of Europe, but let us return to the matter at hand. While it is no small concession, I am prepared to permit American ships to off-load relief supplies at Rotterdam, provided that no American sets foot on land. Let this concession serve as testament to the German Empire's humane governance. I would like this concession acknowledged by President Wilson himself."

Benedict nodded. "The message shall be wired to the president today."

Delia wanted to jump up and shout in triumph, but another

battle loomed. Finn and Mathilde Verhaegen remained locked up in that Gothic horror called Saint-Gilles Prison. Benedict and the baron murmured gracious platitudes while Delia searched through her stack of documents to find the relevant passages that could perhaps free Finn and Mathilde. Her fingers trembled as she slid the papers to Benedict. She held her breath as he began.

"It has come to our attention that you currently have an American pilot under detention. Six weeks ago, Lieutenant Delaney approached you with a gallant, albeit somewhat foolish offer."

Gallant, albeit somewhat foolish. The phrase perfectly encapsulated what Finn had done, and maybe he deserved the punishment he was enduring, but he'd done no harm to anyone but himself. If Benedict could win Finn's freedom, he might walk out of the prison this very day. He could breathe clean air, eat decent food. Her heart thudded as she stared at the general, praying for a sliver of compassion.

"I am aware of the case," the general said coldly.

Benedict proceeded with the same calm, level-headed tone. "As a sign of goodwill—"

"No," the general interrupted. "Lieutenant Delaney will remain a prisoner at Saint-Gilles as long as I am Governor General of Belgium."

Delia couldn't hold her tongue. "What law has he been charged with breaking?"

The general's brows shot up, his eyes wide as if astonished that a female dared to speak to him. Benedict also shot her a surly glare, and she cursed herself for overstepping. But wasn't this the crux of the matter? What Finn did was reckless and ill-advised, but not illegal.

"He is in violation of martial law, legitimately imposed by Germany to keep order among a rebellious population," General Ryckman said, his voice lashing out like a whip.

As usual, Benedict remained calm. "Still, in the spirit of the Hague Convention—"

"Absolutely not," General Ryckman shot back. "Delaney shall remain in prison, and before you waste my time by requesting clemency for the Verhaegen woman, the answer is no. Mathilde Verhaegen is scheduled to be tried next week. She will be found guilty and will almost certainly be executed, which is the appropriate sentence for a woman who spread incendiary lies to keep the rebellion stoked. *La Libre Belgique* has caused the deaths of a great many people on both the German and Belgian sides. She must be made to pay for it."

Baron von Eschenbach's voice was like a cool dash of water, dousing the general's ire. "Don't forget. People all over the world made the English nurse Edith Cavell a saint after you ordered her execution. It would be best not to make Mathilde Verhaegen another martyred heroine who fell victim to German atrocities."

"I have no interest in the opinions of those across the Channel," the general said. "Their minds are set against us. We despise the Allies, and they despise us. The war of public opinion is over, and the only way to maintain control in Belgium is to enforce the letter of the law."

"On the contrary, the war is drawing to a close," the baron said, his voice bleak. "Our long-hoped-for Spring Offensive has stalled, and defeat looms on our doorstep. We suffer from low morale, while the Allies grow stronger with each new shipload of American troops. When the war ends, the world will remember how we treated our enemies. Our survival in the coming years will depend on the mercy we show today. Please, for the sake of Germany's future, show some compassion for the two people who will be turned into martyrs and heroes if you insist on enforcing 'the letter of the law.'"

"I consider it an *honor* to enforce the laws of Germany," General Ryckman snapped. "Do not try my patience, or perhaps I can find a clause to prohibit any American ship from using the Port of Rotterdam."

Benedict cleared his throat. "Forgive me, General Ryckman. We seem to have strayed from our primary purpose for being here today. Now, my secretary has prepared a document to authorize reopening the Port of Rotterdam to ships sent by the CRB. All it needs is your signature."

Delia opened the folder with the all-important letter of authorization. While they had won the argument to allow CRB relief shipments to flow into Belgium, they'd lost in their attempt to save two brave people languishing in prison, isolated and forgotten by the rest of the world.

Defeat made Delia's limbs feel heavy as she climbed into the carriage alongside Benedict and the baron. She ought to be overjoyed by their victory in reopening the port, and yet all she could think about was Finn.

Would the general have granted clemency for Finn had she not offended him? Shooting her mouth off might have cost Finn months or even years of imprisonment. How sanctimonious she'd been when condemning Finn for his inability to control his emotions, and yet at the most important meeting of her life, she'd been equally hotheaded.

"Congratulations on your great victory," the baron said to Benedict. "We shall go home and have a toast to your success."

"Delia deserves credit too," Benedict generously said. "Her knowledge of the treaties made our case unfold like a perfectly choreographed dance."

She managed a smile to acknowledge Benedict's compliment, but it evaporated quickly. Her presence at the meeting could have sunk Finn's chances of clemency forever.

Benedict must have sensed her anguish because he sounded unusually kind as he responded, "Don't torture yourself with regrets, Delia. It's unlikely that anything we could have said or done would have resulted in General Ryckman showing mercy to Finn or Mathilde. The general still wants revenge on the two people who humiliated him."

"Then he's an idiot," the baron said. "The end of the war is near, and he ought to be worried about his reputation after the war rather than exacting his revenge."

Delia's gaze strayed outside the carriage window to a charming café, where the tables were filled with German soldiers instead of ordinary Belgians. She couldn't blame the soldiers or even General Ryckman for this war. Responsibility for the horrors of the past four years belonged squarely on the shoulders of the kings and kaisers who had let the world sink into the abyss rather than sit down and compromise around a table.

What would happen to those kings and kaisers after the war? The Russian czar had been assassinated by his own people. What about Kaiser Wilhelm? Of all the leaders, he had the reputation for being the most belligerent. If Germany lost the war, as Baron von Eschenbach believed they would, things would not go well for the kaiser.

"Why don't we ask the kaiser for clemency?" Delia said, surprising even herself with the audacious proposal.

"Kaiser Wilhelm?" Benedict asked.

"Why not? General Ryckman answers to the kaiser, doesn't he?"

"He does," the baron confirmed.

Delia's heart started beating faster as pieces of her plan started falling into place. "If the war is going as badly as you suggest, Kaiser Wilhelm is probably already fearing for his fate after it's all over. He'll be worried about sitting down at the negotiating table and being forced to answer for the atrocities carried out in his name. He can start repairing his reputation by showing clemency for Finn and Mathilde."

Benedict gave a cynical snort. "Do you think that the pompous, bombastic kaiser will be inspired to lift a pinky finger on behalf of two nonentities?"

"Aren't you a bundle of joy," she teased. A rising tide of good humor lightened her mind. Perhaps their victory in reopening the port gave her inspiration, or maybe a bit of Finn's optimism had rubbed off on her, but yes, she had a bold idea and intended to see it through. "I think it's possible the kaiser will help if he sees it is in his personal interest. What is the harm in asking? Maybe we are insignificant nobodies, but sometimes a nobody can change the world. I refuse to capitulate without a fight. How do I get the kaiser's attention?"

"*You* can't," Baron von Eschenbach replied, his smile laced with confidence. "But I can."

32

Mathilde's trial was to take place at the *Kriegsgericht*, a military court in the center of Brussels. It had once been an ordinary Belgian courthouse, but the Germans had since transformed it. The portrait of King Albert had been replaced with that of Kaiser Wilhelm. Where the Belgian flag once flew, now the flag of Imperial Germany waved with its distinctive black eagle, spreading its wings like an ominous threat. The jury box was empty, as Mathilde's trial would be decided by a tribunal of three military judges.

Delia and Benedict arrived at the courthouse early enough to claim the bench directly behind the table where Mathilde Verhaegen would sit beside Johannes Bakker, the Belgian lawyer defending her.

A German officer marched to the front of the courtroom, pivoted with military precision, and began speaking in a loud, intimidating voice. Delia's inability to understand German was frustrating, but after a few moments, Benedict leaned over to whisper, "He's laying out the rules and warning the spectators to remain silent throughout the proceedings."

The spectators were ordinary Belgian men and women, their

expressions uniformly grim. It was doubtful that any of them personally knew Mathilde Verhaegen, who lived a hundred miles away in a small border village, but these citizens of Brussels had arrived to show their support and so it was standing room only in the *Kriegsgericht*.

When the officer stopped speaking, he snapped his heels together and shouted a command: "*Alle Aufstieg!*"

The phrase needed no translation, and everyone in the courtroom rose as the three officers who would decide the case strode into the room and claimed their seats at the table in the front.

Were they even real judges? Judges were supposed to wear black robes—a sign of their impartiality and legal training—not the uniform of the German Army. Were these men actual jurists, or merely a pack of officers eager to condemn any Belgian who dared lift their eyes from the ground and aspire to freedom?

A side door opened, and two guards escorted Mathilde inside. She was a strong-looking woman with a mass of curly, coppery hair mounded atop her head, the hint of color in sharp contrast to her drab gray prison gown.

The guards directed Mathilde to stand directly in front of the panel of judges. She was joined by her lawyer, who translated the charges as they were read aloud.

The first count was aiding and abetting Finn's escape from Belgium. The second and more serious charge was the distribution of *La Libre Belgique*. Both counts potentially carried the death penalty, and it was unlikely there would be any mercy shown in this trial. Nevertheless, Mathilde remained stoic as she stood to hear the charges read, her attorney quietly translating throughout. Afterward, she and her lawyer were told to take their seats at the defendant's table.

Delia lowered her head to pray.

God, are you here in this horrible courtroom today? Do you see what is happening? Please soften the hearts of the stone-faced men who will stand in judgment of a good woman. Mathilde disobeyed the laws of man, and perhaps she owes a price for that, but please, not the death penalty. She has children . . .

It was hard to pray when the harsh voice of the prosecuting attorney opened his case, pacing before the judges' bench, pausing every few sentences to glare or point at the defendant. Why did people speaking German always sound so angry? The judges paid keen attention, their heads turning to follow the prosecutor as he walked haughtily around the courtroom.

Delia looked away, searching for anything other than the daunting sight of the judges, and noticed an oddly dressed man in the front row of the spectators' section. He wore a red shirt with a black suit and had a yellow daffodil pinned to his lapel. It matched the yellow gown of the woman sitting beside him. Her canary-yellow gown featured a row of black buttons down the front, and a red scarf was jauntily knotted around her neck. It didn't really match.

Delia's breath caught when she took notice of the other spectators in the front row. All of them had something red, yellow, and black incorporated into their clothing. The colors of the Belgian flag.

The citizens of Belgium had been forbidden to fly their flag since the day Germany invaded their country, and this was a subtle sign of solidarity with the woman on trial today.

Delia's heart was moved as she scanned the rest of the spectators. There was a great variety of colors, patterns, and designs among them, but without fail, every spectator in the courtroom wore red, yellow, and black. The embellishments were subtle enough that the Germans probably wouldn't notice. But Delia had spotted it. A black armband, a yellow pocket square, red suspenders, yellow-and-black beaded necklaces, red jewelry, or hair ribbons in tricolor stripes. One woman waved a red-and-black fan, which gently fluttered her yellow neck scarf. As for Mathilde's attorney, he wore a black suit with red cuff links and yellow socks.

Had Mathilde noticed their silent sign of support? Delia prayed she had.

The trial proceeded with shocking speed. The prosecution concluded their case in less than an hour, and Delia didn't know if that was a good sign or not.

Mr. Bakker rose to present the defense's case, which was going to be a challenge since Mathilde had been caught with the newspapers in her possession, and she had confessed to helping Finn escape. Mr. Bakker hadn't completed two sentences when the lead judge interrupted him, and a brief argument ensued.

Benedict leaned down to whisper, "Mr. Bakker tried to present evidence that since Lieutenant Delaney never returned to active combat, Mathilde shouldn't be charged with causing harm to German military operations. The judge said Mathilde couldn't have known that when she committed the crime, so he is letting the charge stand."

It was a blow, but the defense attorney seemed to have plenty of other arrows in his quiver. He immediately launched into another line of attack, yet it was shot down quickly as well.

Benedict explained, "Mr. Bakker tried to claim that distributing *La Libre Belgique* was motivated not by defiance of the law, but to spread comfort and moral support. The judge won't allow it."

Throughout the next hour, Delia kept careful watch on Mathilde. The woman had flawless posture, her shoulders never showing a hint of slumping as the judges systematically demolished the defense's case. It wasn't even lunchtime before the case came to a close. The lead judge announced the tribunal would withdraw to consider the charges and then return with a verdict.

Benedict twisted on the bench to speak in a low voice. "I wish I'd gotten the message about attire. I'd have worn my red waistcoat."

"You noticed too?" Delia asked.

Benedict nodded. "I noticed. I hope Mathilde did as well. It might be the only consolation she will receive today."

"The case is that bleak?"

"A guilty verdict is all but certain," Benedict replied. "The best we can hope for is a merciful sentence. They will proceed to the sentencing portion of the trial immediately after the verdict is delivered."

Delia sighed. Perhaps Baron von Eschenbach would save the day. He'd left to appeal to the kaiser for leniency five days ago, but they hadn't heard anything from him as yet. Whether he had good news or bad, he ought to have wired them a response by now.

Less than twenty minutes later, the court bailiff strode to the front of the courtroom. "*Alle Aufstieg!*"

Everyone in the courtroom stood. Mathilde silently crossed herself as the three judges walked in a line to their positions behind the front table. With a loud tap of the gavel, court was back in session, and every muscle in Delia's body became strung so tautly that she hurt.

The lead judge began reading from a prepared document, his voice as dry as if he were reading a weather report. Yet he was clearly delivering the verdict because a handful of spectators murmured in dismay.

Benedict leaned toward Delia to whisper, "Guilty on both charges, as expected."

Mathilde's lawyer translated the verdict for her. Though Mathilde's expression didn't waver, she swallowed hard and straightened her shoulders.

Without delay, the case shifted to the sentencing phase. Because both charges carried the death penalty, the defense attorney rose to offer his best case for mercy.

Again, Benedict turned to Delia and translated quietly, "Mr. Bakker is pointing out that Mathilde is a mother to three children. Mathilde's husband was seized by the German Army in the early days of the war and is not there to help raise the children. The court will be making orphans of the children if they proceed with a sentence of execution."

Delia watched the expression of all three judges. Their faces might have been carved from granite for all the compassion they showed. The defense attorney then outlined several other reasons for the court to show mercy. To her surprise, Mr. Bakker was allowed to speak at length and was never interrupted. Benedict translated the highlights of the defense's argument for mercy. Mathilde had a spotless reputation and had contributed to her community through charitable works and causes. If she was sentenced to remain imprisoned for the duration of the war, she would cause no additional harm to the German war effort.

At last, Mr. Bakker had reached the end of his prepared argument and gave the judges a deep bow before sitting down.

The lead judge announced something, and Benedict swore under his breath. "They're ready to pronounce the sentence," he hissed. "This was a foregone conclusion all along."

Despair blossomed in Delia's chest when the judge began reading from a prepared document, proof that the sentence had already been decided while the judges were in chamber. The few people among the spectators who understood German began a low, hostile murmuring, and the judge banged his gavel, shooting them all a glare before continuing to render his sentence.

"Death by firing squad," Benedict told her. "The sentence will be carried out tomorrow morning at seven o'clock."

Delia refused to leave the courthouse. They needed to find a way to delay the scheduled execution long enough to hear back from the baron.

Mathilde had been escorted back to her cell, and Benedict intercepted her lawyer for an emergency consultation. Delia joined the two men in a windowless courthouse meeting room that had only a single table and two chairs. Who cared how claustrophobic it felt? They needed to save a woman's life and had less than eighteen hours to do so. The men took the chairs as Delia, too nervous to sit, began pacing the room.

"What about requesting an appeal?" Benedict asked.

Mr. Bakker shook his head. "Appeals require filing paperwork in Berlin, and Mathilde will be dead before we can cut through the layers of red tape to get the necessary signatures. It's how they carried out Edith Cavell's execution before the international community could object, and that is what they're planning to do this time."

Benedict muttered a curse and grumbled about the German love affair with rules and procedures.

Delia mulled over the problem. Their best bet for saving Mathilde's life was a reprieve from the kaiser, but they needed to delay the execution at least until they heard back from Baron von Eschenbach.

Benedict and Mr. Bakker batted ideas back and forth while Delia steepled her hands beneath her chin and continued to pace. Benedict was correct about German adherence to structure and schedules. Delia often teased Inga about her insistence of following recipes to the letter instead of feeling free to experiment.

Perhaps their best chance to save Mathilde wouldn't be found in the lawbooks or pleading for mercy. How could they use Germany's fussy preoccupation with rules and procedures to delay the execution?

The answer blazed in Delia's mind like fireworks.

"The promotion ceremony! Don't you remember?" she asked Benedict. "General Ryckman said the mid-level officers have all been called to Munich to be recognized for their promotions. There will be atrocious accordion music. What sort of officer will be in charge of a firing squad?"

"Captain Weisner has been in the post for the past two years," Mr. Bakker responded.

"And if Captain Weisner is not available?" she asked.

The lawyer glanced around the room as he considered the question. "My guess is that they'd appoint the lieutenant who reports to Weisner."

Benedict's gaze sharpened as he grasped Delia's train of thought. "A lieutenant isn't good enough," he said. "This is a high-profile case, and if they dare use a lieutenant, it would be a significant deviation from military protocol. The Germans can't risk a botched execution or one that is not carried out with the utmost adherence to protocol."

"They'll simply find some other captain in Brussels to stand in," Mr. Bakker said.

Benedict shook his head. "Commanding a firing squad carries a stigma, and few officers would gladly accept the assignment. They will almost certainly await the return of Captain Weisner to assume responsibility for the task."

Delia smiled. For the first time that day, a glimmer of hope had begun to surface.

33

Delia's audacious gambit paid off. The Germans, bound by their rigid adherence to protocol, agreed to postpone the execution until Captain Weisner's return. The good news arrived an hour before the execution, and she listened with relief as Benedict recounted the details to Inga and Bertie, who had arrived in town on CRB business earlier in the afternoon. They were gathered at the bistro outside Bertie's grand hotel—the Hotel Ravenstein, the headquarters for the CRB in Brussels since the start of the war.

"Once I learned Captain Weisner was part of the delegation sent to Munich, I turned to the staff at the Spanish Embassy to lean hard on the Germans." Though Benedict sounded nonchalant, the nervous strain from last night still lingered in his voice.

Delia received a lesson in international diplomacy throughout the tense eighteen hours following Mathilde's trial. As Americans, she and Benedict had little bargaining power with the Germans, but neutral nations like Norway, Spain, and Switzerland were able to act as mediator between the warring nations.

It was how Inga met Benedict in Berlin. The two of them worked in the American Embassy before the United States entered the war.

They did their best to mediate disputes for those caught in the cross fire of war. It was one of those deals that had freed Baron von Eschenbach from a British detention center. Now Benedict turned to staff at the Spanish Embassy for help with Mathilde.

"The Spanish ambassador made a late-night appeal to the *Kriegsgericht*, stressing that if the Germans carried out a botched execution because the captain of the firing squad was carousing in Munich, it would reflect poorly on them. Captain Weisner is not due back in Brussels until Saturday evening, and since a Sunday execution is considered poor form, it has been rescheduled for Monday morning at seven o'clock."

Hearing the time of the rescheduled execution caused a knot to form in the back of Delia's neck. It was Saturday afternoon. The hours were slipping by quickly and there still had been no word from Baron von Eschenbach. The clock on their three-day reprieve was ticking, and barring a miracle, Mathilde would be dead in two days.

"We ought to have heard from Baron von Eschenbach by now," Benedict said darkly. "He understands the urgency and should have at least let us know if he'd gotten an appointment to see the kaiser."

"You think he may have come to harm?" Inga asked.

"It's a possibility," Benedict said. Berlin was four hundred miles away, and the nation was at war. Half the countryside was starving, and he might have appeared a tempting target for desperate and hungry people.

The frazzled waitress with a coffee-stained apron arrived with their lunch platter. The beer was watered down, the bread sliced paper thin. That with a jar of olives rounded out their lunch. Rations were paltry for everyone in Belgium except German soldiers. Every time the door to the inside restaurant opened, the scent of Wiener schnitzel and fried potatoes made her mouth water.

"Is there any butter or jam?" Benedict asked the waitress. His tone was polite, but the waitress gave only a noncommittal shrug before returning inside.

Bertie opened the jar of olives and began distributing them on small plates. "Mrs. Verhaegen's fate is in the hands of God, but allocating thirty tons of oats, flour, and condensed milk arriving from New York is our responsibility. We need to reestablish our network of distribution before the ship's arrival on Wednesday."

"I still have the register of local volunteers," Delia confirmed. "I'll start tracking them down immediately." It would give her something to do rather than obsess over Mathilde and Finn.

She gazed up at the steely clouds scudding across the sky as they morphed and changed shape in the wind. Finn would love to see this. Any moment drops of rain might come spattering down, but he'd love that too. At this very moment, he was trapped in a windowless cell. She'd give anything to allow him a glimpse of these awesome, ominous clouds unfolding above her.

She popped an olive into her mouth and listened to the ongoing conversation about expediting food throughout Belgium, but it was hard to tear her eyes from the awe-inspiring sky. Was it wrong to enjoy the clouds when Finn couldn't see the sky? Or to savor the salty tang of black olives when he was hungry?

The surly waitress returned. "Here is some jam," she said, plopping a mostly empty jar beside Benedict's plate. "And here is a telegram that arrived for you."

Delia's breath caught as Benedict tore the flap open, his stern face tense as he skimmed the lines of the message. He gave a very uncharacteristic pump of his fist and said, "The kaiser has granted Mathilde clemency!"

Inga shrieked in delight and shot to her feet to throw her arms around Benedict. Bertie lifted his glass of watery beer in a toast while Delia simply stared in wonder. Despite the gloomy skies, this tiny corner of Brussels was suddenly an oasis of joy.

Benedict extracted himself from Inga's enthusiastic embrace to relay more information. "Her clemency is contingent on her agreement to house arrest in Switzerland for the duration of the war. As soon as that agreement is signed, she will be allowed to leave the country."

"Does it say anything about Finn?" Delia asked.

Benedict sobered and handed her the message. It was a lengthy telegram. When her eyes found Finn's name, she read it aloud: "No leniency for Finn."

She lowered the telegram to her lap. It meant Finn would remain in his cell until the end of the war. Everyone had told her it was foolish to believe that both Mathilde and Finn would be spared, but a corner of her heart had clung to that tiny flicker of hope.

Now it had been snuffed out, and the despair in her heart expanded as she watched the telegram make its way around the table, everyone dissecting each line of text for additional insight. The baron's delay was caused because the kaiser had left Berlin to hunt for wild boar in the Mecklenburg forests.

"Surely the hunting trip is what slowed the baron down," Benedict said. "Being away from Berlin might account for the kaiser's conciliatory mood."

Benedict and the others continued discussing their next steps, including how they would inform Mathilde's lawyer of her stay of execution, but Delia could not share in their excitement.

Inga placed a hand on her knee. "I'm sorry nothing could be done for Finn," she said softly. "Hold on to your faith. God has a plan for both of you, even though we can't see it yet."

How could imprisoning a man like Finn serve God's purpose? He was trapped in solitary confinement, wasting away. When she saw him during their single visit, he looked so gaunt and thin, even though he'd been imprisoned for just a month at that point.

"If you could have seen how awful he looks, you would understand," Delia said. "I would give everything I own if I could somehow get him on the same train that will take Mathilde to Switzerland."

Inga gave her a warning look. "Any attempt you make regarding Finn will only risk Mathilde's freedom."

"It's only wishful thinking," Delia admitted. She wasn't the kind of person who could break people out of jail or distribute revolutionary newspapers. She was a clerk with an eye for detail and the heart of a coward.

At least she'd succeeded in saving Mathilde. "I imagine Mathilde hasn't been treated kindly in prison," she said to Inga. "She will need clean clothing and some basic supplies before going to Switzerland. Let's go shopping for her. It will help me shake off the doldrums and can be our way of thanking her for saving Finn."

"Absolutely!" Inga said.

When she informed Bertie of their plan to go shopping, he frowned. "I need help," he said. "I sail for New York at the end of the week and need to hire someone to get the CRB back up and running before I leave."

"So soon?" Delia asked. "I thought we were going to spend another month here."

Bertie shook his head. "President Wilson has summoned me home. He has appointed me to head up the U.S. Food Administration."

Benedict whistled. "A cabinet position?"

Bertie flushed, making his baby face look even younger. "I confess, it's a big step, but one I'm looking forward to."

"Who will run the CRB after you leave?" Delia asked.

"Once I've got the Belgian office staffed, I think it will run itself. I asked President Wilson if the U.S. government could kick in the funding for additional CRB staff, and he agreed to it. I told him it was a condition for my acceptance of the new assignment."

That meant Delia was no longer needed for fundraising back in the United States. What would she do now? Working for the CRB had been the most rewarding experience of her life. New York had lost its allure. She had no desire to return to Wesley, and everyone at the Martha Washington hated her.

If Delia were a braver person, she'd volunteer to stay in Belgium to work for the CRB. That would be impossible, though. She didn't speak French, Dutch, or German, so how could she tackle such a job? She'd be alone in a foreign land. She glanced at the table beside them, which was filled with hard-faced German soldiers, an intimidating reminder that Brussels was an occupied city.

And yet Delia possessed the most important qualification. She understood the CRB and had the willpower to carry out Bertie's vision.

"I want to stay in Brussels," she blurted, surprising even herself with the sudden decision.

"Pardon me?" Bertie said.

"You need to hire competent and trustworthy staff in a hurry. I'll stay and help you with this."

Even Inga looked skeptical. "Delia, you don't speak French."

It was a problem, but Delia had spent her entire life enumerating problems on the horizon. She could spot a risk, a pitfall, or a weak link from a mile away. What if she turned that talent into solving problems rather than coming up with excuses to stay within the safety of her routine, predictable life? Perhaps the first step in becoming a courageous person was to simply start doing brave things whether she was afraid or not.

She met Bertie's gaze. "I know the rules and regulations of the CRB inside and out. I have the key contacts of everyone in New York at my fingertips, and I can hire translators when necessary."

Bertie lifted his glass in a toast. "It will be a relief to have someone I trust staffing the base in Brussels."

Delia was determined to do her utmost for the CRB. She would also help Finn while she was at it.

34

Bertie gave Delia the job, which meant she was still in Brussels on the day Mathilde was due to be released.

Delia and Inga had bought the basic necessities Mathilde would need to begin her life in exile: several skirts and blouses, undergarments, new socks, and a nightgown. Delia also purchased a comb, hairpins, soap, toothbrush, and handkerchiefs. Inga, being eternally vain and also quite wealthy after marrying Benedict, bought a jar of shockingly expensive face cream, lip tint, rice powder, and a bottle of perfume.

"I don't care how heroic Mathilde Verhaegen is, a woman wants to look pretty," Inga insisted. "Besides, after spending time in a German dungeon, she deserves a little luxury."

They arrived at the prison the hour before dawn so that they could be sure to catch Mathilde before she was whisked away to Switzerland. Delia climbed down from the carriage first and took a moment to study the fortresslike prison of Saint-Gilles. High stone walls of bleached granite, formidable turrets, and heavy iron gates exuded the stern authority of an earlier era.

And somewhere beneath that imposing castle, Finn lay trapped in an underground cell where he was destined to sit out the rest of the war. She was only a stone's throw away, yet she couldn't see or speak with him.

Getting past the prison guards to deliver the suitcase of newly purchased clothes for Mathilde might prove difficult, but she was determined to make it happen. Inga brimmed with confidence as they approached the two guards flanking the sally port entrance. The tall guard was grim and skinny, while the shorter one had an eye patch and a softer expression. Both had probably been wounded on the front and transferred to guard duty behind the lines.

"We're here to meet with Madam Verhaegen," Inga said in flawless German. There was a bit of back and forth in the language Delia couldn't understand, and yet the guard with the eye patch seemed to thaw under the generous smile and friendly chatter Inga bestowed on him.

The tall guard didn't smile but demanded to inspect the contents of their suitcase. Delia handed it over. After unbuckling the straps, he pawed through ladies' clothes and undergarments. His face remained stern as he sniffed the perfume and rubbed a dab of the face cream between his thumb and finger.

"*Ja!*" the guard said, snapping his fingers and gesturing for Delia to put the contents of the suitcase back together. By the time she'd folded the clothes and secured the straps, the friendlier soldier had unlocked the iron gate and opened one of the creaky doors.

Delia said nothing as she walked beside Inga into the central courtyard of the prison.

"We're in luck," Inga whispered to her. "Since Mathilde is due to leave within the hour, the guards see no harm in letting us personally deliver the clothing to her."

They turned the corner into a grassy area in between the cell-block wings, where the guard had instructed them to wait.

The prison resembled a scary medieval castle with its central courtyard and four wings of cellblocks, each radiating outward like the spokes of a wheel. They were to wait in the dusty courtyard until Mathilde arrived. With each beat of her heart, Delia longed for a way to communicate with Finn, but it was hopeless.

Ten minutes later, Mathilde finally emerged from one of the cellblocks, wearing the same gray gown she'd worn during her trial. Though two guards escorted her, she was not shackled. Her long, curly hair was tied by a bit of cloth, and her expression was cautious as she scanned the prison yard.

"Mrs. Verhaegen?" Delia said, stepping forward. "We have brought you clothes for the journey."

The woman glanced between Delia and the suitcase. Delia unbuckled the straps and opened the case, gesturing for Mathilde to take the clothes.

"*Pour moi?*" Mathilde said.

Delia smiled. "Yes. For you." Mathilde desperately needed a fresh set of clothes. The hem of her gown was filthy, and the sweat stains beneath her arms made it appear as though she hadn't been afforded clean clothes or the chance to bathe since her trial. The train to Zurich was scheduled to depart in an hour. "Ask the guards if we can use the lavatory," she said to Inga.

Instead of charming the guard like Delia expected, Inga swiveled an annoyed glance at the guard and fired off a castigating torrent of German as she gestured to the sorry state of Mrs. Verhaegen's clothing and hygiene. Miraculously, they were granted access to the lavatory inside the guard's cellblock.

White tile lined the floors and walls, with pipes leading to a ceramic sink and a single toilet. It wasn't the nicest place to clean up, but the white enamel sink had a bar of soap near the faucet, and they had handkerchiefs in the suitcase. The floor was the only place in which to set the suitcase, and Mathilde watched with curiosity as Delia opened it once again.

Inga had been right to choose clothes that were frilly and feminine. Even though Mathilde had a no-nonsense demeanor and a sturdy frame that looked as if she could plow a field, she was still a woman. A smile brightened her face at the sight of the silky undergarments and toiletries. But when she touched the pretty jar of perfumed cream, her expression crumpled and she blinked rapidly as a sheen of tears came to her eyes.

"Thank you," Mathilde said on a shaky breath, covering her mouth with trembling hands.

They were the same hands that had dragged Finn to safety. Mathilde probably didn't understand much English, but Delia couldn't hold back. "It is I who should be thanking *you*," she said. "You saved my best friend. I am in awe of everything you did for Finn and for your family and the people of Belgium. You helped inspire a nation, and there are no words for how grateful I am, ma'am."

There was more she wanted to say, but a lump had formed in her throat, making it hard to keep speaking. Mathilde seemed to appreciate the sentiment and squeezed Delia's hands in a moment of understanding.

Inga turned the spigot and began lathering a handkerchief. "We must hurry," she said. "We have only ten minutes before that guard will be banging on the door."

Mathilde wasn't the least bit shy as she shucked the threadbare gown from her body. In short order she ran the soapy handkerchief over her shoulders and beneath her arms. Delia and Inga both turned away as the older woman stepped out of the gown and shed the rest of her clothes.

Once Mathilde was dressed in a new wool skirt and cotton blouse, the three of them went into the courtyard to wait. Language barriers made communication difficult, but Inga filled the time with pleasant chatter in a combination of German and broken French.

Meanwhile, Delia scanned the bleak courtyard, wondering which of the buildings housed Finn. He'd now been imprisoned for more than two months. He had been so brave to come here. While his attempt to free Mathilde hadn't worked, it was still an extraordinary sacrifice. *"Greater love has no one than this: to lay down one's life for one's friends."*

That was exactly what Finn had done. Although it wasn't Finn's actions that led to Mathilde's release, did that make his sacrifice any less valiant? He was a good man. Not always wise or careful, but he had offered his life in exchange for Mathilde's.

A carriage arrived at the top of the hour to take Mathilde to the train station. Inga walked arm in arm with the courageous woman while Delia hung a few steps behind. Admiration mingled with shame as she watched Mathilde board the carriage. The Belgian woman turned back to wave farewell, smiling for the first time since Delia saw her. Delia returned the smile and sent back a hearty wave, but inside frustration began to roil.

All her life she had been a rule follower. Mathilde wasn't. Neither was Finn. Even Bertie occasionally bent the rules when he needed to make things happen. People who saved the world rarely followed the rules or worried about their personal safety. What kind of person was she if she would docilely walk out of this prison, mere yards away from Finn, because a German corporal told her she needed to leave?

She drew a fortifying breath and stared hard at the two German soldiers pacing before the prison entrance. They were casting annoyed looks her way and would boot her out soon.

Courage was such an elusive yet magnificent thing. A person could conjure it out of thin air. Courage could change the world. Courage wasn't the absence of fear, but the ability to overcome her trepidation and act in spite of it.

Bluffing her way into a German prison had scared Delia down to her foundation. But she was tired of being frightened. She drew a deep breath, ignoring the familiar knots of fear beginning to gather, and imagined herself becoming as strong as the granite blocks of the prison walls that held Finn trapped inside.

She turned to Inga. "I want to see Finn, and I need to get past those guards to do it. Will you translate for me?"

35

Finn couldn't believe it when the guard said his American lawyer was here to see him. He didn't even have a lawyer, but perhaps the Red Cross had managed to finagle something to help him.

Finn wouldn't argue. Anything to get out of this tiny cell would be like manna from heaven, even though he had to hold his wrists out to be handcuffed. The soldier's nose wrinkled, and he withdrew a few paces the instant he completed the chore. No doubt Finn smelled pretty rank, although he couldn't smell it anymore. It would be nice to clean up before meeting with the unknown lawyer. Then again, he didn't have any pride anymore. He intended to enjoy the chance to stretch his legs for the long walk down the cellblock hallway to the meeting room, and if the lawyer was appalled at his condition, so much the better. Perhaps it would result in some changes.

Each footstep felt odd, triggering a prickly sensation in his feet as he walked. The tingling in his hands and feet had been getting worse over the past week. Maybe it was just the lack of exercise. His sense of balance was off, and he focused on keeping each footfall steady as the tingles engulfed his feet.

Hope warred with anxiety as the door to the meeting room came into view. One of the guards stepped forward to open it, and Finn angled to peer into the room through the widening gap.

He blinked furiously. Delia? *Delia?* There were others in the room, but all he could see was Delia, who beamed the most glorious smile at him. Why wasn't she in New York? What had kept her here?

Laughter bubbled up inside and echoed in the small room. "Dee!" he shouted through his peals of laughter. "Oh, Dee, look at you!"

"Hello, Finn."

Was this a dream? Yet his dreams never involved handcuffs or tingling feet. He struggled to make his brain piece together a coherent sentence. "I-I figured you'd be in New York by now."

She shook her head. "The Red Cross has rules that lawyers are allowed to conduct random welfare checks on their clients. So here I am."

What a load of rubbish! Whatever had prompted Delia to hoodwink her way into Saint-Gilles Prison was a surprise, but he was determined to go along with the subterfuge. "I'm grateful," he said. And overjoyed. Just knowing she was still in Belgium was a great relief. "You look good, Dee."

He probably shouldn't be saying such things to a lawyer. Some of the guards in the room might understand English, and he needed to pretend she was just an ordinary Red Cross lawyer. Delia took a seat at a small wooden table, and he took the chair opposite her. A guard warned them not to attempt to touch each other or exchange any materials.

Finn nodded his agreement. In light of the guard's ability to speak English, he had to be extra cautious about what he said. He scrambled for a safe topic. The most painful one immediately sprang to mind. "Any update on Mathilde?"

"She's free," Delia said.

He leaned forward, and his eyes locked on hers. Keeping his

voice cautious, he asked, "Is it true? You're not just saying that to make me feel better?"

"It's true," she assured him. "The kaiser granted clemency on the condition she go to Switzerland for the duration of the war. She has accepted his terms and was released this morning."

Finn sagged back in the chair. He ought to be embarrassed by the tears stinging his eyes, but he was too relieved and listened as Delia filled him in on all the details. The trial, the guilty verdict, but also Kaiser Wilhelm's last-minute intervention to spare Mathilde's life. She was on a train to Zurich this very moment.

In his mind's eye he imagined the train chugging through endless green fields, meadows of wildflowers, sunshine, with an impossibly blue sky overhead. The image was so breathtaking it caused a lump in his throat.

"I hope she will be happy there," he choked out, "and that she'll have a view of the mountains and the sky. I'll bet the flowers are in full bloom."

Mathilde deserved every happiness. She'd been imprisoned far longer than he had and deserved the mercy she'd been granted. A pause stretched in the room, and his fingers began a nervous tapping on the tabletop. Was it possible? He hesitated to even ask, yet he needed to know.

"Did the kaiser include anyone else in that clemency?"

The light faded from Delia's lovely face. "We appealed for you but didn't have any luck," she said gently.

It was as he'd expected, but the blow still hurt. The chain on the handcuffs rattled as he clasped his hands to stop them from shaking. He forced a light tone into his voice. "That's all right. Mathilde deserves it. I'm happy for her . . . and grateful to you for pulling everything off."

He stared at her, trying to etch her image onto his soul. He had to keep his chin up lest she sense the crushing weight of disappointment that threatened to choke him. She'd obviously fought hard to get permission to visit him. It should be enough.

His bravado didn't work. Delia could always see right through him. "Finn, I know this isn't what you wanted to hear, but hold tight to the thought that the war *will* someday end, and you'll be alive to walk out of this prison and be a free man once again. The rest of the world is going to need you when this nightmare is over. They'll need your humor and optimism. Finn, they'll need your kites."

He stifled a cynical snort, and she latched on to it. "Yes, they'll need your kites," she insisted. "Right now, the whole world is sore and aching and wounded, and those kites will remind people that there's still joy to be found on any sunny afternoon. When people are tired from rebuilding or tending graves, they can take their children out into the fresh air to watch a kite soar in the air and remember that the world is still an amazing place."

He managed a nod, hoping to God that he'd be there to see such a thing.

"Well, listen to me ramble," Delia said. "I came here for a wellness check. Is there anything you need? Anything that might make this time more bearable?"

Food. He dreamed about food all the time, but all he'd been given since the day he arrived was turnips. Germany could barely feed itself, so they weren't going to give them extra rations, but allowing the prisoners outside to stretch their legs and see the sun wouldn't cost anything.

"Some time outside the cell for fresh air and exercise would be nice."

"I'll see what I can do," she said, and he nodded his thanks, even though it wouldn't happen. Delia wasn't a lawyer, and she didn't work for the Red Cross. Even so, he was proud of her for pulling off this visit.

And yet it had been a risk. She shouldn't gamble her life or her freedom for him. He wanted to warn her but had to choose his words carefully because the guard understood everything.

"I will be forever grateful for this visit," he said. "I think you should return to New York. You'll be safer there."

"I can't do that," she said. "Bertie still needs my help. I'm staying in Brussels to make sure the shipments continue going where they're most needed."

His heart started pounding. There were plenty of people who could have taken a job with the CRB, and the fact that she was staying surely meant something. He didn't want to talk about himself and so pumped her for news from back home. Talk of the war must have been forbidden because she stuck to safe subjects like baseball and how Babe Ruth was hitting home runs like he'd been born for it. She said she was trying to learn French, but it was slow going.

All too soon their ten minutes were up, and regret filled her face. "This is going to be the last time I'll be able to visit you," she said, and a deep, hollow ache settled in his chest. It took effort for him to manage a smile.

"I understand. And hey . . ." The next words were going to scorch. He might not survive the war, so they needed to be said. "When you do go back to New York . . . well, the old guy isn't so bad."

Tears sprang to Delia's eyes, but she was quick to swipe them away. "Stop being so valiant," she said with a little laugh.

He grinned and shrugged. "I can't help it. It's who I am." He sobered and met her eyes. "I'm serious, Dee. I want you to be happy."

She drew a breath to speak, but the guard interrupted. "Your time is up," the guard announced and gestured for Finn to stand.

It took every bit of his willpower to force himself to obey. Nevertheless, he focused on Delia's face, trying to memorize every blessed detail, the curve of her cheek, the magnificent blue of her eyes. He would replay this image in his mind in the weeks and months ahead.

"Take care, Finn. I'll be praying for you every day."

"As always, I'll need it." He gave a final nod and turned away. Despair swamped him as he headed back to his cell. The stench of the underground hall triggered a surge of hopelessness, making it hard to keep walking. How much longer could he take this? For a few minutes today he forgot he was a prisoner, but that was all over now. The sound of the lock sliding back into place sounded like a death knell. Every muscle in his body ached.

A tapping on the ventilation pipe was followed by the priest's soft whisper. "Who was it?"

Finn closed his eyes tightly. He didn't have the strength to talk about Delia right now, not when he was at a breaking point. "Nobody," he answered, then turned his face to the cell wall.

Delia caught the hint of despair in Finn's eyes as he was led out of the cell, and it haunted her all the way back to the Hotel Ravenstein. The heart-wrenching sight confirmed her decision to remain in Brussels. She would stay here and fight to improve his conditions as best she could.

It had been surprisingly easy to win a visit. The guard remembered her from their earlier visit to Finn, and by bluntly declaring she was here to conduct a wellness check, it worked to open Finn's cell door. It wouldn't work again, and this was likely to be the last time she'd set eyes on Finn until the end of the war.

Provided he was still alive. She confided her concerns to Inga on the carriage ride back to the hotel.

"There's something wrong with him," Delia said. "He was so thin, the collar gaped around his scrawny neck, and he seemed unsteady on his feet."

"I'm sure seeing you was a balm for his spirit. And learning Mathilde is safe had to help, right?"

Delia smiled, for Inga always had a magical way of finding a glimmer of good amid the darkness. "Oh, I'm going to miss you."

Inga and the others were leaving on a train for Rotterdam tomorrow morning, leaving Delia all alone in a city where she knew nobody and didn't speak the language.

She and Inga walked arm in arm toward their suite on the top floor of the hotel and were greeted by a surprise the moment they stepped inside.

A huge bouquet of flowers graced the center of the table, an explosion of roses, lilies, and daffodils. A purple bow encircled the crystal vase that held the cheerful blossoms.

Inga glanced at Benedict. "Flowers for me?"

Benedict had a habit of bombarding Inga with flowers, but this bouquet was extravagant even for his hefty wallet.

"They're Bertie's," Benedict said dryly. "The Belgian government has awarded him the Order of Leopold in gratitude for the CRB. Look." He opened a velvet box to reveal a medal in the shape of a Maltese cross with the Belgian lion at the center. It was attached to a ribbon made of the same purple silk that adorned the vase of flowers.

Bertie stood off to the side, looking bashful and embarrassed at the award.

"Congratulations!" Delia enthused. "When did you find out?"

"When the flowers arrived. Although my name is on the medal, in truth it belongs to the hundreds of volunteers who make the CRB possible. Delia, please take the flowers to your room. You earned them."

She stood a little straighter as she gazed at the spectacular bouquet. Serving on the CRB had been the most rewarding experience of her life, but the honor truly belonged to Bertie alone. He was the one who had envisioned the plan and who had the leadership skills and charisma to get it up and running.

"I'll take the flowers, but only because they would require a separate train ticket if you tried to take them with you tomorrow," she teased.

"This calls for a celebration," Inga said, walking to the balcony to fling the French doors open. "This is the last evening the four of us will be together. We must make a toast."

Bertie called downstairs for a bottle of champagne and a platter of cheese. The balcony overlooked the square, and mandolin music floated up from the bistro across the street. So perfect was the summer evening that it didn't seem possible that there was a war being fought not far away.

"Rumor has it the French plan on awarding Bertie the Legion of Honour," Benedict said once they were seated on the balcony. "Soon he will have collected so many awards, he will need a separate trunk for them all."

"That's because everybody loves you," Inga said to Bertie. "Even President Wilson is smart enough to put you in his cabinet."

"Will you ever go back to mining?" Benedict asked. "I should think you'll need to replenish your bank account after all these years of letting the CRB drain your wallet."

Bertie's babyish face turned wistful as he gazed at the sunset. "I became a rich man from working in gold and silver mines, but nothing has given me greater satisfaction than tackling humanitarian issues. For now, I'll do what I can to help President Wilson. After that, well, I don't think I can return to mining. The war has changed me. Perhaps I'll throw my hat into the political arena and see what comes of it."

Benedict frowned. "You'll need a name with more gravitas than *Bertie* if you want to run for elected office. What is your given name?"

"Herbert," he replied.

It didn't sound that much more impressive than Bertie, but Benedict seemed thoughtful as he mulled over the name. "Herbert Hoover," he said slowly. "That has a ring to it. Yes, I could vote for a man named Herbert Hoover."

Delia stepped forward to kiss Bertie on the cheek. "You'll always be Bertie to me," she said. "But I expect you will do well in the political arena."

36

Finn thought he was dreaming when it was announced that all the prisoners in solitary confinement would be granted a daily hour in the exercise yard. There were twelve men in solitary, all of them wraith-thin as they emerged from their cells, staring at one another in hopeful bewilderment, unable to believe this unexpected gift. For the first time, he saw Father Gerhardt face-to-face. The old man was short, blocky, and had a wizened face that was wreathed in a thousand wrinkles when he smiled.

Is this your doing, Dee? Finn silently wondered as he walked through the corridors. It had been a week since her visit, and he doubted this was a coincidence.

The exercise yard was about half an acre of hard-packed dirt with a few patches of scrabbly grass. The cinder-block walls were topped with barbed wire, but none of them could blot out the pale blue sky with its wispy cirrus clouds. It was the most beautiful sky Finn had ever seen. He nearly wept at the sight.

Sweet Jesus, thank you for this blessing. To see the sky again . . . thank you.

An instant bond formed among his twelve fellow prisoners despite the language barriers. Finn was the only native English

277

speaker. The others spoke French, Dutch, Flemish, and German. Finn knew enough French to converse with most of them.

The hour spent in the sunlight had been overwhelming, filling him with unexpected joy. When Finn returned to his cell, he lay on the cot, staring at the ceiling and counting down the minutes until the next day when he could go outside again.

That was when the tremblies hit him again. It had been months since one of these wild surges in emotion struck him. It started in his belly, then moved up to his shoulders and down to his fingertips. The weepiness hit him hard, with waves of grief alternating with laughter over the beauty of the cirrus clouds he saw when out in the prison yard.

That night he spoke about it with Father Gerhardt through the ventilation pipe. "This isn't the first time it has happened to me," he confided. "When I returned to America, the waves of emotion hit me when I thought about my time in Belgium. It's humiliating."

Father Gerhardt was typically astute. "What kind of man would you be if you could remember such calamities and remain impassive? Your emotion shows that you have a heart and a soul."

"It proves I'm turning into a weakling," he replied.

Naturally, Father Gerhardt was ready with a denial. "It isn't a sign of weakness, but one that shows you have a generous heart. Your emotions are proof that your soul remains tender amidst the savagery of war, and that is a gift."

Finn snorted. "I've been trained to be a fighter, someone who stands up for others. Now I get weepy at the sight of some pretty clouds. Sorry, Father, but that's not who I am."

Laughter drifted through the pipe. "And yet . . ." The old man's voice trailed off.

"And yet *what*, Father?"

"Sometimes it takes a strong man to acknowledge that he is weak."

Finn shook his head. "I'd rather die a hero than live as a weakling."

"I pray that isn't your fate."

So did Finn, but he wasn't part of the war anymore. All he could do now was pray for peace and the chance to someday go back to his small-town kite store and maybe win Delia back for good.

37

Delia soon learned that she couldn't remain in the Hotel Ravenstein after Bertie left. Too many local people knew she worked for the CRB, and they came to her with pleas for extra rations. Her work preparing reports for New York were continually interrupted by a steady stream of supplicants and their heartrending appeals. The sweet young lady who cleaned the hotel pleaded on behalf of her twin boys, only three years old and not as robust as they ought to be. The mandolin player at the bistro across the street had a sick mother, who had been advised to eat more meat. People from all over Brussels came to the hotel to beg her for help.

And Delia's inability to speak French proved no barrier, for they brought along translators to make their appeals. Yet compassion was all that Delia could offer, and she took the time to hear each person's case before gently turning them away. Still, it was beginning to sap her spirit. She wished she could magically double in size the scant rations shipped in from Rotterdam. It was easier to move across town where nobody knew her. Besides, she didn't need the grandeur of the Hotel Ravenstein. The Marollen District was more affordable and charming in its own way.

After she moved, she kept to herself and never revealed her role with the CRB, which wasn't difficult since Delia didn't actually distribute the food. That was handled in Rotterdam, where CRB staff off-loaded the ships and transferred food onto barges to be distributed throughout occupied Belgium. Delia's job was to confirm that the shipments had arrived at their destination and then compile the statistical report to be sent to New York.

Because her cramped hotel room hadn't the space to lay out her paperwork, she leased an office that belonged to a lawyer conscripted by the Germans years earlier. She felt guilty about taking advantage of the situation, until the man's wife appeared and assured her that the revenue would be greatly appreciated.

Most of the books lining the shelves of the office were printed in French, but there were a few American lawbooks, and they made her feel at home. With a typewriter, a stack of legal texts, and a view of a flower seller's stall across the street, it was the perfect place in which to work.

She came to love the quaint neighborhood with its flea market, antique shops, and cafés. The cafés tended to be filled with too many German officers for Delia to feel comfortable, so she settled for the same rations as ordinary Belgians. Subsisting on CRB rations gave her firsthand experience of the difficulty living under foreign occupation. She lived on little more than a weekly sack of oats, a tin of sardines, and a loaf of bread. Sometimes she longed for a thick pastrami sandwich like she had in New York, but these rations were surely a bounty compared to what Finn received.

At least she had won him an hour of outdoor time each day. She had taken her request to the Swiss diplomatic representative stationed in Brussels, knowing that a formal complaint from a neutral power was the best way to win better conditions for Finn and the other prisoners. She had requested better food, access to doctors and medicine, and the chance to spend time in the fresh air each day. She provided the Swiss delegate with all the proper citations from the Hague Conventions to make her case, but only the hour of outdoor exercise each day was approved. It cost the Germans nothing to provide, but still, it was something.

The crenellated towers of Saint-Gilles Prison were visible from the roof of Delia's hotel. Proximity to Finn's prison was part of the reason she chose this hotel. Visiting him wasn't possible, but she felt closer to him here. At the end of each day, as the sun melted into the horizon over the skyline of Brussels, she made the regular trek up the rickety fire escape steps to stand on the roof and gaze at the prison.

Sometimes she even whispered words of encouragement to him, praying that somehow he could sense her message.

Hang on, Finn. The war may come to an end soon. The American troops have arrived in France, and maybe the tide will turn soon. Please don't despair . . .

The vacant rooftop was ugly, just a patch of tarred gravel with a few ventilation pipes and a water tank. It was oddly reminiscent of her early years with Finn, when two lonely teenagers stole a bit of privacy to fall in love. Looking back, it had been the happiest years of her life. Despite their poverty and the uncertainty of their lives, she'd been happy.

Why had she let safety and security matter more than Finn? Why had she wasted so many years clinging to anger and bitterness? She prayed that someday Finn would walk out of the prison, allowing her the freedom to offer forgiveness and seek his in return.

Delia's anonymity in her new neighborhood could not last forever. Her affiliation with the CRB was accidentally exposed two weeks after she arrived when she visited the post office to send a telegram to New York.

A bell dinged as she crossed the threshold, the scent of aged paper mingling with traces of tobacco from the cigar shop next door. A stooped clerk with a scowling face and shaggy eyebrows sorted letters into wooden pigeonholes behind the front counter.

"*Excusez-moi*," Delia said, which was about the limit of her French. Luckily, her business wouldn't require much of the language since she had written out the brief text for her telegram. "*Le télégraphe?*" she asked, pointing to the telegraph machine tucked behind the counter.

The postal clerk frowned, shook his head, and let out a long spiel in French.

"I'm sorry, I don't understand."

Luckily, the man spoke her language and switched to English. "We don't send telegrams during the day anymore. My son is the operator, and they took him."

"The Germans?"

He nodded. "Six months after the war started, they marched through town and scooped up thousands of our men, including my son. Most of them got shipped to Germany, but Joseph has a bad leg, so they kept him here to slave for the Germans. At least he gets to come home each night."

The postal clerk introduced himself as Mr. Lemaire, and he offered to pass her message to his son, who would wire it when he got home around nine o'clock that night.

Nine o'clock wasn't too much of a delay, so Delia handed him the message. She rooted around in her handbag for the coins to pay the fee, and by the time she looked up, the clerk gaped at her in surprise.

"You work for the CRB?" he asked.

She could have kicked herself for including that in her telegram. "I would appreciate it if you kept that confidential," she said. Back home, postal clerks could lose their job if they invaded people's privacy, but maybe the rules were different here. Or perhaps the war had rewritten all the rules of normal life.

The sluggishness of the clerk vanished, and he stood a little straighter. "Can you pull some strings to get my son additional rations? He really needs them."

Everyone wanted additional rations, and she drew on her well-rehearsed script to deny him, wondering how long it would take for word to spread and her anonymity to be destroyed. "I'm sorry, but I am unable to make concessions for—"

Mr. Lemaire interrupted her. "My son is a cook at the Saint-Gilles Prison," he said, and Delia's breath caught at the revelation. The clerk continued. "Joseph says the prisoners hardly get anything except turnips. Most of the prisoners are Belgians, so shouldn't they be entitled to rations? They have never gotten so much as a slice of bread from the CRB."

This was what Bertie warned her about. The rationing system had been in place for three years, and if they started making exceptions, the fragile system would start breaking down fast.

But did Bertie know about the POWs? Most of the people incarcerated in Saint-Gilles weren't criminals. They were ordinary men and women who had been swept up in a war they hadn't asked for. If it was humanly possible, she needed to get additional rations into the prison. She was ashamed she hadn't thought of it before.

"I'll wire to the man in charge of rations to ask," she told the clerk. "Where is the nearest operational telegraph?"

This message would go straight to Bertie in Washington, not the administrators in New York. Mr. Lemaire guided her outside to point her to the nearest operational telegraph station, which was almost a mile away.

"I'll be back tonight with an answer," she vowed.

———

Six hours later, a telegram from Bertie arrived at her room, and it wasn't good news.

We can allow no deviations from established allotments.

With regret, Bertie

She should have expected it, but as she trudged up to the roof that night, the sight of the prison's medieval stone towers looked especially harsh. Somewhere in that granite monstrosity, Finn languished—alone, hungry, and ill.

Later that evening, she walked back to the post office to meet Joseph, the telegrapher who'd been conscripted into being a cook at the prison. She couldn't secure more rations for the prisoners, but perhaps she could still do something for Finn.

The neighborhood was almost vacant as she walked the familiar cobblestone street toward the post office, a letter to Finn clutched in her hand. The cafés lacked food to stay open into the night, the theaters had been closed for years, and even the Germans had to return to their quarters by sundown. What a contrast to New York back home, the city that never slept.

Though the post office was closed, a lantern burned inside. A young man with a swath of dark hair hanging across his forehead was busy at the telegraph machine. He was alone, probably catching up on the day's work after returning from the prison.

She tapped on the windowpane, and he looked up, revealing a startlingly handsome face. He had a finely chiseled jaw and gentle eyes, but when he came around the counter to unlock the door, she saw a dreadfully twisted leg that caused a severe hitch in his gait.

"Are you Joseph?" she asked when he opened the door.

He nodded and motioned for her to step inside, speaking a torrent of phrases she couldn't understand. He knocked on the pipe at the back of the post office. "*Vite, vite, Papa. L'Américaine est là.*"

Shuffling sounds could be heard from above, and within a minute the postal clerk came downstairs. It was painful to see the hope in both men's eyes, knowing that she had to disappoint them. Since the son didn't speak English, she spoke directly to Mr. Lemaire.

"I'm sorry. It won't be possible to supply the prison with additional rations."

Both men seemed resigned to her answer, and they thanked her for the effort. Now it was her turn to ask a favor.

"A man I care about is imprisoned in Saint-Gilles," she began, speaking directly to Joseph. If he could see the pain in her eyes, perhaps he'd be willing to help. She held the letter aloft and tried to block the quivering from her voice. "His name is Finn Delaney. Would it be possible for you to slip a letter to him?"

Joseph turned to his father for translation. She heard Finn's name among the foreign words, and the two men exchanged several sentences before the elder man turned to her with regret in his expression.

"He can't do it," Mr. Lemaire said. "Any Belgian worker caught trying to communicate with a prisoner risks getting locked up too. Joseph has heard of your pilot. He's the only American in the prison. The Germans really hate him."

It was a double blow, and she reached for the counter to steady herself. Was Finn so badly treated that even the cooks had heard about it?

Mr. Lemaire noticed her distress and guided her to a bench. Both men dragged chairs over to sit with her. Joseph leaned forward, speaking in French, which Mr. Lemaire translated.

"Joseph says that all the prisoners in the basement cells are suffering. While the prisoners upstairs get cabbage and potatoes, the men in solitary confinement get only turnips. Their legs and feet are swollen, and it is hard for them to stand."

She dropped her head into her hands, covering her face. It had been a month since she last saw Finn, and yes, he seemed unsteady on his feet even then. What ghastly disease was afflicting him?

Sniveling wouldn't do Finn any good. She needed more information, and to think of a way to fix this. She dropped her hands and gathered her resolve and asked, "What are the symptoms of the men in solitary confinement? Please tell me everything you know."

Though translation, Delia learned that the men in the lower cells were the most watched, for they were considered spies and traitors. They got the worst food and had only recently been allowed a brief period of daily exercise in the prison yard—a concession Delia had fought hard for them to receive. Joseph had seen the prisoners being led into the yard, but most seemed too ill for exercise and instead sat on wooden benches in the yard. One man had taken to crawling because his feet hurt so badly.

"Are you ever allowed in the yard when these men are out?" She waited while Mr. Lemaire translated.

"He has seen them once or twice," Mr. Lemaire relayed.

Communicating with the prisoners was forbidden, but Delia couldn't help herself as the words poured out of her.

"If you ever see Finn, please tell him I love him. Tell him I'm sorry for every mean, small thing I ever said to him and that I think he has the biggest, most generous heart in the whole world. He taught me to be brave and to dream and to do bold things. Thank him for befriending me when I was alone and had nobody. And tell him to never give up hope. Never, never, never because I'm working to get him out."

Mr. Lemaire rested his hand on her knee, kindness in his tired, old eyes. "My dear, you know that my son cannot deliver your message. It would put his life in danger."

She realized that, but it felt good to say the words out loud. "I know," she whispered.

The best she could do for Finn was to pray for the war to end soon.

As suspected, after revealing her position at the CRB to the men at the post office, word quickly spread throughout the neighborhood. People loitered outside her hotel whenever she emerged to post a letter, buy a cup of tea, or carry her clothes to the laundress. Some were sympathetic, like the lady who asked if her elderly father suffering from pneumonia could be entitled to an extra ration. Others less so, like the portly man with red hair and the world's widest handlebar mustache who approached her when she returned home from church one Sunday morning.

"Rumor has it that the latest CRB ship to arrive in Rotterdam had a case of chocolate bars aboard," he said, fiddling with the waxed tip of his mustache.

It was more than a rumor. The *Athena* had arrived in Rotterdam last week, and the inventory reported a huge donation of chocolate bars from the Hershey Company. Two hundred crates of chocolate had been sent to various distribution points throughout Belgium, all of it earmarked for children. Milton Hershey was a renowned humanitarian who had a special place in his heart for children, and so the chocolate bars had been designated to go to the youngsters of Belgium, who'd had little enough to smile about during their bleak childhood.

"As always, each crate of the donated food has been sent to locations where it will do the most good," Delia said.

"Forgive me, and allow me to introduce myself," the portly gentleman said. "My name is Frederik Mulder, and my wife has a particular love of chocolate. How might I acquire a crate of the chocolate?"

An entire crate! This man had some nerve. It didn't matter how great a person's love for chocolate, nobody could consume an entire crate's worth. Mr. Mulder clearly intended to resell the chocolate on the black market.

"I'm afraid that won't be possible," Delia replied.

"I am happy to pay a fee," he said, not giving up. "In fact, I shall personally deposit a generous fee directly into your hands. You see, my wife simply *needs* the chocolate. She has a medical condition."

It was an attempt to bribe her, and it was easy to refuse the Frederik Mulders of the world. Far more difficult to turn away were the two cheerful nuns who lived at the church nearest Delia's hotel. Sister Agatha was dressed in a black habit from head to toe, while Sister Gita was a nun-in-training who wore a white habit. The younger sister also wore a short white veil that showed her carrot-colored hair. The sisters had cheerful smiles and arrived with a bouquet of roses clipped from the churchyard garden and a jar of honey. Delia was in her office at the time.

"These are for you," Sister Agatha said, extending the bouquet to her. "As soon as we heard a single young lady had come all the way from America on behalf of the people of Belgium, we hurried over to welcome you to Brussels."

Both women spoke perfect English and invited themselves into her office with peals of laughter. Once they had settled in the chairs opposite Delia's desk, Sister Agatha handed over the jar of honey. "It's linden tree honey from our own beehive," the older nun said.

"Linden honey?" Delia asked. "We have apple blossom honey in New York, but I've never heard of linden honey." Sunlight streaming through the window made the honey look like liquid gold.

The younger novice clasped a hand to her chest. "Then you are in for a treat. The bees love linden trees and become positively drunk on their nectar. Truly, you will be able to taste the joy in their honey."

"Indeed," Sister Agatha said. "We are so glad to welcome you to Brussels and will add you to our list of people to pray for."

My, these women were wonderfully clever. They were clearly setting the stage to ask for something, and Delia steeled herself because these two were both kind and charming.

"We run the orphanage at the end of the street," Sister Gita said. "We have thirty orphaned children in our care, and the food provided by the CRB has been lifesaving."

"Yes, but it's not enough," the older nun added, her expression turning serious. "We would like to request an additional fifty percent added to our weekly ration."

How quickly the tone had changed. Delia set the jar of honey on the desk. "Thank you for caring for the children. I grew up in an orphanage, so I know how important your work is."

Sister Agatha nodded. "Does that mean we can expect additional food, then?"

"I'm afraid not," Delia said. "I cannot deviate from the distribution amounts without taking from someone else."

"But our allotment was set in 1914," said Sister Gita. "At the time we had only twenty-one children, and since then the number has grown. The war has taken a terrible toll, and with so many of the men taken by the Germans, their children can become homeless quickly."

Sometimes saying no was simply impossible. The sisters had an excellent justification for requesting extra rations. If a woman gave birth to another child, she received an additional ration, so it seemed logical that an orphanage who took in more children should also get more.

"I will appeal your case to New York," Delia promised. "Until then, I must stick with the authorized distributions."

"And when shall you hear back from New York?" Sister Agatha asked, her smile still tight. It was good the children had so fierce an advocate on their behalf, but Delia intended to visit the orphanage to verify the number of children before sending an appeal to New York.

"As soon as I can verify the number of children in your care, I will send the message."

Both nuns instantly stood. "Come with us now," Sister Gita said.

Delia couldn't help but admire the two women with their barrage of relentless charm, fought on behalf of their young charges. Working for the CRB had never been easy, and it was likely to get even more heartbreaking as the war continued.

38

Finn placed one foot in front of the other, concentrating on the open door at the end of the corridor. It was time for his hour of exercise in the prison yard. Each step triggered a flash of pain that shot up his leg like fiery needles.

Every day he looked forward to this blessed hour in the fresh air, where he could see the sky and the clouds and the sun. Walking hurt, and his feet were getting progressively worse. The only thing he knew to do for the strange, prickly condition was to walk despite the pain.

He squinted against the afternoon glare as he headed into the yard. His eyesight was getting worse too, but he could still see coils of barbed wire topping the granite walls. It was completely unnecessary since neither Finn nor any of the other prisoners had the strength to scale a wall. All of them were suffering from the same debilitating sensation in their feet and hands.

Father Gerhardt was in the worst shape. The old priest sat on a bench in the shade of a scraggly oak tree. Finn lifted his hand in a wave and smiled when the gesture was returned.

Finn wanted to complete at least two laps of the yard before joining Father Gerhardt. Bracing a hand on the grainy stone wall

291

helped keep him steady as he walked, his eyes fastened on the glorious sky above. It was filled with more cirrus clouds today, those wispy clouds found at high altitudes. He'd read once that they were composed entirely of ice crystals. He had never been able to get his plane high enough to fly through them.

It was a relief when he finally completed the second lap and headed toward the benches. Father Gerhardt had been joined by Lucas de Koning, the youngest prisoner here. Lucas had been a music student before the war but got caught sabotaging a railroad the Germans used to transport weapons. Now he was just another prisoner with swollen feet and bad vision.

Finn lowered himself onto the wooden bench opposite the two men and glanced at Gerhardt's feet, covered only by a pair of socks. The old priest's feet had gotten so swollen that they could no longer fit into his shoes.

"How are your feet?"

"Good," Gerhardt replied. "They don't hurt so much anymore. It's my heart that is bad today. It has been racing ever since I awoke this morning. So fast it makes me dizzy."

Finn winced and looked away. Jacob Vinke, one of the prisoners who'd been here for two years, had complained of the exact same symptoms. The pain in his feet eased, and then his heart started acting strangely. He died a few days later. Jacob had been a young man, but Father Gerhardt was seventy-three. If he didn't get decent medical help, he would probably follow Jacob into the grave.

"Maybe the war will be over soon," Finn said, and Lucas's young face brightened as he leaned forward to speak in a conspiratorial whisper.

"I heard that a German general carried a white flag across enemy lines somewhere in France."

A jolt of hope speared Finn's heart. "Where did you hear that?"

"Some of the guards were gossiping."

Father Gerhardt frowned. "That doesn't sound like the behavior of a German general. They may want peace talks, but they wouldn't ever let themselves be seen carrying a white flag."

Yet was talk of surrender impossible? The American forces were probably at full strength by now. Over a million Americans were destined to be sent to the front, a development the Germans probably never expected when they started the war.

"The rainy season is coming up," Finn said. "That means the tanks will get mired in mud, and the Allies won't be able to break through the German lines."

"No," Lucas said. "The British have better tanks and—"

"Hush," Father Gerhardt said with a quick glance to the door.

A cook with a gimpy leg hobbled into the yard, his limp so pronounced that water in his bucket sloshed over the side. All conversation ceased. It was impossible to know if this fellow was a wounded German sent here for light duty or a conscripted Belgian, but he was headed toward them.

The cook didn't even meet their eyes as he offered a ladle of water to Father Gerhardt, who drank greedily. This was odd. They'd never had someone providing them with water before, and as soon as the priest had his fill, the cook dipped the ladle again, then offered it to Finn.

He took the ladle and sniffed the water. It didn't smell off, and he was perpetually thirsty and couldn't resist.

The water slid down his throat like a cool, blessed stream, alleviating the summer's heat and clearing away the grit that had settled within him. Water from heaven itself surely didn't taste this good.

"Thank you," he said as he returned the ladle to the young man, who still refused to look at him before shuffling away to offer water to other prisoners in the yard.

Fatigue had set in, but Finn still had a little more time outdoors. Talk of a German officer with the white flag was surely a rumor. Belief that the Americans entering the war would magically cause a ceasefire was only wishful thinking. Peace might not come for months or even years, and unless he kept exercising, his condition would likely get worse, and he'd find himself as bad off as Father Gerhardt.

He pushed himself off the bench, waiting for the dizziness to pass before setting off on another lap. Everything hurt, the tingling in his feet feeling like fire. It didn't matter. He had to keep the blood moving through his limbs to stave off the course of the illness. Delia was waiting for him.

But was she? Maybe she took his advice and went back to New York and married the old guy. Even if she did, she wouldn't want him to die in prison. He had to survive, if only for her. The chance to work with her raising money for the CRB had been a gift from God. She'd forgiven him. They loved each other. They might never walk down the aisle together, but he'd made his peace with her.

All too soon the clang of a cowbell signaled the end of their time in the prison yard. They had five minutes to clear the area or else there would be consequences. Finn turned to the benches to help Father Gerhardt, but Lucas was already helping the old man to rise.

Without warning, Father Gerhardt toppled over and collapsed in the dusty grass.

Finn scurried over, ignoring the pain, and knelt beside the priest. "Father, are you all right? Did you hurt yourself?"

Gerhardt panted, staring at the sky. "I'm fine. Just dizzy. And my legs don't work too well."

A pair of angry-looking guards approached, yelling in German. It was obvious the old man was in distress, but the guards didn't seem to know what to do. They stood staring stupidly at Father Gerhardt as he panted on the ground.

"I'll carry him inside," Finn offered, but the guards pushed him away. They exchanged a few sentences with Father Gerhardt, who sent Finn a reassuring glance.

"They are going to send for a stretcher," he said, and Finn nodded.

It didn't take long for the stretcher to arrive. Would they take him to an infirmary? In all the time Finn had been here, none of the prisoners had ever seen a doctor or been treated at an infirmary, if there even was one in this godforsaken place. Everyone stood in silence as the stretcher with Father Gerhardt was carried away.

From the corner of his eye, Finn spotted the cook with the water bucket, who discreetly made the sign of the cross as the stretcher passed him. Then he took his bucket and left the yard.

A few hours later, the clank of the neighboring cell door jerked Finn awake. He bolted upright and strained to listen. Shuffling of feet and a few snatches of German leaked through the ventilation pipe. Finn could make no sense of the words, but the shuffling sounds and the grunts indicated Father Gerhardt might have returned to his cell.

The door slammed shut, and the lock turned once more. Finn counted his breaths, waiting until he could be sure the guards were gone before standing on tiptoes beneath the ventilation pipe.

"Father?" he whispered. If the old man was sleeping, it was best not to disturb him, but mercifully an answer came.

"All good, Finn." Gerhardt's voice was weak but reassuring. It was late and clear the old man wasn't up for more talk.

"Sleep well," Finn whispered before limping back to bed to pray. He'd been praying for Father Gerhardt throughout the day, mostly begging God to keep him alive for selfish reasons. He needed the old priest's company, his wisdom, his humor. This time, however, Finn thanked God.

Thank you for sending me a German to be my companion. I needed the reminder of our shared humanity. I never should have called them Krauts or Jerries. Please, God, keep Father Gerhardt alive. The world is going to need good men like him when this is all over.

The next morning, Finn returned to the ventilation pipe with a greeting, but there was no answer from the other side. He waited awhile before trying again. When still there was no answer, he risked tapping on the pipe. No response.

A little over an hour later, the neighboring cell door opened, followed by shuffling feet and German voices. Finn pressed his ear to the ventilation pipe to listen. He'd learned enough German to know that Father Gerhardt had passed away during the night. They mentioned *Friedhof*, the name of the cemetery on the prison grounds.

Finn pressed his forehead against the stone wall of his cell. He didn't need to hear any more. "Father Gerhardt, you are free now," he whispered. "Thank you for everything you did for me. Thank you for being my friend and my moral compass through this terrible time. I hope that heaven brings you the peace and joy you always spoke about. I hope it looks like the Black Forest of Germany you loved so well. Farewell, Father. Your kindness will never be forgotten . . ."

He dragged in a lungful of air, and the effort sapped him of all strength. He braced himself against the wall as he crept back to the cot, flopping down onto it. He ought to rejoice that Father Gerhardt had gone to a better place.

Instead, Finn worried he wouldn't be able to survive much longer either.

Delia listened to Joseph the cook relay the terrible symptoms troubling the men in solitary confinement. Something needed to be done for them, and the first step would be to identify their affliction. She asked Sister Gita to accompany her to a doctor's office to serve as translator.

Dr. Achen was one of the few physicians left in Brussels, as most of the doctors and pharmacists in Belgium had been forced to go work in Germany. Gita said that the Germans thought Dr. Achen too old to be conscripted into service, and he'd come out of retirement to treat patients. She was grateful for the chance to meet with him, even though his practice was in the parlor of his town house. There was no examination table or bottles of medicine. It was simply a comfortable parlor with a few ancient medical texts on an overstuffed bookshelf.

Delia blanched when Dr. Achen entered the room, his palsied hand shaking on an unsteady cane and his skin so papery thin that a network of veins looked like an ancient map. Gita explained she would be translating for Delia, but it turned out not to be necessary.

"I attended Yale University back in 1850," the doctor said in a scratchy voice. "Tell me how I can help."

Attending medical school almost three-quarters of a century ago did not lend Delia confidence, but she proceeded to explain how the cook at the Saint-Gilles Prison had observed a common illness among the prisoners. She described their swollen hands and feet, their listlessness, and their terrible diet that consisted of nothing but turnips.

"Two of the men have died," she concluded. "Just before death, the pain in their limbs eased and then they developed rapid heart-beats."

The doctor's brows lowered, and he grabbed a fat book from his shelf and flipped through its pages. The book looked even older than the doctor, and she clenched her fists. Could the answer to this strange affliction be in that tatty old book? Her nerves ratcheted higher as the doctor rubbed his jaw and skimmed several pages.

Finally, with great effort he hefted the book closed. "I believe the men are suffering from beriberi. It is caused by lack of proper nutrition. Give the men some pork or fish and perhaps green peas. That should solve the problem."

Delia sagged. The odds of getting such things smuggled into the prison to Finn were nonexistent. "Is there a pill or medicine we can provide them?" If so, she'd figure out a way to smuggle it to the men.

The doctor let out a heavy sigh, reclined in his chair, and closed his eyes. The only sign that he wasn't asleep was the rapid twiddling of his thumbs. A range of expressions crossed his face, and then he straightened in the chair.

He stood and beckoned them both to his kitchen, a tiny space crowded with herbs and copper pots dangling from an overhead rack. Dr. Achen reached for a canister on a shelf above the stove and opened it to show them a brown powder that gave off a sharp odor.

"It's brewer's yeast," the doctor said. "It is packed with the nutritional properties that will help cure beriberi. Mix it into the water your cook gives the prisoners, and it might work."

It didn't sound very promising, but it was worth a try.

Their only way of getting anything to Finn and the other men was through Joseph. That night, Delia and Gita waited in the post office for Joseph's return at nine o'clock. They had been meeting him here almost every evening since persuading him to offer water to the prisoners during their hour in the prison yard. There was always a stack of accumulated telegrams to be sent, and they waited patiently in the tiny post office while he completed the task. Sister Gita hopped up onto the front counter to read the messages while Joseph tapped the sounder in a rapid stream of electronic dots and dashes to send messages all over the world.

Once he completed the task, he'd pass on whatever he noticed about the condition of the men in the yard. Normally he was congenial, but that came to a swift end when Gita asked him to mix brewer's yeast into the bucket of water he served the prisoners. Delia couldn't understand as they argued in French, but the harder Gita pushed, the sterner Joseph became. Gita hopped down from the counter and paced the cramped area behind the telegraph station while Joseph folded his arms and glowered.

"He won't do it," Gita finally told Delia in English. "Ever since he asked permission to provide water to the men, the Germans are suspicious of him. The commandant warned Joseph that if he dared to smuggle notes or food to the prisoners, he will be clapped into chains and become a prisoner himself. He isn't even allowed to speak to the men."

Joseph's fear was understandable, and Delia couldn't even be certain the brewer's yeast would save the prisoners. Dr. Achen was ancient, and the plan seemed improbable. How could she ask Joseph to risk his life for a folk remedy that only *might* work?

"Tell Joseph that he will be a hero if he does this," Delia told

Gita. "Tell him that when the war is over, the CRB will nominate him for the Order of Leopold. The whole neighborhood will throw rose petals in his path."

She listened while Gita relayed the message, and Joseph shoved his chair back from the telegraph machine to pace, his lumbering gait more pronounced than ever.

"He asks what good are medals and glory if he is dead."

Joseph had a good point, but Gita went back to arguing with him, her white novice's habit swaying with the force of her gestures. Joseph sparred, scowled, and shouted. It was a little unseemly to yell at a nun, but Gita stood up to him in an endless series of tart replies. The only time she broke stride was to relay Joseph's latest argument.

"Joseph says his father depends on the income he brings in, and if he is imprisoned, it is his father who will pay the price."

"Tell him I'll pay for a telegrapher if he can't do it," Delia said.

Gita did, and Joseph shook his head. The arguing continued for several more minutes until at last Gita whipped off her veil and threw it against the wall as she continued shouting.

Joseph backed up against the wall, looking stunned. Finally, he interrupted. "*J'abandonne. Je vais le faire.*" Then he limped up the stairs and slammed the door.

Gita looked tired as she went to retrieve her veil. "He'll do it," she said, and yet she seemed annoyed.

"How did you convince him?" Delia asked.

"He doesn't trust you to pay for a telegrapher because you will leave once the war is over. I told him that if he died in the jail, I would learn the trade and do the job for the rest of his father's life."

Delia was grateful for Gita's persistence, but the younger woman did not look happy.

Gita locked eyes with her and said, "We must pray very hard for Joseph's safety because I would rather pick snails from the muck than be a telegrapher."

Delia grinned and gave Gita a hearty embrace. "Yes, my friend. We will both pray very hard."

40

Finn ignored the pain in his limbs as he struggled to complete a single lap in the prison yard. His hands hurt as he braced them against the wall for support. And though his feet were so swollen that they felt like lead weights, he wouldn't stop walking.

At least he could still feel the pain. When his feet went numb, it would mean that death was drawing near. He eyed the cluster of men slumped on the benches beneath the oak tree. Everyone was despondent since Father Gerhardt's death last week. The old man had been a pillar of courage and optimism. With his passing, it felt as though the fragile thread of hope that held them aloft had vanished.

Finn lowered his chin and focused on the far end of the yard. He'd get there even if he had to crawl. The man with the crooked leg arrived and headed toward Finn with his bucket of water.

Finn leaned against the wall to catch his breath. It took a moment to summon the energy to reach for the ladle of water and draw it to his mouth.

He spat it out, gagging as he threw the ladle to the ground. The cook picked it up, wiped the dipper on his trousers, then dunked it in the bucket again.

Finn shook his head. "Bad water," he said. It was beyond bad; it was gritty and it stank. Was this man trying to kill him?

The cook refused to look at him as he leaned in and whispered, "*Boire. C'est un médicament.*"

Finn froze, his cloudy mind trying to parse the words. The cook had spoken in French. He was probably a Belgian, not a German, and he said there was medicine in the water.

It surely tasted bad enough to be medicine, but could he trust the cook? Just because he spoke a few words in French didn't mean he wasn't German. And yet when Father Gerhardt collapsed and had to be carried away on the stretcher, the cook looked genuinely sad. He'd made the sign of the cross as Father Gerhardt was taken away.

Finn took the ladle, dipped it into the water, and drank. The bitter liquid left a grainy residue on his tongue and down his throat. Though his stomach threatened to heave, he drank again, this time holding his breath to ensure everything stayed down.

"Thank you," he said as he returned the dipper. The cook still wouldn't look at him, but he pointed to the other prisoners sitting beneath the tree before heading off in his distinctive, listing gait.

The gesture was so fast that Finn couldn't be sure he hadn't imagined it, but it seemed the cook wanted him to tell the other prisoners about the water. If the other men spat it out or threw the ladle as Finn had done, it would attract the attention of the two soldiers standing guard.

Needles of pain shot up from his feet as he tried to catch up to the cook. He was dizzy by the time he arrived at the bench. Lucas saw him coming and scooted to make room just as Finn collapsed onto the bench.

"The water has medicine in it," he whispered to Lucas. "Drink it. It tastes bad but get it down."

Lucus looked surprised, but he drank without complaint. His

nose wrinkled, and he fought back a gag, but the water stayed down. He then turned to the man next to him, and news about the medicine was passed down the line.

"Are you sure that was medicine?" Lucas whispered.

Finn shrugged. "I hope so. Even if it's poison, we're all going to die eventually if something doesn't change."

Delia settled into a routine as the summer stretched on. The deprivations of war hovered over the city like a dark, smothering cloud, yet life pressed onward. The perfume from the linden trees mingled with acrid coal smoke, a reminder that the commandeered factories of Brussels still produced munitions to power the German war machine. Street vendors wheeled their carts to-and-fro, filled with whatever meager produce they could scavenge from the countryside.

Despite the comradery among most of the Belgians, the black market still thrived. Frederik Mulder, the man who had tried to bribe Delia for CRB chocolate, always seemed to have food to sell. He could be seen strutting around the Marollen District, a jovial smile plastered on his face as he bartered with desperate people for chocolate, coffee, and tins of food. It was sad to see people trade their watches, jewelry, and family heirlooms for a bit of black-market food.

Delia looked the other way. Her job was to track CRB shipments and ensure they didn't fall into the hands of the Germans. She couldn't stop the black market, nor did she even know if that was wise. Who was she to say that a woman shouldn't trade a pair of earrings if her child needed a can of condensed milk?

At least Delia had succeeded in getting more food for the children at the church orphanage. Her appeal to New York for additional food had resulted in several more sacks of rice, oats, and cans of milk.

Delia's daily activities now included making batches of brewer's yeast to give to Joseph. The process involved several stages and took ten days to complete. She met Gita at the orphanage kitchen each evening to move production along. A single lantern cast an amber glow over the white enameled kitchen as they worked long into the night. The muscles of Delia's arms grew strong as she continually stirred the mixture to introduce more oxygen and help the yeast multiply.

Cooking, fermenting, and drying the yeast gave the kitchen a sour, zesty smell. Over time, Delia grew to appreciate the scent because it signaled the growth of lifesaving yeast.

It was hard to tell if the medicine was working. Joseph said the prisoners still complained of worsening symptoms in their swollen limbs, but nobody else had died. Nor did any of the prisoners suffer from chest pain or a racing heart that was the forewarning of imminent death. Dr. Achen speculated that the brewer's yeast could not cure them but was slowing the progression of the disease, so Delia doubled her efforts to produce a steady supply of daily yeast.

Getting sugar was her only problem. Sugar was necessary for the fermentation process, but aside from the black market, there was simply no sugar to be had. It meant Delia had to resort to working with her least favorite person in all of Belgium.

"I shall happily supply you with sugar," Frederik Mulder said brightly. "It will cost you, but I'd love to establish a better relationship with the CRB."

Delia had no idea where Mr. Mulder got the sugar, nor did she care. She paid his exorbitant price for the sugar from her own pocket and put it to work making yeast.

"I hated putting a single franc into that man's grubby hand," she told Gita later that evening as she stirred a cooking mixture. "The first time we met, he implied his wife was ill and only a crate of chocolate would cure her."

Gita rolled her eyes. "He doesn't even have a wife, though I always see him squiring women about town. I suspect they like the sugar and chocolate and whatever other black-market goodies he's got."

Gita added a few more lumps of fermented yeast into a large bowl and began grinding it into a powder with the pestle. "Do you think you'll marry Finn when this is all over?" she asked.

Delia paused her stirring. In the past, Finn's reckless nature scared her away. Sometimes his gambles worked, and sometimes they were catastrophic. And yet knowing him had made her a better person. Braver and more generous. Less focused on herself and her own needs.

"I'd like to," she finally said. "I don't know if he'll survive or if he'll come out of prison a different person, but I've learned to weather storms and to forgive. He may need both when he finally gets out of that dungeon."

"And if he doesn't survive?"

The question hung in the air. Contemplating Finn's death felt disloyal, even if it was a real possibility. She managed a sad smile. "If Finn doesn't make it, maybe I'll become a nun like you."

Gita wagged her finger. "I'm not a nun yet, just a novice. I don't take my final vows for another six months. I can still bail out if I want. There's no shame in it."

"Will you?" It never occurred to Delia that Gita might someday leave the convent and the orphanage.

Gita shrugged. "I still don't know. I came here because God called me to tend abandoned children. Nothing has given me greater satisfaction. But the war has created so many orphans that perhaps I don't need to become a nun to care for them."

If Finn didn't make it, perhaps Delia would stay in Belgium with Gita to help care for the multitudes of displaced children and people. Peace would only be a starting point of the healing. The scars of the war would reverberate for decades, shaping the world in ways no one could yet imagine.

The fluttery call of a nightingale sounded in the tree outside the open window, and Delia wandered closer to listen. Its whistles and trills were lovely, a reminder of the beauty of God's creation.

And yet the nightingale was the bird of lamentation too. Its elegiac call was a symbol of lost beauty, of mourning and remembrance of the dead.

Oh, Finn, please hang on. What a terrible time you are enduring, but someday soon the darkness will lift from the world, and you will be free again. Just don't die . . .

The call of the nightingale haunted her, and for the first time, Delia feared that Finn might not live to see the world at peace again.

41

Finn was coming to accept that he was probably going to die in prison, and he needed to get a final message to Delia. His best shot at that was to meet with Lucas de Koning in the yard today. Lucas was still in good shape and could get a message to Delia once the war was over.

That meant Finn had to fight through unbearable lethargy, sit up, and be ready to get himself to the prison yard when the guard came for him. Sitting upright made him dizzy, and he stared at his swollen, pudgy feet. They looked like they belonged to a different person and were so big he couldn't get them into his shoes. He'd have to go barefoot.

They didn't hurt anymore, which was a sign that the end was drawing near.

When the guard came for him, Finn was ready. The tunnel leading to the yard seemed longer than ever, but he was determined to get there. Once in the yard, he could sit on the bench and talk to Lucas.

It was freezing outside. The autumn wind carried speckles of sleet that slashed on his face. Some of the prisoners had stayed inside, but Lucas was here. Finn hobbled over to the bench to join him. Just lowering himself onto the bench drained his paltry reserve of energy.

"You okay?" Lucas asked.

"My feet have turned numb."

The expression on Lucas's face morphed from shock to grief and then to acceptance in the space of a few seconds. Finn scrambled for something funny to say.

"Hey, at least I won't have to eat turnips after I'm gone."

Lucas didn't laugh. "Are you sure?"

"Yeah, I'm sure," Finn said. If his illness followed the same symptoms as Father Gerhardt, in the next few days his heart would start racing and breathing would become difficult. Time was growing short, and he had to get a message to Delia.

"Lucas, if you survive the war, I want you to get a message to my girl. Her name is Delia Byrne, and she works for the CRB. Tell her that she's getting my kite shop. It's in the will I wrote before I left. Tell her she can do whatever she wants with it . . ." The mental image of his shop caused his throat to close up. He'd painted the ceiling a pale shade of sky blue, just like the shop he and Delia dreamed about when they were kids. The memories were painful, so he cleared his throat to talk again. "Tell her she can do whatever she wants with the kite shop, but I hope she lives there and runs it."

"You've got a kite store?" Lucas asked, a hint of amusement in his eyes.

"Yeah, I do." And it had been great. He loved showing people how to look up at the immensity of the sky and fly, to transcend the bonds that held them down and watch their kites soar between heaven and earth. It would have been better had he run the store with Delia, but they'd been too hotheaded to make it happen. Yet they'd both grown up a lot in the past year, and maybe they could have made it work after all.

He looked up at the sky. The blustery autumn day made for good kite-flying weather. He gathered a breath to keep talking to Lucas.

"Tell Delia how grateful I am that she got the Germans to let us have this hour to see the sky. Tell her that every day I've been able to look up at the clouds and the sun, and I think about how lucky we were to find each other. Despite everything, how lucky we were."

A thick layer of stratus clouds completely blanketed the sky. To the west, muted sunlight shone behind pewter-colored clouds. The sun's bright radiance was trying to break through the gloom, but Finn wouldn't be here to see it. The guards would be back soon, and he'd be shuffled back to his cell.

But for now, he still had a few blessed minutes to enjoy the sky. Yes, despite everything, Finn had been blessed with a wonderful life. He turned his face toward the veiled sun and smiled.

42

Delia was awakened by the ringing of church bells. She rose up on her elbow to see the hint of a sunrise through the filmy drapes. How strange for church bells to be ringing so early on a Monday morning. The bells went on and on, a cascade of clangs in a rhythmic cadence, echoing through the neighborhood.

She threw back the sheets and darted to the window, the tile floor icy on her bare feet. She looked toward the bell tower across the street and spotted Joseph leaving the church, moving as fast as his lopsided gait could carry him. She hoisted up the sash and leaned out into the chilly morning air.

"Joseph!" she called down, but her voice was lost in the ringing of the bells, for he didn't stop as he hurried down the street and around the bend.

Delia grabbed her robe, shoved her feet into a pair of boots, and rushed down the stairs and out the door. The frigid November air hit her, but she ignored it as she ran toward the bell tower.

Inside, the nuns still wore their nightgowns, pulling on the bells' ropes with all their might. Some were laughing, others crying.

Gita noticed her first. "Delia! The war is over!"

Delia clapped a hand over her mouth, her eyes wide and unable to believe her ears. Gita had to shout to be heard over the clanging of the bells, explaining that Joseph had just received a telegram from Paris, announcing that Germany had signed an agreement an hour ago. The armistice would go into effect at eleven o'clock this morning.

Delia fell into Gita's arms and wept. Tears flooded her eyes as she bawled like a baby. Finn was going to get out! He was going to live. He had made it to the end of the war, and God had been merciful to them.

Joseph had gone to spread the news to the other churches, and soon bells were ringing throughout the city. People began pouring into the streets as the news spread like wildfire, and then the cheering began.

Delia wasn't the only person still in her nightclothes, but she was freezing and so ran back to her hotel to pull on warmer clothes. By the time she returned to the street, the celebration had expanded as more people filled the narrow alleys. Strangers hugged and kissed one another. Bottles of wine were uncorked despite the early hour. A trumpeter played the Belgian national anthem, its triumphant melody reverberating through the streets of Brussels for the first time in four years.

Delia and Gita strolled arm and arm down the street, waving at people and exchanging blessings.

"Look!" Delia said, pointing to a window on the third floor of a rooming house, where a man unfurled the flag of Belgium. The crowd below roared as the tricolor flag caught the breeze.

Amid the crowd, Delia spotted Joseph's distinctive limp as he headed back toward the post office. She grinned and waved, hoping to catch his attention.

Instead, he was focused on Gita. A glint of determination brightened his face as he descended on Gita, grinning and wrapping her in his arms and laying a deep kiss on her mouth. Delia's eyes nearly popped from her head as Gita returned the kiss in earnest. Perhaps it was a good thing that Gita hadn't yet taken her vows, for it appeared she was about to embark on a different path in life. She and Joseph babbled to each other in joyous French, talking over one another with laughter.

Then Joseph sobered, spoke a few words, and turned to limp away. Gita still beamed at him as she raised her hand in farewell.

"He's going to the prison," she said. "The men will still need breakfast."

Delia sucked in a quick breath. "Does he know when the prisoners will be released?"

"No," Gita replied. "My guess is that the Germans will still insist on their fussy rules and red tape. It could be days or even longer before they get out."

Delia hardened her resolve. "No, it will *not*," she said. They were in uncharted territory, and chaos was likely to reign for a while, but she was going to get Finn out of that prison. Maybe even today!

A quiet joy lit Gita's face as she gazed at Joseph making his way down the street.

"So," Delia said in a teasing voice. "Joseph?"

A blush colored Gita's cheeks. "I didn't realize he felt the same. I had hoped, but you know how terribly serious he always is."

Delia gave her a friendly nudge. "Just think, you won't have to become a telegrapher after all."

Gita beamed. "A telegrapher's *wife* will be just fine for me."

The euphoria on the streets of Brussels lingered, but after a few hours, reality began to sink in. Churches held prayer gatherings, and many people took flowers to the cemetery to mourn for those who hadn't survived to see this day.

Lines began forming outside the office of the Belgian Red Cross as women demanded the return of their sons and husbands who'd been conscripted by the Germans. A frazzled Red Cross clerk stood on the stoop of the building, squinting to read aloud from a telegram.

Gita provided the translation. "They don't know when the men will be repatriated. The Swiss are offering to help with negotiations."

A woman started screaming, tears flowing down her cheeks as she shook her fists. Gita's eyes filled with compassion as she listened.

"That woman has three sons and a husband who were taken by conscription. She thinks they were sent to the Eastern Front but isn't sure. She demands their return immediately."

Europe would soon be flooded with refugees, returning soldiers, and people like this woman's three sons who'd been conscripted by the Germans. Were they still alive? Who was going to help all these people? Who was going to negotiate the release of the prisoners at Saint-Gilles? Were they supposed to patiently wait for the Red Cross?

Delia grabbed Gita's arm. "I'm going to the prison. Will you come with me? I don't know what we'll find when we get there, but I need you to translate for me."

"I don't speak German, but I'll help however I can."

The half-mile walk took longer than usual. Throngs of people crowded the streets, and automobiles honked their horns, both in celebration and out of frustration with the congestion. A hasty edition of the newspaper had been printed, and people clustered around the newsboy to buy an issue. Children waved Belgian flags and sang patriotic songs. Here and there, German soldiers watched the ongoing celebration with baffled expressions.

A handful of people gathered around a portly man with a familiar handlebar mustache, who was busy selling chocolate from a vendor tray strapped around his neck. With the end of the war, Frederik Mulder no longer feared arrest for dealing on the black market and was openly selling candy bars for five francs each.

Delia shouldered her way through the crowd. "Tell me, Mr. Mulder, where did you get that chocolate?"

Frederik Mulder grinned and gave a good-natured shrug. "Where there's a will, there's a way."

"If you did an under-the-table deal with someone at a CRB distribution center, I will find out and have you both charged," she warned.

Mr. Mulder's face remained the picture of innocence. "Why so glum? Here! A gift from me to the lovely local CRB representative." He tossed up a chocolate bar, and she snatched it from the air. Finn might need it.

She and Gita continued trudging up the cobblestone street toward the prison. As they neared the top of the hill, the massive facade of Saint-Gilles loomed ahead, its formidable towers and barred windows in stark contrast to the revelry in the streets.

They weren't the only ones going to the prison. Plenty of other people had friends and relatives imprisoned, while others were simply Belgian civilians ready to join the stampede to liberate the prisoners. Delia clutched Gita's hand to avoid being separated as they surged up the hill toward the front gate.

Five German soldiers guarded the entrance, nervously pacing and clutching their rifles. Barely older than boys, they exchanged nervous glances when the crowd started shouting at them.

"The people are demanding for them to open the gates," Gita told her.

It was now two o'clock in the afternoon. The armistice was in effect, and it was time to free the prisoners. She wasn't going to wait for some Swiss diplomat or international arbitration panel. Shouts in French and Dutch filled the air as the people yelled at the guards.

About thirty unarmed civilians faced the five armed guards. It was a potentially dangerous situation.

Gita stepped forward, and the agitation from the crowd settled at the sight of her. She was only a novice, but her all-white habit and veil made her look like a nun, and she was afforded automatic respect. With her hands held up, palms out, Gita walked slowly forward to speak to a German sergeant.

"*Nous venons en paix*," she said, but when the sergeant showed no understanding, she repeated it in English: "We come in peace."

"It doesn't look like peace to me," the nervous sergeant replied, also speaking in English. "We're waiting for orders from Berlin. We're not doing anything until we get them. The commandant says we should hear something in a few days."

Delia strode forward and faced the sergeant. "No! Not another day, not another hour!" Her demand rang off the hard granite walls, but she wasn't finished. "We want those men out *now*. Unlock the cells and throw open the gates."

"I can't do that," the sergeant said. "We have orders."

Enough people spoke English so that the sergeant's refusal set off a ripple of anger through the crowd. "You lost the war!" someone shouted. "Let our men go!"

Then a tough-looking young man in the crowd picked up a rock. He stood where the sergeant could plainly see him as he tossed the rock from hand to hand, a clear threat. Others in the crowd reached down for loose cobblestones. The last thing Delia wanted was violence. The people of this city had endured too much for tempers to cause bloodshed this close to the end.

She wanted peace, but she wasn't going to back down either. She took a step closer to the sergeant. "The war is over. Let the men in this prison go home to their families. People higher than us will be meeting for months and years to settle accounts for what happened in the war. If you show compassion now, it will be remembered as a sign of goodwill. And, Sergeant, there isn't much goodwill for Germans right now."

A muscle ticked in the German soldier's jaw. He glanced nervously at the gathering crowd. He could order his men to open fire and end this right now, but there would be a cost for that in the time to come.

The sergeant barked an order to his men, then turned around and disappeared behind a locked door.

Though it was a cold day, sweat trickled down Delia's back. Nobody in the crowd moved. All stood in silence, waiting for something to happen. It felt like forever but was probably only a few minutes until the gate opened and the sergeant reemerged to address the crowd.

"Everyone, stand back," he announced. "The prisoners will be released. Feeding and caring for them is now your responsibility."

A guard repeated the command in French as another of the soldiers pushed the gate wide, and the creak of its hinges was loud enough to cut through the nervous murmurs among the crowd.

At first nothing happened, but after a moment, a pair of bedraggled men came shuffling forward, smiles of relief on their grubby faces.

Applause sounded from the crowd while the men trudged forward. Delia's vision blurred beneath a sheen of tears. It was happening! It was really happening, and any moment Finn Delaney was going to come walking out of the gates and she would be here to meet him. Here with a chocolate bar for him!

More prisoners came trickling out of the prison, blinking in astonishment at their sudden change in fortune. Some looked aimless and confused, as if not knowing where to go.

Delia grabbed Gita's arm. "Someone needs to contact the Red Cross. These people will need shelter until we can get them to their homes." Most were Belgian resistance fighters, but some came from as far away as Italy and France.

The man who had picked up the first rock tossed it to the ground. "I will contact them. I work for the Red Cross."

Gita scowled. "And you were ready to start a riot?"

The man shrugged. "I'm a Belgian first, Red Cross worker second."

Delia urged him to hurry because the trickle of former prisoners had turned into a flood. Delia shielded her eyes from the sun, straining to see each face. Most of the men had beards, and surely Finn would as well.

"Help me search for Finn," she said to Gita.

"What does he look like?"

She and Gita had grown so close over the past months, it was hard to remember that Gita had never met Finn. "He has blond hair that's probably long and shaggy by now. And he's got the bluest eyes; you can drown in them. He's tall and has a bad leg, so he limps when he walks. Not as much as Joseph, but still, he limps a little." She knew she was babbling, but excitement made it impossible to stop talking because in just a few short minutes, she was going to finally welcome Finn back into the world of freedom.

The throngs of prisoners walking out the gates was so thick that she couldn't see them all. She hoisted up her skirts to climb atop a bench. Now she could look down on the steady flow of tired, elated, and bewildered prisoners as they shuffled down the cobblestone street. Most were men, but a few women were in the mix too.

"See anything?" Gita asked.

"No."

It was too early to panic. There were around five hundred people imprisoned in Saint-Gilles, and only a few hundred people had walked through the gates. Ten people were still being held in solitary confinement down in the basement, and perhaps it was taking longer for those prisoners to be released. She must not panic yet, but her stomach felt sour.

Soon Gita joined her on the bench, and the two of them stood there scanning the former prisoners as they slowly plodded down the street. These ones looked thinner and more bedraggled than the earlier prisoners.

Oh, Finn, where are you? Delia silently begged. Maybe she needed to go inside the prison to search for him. The German guards still flanked the entrance, and none of the civilians had entered the prison. But if Delia had to go inside and search every cell, she was going to find him.

"There he is!" Gita called out.

Delia froze and looked to where Gita was pointing. At first all she saw was Joseph, heading their way with a man slumped against his shoulder. He was filthy, his hair covering most of his face, and his feet were bare, swollen . . .

"*Finn?*"

When the man looked up, Delia nearly fainted because it *was* Finn. His face crumpled when he saw her, and he almost toppled over, but Joseph propped him back up. She leaped off the bench and angled her way through the crowds to reach his side.

"I thought you went back to New York," he said, his voice stunned.

"*Never, never, never.* I'd never leave Belgium while you were still here." She opened her arms, and he reached out to grab her, squeezing her tightly. Her heart nearly split at how sharp his bones felt beneath the threadbare coat, but he was out, and he was here. He was hers again.

"Thank God you're alive," she choked out against his shoulder. "I'm going to take you home and take the best care of you. I'll get you cleaned up and feed you something warm and rich and sweet. I'll kiss you and hold you and never let you go again."

His breath caught and was ragged. "Dee, I'm about to start bawling, which is completely at odds with the moment."

She laughed, even as she grieved his frail condition. She clutched his hand and pressed a kiss to his knuckles, and he gasped. It was a gasp of pain, not pleasure, and she immediately let go. "Did I hurt you?"

"I'm not in good shape, Dee," he said with a half smile that nearly broke her heart all over again. "I can't really walk anymore. If Joseph hadn't helped me out of my cell . . ."

Delia knew the cure for his illness. Nourishing food would do the trick, although the best she could offer at the moment was the chocolate bar. When she held the familiar Hershey's candy bar out to him, his face crumpled again, and then he did start bawling in earnest. He buried his face in her neck and sobbed, and she held him gently, stroking his back as tears fogged her vision too.

"It's going to be okay," she soothed. "Everything is going to be okay now."

Church bells continued to peal, and a spontaneous singing of the national anthem broke out among the liberated prisoners. There would be time enough in the years ahead for lamentations and rebuilding. Today, however, was for celebration.

Finn sat on a wicker chair on the hospital veranda, the scent of freshly cut grass and damp earth rising with the soft breeze. With slow, practiced strokes, he used the blade of his pocketknife to carve a slender strip of wood, shaving it down to the perfect curve for a kite's frame.

He had been at the convalescent hospital in Le Havre for two months. His recovery took longer than expected because malnutrition had left his muscles severely atrophied, his nerves damaged, and his heart weakened. The swelling in his lower limbs eventually subsided, but lingering neuropathy in his hands and feet made even simple movements painful.

He was mostly healed now, and making kites had been the perfect task for regaining his dexterity. He was ready to be discharged, but the troopships heading home were fully booked for months, and the hotels in Le Harve had all been requisitioned for the soldiers waiting to sail home. That meant the hospital was the only place for Finn to stay. Every day, he sat on the veranda overlooking the harbor, where a collection of masts, cranes, and ships could be seen in the distance. The same ships that were ferrying troops homeward. Soon he would leave too, but right now he had to wait his turn.

So here he sat, building kites in a seaside villa once meant for holidaymakers, but now used as a convalescent hospital for recuperating soldiers. A row of wicker chairs lined the patio, where a dozen other men dozed or read in the quiet lull of midmorning. Finn passed the time by making the kites, which he then gave to his fellow soldiers as gifts.

The wind blowing off the English Channel was brisk enough to raise the kites with ease, and it was impossible not to smile when seeing them soaring in the sea breeze. One of the doctors told Finn that his kites were some of the best medicine he'd yet seen for war-weary soldiers.

Doctors and nurses in their prim white caps moved among the patients scattered on the lawn, yet there was only one nurse Finn wanted to see.

Each day, Nurse Ellie went into town with requests from patients to pick up various sundries from the commissary or to post letters. This morning she was making a special trip to the jeweler to pick up the engagement ring he had commissioned for Delia. As soon as he had the ring, he could finally propose. This day was more than ten years in the making, and he had prepared for it with care.

Delia visited him for lunch every day, and normally they ate on the sheltered veranda that was crowded with patients sitting at long tables. Not today, though. Finn wanted privacy to propose to her and so had made special arrangements to use one of the quaint round tables in the garden usually reserved for staff. Folks on the veranda might still be able to see him and Delia, but at least they wouldn't overhear their conversation.

The creak of the front gate caught his attention, and he set aside the kite frame he was working on. "Ellie!" The nurse had just arrived, and he walked across the lawn to meet her. "Do you have the ring?"

Ellie grinned and held up her hand, the gemstone flashing on her ring finger. It was a square aquamarine stone, the exact color of the sky on a cloudless day, and Delia's favorite color in the world.

"It's gorgeous," Ellie said and batted her eyelashes at him. "Are you sure you don't want to propose to me instead?"

"Ellie, there are a couple dozen guys here who would love to take you home with them, but my heart is already taken."

She faked a sad face and tugged the ring from her finger. "Have it your way," she said and handed it over. "Hey, I heard a Holland America ship is arriving next week to carry more troops home, and it has lots of civilian berths available. If you get married quickly enough, maybe you can book passage on it instead of waiting for a troopship."

The news was too good to be true. The Holland America line had first-rate passenger cabins, and it would make for a perfect honeymoon. The prospect of returning home never felt closer. Delia's work with the CRB was coming to an end, so she could leave Europe with him.

Now that Belgium had been liberated, the small nation was in no greater need than any of the other war-torn countries. Each day saw more Belgian men and boys returning home, all those who'd been conscripted by the Germans, including Mathilde's husband. It took Mathilde a little longer to make her way home from Switzerland, but after four long years, the Verhaegen family was once again whole.

It was almost one o'clock, the time he asked for lunch to be delivered to the garden table. He returned his kite-making tools and the half-finished frames to the workroom used by recovering soldiers and headed to the table.

All was ready. A cloth-draped basket held warm croissants, and two stoneware crocks each had a crusty layer of melted Gruyère cheese. He lifted a lid, inhaling the scent of caramelized onion. He had even bought a bottle of champagne, which was hidden beneath the table in a bucket of ice. The ring was in his pocket.

He was so eager to get married and go back home that he was tempted to start packing his bags.

One o'clock came and went with no sign of Delia. He shouldn't worry. Le Havre swarmed with thousands of soldiers flooding into the port village for their chance to sail home. The narrow cobblestone streets, built to accommodate horse carts and bicycles, now groaned under the weight of Army trucks and convoys hauling artillery lashed to flatbeds and bundled canvas tents stacked six feet high. All of it needed to be shipped home. Le Havre had never been meant to handle the crush of demobilization, so he shouldn't be worried if traffic snarls caused Delia to be running late.

Finn used the extra time to cut a few azalea blooms for a centerpiece on the table. With nothing else to do, he sat with the basket of cooling bread and bowls of soup. Who cared if lunch got cold? For as long as he lived, Finn would never take a mouthful of food for granted.

Twenty minutes later, Delia hurried across the carpet of grass toward him. Her hair was sloppy, and she looked overheated. "Sorry I'm late," she said, her cheeks chapped from the sea breeze. "It's been a dreadfully busy morning."

"Is something wrong?" It wasn't like Delia to appear so frazzled, and it worried him.

"Nothing is wrong!" she rushed to say. "I've sent letters to all the CRB volunteers throughout Belgium, notifying them to expect no more shipments. I paid the last of the outstanding bills for renting the barges. As of this morning, the CRB is officially disbanded."

A lump rose in his throat, and a suspicious prickle stung his eyes. Working for the CRB would forever be his proudest accomplishment in life, and they had finally reached the finish line. Their work was over, and they had completed the task with honor.

He lifted his glass of water. "Congratulations," he said.

They clinked glasses. It was a toast of commemoration, of joy, of relief. It was time to return to normal life and start rebuilding their world. The engagement ring was burning a hole in Finn's pocket. He was ready pop the question.

"Bertie wants a favor," Delia said before he could pull the ring from his pocket. Her expression was a combination of regret and resignation. Finn owed Bertie his life. The problem was that Bertie knew it and wasn't shy about asking for favors.

He left the ring in his pocket and rested his hands on the table. "Let's hear it."

"Now that the CRB is disbanded, Bertie has turned his attention to the American Relief Administration."

"I know," Finn said. It had been all over the newspapers for weeks.

The war had left Europe in a state of ruin—cities destroyed, fields barren, and millions of people teetering on the edge of starvation. Widows and orphans had been left homeless, and refugees wandered aimlessly throughout the continent, desperate for a safe place to land. Bertie planned on taking what he'd learned from running the CRB to head up an expanded version called the American Relief Administration. Their aim was to provide food, medicine, and shelter to avert the humanitarian catastrophe that threatened all of continental Europe.

"He's looking for people to join the new organization," Delia said. "Plenty have volunteered to work in France and Belgium, but hardly anyone is willing to go to Germany."

Finn folded his arms across his chest, not liking the direction he sensed this conversation was going. "Please don't tell me that Bertie is asking us to go to Germany."

"His telegram didn't exactly ask us. He merely pointed out that he's in dire need of people willing to go, and we are both experienced in relief work."

Father Gerhardt's voice rose to the surface of Finn's mind. *"Blessed are the peacemakers, for they will be called children of God."* A laugh began deep in his belly. "Oh Father Gerhardt, I can finally repay my debt to you," he murmured.

"Bertie said we could go anywhere in Germany we want," Delia continued. "Everywhere is destitute, and he needs people he can trust."

Father Gerhardt came from the Black Forest region of southwest Germany and often spoke of its beauty—of towering firs and mist-laden valleys, of rolling hills and the distant clang of church bells muffled by the thick forest. Towns and villages were abundant in the Black Forest, and they could probably have their pick of assignments.

Suddenly, the comforts of New York and his kite shop seemed far away. "Do you want to go?" he asked.

Her eyes grew luminous, as if knowing the challenge ahead would be great, grand, and daunting. "Yes," she whispered. "But I don't want to go without you."

He thought of the ring in his pocket. It appeared there would be no honeymoon aboard the Holland America ship, but perhaps they could have something better . . .

Sometimes the hardest things in life were the best.

This wasn't a difficult decision. He knew the right thing to do, but he wanted Delia by his side as his wife. He cleared his throat and reached into his pocket. The aquamarine flashed in the sunlight as he set it on the tablecloth beside her plate, watching her eyes grow wide.

"This is about ten years overdue, but, Delia, you're the only woman I've ever loved. I would like to go to Germany with you as my wife. You know how to prop me up when I stumble. You make me feel like a hero even though I've failed a thousand times. Every day is better when you are with me to share it. Will you marry me, Dee?"

Her eyes were a little watery, her smile radiant. "Oh, yes, Finn!" she said, and he took the ring and slid it onto her finger.

Back up on the veranda, dozens of patients who had been watching from afar let out a cheer and clapped their hands. He had made it to the finish line, to a land beyond the clouds where the sun was shining bright.

44

NINE YEARS LATER
NEW YORK CITY • NOVEMBER 6, 1928

Finn squeezed into the nearly full subway car with an overnight bag slung over his shoulder while Delia held their son's hand. They were lucky to find an open bench, although Gerhardt chose to stand and hold on to a support pole.

"What did *you* do during the war?" Gerhardt asked the soldier sitting on the other side of the aisle. At seven years old, Gerhardt became instantly fascinated whenever he saw a man in uniform, although Finn wished his son didn't approach strangers to ask the delicate question. Not all men wanted to revisit those years.

"Shh," Delia whispered to Gerhardt, tugging him back toward their bench. As it was crowded on the subway tonight, a number of people turned to listen.

"It's all right, ma'am," the soldier said with a friendly nod. His face was lined from years of tough living, and he had sergeant's stripes on his sleeve. "I was a signalman who carried radio communications in Italy. Do you know where that is?"

"No," Gerhardt said. "My dad was a pilot in France."

The sergeant sent Finn a quick look of admiration before turning back to Gerhardt. "Well, that makes your dad a bona fide hero." The sergeant stretched out his hand, and Finn reached across the aisle to shake it.

Finn didn't regret his years with the Lafayette Escadrille, but his proudest work came during the years following the war. He and Delia moved to Württemberg, Germany, the same region where Father Gerhardt was raised, and they spent two years serving the people Finn once saw as enemies.

"This is our stop," Delia said as the subway slowed down, approaching the Times Square station.

The sergeant stood too. "Are you folks going to watch the fireworks tonight?"

It was the night of the presidential election, and a firework spectacle would begin once a winner was announced.

Finn shook his head. "We're on our way to a friend's house. Do we know who won yet?"

"I haven't heard anything for a few hours, but I'm rooting for Al Smith," the sergeant said.

"It still hasn't been called," another subway rider said. "Last I heard, Herbert Hoover has the momentum going into the homestretch."

There was some grumbling among the passengers, but plenty of clapping as well. Al Smith was the most popular governor New York ever had, yet he was running against Bertie Hoover, whose meteoric political career had garnered acclaim all over the world. No matter who won, Finn merely prayed for peace.

Finn gave the sergeant a casual farewell salute. "Good luck to you," he said as he shouldered his overnight bag, then led Delia and their son off the subway.

If felt good to stretch his legs as they climbed up to street level, where a sea of humanity was lit by a blaze of electric signs. The marquee for the *New York Times* displayed election updates that scrolled across it with brightly lit bulbs. Shouts of newsboys blended with the honks of car horns.

Finn didn't want Gerhardt getting lost in the throngs of people, and they had several blocks to walk before reaching Benedict and Inga's apartment. He hunkered down and gestured to Gerhardt. "Hop aboard," he said with a grin, and Gerhardt climbed up to ride piggyback. Finn sent a wink to Delia. "Is all this excitement making you miss the city?"

"Not at all," Delia laughed as they set off toward Benedict and Inga's apartment. Despite being born and raised in the city, he and Delia were much happier living above their kite shop in the quaint, touristy town on Long Island. They often returned to the city to visit with friends in Midtown, but it wasn't home anymore.

They were still a block from Inga's house when a voice shouted out from the crowd, "Delia! Over here!"

It was Katherine Birch and her husband, also on their way to the election night party at Inga's house. Before the war, Katherine, Delia, and Inga lived in neighboring apartments at the Martha Washington. Now Katherine worked at her own dental office and shared a town house with her husband in Midtown. Delia and Katherine exchanged hugs while Finn shook Jonathan's hand.

"Have you heard anything yet?" Katherine asked.

Delia shook her head. "Somebody on the subway said the momentum is behind Hoover, but I guess it's still up in the air."

"Inga says that Benedict has already accepted an appointment to Hoover's cabinet if he wins," Katherine said. "What about the two of you? I'll bet he will find something if you want to go overseas again."

Finn smothered a laugh. "Never! I've already done my time. All I want is to get old in my own home."

"Amen!" Jonathan said.

Although neither Jonathan nor Finn had external scars, the war left them both with wounds that couldn't be seen. Jonathan had served as a bomb-disposal expert in France and had seen enough devastation to last a lifetime. Memories of Belgium still periodically haunted Finn, and yet he thanked God for his imprisonment. It taught him patience and humility. It taught him the blessing of nourishing food, of sunlight and freedom. Most of all, it taught him to love his fellow man.

"Look!" Delia shouted, pointing to the ticker display on the *Times* building.

Herbert Hoover Elected 31st President of the United States.

Delia squealed and jumped into Finn's embrace. He laughed and marveled at the fact that two orphaned kids could ever grow up to have rubbed shoulders with an American president. He let go of Delia to hoist Gerhardt up, pointing to the glittering lights announcing Bertie's ascendency to the White House.

"Come on," Katherine said. "Let's go pester Inga and Benedict for something to eat, then head out for the fireworks."

Finn lingered a moment longer, his eyes lifted to the glittering lights of the city against the night sky. He and Delia had been blessed beyond all measure. They had survived a difficult childhood and had endured the heartbreak of war, but all along they'd been blessed by heaven-sent people to light their way. The goodness of Sister Bernadette, of Mathilde Verhaegen and Father Gerhardt and Bertie Hoover. Finn had done his best to emulate their courage and compassion, which was all that God asked of him.

He shook away the poignant memories and hurried after the others, for Benedict and Inga's parties were always terrific. Tonight was meant for laughter, celebration, and hope for all that lay ahead.

Author's Note

Herbert "Bertie" Hoover shot to international fame due to his role in founding the Commission for the Relief of Belgium. He made the dangerous Atlantic crossing forty times during the war to keep the supply of food flowing to Belgium. After the war, the king of Belgium granted Hoover an honorary Belgian citizenship. To this day, countless streets, schools, and public parks in Belgium are named in honor of Herbert Hoover.

In the years following the war, Hoover spearheaded a massive humanitarian mission through the American Relief Administration. Twelve million Europeans were displaced due to the upheaval of the war and the redrawing of national boundaries. An estimated ten million children were orphaned from the combined effects of the war and the influenza pandemic. Herbert Hoover's leadership of the American Relief Administration helped combat famine and stabilized war-torn regions. Although Hoover's tenure as president was marred by the Great Depression, he is remembered for his efforts promoting public works projects such as the Hoover Dam, which began construction during his administration. At the end of his life, Hoover considered his work for the CRB to be the pinnacle of his humanitarian career. He died in 1964 at the age of ninety.

Mathilde Verhaegen is a fictional character based on an amalgamation of actual people who risked their lives to publish *La Libre Belgique*. They carried out their clandestine work in basements and attics, using illegal presses to print issues of the underground newspaper during the occupation. The last issue of *La Libre Belgique* was published on November 12, 1918, the day after the armistice was signed.

La Libre Belgique was revived in 1941 when the nation once again fell under German occupation. The men and women behind *La Libre Belgique* stand as a testament to the spirit of resistance and commitment to freedom even in the darkest of times.

Acknowledgments

I am deeply grateful to the editors and marketing team at Bethany House for their support and guidance over the years. Your partnership throughout the Women of Midtown trilogy has been instrumental in helping me bring each novel to the finish line. My editor, Jessica Sharpe, deserves special thanks for her remarkable gift in balancing honest critique with encouragement and praise.

I'd also like to thank Barb and Hal Massa for their years of fascinating conversations and insights into the German language and culture.

Finally, my heartfelt thanks go to my husband, Bill. Long before publication, his steadfast confidence gave me the courage to keep honing my craft and to persist in the competitive world of publishing. Although writing is a natural pursuit for a dyed-in-the-wool introvert, Bill has a gift for coaxing me out of my writing cave to travel around the world with him. It has filled my life with unexpected adventures and inspired stories I never dreamed I'd have the chance to tell.

Reading Group Discussion Guide

1. In the novel, Wesley is forty-eight and Delia twenty-nine. Is this too great an age difference for a happy marriage? What if Wesley had been thirty-eight and Delia nineteen?

2. At the beginning of the story, Delia's pacifist beliefs make her an outcast among those in her apartment building, yet she stays there because she struggles with change. Have you ever stayed too long in a job, home, or relationship simply because change felt too daunting? What helped you recognize when it was time to move on?

3. Hilde, who leads the war bond campaign, seems to take pleasure in belittling Delia for her pacifist views. Do you think shaming or public ridicule is ever effective in changing someone's beliefs? Can you think of any modern examples of social ostracism? How successful and/or harmful are such tactics?

4. Delia discouraged Finn from leaving his humble job at the fish cannery to move to a place where he could learn to fly airplanes. Why was she so reluctant to see him follow his dream of flying?

5. By the end of the novel, Delia comes to understand that expecting Finn to abandon his daring, impulsive nature is

both unrealistic and unfair. How important is it in a relationship to accept one's partner as they truly are rather than as we wish them to be? Can love truly thrive when one person is hoping for the other to change? Where is the line between helping a partner grow and trying to reshape them?

6. Shortly after Delia musters the courage to accompany Bertie to Belgium, she concludes that God makes some people warriors, while others are destined to work quietly behind the front lines, and yet both roles are worthy. In today's world, who do you see as the "warriors," and who are the ones serving quietly behind the scenes? Are we more inclined to celebrate one over the other? If so, why?

7. Civilians in occupied Belgium often relied on the black market to survive despite it being illegal. Do you think that people who participated in black-market trading should have been punished after the war, or were their actions justified given the circumstances?

8. Delia finally opens her heart to Finn midway through the novel, even though she still worries his reckless nature will likely never change. At the end of chapter 18, Delia reflects, "If she was to fully participate in the wondrous world God had created, she needed to risk getting hurt." Do you think it's possible to live a full and meaningful life without risking emotional pain? What role does risk play in our becoming the people God wants us to be?

9. Forgiveness plays a central role in Delia and Finn's journey. Is forgiveness shown in the story to be a process, an event, a singular decision, or a combination of these?

10. Many war novels and movies end with a declaration of peace, but for those who live through it, this moment often marks the beginning of a new set of challenges. Did this novel give you a deeper understanding of what life was like in the aftermath of World War I?

Read on
for a *sneak peek* at
the next book by

ELIZABETH CAMDEN

Available in the spring of 2027

1

Lieutenant Cooper Wainright saw his share of wounded sailors when he fought in the Spanish-American War, and he had a knack for visiting them in the hospital. These men didn't want to be pitied or handled with kid gloves; they needed someone with a sense of humor and to know that they hadn't been forgotten by their brothers-in-arms.

Cooper would walk into the hospital room of a half-dead man and hunker down beside him. "You didn't need that second leg, did you?" To the guy who had his front teeth blown out in a misfire, Cooper would say something like, "Looks like the tooth fairy is going to owe you in a big way." Cooper was never at a loss for words, and treating a wounded man as though he were still part of the team was the best medicine he could offer.

And yet today's visit was going to be the hardest of his life. Cooper blanched at the sight of his best friend lying in the hospital bed. One leg was elevated by a pulley hanging from the ceiling, and his fractured pelvis was encased by a metal brace bolted to the bed. Jasper Duvall's face was so bruised and swollen, it was hard to recognize him.

Cooper scrubbed all compassion from his voice and barked a question. "Duvall! Are you lying down on the job again?"

The grin from Jasper was priceless. "Just resting up for the next mission," he said. "When can I get back on the job?"

"When you can clean my clock in the fifty-yard dash and not a day before." Cooper plunked a metal chair down beside Jasper's bed. "Is there anything I can get for you? Something to eat? Or to read?"

Jasper lifted a hand and pointed to the bruising around his eyes. "Maybe a better-looking face."

"That's a tall order," Cooper said. "My hand to God, you're getting homelier every day." It wasn't true. He and Jasper had entered the Naval Academy in the same class. They were both blond, clean-cut, and never had trouble attracting female attention. They had been top athletes and star players on the Navy football team.

Jasper lifted his head to squint at Cooper's plain button-down shirt and trousers held up by a pair of suspenders.

"Why aren't you in uniform?"

It was the question Cooper dreaded, and despite himself, his shoulders sagged. "I resigned from the Navy. I'm an ordinary civilian now."

Jasper flopped back on the pillows. "No," he said. "Don't let this be the end of you, Coop. The accident wasn't your fault."

But the accident *was* Cooper's fault. He was the one who had issued the orders that overheated the boilers on the USS *Falcon*. The explosion blew the engine room apart and broke so many bones in Jasper's pelvis and leg that his best friend would probably never walk again. Six other men had been injured, and all of it was Cooper's fault because of a stupid mathematical error. No doubt the mistake was going to haunt him for the rest of his life.

"I've already accepted responsibility," he said. "Captain Holland bent over backwards to save me from a court-martial. He even got me transferred to a decent job at the academy in Annapolis."

"Doing what?"

For the first time, Cooper's mouth twitched into a half smile. "Coaching football."

Jasper choked on his own breath. "Football? I suppose it could be worse."

"*A lot* worse," Cooper agreed. He could have been court-martialed for incompetence or even imprisoned because of the errors he made that fateful morning.

The USS *Falcon* was a sleek, steam-powered destroyer, a heavily armed ship designed to protect larger battleships in a naval flotilla. Cooper had been on the bridge during a training mission when he overestimated the ship's propulsion system. He pushed the engines beyond their operating limits, which led to a catastrophic explosion in the boiler room.

"I wish you hadn't thrown in the towel," Jasper said. "It's not like you to give up like this."

Cooper shrugged, as though it had been easy to stand down and accept responsibility. "I pushed the engines too hard without running the proper load calculations. It was my own fault. Simple calculus, and I got it wrong. There's no chance the Navy will assign me to another ship. As of next week, I'll be Coach Wainright, the man destined to turn around the sorry fortunes of the Navy football team. They've lost to Army four years in a row."

"Don't change the subject," Jasper said. "The *Falcon* was sailing within the parameters of its abilities. Don't let them make a scapegoat of you."

Cooper sighed. "I'm not a scapegoat; I'm the man who gave an order that caused the boiler to explode. Captain Holland pulled a lot of strings to get me the job at the Naval Academy. I'm no longer an officer, but I've got a respectable civilian job and will be the head coach of the football team. It's more than I could have hoped for."

"You'll be a great football coach, but you need to clear your name first."

If Cooper asked for a full investigation, news of his disgrace would get back to his mother. He was her only child, her shining star. She'd cried when he was accepted to the Naval Academy. Sixteen years later, she still had his diploma framed and displayed in the family room as though it were her proudest possession.

His mother had sacrificed a lot to get him into the academy. He owed her, and he loved her. For political reasons, Cooper's name had been kept out of the official accident investigation. If he rocked the boat by demanding the case be reopened, he risked everything, including his chance to land a plumb job at the academy.

"Look," Cooper said, "if I demand a public airing of what happened, my mother is going to find out everything. Do I need to add more?"

Understanding dawned on Jasper's face. Cooper had never been good at math, and acceptance into the Naval Academy depended on mastery of algebra, trigonometry, and calculus. His mother was a high school math teacher and had spent months tutoring Cooper to pass the rigorous entrance exam. He passed by the skin of his teeth, and throughout his college years he leaned on his mother for help mastering calculus.

And it was calculus that had been his downfall that fateful morning on the *Falcon*.

"She'll blame herself," Cooper continued. "It's irrational, but every triumph I've had in my life, she ascribed to my sheer brilliance, and any time I mess up she berates herself for failing as a mother."

Jasper snorted. "The world would be a better place if there were more mothers like Melinda Wainright."

"Agreed," Cooper said. "She doesn't need to know the details of what happened. I'll tell her I got tired of living aboard a ship and jumped at the chance to become the football coach at Annapolis. She'll believe it."

There were upsides to life as a civilian. For as long as he could remember, Cooper wanted more than a life at sea. He dreamed of coming home to a warm kitchen that smelled like vanilla, of golden-haired kids barreling toward him when he arrived home at the end of the day. He wanted muddy boots by the back door, a swing set in the yard, and Sunday afternoons spent refereeing backyard scrimmages with the neighborhood kids. He wanted a wife who'd laugh at his bad jokes, talk him down when he got riled up, and help him build that noisy, joyful family he'd always imagined. A naval career made all that a long shot. The few officers who succeeded in married life had steel-spined wives and children who rarely saw their fathers. Instead of having dinner with their kids each day, those men raised their children through letters sent from distant ports of call. But now, as the football coach for the Navy, he had a chance to put down roots and finally look for the right woman.

He spent the next hour with Jasper, shooting the breeze about their days at the academy and the ridiculous things they'd survived during those four years. They kept the talk light—old pranks, impossible instructors, and the time Cooper got seasick in front of a visiting admiral. Jasper laughed until it hurt, and Cooper was glad to see color back in his friend's face. For a while, it almost felt like old times.

Then Jasper had to spoil everything by circling back to what caused the explosion on the *Falcon*. "Something's not right about how quickly the Navy closed the investigation," he said. "They only interviewed me once, but I think the problem started *before* you gave that final order."

Cooper had read the investigative report, and there was no doubt in his mind who had caused the accident. Settling the matter quickly was best for all concerned. Jasper didn't have any memory of the accident, and the experts had already weighed in, yet Jasper was getting agitated as he grasped at straws, desperate to find an alternative explanation that would exonerate Cooper. Jasper wanted to rake over every detail of that morning, trying to conjure up different theories that had already been examined and rejected.

"Jasper, stop," Cooper finally said, frustration tightening his voice. "I'm going to be okay, and you need to quit obsessing over this."

The argument put both of them in a sour mood. Jasper glared at him, and Cooper only wanted to scrub the memory of that morning from his mind for good. This wasn't the ending he'd wanted for their visit, but a nurse had come to close the ward. He was halfway to the door when Jasper's voice stopped him.

"Hey, Coop. I thought of something you can do for me."

Cooper turned. "Name it."

A genuine smile touched Jasper's battered face. "Next fall, when you take the team up north for the Army-Navy football game, no matter what happens, I need you to *beat* Army. Beat the tar out of them, Coop."

Cooper straightened, brought his hand to his forehead, and saluted. "Message received," he said with a spark of his old energy.

He had his orders. Beat Army. Coach the team. Keep his head down and build something good out of the wreckage he'd caused.

And maybe, if he got it right, there was still a chance for the kind of life he'd always dreamed of, with a woman who could see past the catastrophe of his past and venture into the future with him.

The coming months were going to be hard, and redemption wouldn't come all at once, but he knew where to begin.

Elizabeth Camden is best known for her historical novels set in Gilded Age America, featuring clever heroines and richly layered story lines. Before she was a writer, she was an academic librarian at some of the largest and smallest libraries in America, but her favorite is the continually growing library in her own home. Her novels have won the RITA and Christy Awards and have appeared on the CBA bestsellers list. She lives in Citrus County, Florida, with her husband, who graciously tolerates her intimidating stockpile of books. Learn more online at ElizabethCamden.com.

Sign Up for Elizabeth's Newsletter

Keep up to date with Elizabeth's latest news
on book releases and events by signing up
for her email list at the website below.

ElizabethCamden.com

FOLLOW ELIZABETH ON SOCIAL MEDIA

Author Elizabeth Camden   @AuthorElizabethCamden

Be the first to hear about new books from Bethany House!

Stay up to date with our authors and books by signing up for our newsletters at

BethanyHouse.com/SignUp

FOLLOW US ON SOCIAL MEDIA

   @BethanyHouseFiction